M.E. MORRIS

NO ONE IS SAFE FROM THIS INVISIBLE ENEMY...

BLOOD STRIKE

AVON

EAN

ISBN 0-380-77889-0

9 780380 778898

50599>

"Look at that," Davis directed, pointing forward.

Kohn eased the chopper closer. She could make out several crewmen prone on the weatherdeck, their bodies bloated and bleached. Several more were partially visible through the wide windows of the bridge.

"I think they're all dead." Davis shook his head, obviously puzzled. "Something went terribly wrong aboard that ship."

BIOSTRIKE

BIOSTRIKE

M.E. MORRIS

AVON BOOKS ◆ NEW YORK

BIOSTRIKE is an original publication of Avon Books. This work has never before appeared in book form. This work is a novel. The characters within this work are entirely fictional, although they have been given actions, personalities, and dialogue that reflect the tenor of our times. With the exception of the brief reference to Ben Nighthorse Campbell, the first Native-American member of the U.S. Senate, no resemblance to any other persons, living or dead, is intended.

AVON BOOKS
A division of
The Hearst Corporation
1350 Avenue of the Americas
New York, New York 10019

Copyright © 1996 by M. E. Morris
Published by arrangement with the author
Library of Congress Catalog Card Number: 95-94620
ISBN: 0-380-77889-0

First Avon Books Printing: January 1996

AVON TRADEMARK REG. U.S. PAT. OFF. AND IN OTHER COUNTRIES, MARCA REGISTRADA, HECHO EN U.S.A.

Printed in the U.S.A.

RA   10   9   8   7   6   5   4   3   2   1

———

Dedicated to all the men and women of the armed forces of the United States, who, with shrinking budgets and increased operational requirements, will still maintain the level of vigilance and professionalism that is reflected in this tale

The author gratefully acknowledges the everyday performance of the men and women of the United States Navy, whose duties inspired this story. Also recognized is the perseverance and confidence of my agent, Jane Dystel, for insisting that I accept nothing less than my best effort and holding my feet to the fire; to David Highfill, for bringing this story to Avon Books and providing invaluable guidance; and to my editor, Tom Colgan, for his support and expertise in producing the final product. No author could ask for a better team.

Glossary

1MC—shipboard all-spaces intercom circuit

AC—aircraft commander

ACOS—assistant chief of staff

ASW—antisubmarine warfare

AW—aviation antisubmarine warfare operator

BOQ—bachelor officers' quarters

CDO—command duty officer

CIC—combat information center

CICO—combat information center officer

CINC—commander-in-chief

CINCPACFLT—commander-in-chief, Pacific Fleet

CJCS—chairman, Joint Chiefs of Staff

CNO—chief of naval operations

COD—carrier on-board delivery (system)

conn—the responsibility for steering the ship

CPA—closest point of approach

CPO—chief petty officer

C-5—USAF logistic support aircraft (heavy)

ECM—electronic countermeasures

exec—executive officer

GI—government issue

GQ—General Quarters

HPD—Honolulu Police Department

HSL-47—Helicopter LAMPS Squadron 47

jaygee—lieutenant, junior grade, U.S. Navy (nickname)

JOOD—junior officer-of-the-deck

LAMPS—light airborne multipurpose system

LCDR—lieutenant commander, U.S. Navy

LT—lieutenant, U.S. Navy

LT(jg)—lieutenant, junior grade, U.S. Navy

MCPO—master chief petty officer

NAS—Naval Air Station

NAVAIRPAC—Naval Air Forces, Pacific fleet

NBC—nuclear, biological, and chemical (warfare)

NCA—National Command Authority (president plus SECDEF)

NEX—Navy exchange

NROTC—Navy Reserve Officers Training Corps

NSC—National Security Council

NLSO—Naval Legal Services Office

OOD—officer-of-the-deck

ops—operations or operations officer

0-5—rank designator for commander, USN (also lieutenant colonel; USMC and USA)

PACFLT—Pacific fleet

PACOM—Pacific Command

RAST—recovery assistance, securing, and traversing system: a high-seas method of shipboard helicopter landing using a ship-to-aircraft tether

SATCOMM—satellite communications

SECDEF—secretary of defense

SECNAV—secretary of the navy

SSM—surface-to-surface missile

UCMJ—Uniform Code of Military Justice

USCINCPAC—commander-in-chief, U.S. Pacific Command

USPACOM—United States Pacific Command

0000 Local—Local time based on the 24-hour military system

000000Z—Date-time group based on Greenwich time (Z). The first two digits are the day of the month, the last four the international time. An abbreviation of the month usually follows.

Author's Note

Many have said that there are sailors and there are *sailors*, with the emphasis being on those who brave the blue waters of the deep oceans. If a modern navy is anything, it is a global blue water navy, and this fictional tale concerns such a navy and such a ship and such a man.

OPERATIONAL CHAIN OF COMMAND, USS *FORD* (FFG-54)

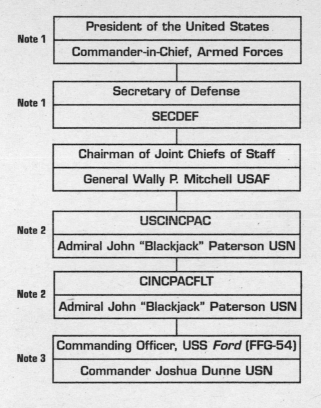

Note 1
President of the United States
Commander-in-Chief, Armed Forces

Note 1
Secretary of Defense
SECDEF

Chairman of Joint Chiefs of Staff
General Wally P. Mitchell USAF

Note 2
USCINCPAC
Admiral John "Blackjack" Paterson USN

Note 2
CINCPACFLT
Admiral John "Blackjack" Paterson USN

Note 3
Commanding Officer, USS *Ford* (FFG-54)
Commander Joshua Dunne USN

Note 1: The president and secretary of defense comprise the National Command Authority.

Note 2: Normally filled by two individuals. Due to unexpected sudden death of USCINCPAC incumbent, Admiral Paterson is temporarily assigned additional duty as USCINCPAC.

Note 3: USS *Ford* (FFG-54) is steaming independently while in transit from Australia to home port at San Diego. Upon arrival, will report to Commander, Carrier *Nimitz* Battle Group for operational control and Surface Squadron 5 for administrative control.

1

"Captain to the bridge!"

Commander Joshua Dunne, U.S. Navy, uttered a mild epithet, sat up, and slid his legs off the side of his sea-cabin bunk. *Damn.* Seventeen minutes past three in the morning. He had only been horizontal—or reasonably so—for forty-three minutes, and that was after seventeen straight hours on the bridge of the guided-missile frigate USS *Ford* (FFG-54). Thirty-four years old, a head-and-shoulders rapidly rising naval officer who had been early selected for both lieutenant commander and full bull, Dunne had only one regret about his first command. *You never get any sleep.* Running one hand through an unruly shock of dark brown hair, he spoke wearily into the bridge intercom, "Whatcha got?"

"Radar contact, Captain. Bearing three-two-zero degrees, twenty thousand yards; speed of advance: sixteen knots; CPA collision."

The last word completely erased any lingering desire to sleep.

Sixteen knots, thought Dunne. *What the hell is a ship*

1

doing at sixteen knots in these seas? Even as he strug-gled to lean over and reach for his slippers, the violent pitching and rolling of the *Ford* forced him to grab a handrail to avoid being spilled onto the deck. Thank goodness he had left night orders for only twelve knots. That was pushing it a bit even though the *Ford* was steaming downwind and downswell, trying to ride out the storm that should be slowly pulling away from them. His immediate mental picture of the situation revealed that the target vessel was steaming almost head-on into both wind and swell. And at sixteen knots, she had to be alternately pitching her bow high above the water and diving into troughs that must be flooding her fo'c'sle with enough blue water to float a destroyer. What kind of captain would do that to his ship and crew?

Dunne managed to stand and pull on his long gray flannel robe. When he wrapped it around him, it ac-cented an athletic build that had yet to surrender to any middle-age spread. He looked more the middleweight boxer preparing to climb through the ring ropes than an overtired naval officer wondering what kind of sea ves-sel was menacing his ship. On the back of the robe were sewn three-inch-high black felt letters: U.S. Naval Acad-emy, 1980.

Dunne flung the ends of the sash into a loose square knot and grabbed for his door latch. His sea cabin was only a few steps aft of the enclosed bridge, but as he stepped into the short passageway he was immediately thrown against the opposite bulkhead, his right shoulder slamming hard against the steel, the impact generating a bolt of nerve lightning that flashed down to the tips of his fingers and flickered off into the red-lighted glow of the passageway. *Shit!* Righting himself, he shook off the pain and stepped forward only to be thrown against the opposite bulkhead. He started to fall backward before regaining his footing. Fortunately, a large swell lifted the stern of the *Ford*, and it was downhill for the last step.

"Captain's on the bridge," quietly announced the bo's'n's mate of the watch as Dunne pulled himself through the hatch. More dim red lights gave night-steaming illumination to the darkened pilot house. It was useless to look outside through any of the windows or ports. A driving rain pouring out of a tumultuous black overcast completely obscured the mountainous Pacific waves and night sky.

Lieutenant "Long John" Childress, a head taller than Dunne and twenty pounds lighter, was waiting and immediately started briefing Dunne as he gingerly led his captain to the large radar repeater scope on the port side of the enclosed bridge. "We've held the contact since about ten minutes after you left the bridge, Captain. Originally at 40,000 yards. She's held a steady course and speed since initial contact."

"Must be taking one hell of a beating," Dunne commented, fumbling with his sash to cinch it tighter.

"Yes, sir," the slim young officer-of-the-deck responded. "I don't know how that captain's doing it without endangering his ship. I would think that at that speed in these seas every plate in the hull would jar loose."

"Have you contacted him?"

"We've been trying, sir, but no response yet."

"He must hold us at this range," Dunne surmised.

"Combat says they're not getting any emissions, sir."

Dunne looked up at Long John. "No radar?"

"Nothing, sir."

"That's just plain irresponsible. Must be a merchant-man."

"We don't know, sir."

"Has to be. No naval vessel is going to go ploughing through this mess at night without some kind of electronic eyes."

Long John shrugged and reached down with a grease pencil to mark a black X over the phosphorescent blip on the scope. It remained aligned with the previous ones. All were leading toward the center of the scope, and in the relative-bearing radar picture the center was the USS *Ford*. "Just over eight thousand yards," he reported.

Dunne estimated about twelve minutes. If neither ship maneuvered before then, they would collide. The *Ford*, under International Rules of the Road for vessels in open seas, could not legally maneuver—not yet. It was the so-called privileged vessel with the right of way in a crossing situation and must hold its course and speed so as not to confuse the other captain. The target ship was closing forty degrees off the *Ford*'s port bow and was obliged, being the burdened vessel, to give way to the *Ford*, either by slowing or turning to a noncollision course or a combination of both. At seventy-five hundred yards, it was doing neither.

"What an ass," Dunne murmured, reaching out with one hand to steady himself against the console as another rolling swell lifted the stern of the *Ford*. The helmsman spun the wheel to stop the falloff of the stern as it surged to port.

"Keep her steady," Dunne cautioned.

The helmsman was ahead of him and the bow of the *Ford* remained fixed on course.

Dunne tried to peer through the pale red light and identify the obviously alert sailor.

"Two Shoes," announced Long John, anticipating Dunne's question.

Charlie Two Shoes. That was good. The slightly built Native-American quartermaster was the best helmsman on the ship. Probably one of the best in the U.S. Navy. He was a key member of the special Sea and Anchor Detail, that assembly of highly qualified bridge personnel always on watch whenever the *Ford* left or entered port, and margins for error were minimal. Good fortune had placed Two Shoes in the midwatch duty section on this night when the *Ford* was apparently about to steam into harm's way in the open sea.

Two Shoes was something of an enigma. A Colorado Ute, he had overcome the disadvantages of being a reservation Indian by doggedly finishing high school and enlisting in the U.S. Navy, despite the lack of a birth certificate. He overcame the obstacle with the help of his senator, Ben Nighthorse Campbell, the first Native-American member of that august body. While Charlie Two Shoes seemed like a stereotype Indian name, the Ute sailor had been named by his grandfather after another Charlie Two Shoes, who strangely enough had been a young Chinese lad adopted by U.S. Marines during the early years of World War II. It didn't make any sense, but it was legal by special congressional action, and it fit. And Charlie Two Shoes had made his grandfather and his bloodbrother senator very proud.

Long John scratched another black grease X on the scope. CPA—still collision.

A voice from the ship's combat information center came over the intercom. "Bridge, combat. CPA in eight minutes. Still collision course, sir." The boys in the dark hole were getting antsy.

"Roger, combat," Long John answered and looked at Dunne.

"Recommendation?" Dunne asked.

"Can't wait much longer, Captain. When the time comes, recommend hard right until safe passage assured."

"I have the conn," announced Dunne loud enough for all the bridge personnel to hear. He was directly responsible now for any maneuver deemed necessary to avoid collision. It was a time-honored and normally routine decision, one the captain of any vessel rightfully made to avoid confusion on the bridge. Until Dunne's announcement, Long John had the sole authority for the maneuvering of the *Ford*, although the captain was always indirectly responsible. With his captain taking the conn, the officer-of-the-deck could breathe a bit easier.

Dunne ordered, "Sound the whistle. Five blasts."

The threat was still slightly over six thousand yards away, but the *Ford* was upwind, and the international danger signal might be heard at that distance even through the noise of the storm.

"Every thirty seconds," Dunne added.

"Every thirty seconds," the bo's'n of the watch repeated. Activating the alarm was his responsibility.

The whistle split the night air with a series of deep-throated blasts that not only tore through the darkness toward the unseen target ship but vibrated through the *Ford* down to its keel. The few sailors who had managed to sleep were now wide awake and undoubtedly alert for the order they all prayed would not come. They knew the five blasts could forecast a disaster. Confirmation would come with a "Collision!" warning order and a few of the supercautious were already slipping trousers and life vests over their skivvies.

The next several minutes were maddening. Dunne knew now that every moment counted. He turned to his talker. "Port lookout, do you see *anything*?"

The sailor activated his sound-powered phone by relaying the question. After a moment, he repeated the port lookout's reply verbatim. "I can't see a hundred yards, sir."

Dunne pressed his face to one of the bridge windows. The wiper was fighting a losing battle, furiously moving the water from side to side, but clearing away none of it. Dunne couldn't even see the bow through the wall of water cascading from the sky, and with the rising and falling of the waves as well as the *Ford*, it was doubtful if he could have seen the other ship with several miles of visibility. He was tempted to grab one of the foul weather slickers and go out on the open bridge, but he knew visibility wouldn't be any better and he would have a firmer grasp of the situation by staying inside. "Range?" he queried.

"Thirty-six hundred yards," Long John answered. Roughly just a shade under two nautical miles.

"Turn, you bastard," Dunne ordered, knowing full well it was an unheard and completely useless command.

Thirty seconds later. "Twenty-three hundred yards." The two ships had a combined closure speed of twenty knots.

Dunne weighed his options. He could not maintain course and speed longer than another minute or so. Maneuvering the *Ford*, as agile as she was, required sea room and he was rapidly running out of that. Turning to port was obviously not an option; that would increase the closing speed of the two ships and risk a head-on collision. He could order more speed, but acceleration in these seas would be sluggish. He could not get out of the way fast enough. Stop engines? That might help, but he would risk being dead in the water and denied any further maneuvering ability. The best tactic would be to turn starboard as his OOD had recommended, thereby decreasing the speed of closure, and pray the other ship didn't at that same moment start its right turn to pass aft of the *Ford*. With its speed advantage, it could plow into the frigate's port quarter.

"Right full rudder," Dunne ordered, his words clear and firm. He needed a very tight turn and he needed it immediately.

"Target bearing three-two-zero degrees, seventeen hundred yards," Long John reported.

The *Ford*, although slowed by its turn, heeled to port as the bow came around.

"Target bearing three-two-zero degrees, twelve hundred yards." Long John's voice had a slight edge to it.

"See anything, port lookout?" Dunne asked. His talker repeated the message.

"Nothing, sir."

"Call out the moment you do."

"Port lookout, aye, sir."

Long John again, "Three-two-zero, nine hundred yards."

Dunne didn't like the tight knot forming in his stomach. *Why isn't the bearing increasing? Surely the son of a bitch wasn't starting a right turn!*

"Seven hundred yards."

The 3,600-ton *Ford* was listing twenty degrees to port under the forces of the hard right turn. "Ahead two-thirds," Dunne ordered. The *Ford* leaned a bit more as her two gas turbines wound upward toward 28,000 shaft horsepower. Although the ship had two engines, they were coupled to a single shaft and screw. Dunne would much more have preferred two shafts at the moment. With two-thirds ahead on an outboard shaft and a compatible reverse on the inside shaft, he could have spun the *Ford* around in a much tighter circle. Nevertheless, the turn was tightening. The heading had come around forty degrees.

"Five hundred yards," Long John called.

Although the drag of the sharp turn in heavy seas had initially slowed the *Ford*, she was beginning to accelerate nicely with the application of more power. Still, the other ship was bearing down at sixteen knots, and as the *Ford* began to come around into the swell she was rolling and pitching like a wild bronco with a dozen burrs stuck in its flanks.

The bearing has to change! prayed Dunne. He had made his decision. He could do no more. All ahead full while coming broadside to the wind and swell could capsize the *Ford*.

"Three hundred yards ... three-two-zero degrees. Three-two-zero. Three-two-zero degrees and holding ... two hundred yards. Two hundred yards ... two hundred yards . . . three-two-*five* degrees! Range steady . . . three-*three-zero* degrees.''

The bearing *was changing*.

''Three-four-zero degrees,'' Long John continued.

The *Ford* passed through the other ship's heading and began to swing its bow further north.

''Two hundred yards . . . one hundred and seventy-five yards . . . one hundred and fifty yards.''

What was happening? Why was the range again decreasing while the bearing was increasing? It took only a moment for Dunne to reason it out. The target should clear them, but it had yet to reach its closest point—and just how close would that be?

With the exception of Long John's voice, there was absolute silence on the bridge. The *Ford* was committed. Either Dunne's decision was correct, or the two ships were less than two minutes away from collision. The bo's'n prepared to sound the collision alarm. Dunne crossed to the port side of the bridge and peered off the port quarter. He could see nothing.

''One hundred yards, Captain . . . holding one hundred . . . range is opening, sir!'' Long John was having difficulty keeping his voice down. ''One hundred fifty yards . . . we've passed CPA, sir,'' he said, a noticeable strain still in his voice of relief.

At the moment, one hundred yards seemed as narrow as the thickness of another coat of gray paint on the hull of the *Ford*. Dunne sucked in a dry deep breath. He should have had the collision alarm sounded. But the Man Topside had been with him. ''You have the conn, Mr. Childress,'' he announced. ''Steady up on zero-one-zero. Make turns for ten knots.''

''Aye, aye, Captain.'' Then Long John announced his return to full control of the *Ford*, ''I have the conn. Steady on zero-one-zero. Engines ahead one-third, make turns for ten knots.''

Charlie Two Shoes and the sailor manning the engine-order pedestal repeated Long John's orders to insure confirmation.

Dunne hurried outside to the port wing of the bridge and stood next to the soaked lookout. He could see nothing but windswept rain, swirling low scud, and darkness. But something was out there, just off the port beam, and less than two hundred yards away. The Ford was 413 feet long at the waterline, but her hull stretched for another forty feet under the surface.

"I can't see any running lights," Dunne muttered to the lookout who had dripping binoculars pressed against his eyes.

"I see it, Captain!" the sailor called out.

"What is it? Can you tell?"

"No, sir, just a big black form, maybe a merchantman . . . yes, it's a merchant ship . . . I can see kingposts."

"Any lights?"

"None, sir, none at all. She's running completely darkened." The lookout passed his glasses to Dunne.

For a moment, Dunne thought he could see a vague shiplike form, but it dissolved into the blackness before he could make out any detail. The Ford began a complex roll as the other ship's wake reached out and rocked the frigate. Whatever the ship was, it was gone. Unbelievable. A completely unlit ship running at sixteen knots in heavy weather and darkness with apparently no concern about any other traffic. And in a shipping lane just two hundred miles southwest of Oahu. Dunne knew that some shorthanded merchantmen routinely put their vessel on automatic pilot and cut back on their bridge watches, but very seldom after sunset, and certainly not in this weather without a radar watch set. The captain of that ship was criminally negligent. If the Ford had not maneuvered at the last minute, there would have been a collision at sea in the very early morning darkness in the midst of a violent storm. The loss of life would have been catastrophic. The more Dunne realized what had happened, the angrier he became. Anger now so deep that any thought of sleep was hopelessly buried.

He pulled himself up into his bridge chair and sensed a presence beside him. The strong aroma of navy coffee triggered his response as he took the hot mug from the bo's'n of the watch.

"Thanks, Boats." The bridge chronometer read 0348. Dunne had just lived a lifetime in thirty-one minutes.

The familiar feel of the high-pedestaled, leather-covered bridge chair comforted Dunne. From it, he could perform all of his functions as commanding officer, and it was at once his bridge station, administrative office, and traditional seat of authority whenever the *Ford* was underway in situations that required the captain's presence on the bridge. A similar chair was located in CIC, often his battle station when fighting the ship. The bridge chair was sacrosanct, and only the captain ever occupied it. Even in the darkest, dullest, and most routine night, no enlisted or officer crewman would ever presume to seek its soft, six-way adjustable comfort. In some ways, it could even be thought of as a throne, for the commanding officer of a man-of-war at sea was one of the few remaining absolute reigning monarchs. His voice was law, his words edict, and his responsibilities were never shared. His utterances from the chair carried the weight of a papal encyclical and were never to be disregarded. And when he was absent from the bridge, the chair was a constant reminder of his omnipotent presence elsewhere on the ship. In addition, the commanding officer of a deployed U.S. Navy vessel was the sole remaining military authority who carried the presence of the U.S. legal and political system with him wherever he sailed. His ship was in essence U.S. soil, and he was empowered in times of criticality to represent the United States in such diplomatic responsibilities as refuge for foreigners and protection of U.S. citizens.

But the chair did not sit on the high steel pedestal for

the sake of prestige. It sat tall to insure that the captain
had an unobstructed view over the heads of the bridge
personnel and visual access to the great expanse of sea
through the windows and portholes of the enclosed
bridge. And the chair was not pretentious; it was luxu-
riously soft with multiple adjustments only because on
occasions the captain would be spending long hours in
it, and its comfort would rest him despite his demanding
duties and responsibilities. The captain's chair was as
essential a piece of bridge equipment to efficient ship
handling and fighting tactics as were the helm and engine-order pedestal and radar repeaters and all of the
other communications and operational equipment. The
captain was not confined to it, of course, when he was
on the bridge, but it was always there when his need
arose. Of the seventeen continuous hours Dunne had
spent on the bridge just prior to retiring to his sea cabin,
only to be awakened by the collision course incident, he
had spent twelve in the chair. He had taken his meals
there. He had kept up with his endless paperwork there.
And he had counseled, and taken counsel of, his officers
there. Within the great depth of naval tradition, when
the captain was in his chair, it was only a slight exaggeration to say that all was well with the world.

Ten minutes later, the *Ford* was settled on a northerly
heading with the mystery vessel off to port at two thousand yards and opening. Both ships were on a general
course for the Hawaiian Islands and riding the aft edge
of a building tropical storm that also seemed to have its
course set for Hawaii. Dunne squirmed to settle into his
seat. "What's the latest on the storm, Mr. Childress?"

Long John was standing to the right and just behind
the captain's chair. "Gaining strength and momentum,
Captain. The latest satellite picture shows the eye ninety
miles southwest of Oahu. They're already experiencing
forty knot winds at Pearl."

Surprisingly, the *Ford* was riding well despite plow-

ing into the wind and swells. Both seemed to have sub-
sided somewhat, although that was contrary to the
normal nature of such storms.

Dunne continued. "I suspect Pearl is battening down
the hatches. What kind of time do they have if the thing
continues on course?"

"Less than four hours I would say, Captain."

Try as he might, Dunne could not settle back into a
normal routine. His Irish dander was up and he was determined that the rogue merchantman was not going to
get away with such reckless conduct. The storm ahead
of them should be slowly pulling away if its speed of
advance was the reported twenty-five knots. The merchantman that had given them the scare was making sixteen and the *Ford* ten. Both ships should be falling
behind the storm unless it was building extremely rapidly. Why not launch the ship's helicopter at daybreak
and identify the violator—provided there was sufficient
ceiling and visibility, of course? At the very least, Dunne
reasoned, he could file a violation against the captain of
the merchantman. That thought appealed to him. Dawn
was no more than two hours away. The merchant ship
would be only fifteen miles or less from the Ford. Dunne
had been tempted to increase speed and make the identification with his own eyes, but on second thought that
would be foolish. He hadn't been able to see the intruder
at one hundred yards. Besides, sixteen knots would beat
his crew to death even if the *Ford* was riding reasonably
well at the moment. Yes, it would be much more sen-
sible to launch the chopper.

"Why don't you try again, Captain, and get some
rest?" Long John suggested.

"Too keyed up, John. Actually, I'm mad as hell. Such
irresponsible behavior on part of that captain. I want a
chunk of his ass. Whaddya think about launching the
chopper at dawn and ID-ing the bastard?"

Long John was the ship's First Lieutenant; his area of

expertise was the deck force and their responsibilities in seamanship and ship's upkeep. "Not in my area, Captain."

Dunne knew that. His question really had been addressed to himself. "Well, have your relief break out the ops officer in an hour or so and I'll see what he recommends. Weather permitting, I'd like to run an intercept and ID him."

"Aye, aye, sir."

"And John, I could use a plate of eggs—maybe some bacon."

"You got it, Captain."

Dunne let the high seatback recline a notch. While he wasn't in the mood to retire again to his sea cabin, he was all but overcome with a bone-aching fatigue. Maybe, if he could just close his eyes for a moment . . .

One hundred and ten miles ahead, there was a third eye, but it was not about to close. It was the eye of the rapidly developing tropical storm and it had survived the night by feeding on several squall lines that had added their turbulence and updrafts to the storm as it passed. With the rising of the sun, there would be a renewal of surface heat and the storm would grow and turn tighter onto itself, winding into a vicious, cyclonic disturbance that would gather even more energy. It was on a course directly toward the island of Oahu and held there by the clockwise winds of a high-pressure cell to its right and the counterclockwise winds of a sister low-pressure cell to its left. The two complimentary systems provided a steep pressure gradient that added even more thrust to the storm's northeastward travel.

Already, CINCPACFLT—the commander-in-chief, Pacific fleet—had set Storm Condition Two, and a number of the naval ships berthed in Pearl Harbor were making preliminary arrangements to get underway. If the approaching storm continued on its present course, it would hit Oahu; but prior to that time, Storm Condition One would be set and a number of ships would slip out of the harbor to ride out the storm at sea. Military aircraft from Hickam Air Force Base and the navy over at Barber's Point, as well as the marine corps air station at Kaneohe on the windward side of Oahu, were also preparing to evacuate to the airports on the big island of Hawaii and incoming Honolulu-bound commercial aircraft would soon be diverted to other islands in the Hawaiian chain.

2

Long John Childress spoke softly. He didn't want to startle his commanding officer, but he did want to wake him. "Your eggs, Captain."

Dunne's eyes were closed and he was in that inbetween state where he was almost asleep but could still feel the rolling and pitching of his ship, and he could vaguely hear the slapping noises of the sea, wind, and rain that were pounding the *Ford*.

Long John tried again. "Your eggs, sir."

Dunne involuntarily released a sound that was part snore and part grunt. It jarred him back to the real world. "Excuse me . . . oh, thank you, John."

He pulled the lever that erected his seatback and took the eggs. As usual, his messman had heated the china plate to insure that the food did not get cold before it reached his captain. A folded white cloth napkin kept the plate from being too warm to handle. The scrambled eggs were firm yet mildly moist, the bacon crisp, and the toast generously buttered, with just a dab of cherry preserves in the middle of each of the two pieces. Dunne ate hungrily, washing his early breakfast down with frequent swallows of hot coffee. He handed the empty plate back to Long John but kept the coffee. The chronometer indicated that he had "rested" for almost half an hour. The bridge was still dark and the sky outside even darker.

"That was good. I was hungry." Dunne looked around curiously. "It's after four, John, did your relief show up?" Childress' watch had been over at 0400 and it was now well past that hour. Then Dunne realized that the ship's CIC officer was standing in the shadows on the other side of Long John.

"Yes, sir, Captain. I have been relieved. I was just getting ready to go below."

"I have the deck and the conn, Captain," added the figure in the shadow, Lieutenant Dave Shepard. Long John touched the brim of his bridge cap. "Goodnight, Captain." Dunne nodded in acknowledgment of the casual salute as Long John left the bridge. Shepard moved a step closer to his captain and the chair. Blond, ruddy-faced, and sporting an ugly yellow mustache that detracted from his boyish good looks, Shepard was a Stanford NROTC graduate, well-seasoned in his surface warfare specialty, and a bridge buff who, when off duty, was always trying to scare up a wardroom game. Regrettably, most of the *Ford*'s small complement of sixteen officers were normally on watch or desperately trying to keep up with their administrative and division officer duties.

"How're the sea legs?" Dunne asked. He knew that Shepard, as well as a good number of the crew, had been bothered by the long stretch of heavy weather.

Shepard pointed to a small circular Band-Aid patch behind his right ear. "Doc fixed me up. I feel fine, sir."

"It's been a long night."

"Long John gave me a full briefing on the crossing incident. I heard the whistle, of course. Then that hard right turn caused me to review my past sins. I was already up and getting ready to relieve Long John, but when I didn't hear anything on the speakers I figured things were okay. Sure wakes a fellow up, though. I can't imagine a darkened ship plowing through this stuff at sixteen knots. We still hold him, sir; thirty-five hundred yards off the port bow and opening.''

"I want to see the ops officer at first light."

"Aye, aye, sir."

The *Ford* had a new bridge watch. In addition to Shepard, all of the other positions had been relieved. Stepping down from his chair, Dunne crossed over to the bridge's navigation table. He recognized the quartermaster overseeing the charts as Petty Officer Third Class Harold Cooper, a personable black Georgian who had some minor disciplinary problems early in the cruise but overall was a good sailor.

Dunne leaned over the chart and studied the *Ford*'s track and latest position. The track of the near-miss vessel was also being maintained. Cooper remained respectfully quiet.

"He damned near hit us," Dunne said as he analyzed the surface plot.

"Yes, sir."

"You did good, Cooper. Take care of that plot. I want to bring charges against that ship's captain. Your plot may wind up to be our number one exhibit."

"Yes, sir."

"We're going to be a few hours late with this storm," Dunne commented casually.

"Yessir." Cooper agreed.

"How's your mother?" Dunne asked. His exec earlier had briefed him concerning Cooper's problems regarding his mother's terminal illness. He also knew that Cooper, being single, sent almost all of his pay home to help with the medical bills.

" 'Bout the same, Captain."

Dunne, trying unsuccessfully to stifle a yawn, turned

and leaned back on the plot table. "When we get to Pearl, I want you to take some leave and go see your mother. I regret that the ops with the Aussies didn't allow us to spring you loose then."

"That was okay, Captain. But I'll have to go one day soon, though."

Dunne kept his voice low. "Cooper, I know you're short of funds. Sailors always are. When we get to Pearl, you see the exec. I've already talked to him. We've got a few dollars in the Morale Fund. Enough to get you home for a couple days."

"Captain, I owe everybody already. That's why I got into trouble in Sydney."

"I know, but the ship's fund is there for people like you. You don't have to repay it."

"I appreciate it, Captain. I really do, but I'll have to go home for the funeral . . . whenever."

"You need to see your mother now, not after she's gone."

"Yessir. Thank you, Captain."

"But don't you screw up again."

"No, sir."

"I mean it. You're a good sailor, Cooper. Your division officer has gone to bat for you with the exec. Exams are coming. I'm told there's no reason why you shouldn't make second class."

Dunne knew that Cooper was nervous talking directly to his commanding officer about his personal situation. But Dunne also knew that a word of encouragement at the right time could be just the support Cooper needed. The navy was struggling to retain good people with the long deployments, heavy operational schedules, declining manpower, and a bare-bones budget. From what he had been told, Dunne reasoned that Cooper was a petty officer well worth some of his personal attention. He also knew that his men were his greatest asset. If he survived the twelve months of command and went on to bigger and better things, it would be because men like Cooper worked long hours, around the clock when required, gave up their personal comfort, often disregarded their own needs, and jeopardized their personal safety on too many occasions during operations at sea. While the American sailor was probably the most profane, irreverent, independent, hard-living, constantly bitching member of the armed forces, he was also a most proud, hardworking, self-sacrificing individual who loved his country shamelessly and flaunted the bell-bottomed traditions of the sea service at every opportunity. On shore, sailors didn't walk, they swaggered—with the confidence that they could stay at sea for months and recoup all their lost fun and opportunities in one night. Some of the young ones drank too much and constantly sought excitement between the thighs of some aggressive female, but most matured fast in spite of their hormones and soon discovered the advantages of discretion and temperance in their liberty conduct. If they didn't, they were sure to receive the attention of the real backbone of the navy, the chief petty officer. Like a priest who has heard it all at confession, the chief had done it all in his youth, and now had the wisdom to rein in his young charges with tactics that ranged from simple but sincere advice and guidance to an old-fashioned physical session on the boat deck in the middle of a dark night. The latter didn't happen too often in the contemporary navy, but there were always enough sea stories around to convince the young male sailor that it *could* happen. Of course, that tactic wouldn't work with female naval personnel, but the *Ford* wasn't faced with that situation yet. Too small to be assigned any significant numbers of female sailors, the *Ford* had only one enlisted woman in the ship's company and she was a chief petty officer herself. So, the tradition was intact even if somewhat outmoded. If there were a problem the chief couldn't handle, then the man's division officer became the next responsible party, who had additional tools at his disposal.

By way of encouragement, Dunne touched Cooper lightly on the shoulder as he walked away and made a mental note to have his exec follow up on the situation when they reached Pearl.

As Dunne walked forward, Shepard commented, ''We're not going to see the dawn.'' His face was almost touching the glass in the large rectangular bridge window. The heavy sea spray was coating it, and the saltwater was mixing with the driving rain as waves swept across the bow. The *Ford* was still riding surprisingly well, although the sea state did not appear to have diminished. Shepard silently thanked the naval designers who had come up with such a seaworthy hull. He had suffered much worse rides on larger ships.

Dunne climbed back onto his chair and crossed his legs. It was still only 0445, but the hot breakfast had given him a renewed lease on life. Once more he had his hands cupped around a hot mug of black coffee. This dark, quiet bridge, despite its erratic dips and rises, was his home. It had been so nearly every day since they had sailed from the West Coast southwest across the great blue expanse of the Pacific Ocean and joined the Australians in six weeks of concentrated antisubmarine exercises. The Aussies were good, and the *Ford* had been stretched to keep up with their level of expertise. The submarine, a U.S. nuclear attack boat, had been an extremely elusive quarry, even though it had been restricted by the conditions of the exercises. If it had been the real world, Dunne knew, the task would have been even more difficult. And had it been a massive Russian Typhoon, the small allied task group of eight ships and a half-dozen helicopters would have had an impossible task. But it had been just an exercise, a game to sharpen the skills of the Aussie and Yank seamen. To that end, it had been quite successful.

Too bad the New Zealanders hadn't participated. In years past, before the collapse of the ANZUS (Australia-New Zealand-United States) pact, they always added a dash of colorful but exquisitely professional seamanship to such joint exercises. And the inevitable parties ashore had always been the best when hosted by the Kiwis. But officially they were offended by the U.S. Navy's nuclear weapons and now refused to participate or even allow the *Ford* to make port in their multi-islanded home.

For the first time in nine hours there was a very slight lightening of the darkness outside. Somewhere to the east the earliest rays of the rising sun were spreading over the surface of the water but unable to significantly probe through the thick wet cloud cover of the tropical storm that engulfed the *Ford*. Dunne noted that the wind was coming a bit more from the west, although the velocity was remaining steady. That disturbed him, for the westerly swing indicated that either the storm was slowing down or it was building in scope and intensity. Either situation would mean more rough riding for the *Ford*.

"Mr. Shepard, what's the position of our near-miss?"

"Opening fifteen degrees off the port bow, Captain. Range is 24,000 yards, sir."

"Still sixteen knots?"

"Yes, sir."

Dunne shifted to a more comfortable position in his chair. "Dumb bastard. He must have to get somewhere in a hurry."

One hundred and ninety nautical miles to the north, the island of Oahu was awakening early and the people along the southwest shore were beginning to secure loose yard objects and scrounging around for scrap plywood to nail over their windows. It wasn't certain that the storm would come ashore there but it was highly possible, and the early morning weather reports had announced that the threatening disturbance was now officially a hurricane and worthy of the name Kahiki, loosely translated as "the foreigner," and the storm was truly that, an unwelcome outsider who was picking up energy and more moisture as the sun rose and winds near the eye were reported in excess of one hundred knots.

The citizens of Waianae, nestled on tiny Pokai Bay on the island's west coast, had canceled their annual Chamber of Commerce luau and some were already trying to call their relatives over on the normally windward side to reserve bed space. But few of the calls were being answered, since their windward cousins were grabbing their boards and piling into minivans for the thirty-minute ride over the Koolau mountain range to the west coast to take advantage of the unusual and very rare storm waves that were already providing unbelievable surfing opportunities.

It was 0600 and probably about as light as it would get when the *Ford*'s operations officer reported to Dunne on the bridge. The cloud cover was just too intense to allow the sun's rays any more penetration, and the gray dawn would give way only to a gray morning.

Lieutenant Commander Bill McGregor was a seasoned frigate sailor, and his performance in the recent operations with the Aussies had convinced Dunne that McGregor was a suberb tactician and as good an ASW operator as any Dunne had worked with. A thin-haired redhead, the Scot was a born seaman, and his knowledge of frigate helicopter operations had earned him the respect of not only his captain but the somewhat prima donna aviators who flew their complex charges off the small helipad on the stern of the *Ford*. The marriage of the rotary-winged weapon and the seaborne frigate was not one of convenience, for flying off and onto the tiny square platform in pitching and rolling seas was as demanding and dangerous as any mode of naval aviation. Rather, the wedding was one of operational necessity, a coupling that gave the ship a deep over-the-horizon perimeter for submarine hunting and a stealth approach that when properly conducted could give the ship-aircraft team the advantage of tactical surprise.

McGregor pulled his right hand from his green foul weather jacket to give Dunne a morning salute. "G'mornin', Cap'n."

"Good morning, Bill. You up to speed on the near-miss?"

"Yessir. Long John briefed me. Sounds like some merchantman needs his shorts yanked up a notch."

"That's my view. What do you think of this for flying weather?"

"Lousy. We've got a good two-hundred-foot ceiling, but the visibility's garbage and it's pretty bumpy out there."

"We've operated in worse, Bill."

McGregor shrugged. "True, but that was operational necessity."

"Well, I don't want to push the *Ford* to catch that guy and get a visual, but I do want an ID. He's a menace. I want to file a complaint."

"I understand, Cap'n."

"Is the helo crew up?"

"Yessir. The plane captain is preflighting the bird, and the pilots are in the wardroom. I didn't tell them that it's a definite go yet."

"It isn't. But let's pursue it. The bastard is opening on us at about six knots. The farther he pulls away, the longer the airborne time. That's a consideration."

McGregor studied the rise and fall of the bow for a moment. "With these seas, I think the pilots should make the decision on this one."

"I heartily agree with that. I don't intend to send them

off against their recommendation. Why don't we get
Lieutenant Kohn's thoughts?''

McGregor stepped back to the bridge phone and
picked up the handset.

Lieutenant Sheila ''Frosty'' Kohn was not overly enthusiastic about the early wakeup. Operations were over.
This was supposed to be a leisurely cruise back to the
west coast via Pearl. True, the routine would be only
slightly altered for ship's company, but she was the officer in charge of the two-aircraft, sixteen-man helicopter
detachment. The *Ford* carried two ASW helicopters, but
one was in a DOWN status due to its need for an engine
change. Kohn had allowed the crew of the disabled cop-
ter to leave the ship at Sydney and fly military air back
to San Diego. No reason for all of us to be miserable,
she had mused. The long sea voyage home could be
monotonous for the aircrews, despite her plans to use
the time for catch-up administrative and maintenance
chores. But the storm-whipped seas of the past thirty-six
hours had interfered with that. And now the old man
wanted her to go flying?

Kohn had scrubbed her face, brushed her teeth, and
combed her short auburn hair into some semblance of
order before slipping into her flight suit. There was a
very pleasant looseness to its fit. The busy flying routine
over the past weeks with the Aussies had burned away
several pounds in just the right places, an operational
bonus that partly made up for the hasty meals and long
hours with her hands wrapped around the collective and-
cyclic controls of her helicopter. It had been nice not to
watch every calorie.

A few drops of Visine had cleared the faint traces of
red from the white around her cobalt irises, but there
was still a stinging sensation that caused her to lower
her lids and hold them there for a moment. Probably a
result of the late-night reading and the rough ride in the

sack, holding on for dear life as the *Ford* stubbornly fought the swells and plowed through the surface waves of a turbulent sea. The *Ford* was due for some in-port time when they returned to San Diego, and Kohn was looking forward to letting her nails grow a bit. She kept them filed short and well groomed, but for a few weeks of shore duty she could bring back a bit more of her femininity. Then, when she went back to flicking switches and pushing circuit breakers, she would file them shorter again.

Just as she pushed back her chair to grab a coffee refill, one of the wardroom messmen motioned to her. "For you, Lieutenant," he said.

She took the handset. "Lieutenant Kohn . . . Good morning, Commander . . . Yes, sir, we're right here . . . on our way, sir." Another cup of the thick black coffee would have completed her morning ritual but she reluctantly set the empty mug on the self-service counter. "Let's go, Beaver," she called to her copilot, who had listened intently to her remarks and was hurriedly scooping up the last of his scrambled eggs.

LT(jg) Phil "Beaver" Davis had not scrubbed his face, brushed his teeth, nor combed his hair. He had splashed water on his head, patted down the confused abundance of blond hair, and rubbed a dry finger across his slightly protruding front teeth. Realizing now that he had probably missed his opportunity to properly brush the night off his teeth, he popped a breath freshener into his mouth and picked up the last piece of toast as he rose to join Kohn. "I thought we were gonna have a little holiday routine today, *Loo*tenant."

"Don't you wish."

Davis stuffed the toast into his mouth, wincing at the unanticipated mint-toast flavor combination and followed Kohn forward toward the bridge. "I don't think I slept five minutes all night," he remarked to no one in particular.

Their path was along a port passageway, forward through two watertight hatches, up a pair of ladders to the bridge level, and then forward past Dunne's sea cabin. Both shook their heads in awe as they caught their first glimpses of the outside world. Not good flying weather at all.

"Kohn," McGregor began, "the captain wants your evaluation of the weather. We need to intercept a merchantman and ID him. He's up ahead about fifteen miles and pulling away."

"Good morning, Captain," Kohn greeted. *Protocol first.* Beaver Davis repeated her words and stood respectfully beside her. "Not good," Kohn continued. "Ceiling and visibility not *too* bad, but we could have a rough time getting off the pad—and back on. The RAST is still down for parts we're supposed to pick up at Pearl. Without it, we're a little more limited in what kind of seas we can tolerate."

Dunne nodded. "The wind has been lessening the past hour," he said.

"Is the bird up?" McGregor asked.

"It should be," answered Kohn. "Kosickny is pulling his preflight." As she spoke, Kohn looked around the bridge, examining as much of the sea and weather as she could see. It was flyable but could get touchy.

"It's important, Lieutenant Kohn, that we ID the ship," Dunne said. "We came very close to a collison early this morning. It could have been a disaster, and that captain deserves to hear about it."

"That's what the whistle and hard turn were all about?" Kohn asked.

"Yes. We had to maneuver at the last minute, and he was running dark—no lights at all. We had no contact."

Kohn nodded for a moment, giving the weather and seas another silent evaluation. "Then I say we go get him, sir. If it looks too dicey when we're ready to launch, we'll abort." Kohn felt the sharp probe of Davis's elbow in her side.

"It's your call, Lieutenant. Safety is the governing factor," Dunne concluded.

You've covered your ass, thought Davis, not at all anxious to fly just so the captain of the *Ford* could have the satisfaction of placing the other captain on report.

"Why don't we wait another half-hour, just to see if it lets up outside," McGregor suggested.

"It'll take us that long to preflight and get ready," Kohn replied.

"Sounds good," Dunne acknowledged. "Let us know when you're ready and we'll give you the best sea and wind we can."

"Aye, aye, sir," Kohn answered and preceded Davis off the bridge.

Dunne leaned toward McGregor. "I don't want her to push it."

"Lieutenant Kohn is all professional, Captain. If she thinks we shouldn't launch, she'll tell us. I guarantee that."

"Good."

"Holy Christ, Frosty," Davis protested as he and Kohn grabbed for support while making their way aft. "This'll be like operating from a fucking cork. I don't like this and I don't like the fact that the RAST is down. That tether is my security blanket in this kind of shit."

"You got a filthy mouth, Beaver."

"Only when I know I'm heading into certain doom. I apologize."

"It sets a bad example for our enlisted troops. I've told you before. I don't care for it. We better stop by our rooms and get our flight jackets. It's going to be wet and maybe chilly. I'll see you on the pad."

Davis veered off toward his room, pausing only to watch Kohn proceed aft down the passageway and step across the lip of one of the watertight hatch openings. The movement stretched her flight suit across her buttocks and caused Davis to smile in admiration. It was the best-looking tush he had ever seen on a naval aviator, the firm round delicious kind you just wanted to reach out and pat. As she passed out of sight, he wondered if any male had ever patted Frosty Kohn—and lived. Certainly, he was not going to. Her reputation in the U.S. Navy was that of a naval officer first, a naval aviator second, and a woman a distant third.

At the moment, however, there was a consolation. Davis was as professional as any of his contemporaries when it came to flying and that included his judgment as well as his skills. While he would just as soon sit this mission out, if he had to go, Frosty Kohn was the one aviator in whom he had absolute trust and confidence. Sure, there were times when he felt she really needed a man, but it obviously wasn't going to be him. He had found that out as soon as they had started flying together. After his first few disastrous attempts to establish a relationship other than that between professional aviators, Kohn's response had been such that he had been tempted to call her Frigid rather than Frosty. They had served together in HSL-47 (Helicopter LAMPS Squadron Forty-Seven), their parent squadron back at the North Island Naval Air Station in San Diego, for over a year now, and he had jumped at the chance to deploy with her aboard the *Ford* when her regularly assigned copilot had rolled his Porsche, with the result being the jagged end of a broken tibia puncturing the thick flesh of an inside thigh.

To Davis, Kohn was a natural aviator, that rare breed of pilot who adapted to the laws of aerodynamics and skills of flying as easily as she had learned to breathe. Frosty didn't merely strap on an airplane, she became a component, as much a component of the complicated flying machine as any other system: hydraulics, electronics, computer, engine, whatever. She was the flesh-and-blood component, the thinking and decision system whose five senses instantly read every demand and reaction of aircraft performance and immediately responded to make the craft do exactly what she wanted it to do. Her initial assignment had been with a composite squadron, and Frosty had checked out in every one of the five different aircraft types assigned. She had qualified as an aircraft commander in multiengined Grumman C-2 COD operations before she had amassed her first eight hundred hours of flight time, and as a relatively junior jaygee she had regularly delivered the high-strung F/A-18 Hornets aboard carriers at sea as easily as the more docile A-6 Intruders. It was a rare day when Frosty didn't get a CUT! and grab number-three wire on her first pass. Most naval aviators reached the grade of commander before they acquired a service-wide flying reputation; yet Frosty was known throughout the fleet by the time she made the lieutenants' list, and her envious contemporaries had shaken their heads in confusion when she had requested cross-training in helicopters. Her only explanation was brief and simple: she wanted to fly *everything*, and she wanted to go operational. And as he honed his chopper skills flying with HSL-47, Davis was smart enough to realize that an operational tour with Frosty as his mentor would make him a much better aviator. So while he occasionally pulled her chain just to remind her that they carried different sets of hormones, their relationship had taken on an aspect of mutual professional respect and, along with a young, highly skilled enlisted tactical control-sensor operator, they were a very capable and respected flying team. While Davis did have a few reservations about launching on this particular stormy day, especially when he felt there was no operational requirement for such a flight, he was actually looking forward to watching and learning once more from Frosty when she would be at her best.

By the time he reached the pad, Kohn was performing her customary, methodical walkaround inspection despite the wind and rain and slippery deck, carefully checking the security of inspection panels, eye-balling hydraulic and electrical lines, patting and feeling the SH-60B Seahawk helicopter as would a doctor probe and look into all of the orifices of his patient for any irregularity. The ASW helicopter, with its dull-gray finish and short landing gear, seemed more a giant grasshopper squatting in a futile attempt to ward off the fury of the storm than a sophisticated war machine that with a crew of three could hunt and fight its underwater prey with awesome patience and weaponry.

Davis stepped into the left-hand seat, strapped in, and began the pre-start procedure. He checked in with the *Ford*. "Sundance, this is Lightray, ready to launch."

The *Ford* began a wide turn as Dunne brought her around to provide the safest wind and swell combination for liftoff.

A moment later, Kohn climbed into her seat and joined Davis in the check procedure. AW3 Eric Price, their crewman, was already on board and their plane captain, Chief Petty Officer Andy Kosickny, a stocky Pole whose grandparents still lived in Warsaw, also climbed aboard and secured the side hatch. He normally did not fly on operational ASW missions, but he could be of value on this interception. The helicopter had a personnel hoist stowed in the aft cabin in event a search and rescue mission required a pickup at sea, and Kosickny was well-versed in its rigging and use.

The LAMPS III Seahawk was still secured to the pad and chocked. With the erratic rolling and pitching of the *Ford*, it would be unsafe to untie it until the engines were started and the rotors engaged. Even then, launching would be a tricky and dangerous operation.

The start procedure went smoothly, and after a thorough check of the engine instruments, Kohn nodded and

Davis answered with a thumbs-up. The Seahawk took on a life of its own, and after a test of control response, Kohn directed the crewman outside to untie the chopper. With positive control established, she began to load the main rotor as the *Ford* steadied on course.

"Lightray, this is Sundance. You're cleared for liftoff, your discretion."

"Roger, Sundance," Davis answered.

The stern of the *Ford* reached its apogee, and at the exact moment it started back down Kohn twisted the throttle into full power and smoothly lifted the collective control arm, simultaneously giving the cyclic control a gentle back pressure. The Seahawk lifted free smartly as the stern fell. Kohn banked away from the *Ford*. They were clear—and fully in the grip of the storm winds.

"Holy shit!" Davis exclaimed. He had marveled at the ease with which Kohn had executed the difficult launch, but now he was being thrown repeatedly against his straps as Kohn fought the turbulence. They were just below the base of the clouds at two hundred feet and the visibility was no more than a half-mile.

"Lightray, vector three-three-five, target fourteen miles." The voice from the *Ford* was calm and professional. Why not? Davis thought. The speaker was safely tucked away in the combat information center of the *Ford*, warm and dry and encased in a steel hull that was impervious to the violent winds that were tossing the Seahawk around like an aluminum can.

"Roger," Davis responded.

Fourteen miles would be only a few minutes away, and in the custom of airmen the four began to adjust to the rough ride as Petty Officer Price busied himself with monitoring the helicopter's search radar scope. The target had appeared almost immediately after liftoff, and the yellow blip on the radar scope was dead ahead and closing. There was a clutter of sea return around the center of the scope, but by adjusting the brilliance and antenna tilt, Price could maintain a clear target return.

Kohn dropped to one hundred and fifty feet as the cloud bottoms became ragged and wisps of gray condensation dropped down almost to the surface. The constant rain was alternately heavy and damn heavy.

The target was less than a mile away when Davis first saw it. "Visual dead ahead," he reported.

Kohn took her eyes off the instruments and immediately nodded as she also picked up the fat hull of a freighter plowing though the heavy seas. It was riding high with plenty of freeboard, probably empty or near so. That was odd. In these seas it needed a lower center of gravity. Kohn positioned the Seahawk to approach the ship from astern and to port. "Okay, Beaver, give 'em a call on international distress," Kohn directed, slowing to just a few knots above the freighter's speed.

"Hello, *Salinika,*" Davis called, reading the name on the stern of the ship, "this is United States Navy helicopter five-three-seven-two-niner, close aboard your port quarter. Do you read? Over."

"Athens," Kohn murmured, reading the port of origin under the ship's name.

Davis repeated his call. No response.

Kohn eased the chopper closer aboard and inched forward until she was abeam the bridge superstructure. Her "my God" was involuntary. She could make out several crewmen prone on the weatherdeck. They were moving slightly but only because the freighter was rolling and pitching in the storm. Kohn's mouth remained open as she could see that they were obviously dead, their bodies bloated and bleached. Several more were partially visible through the wide windows of the bridge, but her view was limited and she could not tell how many.

"Look at that," Davis directed, pointing forward. Kohn blinked her eyes to clear them and make sure she saw what she saw. An aircraft! A black unmarked shape that she immediately recognized as a Russian-built Yak-

36 Forger. She was completely confused. *What is all this? A Greek freighter with a Russian VTOL fighter on deck?* The Forger had apparently been housed in some sort of prefabricated deckhouse, positioned just about where the forward kingposts would have been. The sides of the deckhouse were collapsed and lying flat on the deck, the Forger fully exposed.

"I think they're all dead," Davis surmised.

"You suppose anyone's alive below decks?" Kohn asked.

"I dunno, but that would explain why they were running with no lights and no apparent control. What the hell's happened?"

"Must have been some sort of sickness."

"Shit, Frosty! There's a pilot in the Forger!"

"I don't believe this. I can get a little closer. Make a contact report to Sundance."

Davis keyed his mike. "Sundance, this is Lightray. We have a visual on a freighter. The ID is *Salinika*, out of the port of Athens. We have dead crewmen on deck and on the fo'c'sle an aircraft. It is a Russian Yak 36 Forger, no markings."

"Lightray, this is Sundance. Did you say it is carrying an aircraft?"

"Affirmative. ID is a Russian Yak-36 Forger. Do you copy?"

"Copy. Stand by."

Joshua Dunne was as puzzled as everyone else on the bridge and in the combat information center. He spoke to his exec. "Jim, draft me a priority message to CINC-PACFLT. I don't know what this is but we need some guidance." Turning toward his OOD, he ordered, "Let's see how we ride at twenty knots. Set your course to intercept. I think we ought to board the ship if it's feasible. If anyone is alive, they need help."

As the *Ford* accelerated, Dunne issued further orders,

"Double check storm condition one. I don't want *any-one* out on the weather decks." He triggered the inter-com to CIC. "Combat, have Lightray return. Let me know when she's ten minutes out."

"Combat, aye, sir."

Dunne spoke again to his exec, "Break out the board-ing party, and we better include the doc. Have them muster in the wardroom in twenty minutes. I want the department heads there, and the ship's bo's'n."

"Aye, aye, sir."

"I count a total of eleven bodies," Beaver Davis re-ported. "How about you, Chief?"

"Eleven, but there may be more on the bridge," Ko-sickny replied. He had the starboard sliding door open but was desperately hanging on to his safety strap as the Seahawk danced in the wind like a fish on the end of a line.

With some difficulty Kohn maneuvered the chopper down and as close abeam the Forger as she dared. "Could he be alive?" she asked. Kosickny leaned out as far as he could. "He's not moving, but I can't see his face with the helmet and mask on."

Davis added, "He'd be waving his arm off if he were. He'd have to see us this close. This is some kind of weird. Frosty, I'm really uncomfortable this close."

Kohn moved out to a more comfortable position. "Do we have a camera on board?"

"No, ma'am," Kosickny answered, "unless Price has a personal one."

"Not me."

The voice of the *Ford* came over the tactical fre-quency. "Lightray, return to home plate. Over."

Kohn nodded her head in acknowledgment, but she had a slight delay in mind. "Beaver, tell 'em I want to make a pass up the other side."

"Sundance, we're going to make one more pass . . . will be departing in five minutes."

"Roger Lightray. No problem. Upon departure, vector one-five-zero."

"Roger, one-five-zero." Beaver scribbled the heading on his kneepad.

Kohn let the helicopter slide aft and then crossed over to the starboard side of the ship. As they flew alongside, they picked up another body previously hidden by the superstructure, and Kohn steadied the helicopter once more opposite the Forger.

Davis strained to make out the apparatus underneath the Forger's wing. There was some kind of piping running spanwise. "What is that?" he asked.

"What is what?" countered Kohn.

"There's some kind of piping under the wing."

"I can't see it from here. I wonder if the pilot was trying to get away from the sickness."

Davis lifted his arm and pointed. "Look at the canopy! There's a hole broken in it just opposite him. I think that's a bullet hole. Somebody shot the bastard!"

"There's a body on the deck just behind the trailing edge of the wing," Kohn added.

Davis was shaking his head, obviously puzzled. "Something went terribly wrong aboard that ship. Maybe a mutiny."

"I don't see how that would account for *everybody* being dead. And look how bloated the bodies are."

"A few days in the sun of these latitudes would do that," Davis speculated.

"Well, let's get back to the ship and see if we can sort it out." Kohn started a turn to the right, fighting the controls as the relative wind began to change along with her heading.

Davis kept twisting in his seat to keep his eyes on the freighter as he gave his report. "Sundance, Lightray departing at one-three."

"Roger, Lightray."

At least the return trip would be shorter with the tail-wind. That was small consolation. The winds were even more confused and violent than before.

Kohn directed, "Let's try the autopilot."

"Rog—" Davis couldn't complete the word as a particularly strong gust tried to lift the Seahawk while the autopilot tried to compensate for it. The result was first a strong positive G effect then an even stronger negative G that lifted the crew's stomachs almost into their throats.

"Negative, autopilot," gasped Kohn, disengaging the system. She could fly manually more smoothly than that. "Too much for that system."

"Too much for *my* system," Davis added.

Kohn worked the cyclic and collective like a spastic video game player. Davis rode the controls but could do little to assist her. Besides, as rough as it was, Kohn was managing to stay fairly ahead of the airplane.

Most of the time.

"Whooaaaaa . . ." Kohn was showing stress for the first time. The chopper had rolled almost sixty degrees.

Davis stared down at the angry sea only a scant twenty yards away. "Let's get out of this shit, Frosty!"

Kohn was too busy to reply. Now the Seahawk was jolting up and down like a yo-yo with a knotted string.

"Speed bumps," announced Kohn, refusing to abandon her sense of humor.

Price and Kosickny were tightly belted in with their arms wrapped around the nearest piece of equipment-rack railing.

Despite her cry, Kohn was grinning and fighting the storm with obvious confidence. *My God!* thought Davis, *she's enjoying this.*

Within eight minutes, they had the *Ford* in sight. It was turning to give them the best landing conditions.

"Lightray, we have you visual. You're cleared to the pad."

Davis responded promptly, "Roger, Sundance. Are you steadying on one-eight-zero?"

"One-six-five looks about the best."

"Roger, thank you."

"Landing check," Frosty ordered as she swung the bucking chopper into position aft and downwind of the *Ford*.

The check completed, she began her approach. The stern of the *Ford* was in a state of perpetual motion, rising and then falling. Kohn gauged the cycle to be about ten or fifteen feet with about one cycle every fifteen seconds. The rain was showing no mercy, and at intervals so intense visibility was severely restricted. She could see a yellow-shirted crewman on the pad, braced against the wind and shielding his face from the rain with one hand while attempting to direct her with the other. It was an impossible task. "Sundance, get the crewman off the pad," Kohn ordered. "It's too dangerous for him; we're all over the sky here."

Kohn saw the crewman give a farewell wave as he left the pad, in all probability one very relieved sailor.

Hovering about ten feet above the reach of the rise of the stern, Kohn began a series of descents to try and match the fall of the pad. After several evaluation attempts, she followed the pad down, dropped onto it just before it hit bottom, briskly lowered the collective all the way, closed the throttle, and stood on the brakes. Perfect timing. The stern started up, immediately canceling out any tendency for the helicopter to bounce. Two crewman quickly climbed onto the pad as soon as the main rotor stopped, and they began tying the Seahawk securely to the deck. With their thumbs-up signal, Kohn shut down the chopper's engines.

Davis sat there shaking his head in unabashed admiration. "That was beautiful. I thought we were going to hit so hard the landing gear would be up here sharing some cockpit space with my private parts.''

Kohn's grin was that of the cat that had not only swallowed the canary but was relishing the sweet taste. ''Oh, ye of little faith,'' she purred. ''Now it's coffee time.''

Everyone stood as Dunne entered the wardroom. ''Please,'' he said, ''as you were.'' He took his seat at the head of the long table and a messman placed a cup of coffee in front of him on the green felt cover. ''Thank you,'' said Dunne.

To his right sat the exec, the ops boss, and beyond him, Lt. Kohn and Lt. (jg) Davis. On Davis' right sat Chief Kosickny. To the left of Dunne sat the ship's engineering officer, LCDR Patrick Sullivan; the navigator, LCDR Jason Sims; Long John Childress; Lt. Holly from admin; communicator Lt. Murray; and finally, the ship's bo's'n, Chief Warrant Officer Lombardi.

''I've just been talking to PACFLT and they're aware of the situation,'' Dunne began. ''I recommended that we board the *Salinika*, check for any surviving crewmen, slow her down, and change her course toward fair weather. The CINC is up to his eyebrows in hurricane evacuation procedures, but he does concur, and we've been ordered to stay with her until PACFLT can get a salvage crew out to bring her into Pearl. That may be as long as twenty-four hours or more since the storm is sitting right between us and Oahu.''

''We can't board her by boat in these seas, Captain,'' Lombardi stated.

''I know that, Boats. Sheila, can you get a team aboard?''

''We do have a hoist on board. If it doesn't get any worse, Captain, we should be able to put them aboard. There's plenty of clear deck forward where they have removed the kingposts and secured the aircraft. We could risk the danger of not being able to get them back off, however. It's marginal out there.''

Dunne sipped his coffee. ''I think we should try. We have a humanitarian obligation. Worst case, if we can get aboard, is that the boarding team will have to stay with her until we can get to fair weather.''

McGregor was obviously uncomfortable with the way the discussion was going. He had shifted twice in his seat and was leaning forward waiting for an opening to speak. ''Captain, we don't know what killed those men, but suppose it's some sort of sickness. It could be highly contagious. We don't want to bring it back to the *Ford*.''

''I've been thinking about that. We'll put the team in biological warfare protective gear. It's bulky. Can we still get them on board, Sheila?''

''They should be able to ride the rescue seat down. That way they won't have to rappel and we can hoist them back up.''

''Long John, you're the officer in charge of the ship's boarding party. You want the whole group?''

''I don't think we need all of the security people, and with this weather we should take only a minimum team.''

''Name it.''

''Quartermaster, a chief engineman, and a corpsman.''

''She's a steamer. Can one man handle the boilers?'' Dunne asked.

''I'll send Chief Gantry,'' engineer Sullivan answered. ''He has merchant marine experience.''

Bo's'n Lombardi lifted a hand. ''I'd like to go in place of a quartermaster. That'll give us more versatility.''

''I buy that,'' Long John agreed.

''Do we really need a corpsman?'' Beaver Davis asked. ''It looks like they're all dead. And each man adds to the time frame and danger of getting on and off.''

"Definitely," Dunne responded. "We don't know if they're all dead. And we'll need some kind of medical evaluation. In fact, I want a body brought back if feasible."

McGregor objected. "I'm not sure that would be a good idea, Captain. We don't know what kind of bug they could bring back. I don't see why we need a body. Let the salvage crew take care of that."

"Use a body bag," Dunne countered. "There's a factor we haven't considered here. 'Doc' Abbot might be able to determine what it is, and then we could inform the salvage party. It could make their job safer."

"Doc is a physician's assistant, not a doctor, Captain. I don't think he has the expertise for something like this," McGregor argued.

Dunne reconsidered. "All right, we do this. Doc goes along in the corpsman slot. If he feels we should bring a body back, we do—provided getting him into the chopper doesn't jeopardize the safety of the operation. It'll be his decision—and Sheila's, of course." Dunne looked around for further protest. There was none.

McGregor reasoned he could live with that, and he'd be damned sure to speak to Doc Abbot before the party boarded the helicopter. It might be Abbot's decision, but there would be one hell of a strong executive officer input. Bringing a contaminated body back to the *Ford* was just plain stupid.

3

Admiral John J. Paterson, Commander-in-Chief, Pacific Fleet, and acting USCINCPAC since the previous incumbent had suffered a fatal heart attack only three days prior and his successor had yet to be named, would have liked to have given the predicament of the USS *Ford* a bit more of his attention. But, with just under one hundred naval vessels currently operating out of Pearl Harbor and one hellacious hurricane bearing down on Oahu, he had the overall safety of the fleet as his first concern. Blackjack Paterson, his nickname reflecting much more his stern demeanor rather than the color of his skin, listened intently as the command duty officer read off the disposition-of-ships list. Thirty-one were at sea on operations, all of them aware of the storm and well clear of its path. Twelve, including the aircraft carrier *Abraham Lincoln* and three nuclear-powered cruisers, had cleared the harbor entrance in the early morning hours and were steaming east where they would remain until the storm passed. Another cruiser, the USS *Sterret*, was not ready for sea, because her prop shaft bearings were being upgraded with new seals. She should be safe in the dry dock. The two resident submarines, both *Los Angeles*-class attack boats, were underway but not yet clear of the harbor. Should be no problem there as they could submerge and ride the storm out once they made open water. The rest were mostly small auxiliaries, tugs, and yard craft, and all would have to ride out the winds securely moored to buoys or at pier side.

"Thank you, Commander," Blackjack said. "I want an update every hour."

"Aye, aye, sir." The briefing officer gathered his papers together. Satisfied that the admiral had no other comments, he excused himself and quietly left the office.

Paterson was also concerned about the naval shore stations in the area, but all commands had reported secured and ready. Nevertheless, the admiral was quite sure that a few commanders were still running around checking on last minute details. You were never one hundred percent ready for a hurricane. The memory of the 1991 storm, Iniki, was still fresh in the minds of some and hard-hit Kauai had only just recently recovered its full tourist capability. But it appeared that unless the storm took a turn to the north, Oahu would take the hit.

His PACOM headquarters at the Marine Base, Camp H. M. Smith, just a few miles north up the Halawa Heights Road from Pearl Harbor, should have no great difficulty in riding out the storm, although there were still some World War II type buildings with feeble survival capabilities.

As for the *Ford*, Blackjack reasoned that the frigate was in good hands. He knew Joshua Dunne like a son, and indeed that was the admiral's feeling toward the skipper of the *Ford* who also happened to be the husband of his only child.

Operating independently under the temporary operational control of CINCPACFLT, Dunne was the commanding officer of a man-of-war at sea and as such was fully capable of making tactical decisions. If the circumstances of the *Ford*'s encounter with the *Salinika* were as reported, and there was no reason to second-guess them, Blackjack was content to monitor the situation and provide moral support and approval as requested; there was little else he could do at the present and it seemed to him that little else was required. He didn't envy the *Ford*'s decision to place a boarding party aboard the runaway *Salinika*, but he did approve of it. And in the way of a sailor who had met his own challenges during thirty years walking the decks of thirteen ships, including destroyers to battleships, the admiral envied his son-in-law commander.

Blackjack stared out his office window, watching the rain pour from the dark clouds approaching from the south, reliving a score of past experiences where he had fought a rough sea and a fearful wind. He would forever savor the memories of a good ship and a good crew working together and sharing the pride of accomplishment. For all of his duties, the ones that had given him the most satisfaction were those when he had been the commanding officer of a U.S. Navy combatant at sea. That was the goal of every naval officer, and although higher command normally followed, there was never again that same excitement, that same very proud and—yes—egotistical feeling of accomplishment. In all of the military, there was no other job that carried with it such personal and professional around-the-clock responsibilities. In no other job was the naval officer so empowered—and so encumbered—by the awesome responsibilities of the welfare of a ship and, in the case of the large carriers, as many as six-thousand crewmen. It was the ultimate challenge.

Well, Blackjack reasoned as he ended his brief reveries, at the moment Joshua had his problems—and he had his. And there was one very personal dilemma that they both shared. He glanced at the brass chronometer on the far wall of his office. It would be almost noon in San Diego. That should be a convenient time. Chemotherapy was normally administered in the morning hours. He dialed the naval hospital at Balboa and asked for his daughter's room.

4

Again, Beaver Davis marveled at the skill displayed by
Kohn as she aggressively lifted the Seahawk off the
Ford's pad. If anything, the sea was a bit rougher than
before, but Kohn's judgment and technique were superb,
and she swung the chopper around in a sweeping turn
that provided maximum safety in the gusty winds and
took up a course for the *Salinika*. Behind the two pilots,
Petty Officer Price was again manning his radar and sen-
sor position. Chief Kosickny and the four-man boarding
team crouched low and held on for dear life.

The Seahawk had not been designed to transport eight
people. Most of the crew space (normally occupied by
just Price, although there was one meager jump seat)
was crammed full of electronic search and detection
gear, and the cramped compartment was made even
more so by the NBC protective suits worn by the passengers. The bulky oversuits that encased the navymen
from head to toe were partially compressed by the aviation life jackets. Only Price and Kosickny were
strapped in. The others managed to grab secure hand-
holds, however, and made themselves as comfortable as

46

possible. A conscientious aviation safety officer would have had a foaming fit at the arrangement, but Kohn considered the flight an emergency operational requirement almost on a par with combat necessity. If she had to stretch a rule, she wouldn't be setting a precedent.

Kosickny had rigged the hoist davit, which required that the sliding door remain partially open, and the incessant rain was intermittently swirling into the cabin area. The black rubber body bag was rolled tightly and secured to the deck by two straps. It served as a cushion for Long John, who would have preferred an open boat in the rough sea to an air machine that was pitching and tossing and rolling about like a ping-pong ball in a bingo cage. He had always had an aversion to flying, particularly in a craft that seemed to be coming apart even as it took off from the pad. Bo's'n Lombardi had one arm around Long John and the other firmly anchored to a bracket that held some kind of black box. Doc Abbot felt quite secure in the middle of the packed compartment; before the turbulence tossed him out, several others would have to go first. As for Chief Gantry, the engineman, he was reevaluating the power of prayer and had decided that it certainly couldn't make things any worse. Unfortunately, the only formal spiritual plea he could remember began "Now I lay me down to sleep. . . . ''

To the relief of all, the *Salinika* appeared ahead after only six minutes, and once more Kohn set up a run along the starboard side of the ship. When she reached her position abeam the Forger, she held it while evaluating the situation. After a few minutes fighting through several approaches in the shifting wind, she lifted and crossed over to the port side.

"This is better," she announced. "We can move in and lower the boarding party one at a time. I don't think it's too bad. But that is one waterswept and slippery deck. Kosickny, warn everybody to really take it easy!"

She inched the Seahawk into position. "Okay, let's do it!"

First over was Long John. Holding desperately to the three-pronged steel rescue seat, he was placed precisely in the center of the clear area. First ensuring that he had a secure footing, he released the device and took refuge behind one of the raised cargo-hold lips.

Next was the bo's'n, who arrived with a mile-wide grin; this was the way the navy was supposed to operate—on the edge! Long John steadied him, and the device was pulled up for Chief Gantry, who also was lowered without incident. Doc Abbot was not quite as fortunate. Still three feet above the deck, he dropped and hit hard as a terrific gust killed some of the Seahawk's lift and it dipped several feet before Kohn could counter its descent. Long John had the handheld radio and reported to Kohn and crew.

"We're all down. The Doc hit hard and may have a sprained ankle . . . says he can go on okay . . . we'll give you a preliminary report as soon as we can."

"Roger, John. I'm going to slide out to port," Kohn advised. On that side she would have a direct view of the activity on the weather decks.

The four *Ford* crewmen huddled together against the side of the cargo hatch.

"Boats, get up to the pilot house and check it out," Long John directed. "Chief, make it down to engineering and give Bo's'n Lombardi a call when you're ready to throttle down. Doc and I will check the bodies on deck and then the aircraft before meeting on the bridge. At that time we'll slow her down and make our course change. And be careful—this deck's as slippery as the proverbial owl shit."

All nodded concurrence and the group separated. Lombardi found the pitching and rolling of the merchantman much more unpredictable than that of the *Ford*. The gusting winds against the high freeboard of the hull shook the merchantman from stem to stern, and without anyone manning the rudder, she was wallowing along in the manner of a drunken whale. These were the kind of seas that poor seamanship could find fatal, and the *Salinika* had the misfortune of no guiding hand at all.

Despite Long John's warning, Lombardi slipped and fell twice moving across the open deck toward the bridge ladder. Firmly gripping the wet siderails, he climbed to the enclosed bridge and entered. It was manned by corpses, all similar to those on the exposed main deck, except that they wore less foul-weather gear. The inside of the bridge was well protected from the rain, but there was a coating of some greasy substance over the deck, overhead, bulkheads, and all of the bridge fixtures. But what caught Lombardi's eyes was the helm. The wheel was chained in position, the chains secured by several large steel locks. *Why was that?* he thought.

Chief Gantry entered the first hatch he came to as he reached the aft superstructure, and once inside he made his way down the ladder. The *Salinika* was a neglected ship, and inside she was more rust than clean steel. As Gantry hit the last rung, his foot slipped and he tumbled forward onto the landing. One shoulder struck a stowed fire axe and the blade ripped a six-inch gash in his protective suit.

"Oh . . . shit," he cursed. One of the leg pockets held some adhesive repair tape and he ripped off a piece to close the gap. Fortunately, next to the axe was a battle lantern, and he grabbed it before proceeding aft and below. The passageway lights were on but he wasn't sure what he would find as he carefully made his way down toward the engine room in the bowels of the ship. The damned deck, bulkheads, and ladders were coated with some kind of slimy substance. It had the consistency of very fine lubricating oil. *What the hell was it?* And why was it applied over rust? Even the dumbest deck ape would know you chipped rust first, then applied a preservative, if that's what the stuff was.

The familiar roaring noise and increasing temperatures gave him some guidance, and he only made one false move before entering the large two-deck-high boiler room. Looking down through the latticed walkway, he searched for the boiler tenders. "Hello!" he yelled. "Anyone there?" Someone had to be tending the boilers. At sixteen knots, the *Salinika* had to have on a full head of steam. He made his way forward and took a branch of the walkway leading to a ladder, which in turn led down to the boiler control panel. Clumsy in his protective suit, he stumbled again but caught himself before dropping to the steel matting. "Shit . . ."

There! A blue-dungareed leg lay around the corner of the panel. Gantry managed to reach the boiler room deck and walked toward the leg. The rest of the body came into view. Then Gantry saw another one, and another, and another, and a fourth, all crumpled on deck in awkward positions, their flesh chalk white, their bodies ballooned as if intended for use in some kind of macabre Macy's parade, and each man was quite dead. At the foot of the control panel lay the body of the engineering watch officer.

Gantry was mystified. *What in God's name has happened? It must be the same thing down here that killed those poor bastards on the weather deck.* But what was it? And how had it spread so fast that the crew died at their duty stations?

Gantry leaned over to more closely examine one of the men. He felt for a pulse. The poor soul was dead beyond any doubt. The skin had lost its elasticity despite being drawn tight by the swelling. Gantry pulled down the man's eyelids. Gantry stood and surveyed the area. He saw nothing unusual except for the same oily residue he had found in the upper passageways and on the ladders. He traced a gloved finger in the greasy substance and looked at it closely. It was almost clear, with just a hint of a pink tint. He couldn't smell it, not from within the confines of his NBC suit.

There was death down here; there was death all over the ship. He coughed, surprised at the dryness of his throat, although that was to be expected while breathing filtered air. He had anticipated the overpowering heat and extremely high decibel noise. That was a boiler room's standard environment. But he was unprepared for the suffocating effect of his protective suit. It was bad enough that his peripheral vision was limited by his protective headgear. He found himself breathing through his open mouth, and when he closed it there was a soreness in his chest. This was not the time to come down with a cold.

Meanwhile, as they made their way forward to the Forger, Long John and Doc Abbot checked several of the bodies. The crewmen had suffered an agonizing death. Their eyes were open, and two had clawed at their throats until they had dug though the flesh and exposed their windpipes.

"What is *that*?" Abbot asked as the two men approached the Forger. A length of three-quarter-inch diameter pipe was fixed to the bottom of the wing, running spanwise. Another curved section came from the bottom of the fuselage and was welded to the crosspiece. At two-foot intervals there were tiny nozzles.

"It looks like spray apparatus, like a crop duster would have," Long John observed. "Why would a high-performance jet fighter be rigged for aerial spraying?"

"Beats the hell out of me unless it was for high plateaus or mountain tops. I wonder who they were delivering it to. Let's check the cockpit."

Long John followed Abbot onto the wing and they peered through the Plexiglas at the pilot. He looked normal, except for the gaping holes in the canopy and the side of the pilot's helmet.

"I found this beside the guy under the wing," Abbot said, holding out an unfamiliar 9-mm handgun.

"Why did they shoot the pilot?" Long John wondered aloud.

"The skipper said bring back a body. Why don't we take him?" Abbot suggested. The exec had specifically ordered him to disregard Dunne's request if there was evidence of a disease. The pilot probably had escaped it and had been trying to save himself.

Long John began rubbing one hand along the forward fuselage. "There's an emergency hand release for the canopy here somewhere." Despite the dull-black overpaint he could see several access panels. One had the shadow of a flat arrow pointing toward a small recessed panel near the front edge of the canopy. He lifted the thumb latch and opened the panel to expose a toggle switch. He moved it and the canopy lurched backward with a startling whump! and then rose smoothly to a full open position. Abbot reached in and pulled off the pilot's oxygen mask. He was neither disfigured nor discolored and had the dark skin and prominent facial features of a Mediterranean. Together, the two men unstrapped the corpse and lifted it free of the cockpit and off the wing. Abbot had the body bag tightly strapped to his back and he removed it. The pilot had a kneepad strapped to the front of his right thigh and Abbot started to unbuckle it.

"No," Long John objected. "Leave it on. It might give us some idea of what was going on."

They placed the corpse in the bag, pulled it together, and zipped it.

Long John placed his radio uncertainly in front of his face. Communications with an aircraft was usually not one of his duties and he felt awkward. He started to call Kohn by name but decided it was more proper to use the chopper's tactical call.

"Lightray, this is Long John. Over." He didn't have a tactical call.

"Roger, John, go ahead."

"We have a body. Suggest you take it back to the *Ford* while we complete our inspection of the ship. Otherwise, I don't know where we'd put it."

"Roger, John. I concur. I'll move in and we can lower the seat. I'll have Price come down and bring up the bag."

Kohn managed to hover the Seahawk once again over the clear deck space and Price rode the seat down.

"This is going to be difficult," Price observed. "Do we have to keep him in the bag?"

"Definitely," Abbot answered. "You stay on the seat and we'll place him across your legs."

"No," objected Price, wiping his soaked face with both hands. "God, I wish this would let up. Let's wrap him around the prongs and I'll sit on top of him. That'll be better."

Abbot agreed. "Okay."

Kohn's voice came over the headset. "A little hustle, folks. I can't hold this thing very looooong. . . ." Her last word dragged and undulated with the pitch changes of the helicopter as she temporarily forgot to release the microphone button.

"Roger," Long John replied. He helped lift the body high. "She's really fighting it up there."

The body was bendable but its flexibility was limited. Abbot and Long John were forced to hold it in position while Price climbed on top, locked his legs around the bag, and wrapped his arms tightly around the cable. Long John gave Chief Kosickny a thumbs-up, and the chief activated the hoist. As Price and the body bag rose, Kohn let the wind take her away from the ship and started her turn while Kosickny pulled them aboard.

Long John suggested, "Let's go see what Boats and the chief have found."

"Wait!" Abbot said. "Look back here—on the side of the fuselage."

The faint outline of an insignia was visible under the thin paint, a large upright triangle outlined by a darker two-inch wide border and with some sort of intertwined line-design inside the border. The black overpaint had obscured any colors, although at the apex of the shape there seemed to be a touch of green where the overpaint had weathered.

"What is it?" Long John asked.

"I don't know. I don't recognize it."

"We'll take back a sketch. Let's hit the bridge."

Bo's'n Lombardi was puzzling over the chain-wrapped wheel when Long John and Abbot reached the bridge.

"What the hell is that?" Long John asked.

Lombardi shrugged. "They chained the bastard. Must have known they were dying and just set a course."

Long John looked confused. "How on earth could this ship survive these seas at this speed with no rudder control?"

"Divine guidance," Abbot murmured.

"There's nothing about this vessel that suggests a holy mission," Lombardi observed.

Long John caught himself just before a violent roll of the ship toppled him against the aft bulkhead of the bridge. "We better get her slowed down. Have you heard from Gantry?"

Chief Gantry was gasping for air and trying to fight off panic. He wanted to rip off his protective head cover but he first had to get out of the engine room. His whole body seemed swollen, so much so that his protective suit was actually tight around his waist and neck. Something was terribly wrong. The closest ladder leading up from the boiler room was only a dozen feet away but he couldn't coordinate his legs. By grabbing safety rails he could pull himself along, however, and he half-staggered, half-dragged himself to the ladder. There was no way he could step up onto the first rung. His throat was closing. He *had* to take off the head cover.

It didn't help. Even with his head exposed, he could not breathe except for an occasional desperate gasp that only teased his lungs. He was dying. *God! I have to breathe. I have to open my throat.* He fell to the deck, barely conscious. Next to him was the body of one of the boiler tenders, and sticking point-up from the man's rear pocket was a large screwdriver. Gantry grasped the tool and began plunging it into his throat.

On the bridge, Lombardi tried to contact the engine room, first by the phone circuit, then the voice tube, and finally by the engine-order telegraph, running the engine signal levers full aft and then back to one-third ahead. There was no response from the engine room indicators.

"Maybe he's not down there, yet," suggested Abbot.

"Possible. But it's been forty minutes. What do you think, John?"

"I think maybe one of us should go check. The chief's an old merchantman and shouldn't have any problem getting around on this size ship."

"I'll go," Lombardi volunteered.

Long John placed a restraining hand on the bo's'n's chest. "Take it slow," he said. "I don't have a good feeling about this. He could have run into something."

"I think maybe he found someone alive and may be trying to assist him. I don't see what could have gone wrong. I'll be careful."

Long John and Abbot watched Lombardi go through the hatch in the aft bulkhead and start down the first of a series of ladders that appeared to lead to the engine room spaces.

"This is really spooky, John," Abbot declared.

"You know, that gun you picked up on deck probably wasn't the only one on board. There's all kinds of possibilities as to what may have happened to Gantry."

"We woulda heard a shot. Besides, why would any survivor attack a rescue party?"

"I don't know what the hell anyone would do after being involved in all this, Doc. Where's this ship heading? She can't have any cargo to speak of. She's riding too high."

"It has to be the west coast . . . unless it's Hawaii. We don't know how long back she was chained on course, and with the effect of the ocean currents her original destination could have been anywhere in the Pacific."

"I don't know. It has to be some kind of south-to-north run. The currents might not have thrown her off course significantly. She's old . . . no autopilot and her radar gear is almost turn-of-the-century. Even I can see that." Doc Abbot's exaggeration, for the sake of emphasis, was certainly indicative of all of the electronic equipment on the bridge.

Long John looked around the enclosed area. "How on earth is this old bucket making sixteen knots?"

Abbot responded. "She's riding awful high. Must be empty."

"And boilers going balls to the wall. Shit, the sea's not getting any better." Long John took a firm hold on the engine order telegraph. The bow of the *Salinika* was cresting a massive wave and starting down as if she intended to plunge to the bottom of the Pacific. "Hold on!"

As the bow dove into the trough, blue water rose in a great cascade to engulf the fo'c'sle and the Forger. When it cleared, the aircraft's canopy that had been left raised was gone and one side of the horizontal stabilizer was bent downward at a sixty-degree angle.

"The sea's going to tear up that airplane," Abbot declared.

"And this ship, if it keeps steaming at full speed into this storm."

Three shrill rings split the air inside the enclosed bridge and a light began to flash by the phone on the pedestal of the engine-order telegraph. "That must be Gantry," Long John exclaimed, picking up the handset. "Bridge . . . this is John. Is this you, Gantry?"

"No, it's Boats. Gantry's dead. I'm in the boiler control room. Gantry's ripped his throat open with a screwdriver. Whatever killed this crew got to him . . . his head cover's off and he's white and starting to bloat like the rest . . . we got to get the hell off this ship . . . I'm coming back up. Recommend we meet on deck . . . stay out of enclosed spaces."

Long John and Abbot exchanged worried glances. "Jesus, what're we into?" Abbot asked. "Gantry had on a protective suit and something still got him."

Long John shook his head. "I dunno, but I agree with Boats. He sounds terrified." He spoke again into the headset, "The sea's picked up, Boats."

"I know. It's throwing me all over down here. I don't see any evidence of any sprung plates, but they're groaning and snapping like they could start to go any minute . . . I'm outta here, Long John . . . see if you can raise the chopper. We gotta get off this ship."

Long John looked at Abbot, and the physician's assistant could read his companion's eyes. "Gantry's dead," Abbot said.

"We have to get off this ship. Come on!"

The two men bolted from the bridge and down to the weather deck. Lombardi joined them only a minute after they reached the partial shelter beside the forward hatch cover. Long John began calling on the radio, "Lightray, this is John. Do you hear me? Over."

There was no answer and Long John repeated the call. Still no answer. Fear had him chewing cotton balls. Where were Kohn and the Seahawk?

* * *

Kohn headed away from the *Ford*, vectored toward the *Salinika* by the calm baritone voice from the ship's combat information center. She reported, "Sundance, we've got less than a hundred feet and it looks like we're not going to get any more." She had managed to deliver the Forger pilot's body but had been unable to actually land on the pad. The *Ford* was riding too roughly to accept the Seahawk, and she had instructed Kosickny to just let the filled body bag drop from the chopper. Even a six-foot fall wouldn't bother a dead man.

The *Ford* responded, "Roger, Lightray. We're altering course southwest and will see if we can find some better water before you return. What's your fuel state? Over."

"One plus thirty . . . er . . . thirty-five or so."

"Understand one plus thirty. Your orders are to effect a pick-up as soon as possible even if the course change or speed reduction has not been made. Over."

"Concur on that. I'll report over the *Salinika*."

"Roger, Lightray . . . safe flight, Lieutenant Kohn. . . ."

"Thanks, Sundance." The personal reference came through like a warm hug. "Beaver, we're going to earn that flight pay before this day is over."

"For sure. One more approach like that last and the ship's laundry is going to be overworked when I get back on board. That was rough, Frosty. I gotta hand it to you. I would have been tempted to look for a piece of land somewhere. We must be within a hundred miles of Oahu."

"We'd have to fly through the hurricane. We can't do that and I don't think we have enough fuel to make Kauai or even Molokai with these winds. We're just too far out. Besides, we have to get Long John and his crew off the *Salinika*. She's heading into the worst of the storm. The skipper'll find us a soft spot before we get back."

"What if he doesn't?"

"I'll get 'er on, Beaver . . . but you just might lose those two front teeth and we'd have to give you a new name."

"Yeah . . . like the *late* Beaver. . . ."

"No way. We might bend Uncle Sammie's airplane but we'll get back aboard." Kohn wished she had more confidence in her own words.

Long John tried the radio again. This time there was an immediate response.

"John, this is Lightray. We're about five miles out. What kind of visibility do you have?"

"It varies, Lightray, and it's hard to tell with no references but I'd say a quarter-mile or so . . . heavy rain . . . very heavy rain, and the seas are unbelievable."

"Piece of cake, John—is everybody ready?"

"Chief Gantry's dead. We hade to leave him below decks."

"What happened? Have you been able to reduce speed and change course?"

"Negative . . . it's hell down here, Frosty . . . for God's sake, hurry! We'll fill you in when we get back on board . . . just don't waste any time."

"We should see you momentarily, John . . . yes, I have the wake . . . we're coming up astern. . . . Contact! . . . can you see us?"

"There!" Abbot called out. The long, thin, gray shape of the Seahawk was emerging from the mist and rain barely fifty feet above the surface of the waves. He could see it move out to starboard and start a slow approach toward a spot abeam the pickup point.

Long John shouted, "Let's go!" and the three headed forward.

The chopper moved over the clear deck area but obviously was having difficulty holding its position. Suddenly it tilted, slid away in a sort of scooping movement, and then started back in.

Davis's voice came up on the radio. (Kohn was most probably too busy to continue handling communications). "No sweat, John, it's just a bit shifty up here ... as soon as we get the seat down, first man grab it and hold on like it's one of those short-time girls in Sidney because we may have to move out smartly ... okay?"

"Roger!" Long John motioned to Abbot. "Doc, you're number one. All ready?"

"I'm ready!"

"Here they come!"

Kohn placed the seat squarely in the middle of the clear spot. Abbot jumped up and wrapped his feet together as he tightly held on to the shaft of the rescue device. As soon as he was a dozen feet in the air, Kohn let the Seahawk seek its own stable position while Chief Kosickny helped Abbot climb aboard. Then she moved the Seahawk back into position.

"You're next, Boats," Long John ordered.

"You go, Lieutenant ... I'm fine ... I'll be right behind you."

"Bullshit, Boats—no heroics."

Lombardi grabbed Long John by the shoulders. "John, I'm a bachelor. You've got a pair of curtain climbers back home to think about. If worse comes to worse, I can ride this tub until the salvage crew gets on board."

"Sure you can, and wind up as another dead marshmallow. No one stays. Get your ass on the hoist, Boats!"

Once more, Kohn had the seat in position. Lombardi mounted it and waved for a lift. Kosickny started him up and the Seahawk drifted out again to open the distance between it and the ship; then it returned.

Long John jumped and grabbed the seat before it was fully lowered and pulled himself onto it with one giant yank of his arms. *Oh, this feels great! Frosty, take me home!*

For the first time, Joshua Dunne was considering his options if Kohn could not get back aboard. He knew her fuel state did not give her the option of making land. If she had been able to pick up the boarding party immediately upon reaching the *Salinika*, she should be on the way back now. He had ordered the new course—southwest—which should take the *Ford* into calmer seas, but he had only an hour's steaming time before the helicopter would have to commit itself to a landing. He could go to "full speed ahead," but that would give him only another eight or nine knots and would significantly increase his fuel consumption. After the long haul north from Sidney and the unpredictable nature of the storm between him and Oahu, he could wind up with a marginal fuel problem of his own. The bottom line was that a twenty-mile advance would have to do. The voice from CIC interrupted his thoughts.

"Bridge, combat. We have Lightray returning, eleven miles out, fuel state one plus zero, seven souls on board."

Seven? "Combat, this is the captain. There should be eight."

"Stand by, sir."

It could have been a mistake, but Lt. Kohn wouldn't make that kind of mistake. Perhaps combat heard it wrong.

"Bridge, combat. Seven is correct. They lost Chief Gantry, sir."

How? Now was not the time to ask, especially over the radio, where the details could be picked up by some eavesdropper. The name should not even have been mentioned. There were procedures to follow. The next-of-kin. *What could have gone wrong?* Dunne turned to his OOD. "The exec is back at the pad with ops; see that they are informed."

"Bridge, combat. We hold Lightray five miles out. She's requesting landing clearance."

"Negative. CDR McGregor is back at the pad. Have him report to combat. Inform Lightray that she is to hold parallel to the ship. She knows we're anticipating improving conditions."

"Combat, aye, sir."

"Combat, this is the captain, again. Were they able to adjust the *Salinika*'s course and speed?"

"Lightray informed us that is negative, sir, and we're still tracking the *Salinika* on the same course at sixteen knots."

"Thank you." *Great . . . we accomplished nothing and lost a good man.* Dunne was not the type of person to second-guess his own decisions once made, but Gantry's death served no purpose. This was peacetime and the *Ford* wasn't even steaming in a training or operational mode as far as her primary mission was concerned, and now she had lost a crewman. Dunne knew that such a thing had happened too many times before; it had happened to him before. But one didn't adjust to such tragedies. Certainly, it was the nature of naval operations because of their demanding pace and unexpected contingencies, and that was the price some payed for their devotion to duty and country, but it always seemed to be so unnecessary. A man overboard in rough seas; a flight crew disappearing on a stormy night; a sailor falling and breaking his neck while a thousand feet down in a ballistic missile submarine; a hundred unanticipated ways to lose a hundred men.

Thirty minutes later there was no noticeable improvement either of the seas or weather. Dunne's executive officer had joined him on the bridge.

"Did you get the casualty report off, Jim?"

"Yes, Captain."

"Gantry's family?"

"His records show his wife lives in National City."

"Kids?"

"Two, one twenty, one twelve. The naval base will handle notification."

"I'd like to write the letter."

"I can do it, Captain."

"No, it's my responsibility. I lost him. And for what?"

"Skipper—it's the name of the game."

"I know that, Jim, and it's a dirty game at times."

Kohn was very tired, although she and Davis had shared the task of keeping the Seahawk within a safe flight envelope. They had tried the autopilot for a short while, but in such turbulence and only a bare rotor-diameter above the Pacific, it just wasn't a safe procedure. "I think it's smoothed out a bit," she estimated.

"I dunno," Davis added, glancing back at the others. They were quiet, not even talking to one another. The boarders still had on their protective headgear, but Davis could see their eyes. Something on the *Salinika* had scared the shit out of them. Long John's breathing was so labored, his suit shook. But Davis had a more immediate concern. The jolting and yawing was churning up the acids in his stomach. Oh, he wouldn't throw up, but he would just like to forget the whole thing and lie down. Though there was no way of that happening.

"You don't get used to riding inside a blender," Price remarked. "I figure we got another half-hour, Lieutenant."

"Yes . . . and I don't want to be pressured by a low fuel state. We'll wait another fifteen minutes and then inform Sundance we need to come aboard. You want to take the first shot, Beaver?"

Davis couldn't believe what he'd heard. Was Kohn serious? She had a delicious sense of humor normally, but this situation seemed much too serious to joke about. She appeared to read his mind.

"I'm serious. This is going to be rough but you're a good driver. You handled some tough ones when we were operating with the Aussies."

"Nothing like this, Frosty. We always had an alternative. I don't think it would be fair to the crew or our passengers."

"That's a good judgment call, Beaver. I've no doubt you could handle it if you had to. You're coming along all right. But never give your crew anything but the most favorable conditions. They place their lives in your hands every time you twist the throttle and lift the collective. I'll take it in, but I want you to stay right on top of everything. If at any time you think I'm pushing too hard, you sound off and we'll back away and try it again. We have two experienced pilots on board; let's use the resources of both of us."

"You can count on it."

"Good—but no hysterical screaming, okay?" The gentle needle was typical of Kohn. She was trying to remove some of the stress.

Ten minutes later, Kohn called the *Ford*. "Sundance, this is Lightray. I don't think it's going to get any better, and I want to make a couple evaluation passes before I set it down. Request you slow to twelve knots and find me the best direction you can. I believe one-six-zero will give us the best wind-wave combination."

"Roger, Lightray, we're coming around to one-six-zero, slowing to twelve knots. You're cleared at your discretion."

Kohn remained fifty yards behind the *Ford* as it steadied. The ship was still tossing about, but the cycles of pitch had slowed and with the high wind speed, which must have gusts approaching forty knots, the relative wind would be about the same, thirty degrees off the starboard bow. She could live with that.

"We'll try it from here," Kohn announced and began to ease the Seahawk forward, its nose cocked into the wind. She reached her hover position and held the helicopter in place as she evaluated the rise and fall of the stern. "Damn!" The erratic wind was shifting and she had to point her nose more to the left; that gave them a forty-five degree difference between the heading of the helicopter and the *Ford*. It might be manageable, since the only motion the Seahawk would recognize as they touched down would be the movement of the aircraft relative to the pad. That would have to be zero. But Kohn was uneasy with the gusts. "Let's back off a minute," Kohn decided, concerned about the effect of the wind once she was on deck. The pad was covered with water an inch or so deep, and the rain was continuing to deluge across its surface. If there was insufficient braking friction, the wind could slide them right off the pad.

"Sundance, let's try one-eight-zero. Over."

"Roger, Lightray . . . the pitching may be worse. Over."

"I understand."

The *Ford* eased starboard to her new heading.

Kohn started her second approach. She soon hovered over the ship, and then began to ease the Seahawk into a series of descending and ascending oscillations, trying to catch a favorable pause of the stern at the peak of its rise. It came several times but simultaneously the ship was in the grip of a roll and Kohn needed a level pad, at least with respect to the horizon ahead. *There! a momentary lull in the pitch cycle and she had a level deck!* Kohn lowered the collective and the Seahawk reached for the pad.

"Abort, Frosty!" Davis called, frantically pointing toward the bow of the *Ford*. A huge wave was bearing down and was only seconds away from crashing into the ship. Kohn powered her way straight up to safety just as the wave hit and instantly cut the *Ford*'s speed by several knots as well as raising the bow until it seemed the stern was going underwater.

Momentarily dismayed, Kohn admitted soberly, "I was concentrating on the pad." There had been an uncharacteristic mental lapse in her thought processes. "I should have seen that . . . good call, Beaver. Thanks." She checked her fuel gauges; still fifteen minutes left.

For the third time she brought the Seahawk over the pad.

"Third time's a charm," Davis muttered.

For several minutes, Kohn held her position, then the cycles of pitch and roll momentarily dampened themselves out. She lowered the collective and met the pad on the peak of its rise. *Off on the throttle! Drop the collective! Stand on the brakes! Shit!!* The airspeed indicator jumped forty knots as the gust hit and the Seahawk began sliding backward across the slippery pad. Kohn quickly added power and began to reload her rotors, but her tail gear dropped off the back of the pad and the rear fuselage crumpled. The impact also caused a violent twist and the rear rotor drive shaft bearings seized the shaft and it tore itself in two. The Seahawk struggled into the air, but without the tail rotor it instantly began a violent torque spin against the direction of the main rotor.

"We've lost our tail rotor!" Kohn wailed. There was no way she could counter the effect of the main rotor torque and deadly gusting wind with her cyclic; she needed tailrotor control. The Seahawk began a series of maddening oscillations around its vertical and horizontal axes, and within seconds rolled ninety degrees. The main rotor caught the surface of the water and all four blades separated as they flailed into the waves. The fuselage crashed into the sea.

On the wing of the bridge, Dunne had witnessed the entire sequence of events and even before the chopper had hit the water he had shouted, "Sound crash alarm! I have the conn! Right full rudder!" Instinctively, he reacted to standard Man Overboard Procedures, starting a hard turn to the right to swing the stern of the *Ford* away from the crashed helicopter. He would let the turn go ninety degrees, then shift his rudder to come about to port and reverse his direction, steaming back up his wake to the crash site. Simultaneously, a motor whale boat would be manned and made ready for lowering.

The well-trained bridge crew responded instinctively. The bo's'n sounded six short blasts on the ship's whistle and the signalman ran the OSCAR flag up one of the halyards. Both gave the same signal, "Man overboard"—in this case, an entire aircraft crew. There were no other ships in sight to hear or see, but routine was routine and tradition was tradition and professionalism was professionalism. Crew members near the helo pad had braved the heaving deck—even against Dunne's orders to stay sheltered—to heave over several life rings and smoke lights.

Dunne barked, "Shift your rudder!" Even as the bow began to reverse its direction, he knew it would be suicide to put a boat in the extremely turbulent water. Lt. Holley was his officer-of-the-deck. "Mr. Holley, tell them not to lower away. See if they have any swimmers rigged."

"Aye, aye, sir."

Dunne was on the inside wing of the bridge as the *Ford* came around toward its wake. He could see a swirl at the crash site even in the high seas, but he could not make out any structure or personnel. Thank God there was no fire.

Kohn had screamed "Brace yourselves!" even as the Seahawk had rolled right for the water. She was surprised that she didn't feel any impact, only that she was suddenly submerged, clawing at her door with no idea whether she was rightside up or not. She had a vague impression of movement behind her, and when she partially exited she turned and could see an arm reaching toward her from Davis's side of the aircraft. She grasped it and pulled, but there was no give. She pushed herself back inside and fumbled for Davis's harness release but couldn't reach it. His side of the door frame had been pushed into his lap and he was pinned. She grabbed the arm a second time but it was limp and the increasing darkness told her she was riding the chopper downward. She clawed her way back out her door, starting to swallow salt water. There was no air left. *Oh, dear God, I'm drowning! Please . . .* She reached down and pulled her life vest inflation toggles and felt a mighty surge upward.

"We have two swimmers rigged, Captain," reported Holly from inside the enclosed bridge.

Dunne ordered, "All stop." He would let the *Ford* slow to just bare steerage speed and order just enough shaft turns to keep it there. The impact point was ahead at about three hundred yards and the *Ford* was closing nicely. "Who do we have for swimmers, Mr. Holly?"

"Chief Sulley and Charlie Two Shoes, Captain. They're on the port side, sir."

Good, both men were superb swimmers and had even bested the Aussies during a match back at Manly Beach near Sidney. The young Indian was the most powerful stroker Dunne had ever seen, although he was wiry and underweight. "Right ten degrees rudder," Dunne ordered. He would swing the bow a few degrees starboard and let the quartering wind drift them to the site. Along with the port lookout, the bridge bo's'n, and his exec, he searched the waves ahead. They were so high and confused that there was a real danger that the *Ford* could drift right onto any survivors if they were not sighted in time.

The port lookout had his binoculars glued to his eyes

and suddenly grabbed Dunne's arm. "Sir, I have smoke, eleven o'clock, one hundred yards!"

Kohn had broken through the surface with such force that she rose more than halfway out of the water but was immediately swamped by a huge wave. She gasped and choked and vomited until her throat was raw and she was spitting blood, alternately being lifted and dropped with such force that only the buoyancy of her life vest kept her relatively upright. She regained her vision and her heart almost stopped; the *Ford* was making bare steerage down its wake and less than two hundred yards away. Kohn yelled and waved her arms, then popped one of her two smoke lights after carefully feeling for the daylight end. Thick orange smoke billowed upward as she held the light at arm's length, but it quickly dissipated, broken up by the strong wind. The *Ford* was yawed such that it was drifting toward her. There! She could see figures on the wing of the bridge and they were waving! The frigate seemed like the largest ship in the world as it loomed over her and she saw two swimmers hit the water, their life lines being played out by men on the deck of the *Ford*. She started stroking toward the lead swimmer, crying with joy and laughing hysterically. The swimmer reached her and the arms he wrapped around her waist were the strongest she had ever felt. Their two life vests provided plenty of buoyancy as they were pulled to the side of the ship. Two other men were suspended by ropes down the side, and they reached down. Her rescuer gave a mighty shove as they both were swamped by another wave, but she felt her arms being grasped and she was jerked clear of the water. Four arms felt even better than two and she hugged and kissed the two sailors as the three were pulled up and over the lifeline. She felt as though her body was about to burst with adrenalin and she jumped and reached toward every mate there. "Oh, God, thank you! You guys are great. . . ."

"Lie down, ma'am, in the litter."

She felt herself being gently wrapped with several blankets and lowered into the wire basket. She could see a dozen faces smiling down on her, the most handsome faces she had ever seen. "Go, Navy . . ." she gasped, and with a giant shiver that shook her from head to toe everything faded to black.

Back on the wing of the bridge, Dunne and his crew continued to search the seas. "Dear God, let there be more than one. Mr. Holly, find out who they pulled on board."

"I just got the report, Captain. It's Lieutenant Kohn."

"Thank you." There just weren't any other bobbing heads or smoke to be seen. Six more gone, thought Dunne, his stomach acids churning with anger and despair. *Six more of the nation's finest and we haven't accomplished a goddamned thing.* He turned to his exec. "I'm going down to sick bay, Jim. Would you take the conn?"

"Certainly, Captain."

"Continue the search. Let me know if there is anyone else."

"Will do, sir." The exec stuck his head into the open hatch to the enclosed bridge. "Mr. Holly, I have the conn, the captain's going to sick bay."

"Aye, aye, sir."

Two of the *Ford*'s hospital corpsmen, Chief Juanita Martinez and First Class Tom Daley, were stripping Kohn of her wet flight gear when Dunne arrived at sick bay. "How is she?" he asked.

Chief Martinez started to ask Dunne to wait outside but decided that would be a sexist decision. Lt. Kohn was one of his officers and he was understandably concerned. The fact that the lieutenant was momentarily nude should not be a consideration under the circumstance. It didn't seem to be so with the captain. Martinez announced, "We need to get her dried off and wrapped up, Captain."

Kohn was only semiconscious, and the two corpsmen quickly enveloped her in a blanket and placed her in one of the bottom sick bay bunks. While Daley covered her with the sheet and a second blanket, Martinez prepared an IV bottle and inserted the needle into the back of Kohn's right hand. Daley lifted Kohn's head and placed a pill in her mouth. "Swallow this, Lieutenant; you'll rest."

Kohn had to be coaxed to keep the pill in her mouth, but after a second urging she sipped some water to ease the pill down. The effort had brought her closer to an awareness of what was taking place and she looked up at Dunne, who was standing behind the two corpsmen. "Captain . . . I . . . I . . ."

"Hush, Sheila, don't try to talk. You're all right now and everything is under control."

Kohn needed no further urging. She closed her eyes and Martinez wiped the tears from Kohn's cheeks. "She doesn't seem to have anything but some minor abrasions. She's one very lucky aviator." The stocky Hispanic chief was Doc Abbot's number-one assistant. "Is she the only one, Captain?"

As if providence were listening, Dunne felt the *Ford* shudder. The frigate seemed to be backing down. He switched the command intercom to the bridge and called, "Bridge, this is the captain. You're maneuvering to pick up someone?"

"Yes, Captain, this is Lieutenant Holly. We have another survivor. The swimmers are just bringing him aboard."

"Do we know who it is?"

"Not yet, sir."

"Is the exec on the bridge?"

"Yes, sir."

"All right, I'll remain here in sick bay until they bring the survivor down."

Chief Martinez was crossing herself and had her eyes closed in prayer. "Dear God, let it be Mister Abbot. . . ." Turning to Dunne, she apologized, "I'm sorry, Captain, that is selfish of me. I want them all saved."

"Of course, Chief, and your prayers are mine."

Martinez busied herself preparing the examination table, her ample girth reflecting her tendency to gain weight at the mere mention of food and reminding Dunne that there was some justification for the crew often referring to her as Mom Martinez rather than Chief. Privately, Martinez was very proud of the nickname and her closeness to the crew, but she was very quick to loudly defend her rank as a chief petty officer. "If I were your mother," she would often declare afterward, "you would still be a virgin and a much better sailor."

The door burst open and four litter bearers entered and placed the wire litter on a collapsible gurney next to the examining table. Martinez took charge and supervised the transfer to the table. It was Long John. His right arm was held rigid by an inflated plastic splint, and there was a large bandage bound tightly around his head, though blood still was flowing through and from beneath it. Martinez quickly cut the saturated cloth away and pressed a square pad over the deep cut. "Let's rewrap," she ordered, "and then we need an X-ray." The sick bay aboard the *Ford* was small and cramped, but it was equipped with a state-of-the-art compact X-ray machine, and as she cut away Long John's NBC suit and clothes, Daley placed the X ray in position. "Okay, everyone else out of here now. Captain, you can stay, sir, but move over there while we shoot his head."

The litter bearers left and Dunne did as instructed. Chief Martinez was in absolute command of her domain.

Once Long John was stripped, dried, examined, and X-rayed, he was placed in a lower bunk across from

Kohn. Daley had removed the plastic immobilization device and was applying the last touches to a plaster cast around Long John's arm.

Martinez tried to console Dunne. "His vital signs are all stable and good, Captain. He has some severe bruises around his right rib cage, but I don't believe any are broken. The right humerus, his upper arm, is fractured, but it's a clean break and Daley has it in place nicely. That head cut is deep but not severe, and there is no sign of skull damage, although he could have a concussion."

"Should he remain unconscious like that with a head injury?"

"It's mostly fatigue, Captain. His body just doesn't have anything left at the moment. We'll watch him closely, and you should be able to talk to him in a couple hours."

"All right, Chief. Thank you." Dunne spoke again to the bridge. "What's the status, Mr. Holly?"

"We're holding in the area, Captain, but no more survivors in sight."

"Very well, I'm on the way back up."

Commander Jim Sessions was not just Joshua Dunne's executive officer, he was an ardent admirer of his boss and he had never served under a more professional naval officer. Although a year senior to Dunne with respect to academy class, Sessions was a year junior by virtue of the whims of the commanders' selection board, and at the moment he was deeply concerned about several of Dunne's decisions. Had identifying the *Salinika* been worth the lives of six of the *Ford*'s crewmen, including the flying types? Was the decision to launch in such high seas a prudent one? In an instant, Sessions felt like a fool. He had said or done nothing when Dunne was faced with the situation. If he had misgivings, he should have voiced them then, not now with the one hundred percent accuracy of hindsight. There would certainly be an inquiry. And an accident investigation with respect to the loss of the helicopter. Promising careers had been abruptly cut short under less damaging circumstances. And when a commanding officer at sea committed a tactical error that resulted in the loss of life, there were almost always contributing factors attributable to one or more of his officers. Where would Sessions stand under the bright lights of a naval board of inquiry? He felt concerned and angry that he had not spoken up, but most of all he felt ashamed. He had violated the first duty of a naval officer: loyalty. And even at this moment, he was placing his own well being above that of his shipmates—all of whom had at the very least acted in good faith and with humanitarian interests toward the poor dead souls on the *Salinika*.

Dunne entered the enclosed bridge and was surprised to see his exec deep in thought, staring out one of the forward windows. Hehad expected that his second-in-command would have been out on the open bridge adding another set of eyes to the search—despite the weather. Perhaps Sessions was just reacting to the tragic events of the past two hours. But that was no excuse for anything less than optimum performance. "You all right, Jim?" Dunne asked.

Sessions turned abruptly. "Yes, Captain. I was just thinking about Boats and how damned cheerful he was and how he performed best when under a strain."

"You tried to comfort me, Jim, when we first heard of Chief Gantry's death. It was good advice. It should help you, too. This is, indeed, the nature of our profession, and if we are worth our salt, we do perform best when the strain is greatest."

Sessions pulled the hood of his foul-weather jacket over his head and walked out onto the rainswept wing of the bridge. Dunne followed. Looking back and forth across the confused seas, blinking his eyes in response to the rain that was still torrential, Sessions turned his gaze down the port side of the frigate where amidships the rescue party was still manning the main deck lifelines. "There isn't anyone else out there, Captain," he said slowly. "Only Kohn and Long John made it."

"Two that would not have made it if we had not done exactly the right thing, Jim. We have to say we lost six, but we *saved* two. We saved two because we reacted well under stress. Kohn and Long John could easily have been lost in these seas and weather unless we did everything exactly right. And we have done everything we can do. I agree—there is no one else out there. But we still have a big problem. The *Salinika*. From what little preliminary information we received from Kohn when she brought the body bag back and the loss of Chief Gantry, I would say that our business with the *Salinika* is not over. I want you to monitor Kohn and Long John, and as soon as they are able to talk to us we need to find out what went on aboard the *Salinika*. You go below. I'll draft an amplifying report on casualties to CINCPACFLT."

"Aye, aye, Captain. Thank you."

Dunne caught the eye of Lt. Holly. "You have the conn, Mr. Holly. Where is the *Salinika*?"

It took a moment for Holly to check the bridge radar repeater. "Twenty-six thousand yards, bearing zero-one-zero true, Captain."

"Maintain the relative bearing, Mr. Holly, but no speed increase. I'll be in my sea cabin. Advise me if we pick up any contacts within sixty-thousand yards."

"Will do, Captain."

"I beg your pardon?"

"Aye, aye, sir."

Dunne turned away, pleased that Holly felt secure enough to improvise his response to an order but displeased with the wording. You never tolerated any relaxation of bridge etiquette, even if your OOD were a competent and personable officer like Holly. There were always lessons to be taught, and now, Dunne remembered with a sigh, there were letters to be written. Letters to the next of kin of Doc Abbot, Chief Gantry, and Boats Lombardi. They would be mailed once he knew the families had been notified. He didn't envy Kohn. By tradition, she would write the ones to the families of Lt. (jg) Davis, Chief Kosickny, and Petty Officer Price. And such obligations, as painful as they were, could not wait.

5

Blackjack Paterson was not in the best of moods. The west coast of Oahu was under siege by an enemy he could not engage, and the great Pacific naval base of Pearl Harbor as well as numerous other military installations on the island were already being pounded by winds and rain that were worsening by the hour. True, his commanders had responded as expected, sending home all unessential personnel, scouring their bases clean of any loose supplies or debris that could become projectiles, boarding up fragile glass areas, moving as many vehicles as possible into sheltered areas, hoarding fresh water, and placing damage-control parties in strategic locations.

There was the smallest of blessings: Kahiki had taken a shallow turn to the north in the last hour. Now the eye would pass just to the west of Oahu instead of roaring in over Honolulu as had been its apparent intent since early morning. The city would take terrible punishment, but the preventive measures were the responsibilities of the city leaders. Still, Blackjack knew that if the expected devastation became a reality, the military would

77

share in the security and cleanup tasks that were certain to follow. To that end, he had already activated the command's disaster team, and his assistant chief of staff for operations had a civilian-liaison command center manned and ready.

The remaining PACFLT ships had taken whatever preventive measures were open to them; a few would even ride out the storm at anchor or moored to buoys in the harbor. With capable watches on board, they had a good chance of surviving with minimum damage.

The civilian cruise ships had sailed for open water, and as many as possible of the larger pleasure craft had hurried east to sheltered bays around Molokai.

Paterson knew that if he could see the waters of Pearl Harbor, which he couldn't at the moment because of the rain, it would be as empty as it had ever been. The real tragedy, he reasoned, would be the destruction of suburbs surrounding Honolulu and the small towns that dotted the southern and western sides of the island. Despite the sophisticated growth of cosmopolitan Oahu, there were still thousands of shacks and fragile residential and mom-and-pop business buildings, particularly along the west coast, that would simply disappear.

The office intercom announced the arrival of the latest briefing team, and after a polite knock Paterson's chief of staff entered, followed by the command meteorologist and the command duty officer. The chief of staff and the CDO sat at Paterson's invitation while the weather-guesser placed his charts on an easel and began his briefing.

"Admiral, Kahiki has just in the last hour shown some signs of weakening; the maximum winds are now in the seventy-five to eighty-five miles per hour range. The latest position of the eye is here—forty-seven miles southwest of Oahu. The storm has grown in physical size to the south with the cloud cover and resultant rains now extending outward nearly one hundred miles. We estimate the maximum wind velocity will hit the western half of Oahu in about three hours as the forward progress of the storm has slowed to fifteen knots. Our winds here are forty-five to fifty, and the west coast has gusts to sixty-five.''

Paterson spoke to the CDO. ''What's the latest position of the *Ford*?''

''She's still tracking the *Salinika*. Her position report on the hour put her eighty miles southwest.''

''God, she's having one hell of a rough ride,'' Paterson interjected. ''What about the *Salinika*?''

''She's about twenty miles northeast of the *Ford*.''

''And still afloat? Incredible. I'm not sure the *Ford* should continue her efforts to assist the ship in the light of the casualties she has already suffered. There doesn't seem to be any crewmen alive to rescue, even if the *Ford* were capable. I don't see how any small freighter can survive in those seas much longer; if she goes down, we'll never know what hit the crew. Chuck, how about the coast guard?''

Rear Admiral Charles Reedy, Paterson's portly and balding chief of staff, replied, ''Admiral, they launched a C-130 Hercules from Molokai about a half-hour ago. It will give us a current position on the eye, and then it will try and make contact with the *Ford*. I doubt that they will be able to get a visual, nor is there any assistance they can render. Their cutter and a chopper are busy to the west with several small boat emergencies and they will probably steam clear of the storm with the survivors.''

''All right. Commander,'' Paterson began, addressing the weather officer, ''thank you. I'd like an update every half hour; you don't have to brief me personally, just see that I have the latest on the position of the eye, projected movement, and winds. You can just feed it into my office terminal if you wish.''

''Aye, aye, sir.'' The meteorologist gathered up his

charts. As the man left, Paterson shook his head in concern. "We've done all we can do. But this *Salinika* thing is driving me looney. If she survives the storm, she's going to plow head-on into the island. There is no way we can board her by surface means, and she's already in an area where trying to send out a helicopter would be suicide."

"That's something I wanted to mention to you, Admiral," the CDO interrupted. "We checked with the port authority and there is a ship by that name due in two days, but there is no such ship listed in the Greek registry."

"What do you suppose that means? And why is she scheduled to make port here? Have we looked into that?"

"No, sir. Perhaps, it is to take on fuel and stores."

"Well, that is not of immediate concern, but her inability to change course and speed is, with respect to her being a navigational hazard; of course, that is almost academic. No other fool will be steaming into the storm, and we have the *Ford* in position to ward anyone off if it did happen. So that leaves us with the possibility of her going aground on Oahu. And it is really a coast guard problem."

"Shall we continue to allow the *Ford* to track her?" the chief of staff asked.

"Well, it shows we're doing something. And we'll have to let the skipper of the *Ford* decide to abort if it gets too dicey. In fact, let's send him an advisory giving him that leeway. I assume all of the casualty report messages have gone out."

"Yes, sir," the chief of staff replied.

"That's rough, losing a helicopter and crew and ship's company sailors in a peaceful transit after a demanding operation with the Aussies. Are we prepared to look into things when the *Ford* arrives?"

"Yes, sir, and NAVAIRPAC has a Field Naval Aviator Disposition Board waiting on the West Coast; they'll leave as soon as the storm passes.''

"All right, Chuck. See that my quarters in the command post are ready. I'll sleep there until this thing is over.''

"Yes, sir, Admiral.''

6

Joshua Dunne sat in his sea cabin wrestling with the next-of-kin letters when his exec called.

"Captain, both Long John and Lieutenant Kohn are awake, and from what Long John has just told me you better come down here immediately."

"I'm on the way, Jim."

When he entered sick bay, Kohn was sitting in a chair wrapped in a GI gray blanket and looking very worried. Long John was still in his bunk but propped up on several pillows and holding a mug of hot coffee in his good left hand. Dunne was shocked at the complete lack of color in Long John's face and his eyes had a very frightened look, as well they should. Only an hour before, he had ridden the out-of-control Seahawk into a raging sea, found himself sinking rapidly into the darkness of the Pacific with a useless right arm and a throbbing head injury, thrashed around until somehow he managed to clear the twisted wreckage and finally activated his life vest. He was full of sea water and semiconscious when Kohn was picked up, yet had managed to wave frantically until the men on the *Ford* also sighted him. The

82

sedative should have kept him asleep for another hour at least, but he had awakened with such a cry that Chief Martinez and the exec both thought he was in extreme pain. Yet this was self-agony; and after his first few words to Sessions, the exec had sent for Dunne.

Soon Long John began to regain his composure, perhaps in part revivified because of the hot, black, and bitter coffee. "Captain," he began, "that ship is a death ship . . ."

"Take it slow, John," Dunne cautioned. "We know that."

"No, you don't know," Long John disagreed. "The crew died from some disease. It got Chief Gantry somehow." Obviously still shaken, Long John looked anxiously up at Dunne. "His protective suit didn't help. . . ."

Dunne placed his hand gently on Long John's shoulder. "John—take an even strain. You're all right. Breathe slowly. Start at the beginning."

"We got on board. Gantry left for the engine room and Doc and I proceeded toward the bridge but first inspected the airplane. That's when we pulled the pilot out and sent him back to the *Ford*. When we got to the bridge, everyone was dead and the wheel was chained so it couldn't be moved. We found residue on everything inside the bridge superstructure . . . that's when Boats called from below. He had found Gantry and had come to the conclusion that whatever had killed the crew had killed Gantry and was still present on the ship."

"But how, John? How did it start?"

"I don't . . . know . . . Captain . . ." Long John's words slowed and he just stopped talking. He began to shake and Chief Martinez took his coffee mug and eased him down on the bunk. Long John, turning his head rapidly from side to side as if looking for something or someone, began gasping for air. Martinez quickly prepared a syringe, filled it with a pale pink fluid from a vial, and injected it into Long John's upper left arm.

"This is a stronger sedative, Captain. He really shouldn't talk now. We have to give his body a chance to bounce back from the trauma. He's much too excited, and I'm afraid too much exertion can send him into shock, but he insisted on seeing you."

Dunne could understand why. He watched Martinez pull the privacy curtain and then turned to Kohn. "This all fits in with what you saw, doesn't it?"

"Yes, Captain."

"Chief, the pilot from the *Salinika*. Where do we have him?"

Martinez pointed to a remote corner of sick bay. "Sealed in plastic and still in the body bag. We don't have any refrigeration capability. He'll keep fine until we hit Pearl, assuming this storm doesn't keep us at sea any extra days."

"Do we have his belongings? Were there any papers? ID?"

Martinez nodded and walked over to a small white enameled cabinet. "His personal effects are in here." She retrieved a ziplock bag and handed it to Dunne. Inside were a passport, a small black leather folder similar to a wallet, and the kneepad that had been strapped to the pilot's leg.

"What nationality is he?"

Martinez shrugged. "I don't know. We didn't examine his papers. He looks Mediterranean—dark complexion, dark hair, dark eyes. Trace of a beard."

Dunne turned the plastic bag over several times examining the outside of the contents.

"Captain," interjected Kohn, "on the flight back, Long John showed me a sketch of an insignia that was on the plane. The black paint had been a very thin overcoat and you could see the insignia outline if you got up close to it."

"Do you have the sketch?"

''No. It might be in Long John's gear. I can redraw it.''

''Good. Do it right now. Did he say anything else other than what he just told us?''

''Only that he had to see you as soon as we landed. He was really nervous, but I thought it was just the concern about getting back to the ship. John doesn't like to fly.''

''He'll like it less, now . . . Listen, Sheila, I'm going to get together with Commander McGregor and several other officers to see if we can work this thing out. If you feel up to it, we'll gather in the wardroom in an hour or so. I need your input.''

''I can be there, Captain.''

''Good, but if you're still queasy, stay here. I'll come back and talk to you. Chief, you take care of her and make her behave. If you need me, I'll be in my sea cabin or on the bridge for the next hour or so.''

''Yes, sir.'' Martinez followed Dunne out into the passageway and closed the sick bay door behind her. ''Captain, I'm concerned about Lieutenant Childress. I think he may have serious internal injuries that I have no way of determining or treating. When will we make Pearl?''

''Well, the storm is hitting there about now, so we're looking at several hours before it passes. We may have some further obligation with respect to the Greek ship; I just don't know yet. But we're probably looking at fifteen hours at least.''

''Thank you, sir.''

''Let me know immediately if he becomes worse.''

''I will, sir.''

Dunne sat once more at the head of the wardroom table with his exec; Bill McGregor, his ops boss; CICO Dave Shepard; the ship's communications officer, Lt. Murray, whose collateral duties included that of the ship's intelligence officer; and Lt. Kohn, who had slipped on a fresh flight suit as it was more comfortable than the uniform of the day. She felt weak and every muscle in her body was aching, but she had come to a conclusion about the *Salinika* and was very anxious to contribute to the discussion. Seated around one of the other wardroom tables were the remainder of the *Ford*'s officers not on watch.

Dunne began. "We know from PACFLT information that there is no *Salinika* on the Greek registry of ships, so we can assume the ship is sailing under a false flag. Also on the pilot's kneepad was a diagram of the island of Oahu with what we believe are track lines for an aircraft overflight mission." Dunne passed the chart to the ops boss, who in turn circulated it around the tables. "Murray, tell everyone what you told me."

Murray nodded. "There is no Sal-*i*-nika in Greece. There is a Sal-*o*-nika. It is the archaic name for a port city in northern Greece; the current Greek name is Thessalonika. It's the second most populous city after Athens."

Dunne held up a forefinger. "Piece number one: a Greek crew on a Greek ship would not tolerate a misspelling of the ship's name. The insignia on the Forger, Mister Murray?"

"Iraqi, but it's painted over. The airplane could belong to anybody, but it's origin—after the Soviet Union—is Iraq. And from the way it's rigged, I'd say that it is capable of aerial spraying. Pretty obvious."

"Piece number two." Dunne held up two fingers. "I have papers here that we found on the pilot and he is obviously Arabic—but from where, I don't know."

"Iraq," McGregor announced.

Dunne shook his head. "Not necessarily. Let's not get ahead of ourselves. Let's look at piece number three. All the crew are dead. Apparently from an illness and a particularly lethal one at that, with rapid onset. Almost immediate incapacitation. Gantry didn't even have time to call the bridge." Dunne paused to study the faces of his officers. "I don't believe that what happened to the crew of the *Salinika* was from a natural disease."

"My God," McGregor interjected, "I said we shouldn't bring back a body."

Dunne signaled his displeasure at McGregor's attitude of I told you so with a quick flick of his eyes. "That, you did. I overruled you. I take the responsibility. The body is quarantined."

The exec quickly brought the discussion back on track. "We have three pieces. . . ."

Dunne summarized: "All together, we have a fake Greek ship with an all dead, probably Arabic crew, and a modern VSOL fighter plane capable of aerial spraying."

The only sound in the wardroom was the soft hissing of the air ventilation system.

Dunne continued. "I believe the *Salinika* was on a terrorist mission, and I further believe its target was one of the Hawaiian islands, most probably Oahu. I think the ship intended to approach the island under the cover of darkness and a false shipping schedule and launch the Forger to spray Oahu with a biological warfare agent."

No one broke the silence.

"I would guess that the ship was engaged in some sort of dress rehearsal when something went terribly wrong. Either the aircraft system malfunctioned or the pilot inadvertently activated the spray system and released the agent. With the aircraft on the bow of the ship and sixteen knots of wind across the deck, the agent immediately covered the weather decks and also was drawn into the interior of the ship by the ventilation system. That's the greasy residue found. The pilot, encased in flight gear and in a pressurized cockpit, was unaffected but one of the crewmen, probably incensed at what had happened, managed to kill the pilot before drawing his last breath."

"Bingo," Kohn said quietly.

"Sheila?" Dunne queried.

"I reached the same conclusion after you left sick bay. I had become suspicious while we were still in the air. Long John's words filled in some of the gaps. I didn't know the nationality involved but figured it had to be Libyan, Iranian, or Iraqi."

"It all fits," McGregor added, turning in his chair to address the officers at the other table. "We know Hussein has chemical and biological weapons and has used them before, even on his own people. And he could have supplied them to anyone. It's a beautiful operation. No one would have suspected the *Salinika* if she hadn't crossed our path, and she would have steamed right up to Oahu and launched the attack."

"But wouldn't our military on Oahu have picked it up?" one of the wardroom officers asked.

"Very doubtful," Dunne answered. "There's no increased readiness condition. It's peacetime. The port of Honolulu had the projected arrival of the ship despite the fact she's bogus, so her appearance in the area would have been perfectly normal. She would most probably have planned to be just a few miles offshore when she launched the attack, undoubtedly under cover of darkness. Even if some sharp radar observer picked up the Forger, there would be no cause for suspicion and certainly no time for an intercept if there were. There would be no visual and it would be all over before anyone could react. The Forger would return to the ship, which would then leave the area. With the chaos, panic, death, and confusion going on, no one would even think of how the attack occurred."

"And the goddamned fanatics never gave up, did they?" the exec mused. "They chained the wheel on a course for the Hawaiian Islands and went to full speed ahead before they died, realizing certainly that any damage they could inflict would be a matter of chance."

Dunne added, "And unless we stop that ship, they just might see their dreams come true."

"If you can see this world from hell," McGregor uttered.

Dunne leaned back in his chair. "So, what do we do? Number one, we get off a message to CINCPACFLT with our conclusion. Flash precedence, top secret—and we ask permission to sink the *Salinika*."

There was an audible stir in the wardroom. Everyone present knew the political ramifications of such an act, despite the threat posed by the *Salinika*.

"We don't have a hell of a lot of time, Captain," McGregor said, "and I don't think CINCPACFLT has the authority to grant us permission."

"No, that will have to come from Washington."

"Sweet Jesus, by the time they act, the *Salinika* could steam all the way to the West Coast," McGregor continued.

"When we secure from this meeting," Dunne directed, "I want a battle stations drill. We'll plan on using Harpoons. As soon as we get a go, I want everything to be thoroughly rehearsed and all systems and circuits double-checked. Remember, we had a theoretical misfire with the Aussies. That was only embarrassing; this time it's critical—it's for real. Any questions or comments?" Dunne looked around the wardroom at the smiles. This would be a perfect mission. A real threat destroyed, no one shooting back, and no casualties would be inflicted—everyone on the *Salinika* was already dead. As if to remind them that there were other considerations, the *Ford* plowed into a giant wave and its bow was thrust sharply upward, then it dived into the trough. The double impact threw loose objects around the wardroom and almost knocked several of the officers from their chairs.

"I'll be on the bridge," Dunne announced and hurried out.

"Oh, showtime is about to start," an anonymous voice declared.

It was 1:35 P.M. Oahu time, and outside of Blackjack Paterson's Camp Smith headquarters the hurricane was laying waste to every tree, brush, and shrub and assaulting the weaker, wood-frame buildings with such force that several had already lost their roofs and the air was filled with flying debris. The admiral had shifted his flag to the USMC compound. Those on watch with Paterson in the PACOM command center, however, were insulated from the winds and rain and noise by an underground bunker of reinforced concrete eight feet thick. A steady stream of damage reports was coming in from the military installations all over the island, army and air force as well as navy. All were a concern for Paterson, since he also temporarily wore the hat of the commander-in-chief, Pacific command, a unified command in which as CINCPACFLT, he was his own naval component commander. Winds were a steady seventy miles per hour with frequent gusts into the low eighties. But the storm's course had remained fixed after its northerly turn, and the eye was now projected to pass twenty miles west of Oahu.

Despite the havoc and increasing danger when the wind velocities peaked, Paterson had an even more important crisis on his hands. He was holding and rereading a message from the USS *Ford*. His chief of staff was standing quietly to his right.

FLASH FLASH FLASH
TOP SECRET
052303z SEPT

FROM: USS FORD (FFG-54)
ACTION: USCINCPAC/CINCPACFLT

COMMANDING OFFICER USS FORD SENDS X SALI-
NIKA IDENTIFIED AS ARABIC TERRORIST SHIP X
POSSIBLY IRAQI X TARGET OAHU X TYPE OF AT-
TACK AERIAL DELIVERY OF BIOLOGICAL AGENT X
ATTACK NOW CONSIDERED IMPOTENT DUE TO
DEATH OF ALL HANDS ON BOARD SALINIKA DUE
TO ACCIDENTAL OR INADVERTENT RELEASE OF
AGENT X BOARDING PARTY UNABLE TO CHANGE
COURSE AND SPEED OF SALINIKA DUE TO CHAINED
RUDDER AND PRESENCE OF AGENT IN ENGINE
ROOM RESULTING IN DEATH OF CHIEF GANTRY X
PRESENT COURSE OF SALINIKA WILL RESULT IN
GROUNDING ON SOUTHERN COAST OF OAHU IN AP-
PROX FOUR HOURS X REMAINING BIOLOGICAL
AGENT ON BOARD SALINIKA PRESENTS LETHAL
THREAT TO POPULATION OF ISLAND X IN LIGHT OF
NO LIVING SOULS ON BOARD SALINIKA REQUEST
AUTHORITY ASAP TO SINK VESSEL IN DEEP WATER
X

"My God, is Commander Dunne sure of this?" Paterson asked, his voice quivering with shock and disbelief. "We need some kind of verification. Why would
the Iraqis try something like this when their representatives are meeting this very moment with our State Department people in Washington? For Christ's sake,
Saddam has offered to back off of the Kurds and Shi'ites
and sign a nonaggression pact with Kuwait if all the UN
sanctions are lifted."

"And we pay him two billion dollars in reparations,"
added the chief of staff. "It's just a power play."

"A power play we have to respond to. The president
will make him a counteroffer if it is determined Saddam
is serious. Practically the whole Arab world has encouraged us to consider the proposal. Every intelligence brief
we have received in the past three weeks has indicated

that there is a very real possibility there is some credence to the offer. Now this. It doesn't make sense."

"Maybe the *Ford* is mistaken and it isn't Iraq. Extremist Muslim groups have been standing in line for just such an opportunity as this."

Paterson shook the dispatch in the face of his chief of staff. "Anything's possible. The bad guys are standing in line. Iraq has the sophisticated weapons and people to pull it off. But so may others now. We have to talk to Dunne. Raise him on the satellite secure system. I have to report this immediately to the chairman of the Joint Chiefs, and I surely can't do that on the strength of just this message. We have to be damned sure we have all the facts when this goes to the president. Why is the *Salinika* suddenly a threat to our security when all along it's been treated as a navigational hazard?"

"Admiral," the chief of staff replied, "this has been a rapidly developing situation and certainly aggravated by the storm. Dunne has endangered his ship and lost a helicopter and six men working on this thing, and I suspect he pulled it all together only in the last hour or so. You know him personally, Admiral. Would he send this if he weren't certain?"

Paterson knew Dunne would not have. But he needed something concrete, some piece of hard evidence to back up Dunne's conclusion. He believed his son-in-law without a doubt, but there was the problem of convincing the chairman of the Joint Chiefs and then the secretary of defense and *then* the president. Sinking a merchantman in international waters, regardless of a possible threat, would require national command authority approval, and that would involve the National Security Council.

The command center watch officer had set up the secure circuit even as Paterson and his chief of staff were talking. "Admiral, we have Commander Dunne on secure tactical."

"Lightray, this is Admiral Paterson. Joshua, we have your flash message here in the command center. I'm sure you can understand the need for some verification. This is a terrible development, and as soon as I go to the chairman of the Joint Chiefs, he is going to want something to back this up. Do we have any physical evidence? Over."

Paterson listened carefully to Dunne's reply. "Admiral, it is a conclusion based on what we have seen and what members of the boarding party experienced. We have positive identification of the aircraft as formerly Iraqi Air Force and the pilot as Arabic. We have his papers and kneepad briefing material that indicate the target was Oahu. No one on board reads Arabic, but considering the events that have taken place, there can be no other conclusion. Over."

"Do you have photographs?"

"Negative, sir. They went down with the chopper."

"You indicated earlier that you would recover a body for medical examination."

"We have a body, sir. The pilot—but he was not affected by the biological agent. Someone shot him in the head while he sat in the cockpit of the Forger."

"You think he is Iraqi?"

Paterson was disturbed by the hesitation before Dunne answered, "Absolutely? No, sir. The aircraft has overpainted Iraqi markings; our intelligence officer has identified the flight gear worn by the pilot as that similar to Iraqi gear—it's modified out-of-date Soviet-issue but everybody in the Middle East has that gear. There is a Lebanese passport with stamps from Syria, Italy, and Greece. I suspect it is false."

"I want a secure fax of all the papers immediately. How many eyewitnesses do you have that can testify to the *Salinika* being a terrorist ship?"

"Two, Admiral. The officer-in-charge of the boarding

party and the helicopter pilot. They are the only survivors of the crash.''

"Can your medical people verify the existence of a biological agent?''

"No, sir. My senior medical officer was a warrant physician's assistant. He was lost in the crash, although he had verified to the others that to him it was evident aboard the *Salinika*.''

"Then, you yourself are basing your conclusions on the testimony of your people and the articles found on the pilot?''

"That is correct, Admiral, and all of my people concur with my evaluation.''

"Very well. Contact me immediately if you think of anything else or there are any further developments. I'll get back to you, Joshua.''

"We don't have much time, Admiral. The winds and waves have slowed the SOA of the *Salinika* to fourteen knots. That gives us about three and a half hours before she reaches Oahu.''

"I understand—and get those papers to me now!''

"I will, sir.''

Paterson shook his head, obviously concerned about his conversation with Dunne. "Chuck, we have to go with what we have,'' Paterson said, addressing his chief of staff. "With this weather and the position of the *Salinika*, there is no way we can get visual confirmation of the configuration of the ship or disposition of the crew unless that Coast Guard C-130 is able to conduct a flyby. We do have radar verification of her course and speed and we do know she is on a collision course with the island.'' Paterson paused for a moment of thought. "I believe Commander Dunne, and we have two problems. The first is to decide if it is truly an Iraqi operation. The second is to obtain permission to sink the *Salinika*. And we may have to solve the second problem before we do the first.''

"How soon do you want to talk to General Mitchell?"

"Well, it's almost 7:30 P.M. in Washington. Give me twenty minutes to collect my thoughts and make some notes. We have one hell of a selling job to do if we push this as an Iraqi attack—especially with their peace delegation in Washington—but I really think that they are the only ones with the organization and assets to pull this off. God, it's clever. Hawaii is the perfect target. Readdress the *Ford*'s message to the Joint Chiefs, same precedence, and add that I will call General Mitchell at . . . four zero past the hour. I'll be at my desk when you have his office on the line."

"Yes, sir, I will."

Paterson stopped by the coffee station before proceeding into his tiny cell of an office off the main room of the command center. One of the enlisted watch standers rushed over to pour.

"This is one hell of a storm," the sailor said, taking care to fill the cup only half full. The admiral never finished a full cup.

"That's for sure. Thanks."

"You're welcome, Admiral. Can I get you anything else? We have a whole tray full of fat pills."

"Think you can find me a doughnut?"

"Yes, sir," the sailor replied with enthusiasm. He pulled a large white napkin off a tray by the coffee urn, picked out the largest doughnut and placed it on a saucer before handing it to Paterson.

A glazed, raised doughnut practically the size of an Olympic discus was the last thing Paterson would normally eat, but this was one of those what-the-hell times. As USCINCPAC, in light of Dunne's message, he had specific duties with respect to his contact and recommendation to SECDEF. As CINCPACFLT, he had a rare operational responsibility for providing tactical direction to the *Ford*. With a hurricane bearing down on Oahu, he had additional liaison and support duties with the civil authorities. No wonder the two commands had been placed under separate CINCs back in 1958. Prior to that time, one officer had filled both posts just as Blackjack was doing now. Poor bastard must have met himself coming and going, Paterson thought at the moment.

He sat at his desk and chomped on the doughnut. It tasted like a sick bagel.

Dunne took off his steel pot and handed it to his OOD. "Secure from General Quarters," he directed, and the OOD had the word passed over the *Ford*'s 1MC speaker system. The drill had gone well. Theoretically, his crew had acquired a target and fired a Harpoon SSM. It had been a smooth, professional exercise despite the high seas, the only modification having been a prohibition of manning any stations on the weather decks.

Dunne was very anxious now. Before he had decided to recommend sinking the *Salinika*, before he had evaluated the threat, he had been preoccupied with the helicopter operations and keeping his ship from exceeding her limits in the waters churned into a maelstrom of frothy waves by the hurricane Kahiki. Time had passed very slowly then, each minute dragging by as if it were an hour. Now, with his decision made, time was speeding by, the minutes seemed seconds as he watched the *Salinika* approaching the coastline of Oahu. He would need some lead time once he received permission to shoot, although not much. Fortunately, there was deep water almost up to the southern coastline. But in his mind, he could wait only two hours. That would put the *Salinika* only sixteen miles off Oahu. If he did not have permission by then, he would have an awesome responsibility.

The latest satellite printout showed the eye passing to the west of Oahu; the west coast was feeling its full force now. The *Ford*'s surface-search radar indicated the *Sal-*

inika to be twenty-five miles ahead of the *Ford*, her bow pointed toward Honolulu just forty-eight miles further northeast. On the other side of the ledger, Kahiki had picked up speed and was now being clocked at twenty miles per hour. That would lessen the time that the winds battered Oahu, although it meant that there was little chance they would diminish until the eye passed abeam the island. But the storm was drawing away from the *Salinika* and the *Ford* at the relative speed of four knots. Thus, there was a chance the frigate would encounter lesser winds and a less violent sea when the time came to fire the Harpoons. It would not be a big difference, but any improvement would improve the chances of a successful one-launch kill. It was one thing to conduct a textbook perfect drill, but the Harpoon was a flying machine like all other flying machines. Dunne had never heard of a firing in extremely adverse weather.

Suddenly, the voice of his combat information center interrupted his deliberations. "Bridge, combat, we have a Coast Guard C-130 overhead. He will be penetrating and fixing the eye every thirty minutes and is asking if the ceiling and visibility are suitable for him to make a low pass by the *Salinika*. He has been ordered to get some photographs."

Dunne waved back his OOD. "This is the Captain. Give him our conditions and inform him that we don't know the situation at the *Salinika*; however, we would anticipate that it would be no better. Tell him to expect extreme turbulence."

"Combat, aye."

"And patch him to the bridge so we can listen in."

"Aye, aye, sir."

The C-130 was at 36,000 feet and nipping the top of the storm clouds when it began to descend. Fourteen minutes later it was at 8,000 feet and beginning to slow its rate of descent. The bridge speaker monitored its attempt to obtain a visual sighting of the *Salinika*.

"Lightray, we're passing five thousand. Over."

"Roger, coast guard one-three-five. We have the *Salinika* at your eleven o'clock position, twenty-two miles."

"We concur, Lightray. Verify his course as zero-one-zero, please."

"That's correct, you'll be coming up dead astern."

"Roger that, passing three thousand."

Dunne crossed his fingers. A good photographic pass would give Admiral Paterson further evidence of the identity of the ship and the Forger on the bow. A few minutes later, the C-130 gave a progress report.

"Lightray, we're at five hundred feet, seven miles astern the *Salinika*. Experiencing extreme turbulence . . . heavy rain . . . no contact with surface yet."

One minute later: "Lightray . . . we're at two . . . whoa! . . . two hundred. No . . . visual as . . . yet . . . three miles."

Dunne gripped his lower lip with his teeth. The Coastie crew was playing guts ball. He certainly didn't envy them at the moment.

An eighty-ton, four-turboprop cargo carrier, the C-130 Hercules was aptly named. The coast guard regularly used it for hurricane penetration, its awesome strength and unequaled controllability for such missions legendary. The classic Hercules had started rolling off Lockheed assembly lines in 1954, and most of the many thousands built were older than their crews.

Coast guard one-three-five was relatively new—manufactured in 1978—and ordinarily was right at home in turbulent air and wet clouds; but now, roaring along at two-hundred and fifty knots a bare two wingspans above the ferocious Pacific, it was truly going in harm's way.

The seasoned aircraft commander—a lieutenant with over 2,600 hours at the controls of the big craft—was giving careful consideration to aborting the flyby, though another fifty feet perhaps would put him below the cloud layer—and PACFLT had specified that photographs of the *Salinika* were strongly desired. He muscled the Hercules down another fifty feet. He was now flying just a bit over one wingspan above the water. His cockpit radar repeater showed the *Salinika* to be one mile ahead and slightly to port. His copilot was also monitoring the flight instruments; if there were the slightest inattention the severe downdrafts could preempt the hesitant reactions of the pilot and plunge them into the sea.

The flight engineer, strapped in his thronelike seat aft and between the two pilots was devoting one hundred percent of his attention to the overhead panel, where diverse gauges and switches showed the status of the aircraft's electrical, hydraulic, and fuel systems. On the left side, behind the AC, one of the enlisted aircrewmen had strapped himself to the cabin structure and was standing ready with a large aerial camera.

"One hundred feet," the copilot announced in a calm voice, his anxiety filtered out by the time his breath passed through his voice box. The aircraft finally had visual contact with the surface but was less than a wingspan above the water. The noise of the solid sheets of rain striking the aluminum fuselage was making communications, even over the intercom system, almost impossible.

"There it is!" the pilot called out. They were close aboard the starboard side of a shadowy form that could only be the *Salinika*, and although the AC had slowed the Hercules to one hundred and eighty knots, the form disappeared as suddenly as it had materialized. The Hercules rocked and pitched and shook with the impact of wind gusts that were fifty knots above the average winds, the airspeed indicators fluctuating between one-seventy and two-ten. The AC had enough. He eased back on the control yoke. "Gimme climb power; we're outta here!"

The Hercules nosed upward and began a powerful climb.

"Did you get any pictures?" the AC asked over his shoulder.

"Time for two shots, but I doubt that we got anything with a degree of clarity. All I could see was what vaguely looked like a hull with an aft superstructure."

The copilot, sitting on the far side away from the *Salinika*, shook his head. "I didn't see a goddamned thing. Skipper, when you said 'give me climb power,' my muscles were so taut I wasn't sure I could move the power levels forward."

"You didn't seem to have too much trouble," the AC remarked with a chuckle.

"That was rough," the cameraman stated, obviously relieved that with each passing second they were farther above the waves and the same distance closer to the clear air above the storm clouds.

"Better check out with Lightray," the AC ordered.

Dunne was pleased to hear the C-130 was safe but disappointed at the report. "Lightray, we made one pass although I don't know how the pictures will come out. We were at one hundred feet and there was only a glimpse of the ship. I don't think we'll go back down for a while. Over."

"Roger, one-three-five. We were concerned about you."

"Thank you, Lightray."

Dunne called CIC. "Ask them if they could see the aircraft on the bow."

The answer from the Hercules was not encouraging, "Negative. We really only saw a form that looked more like a ship than anything else. There is practically no visibility with all the moisture coming down."

For the time being, Blackjack Paterson would not have his pictures.

* * *

It was the dinner hour in the District of Columbia, and the chairman of the Joint Chiefs had been at a reception for some visiting military personnel from Chile. It took him a half hour to reach the Pentagon command center. The red line to USCINCPAC was open, and Admiral Paterson was on the other end waiting.

"Yes, Blackjack?"

"Have you seen my flash message, General?"

"It was just handed to me. Is this for real?"

"Yes, sir, and we're really squeezed for time."

"I've just sent word to SECDEF. Bulldog is meeting with a congressional delegation on the Iraqi proposal for a withdrawal of UN troops." The chairman had used the code name "Bulldog" for the president. "I haven't had time to digest this message yet, but you obviously have evaluated it. Do we have anything other than the report from *Ford*?"

"No, General Mitchell, we do not and we are not going to get anything else. The coast guard had one of their weather planes make a low pass to try and get some photographs, but the pictures are not conclusive at all. Both the *Salinika* and the *Ford* are steaming into the hurricane that is hitting Oahu, and there is just no visibility for photographs."

"How on earth was a merchantman going to conduct an aerial attack?"

"A Yak-36 Forger—it has vertical takeoff and landing ability—was housed in a collapsible deckhouse on the forward weather deck. We have eyewitnesses to that."

General Wally P. Mitchell, U.S. Air Force, CJCS, instantly recognized the dilemma. Before the NCA would even consider ordering the sinking of the *Salinika*, the National Security Council would have to be consulted, yet at least half of them were out of town. The vice president was available, and the secretary of state. The

secretary of the treasury was in San Franciso, and the
director of central intelligence was airborne somewhere
over east Texas returning to Washington. Also absent
was the president's national security adviser, although
he would be present for the morning discussions with
the Iraqi representatives.

"We have less than two hours, General," Paterson
said with some irritation.

Mitchell did not have to be reminded nor did he appreciate the tone in Paterson's voice. "Admiral, I will
contact Bulldog's staff immediately, and as soon as
SECDEF arrives here I will brief him and we will request a meeting with Bulldog."

"General, put it to Bulldog in these terms. Unless
directed otherwise, I intend to order the sinking of the
Salinika before she grounds on Oahu."

"Bulldog will not like any intimidation, Admiral. He
barely communicates with us now. I'll be lucky if he
agrees to let me accompany SECDEF to the meeting.
You know how the game is played these days."

"This is bigger than any crisis Bulldog has faced—
bigger than any of us have faced since the new administration has taken over. It certainly is not the time for
any petty dislikes or power plays. We are talking about
a threat to several million American citizens. I don't
know how I can make it any clearer."

"Admiral, I'll have them keep this line open. We can
put watch officers on each end, and I'll get back with
you as soon as I have a decision."

"Thank you, General. I'll be waiting."

The chairman of the Joint Chiefs had alerted his deputy and the chief of naval operations, and by the time
SECDEF arrived at the command center they had evaluated the situation, prepared some briefing material, and
discussed the options. Mitchell had also placed the other
Joint Chiefs on alert; however, SECDEF saw no need
for their input to the discussion. It was obviously a naval

problem. The SECDEF was brief and to the point. "Let's keep inputs to a minimum; I want the facts to present to the president and a recommended course of action."

General Mitchell had no hesitancy in presenting his view. "Sir, even though I would like more hard evidence, I believe we have to assume that the situation is exactly as presented by the commanding officer of the *Ford*. As to the culpability, I'm not as certain, but with the Iraqi input to the bombing of the World Trade Center, the plot to assassinate President Bush in Kuwait, and the bombing aboard the Caribbean *Princess*, it falls right into the pattern."

"Then what are our options?"

Mitchell's sigh forecast his reply. "We sink the *Salinika* or we allow it to hit Oahu. No other options."

SECDEF shook his head. "No, I feel that there is another option—and that is to do nothing. There are two other possibilities we have to consider. One, that the storm winds will drift the ship so it passes clear of Oahu and two, that if it grounds itself on the island, there is no spread of the agent. In the first situation, we gain time to gather international support for sinking the *Salinika* in the open sea north of the islands—it could even be a United Nations action. In the latter situation, we could have decontamination teams on the site and cordon off the area. We could even evacuate any endangered communities."

General Mitchell was having difficulty with the SECDEF's reasoning. He selected one of the large charts on a nearby table. "Mister Secretary, this is the latest satellite photograph of the storm. I had the islands plotted and the positions of the two ships along with the projected course of the *Salinika*. It leads right to Oahu along the Waikiki-Diamond Head shoreline, the most heavily populated region of the island."

SECDEF again shook his head. "The scale is too

small and the plotted positions are too broad. A pencil point covers a mile or so.''

Mitchell continued his argument, ''I am having a more detailed plot prepared. It will be ready momentarily. Meanwhile, I would like to point out the position of the eye of the storm. The winds around the eye run counterclockwise. You can see that at the present time with the eye almost abeam the island to the west. In the heavy seas, the *Salinika*'s speed of advance has slowed to fourteen knots, which gives us a bit more time. She's headed for the southeast shoreline, but her drift can alter her course. *If* the winds increase, the only thing that will possibly change is the grounding point—to the Pearl Harbor or Barber's Point area at best. Besides, we have been observing her track as well as her projected course. Regardless of where her bow is pointed . . .''

''Excuse me, sir.'' A crewcut army colonel placed a detailed navigational chart on the table with storm and ship positions plotted relative to Oahu.

Mitchell glanced at it for only a second before continuing, ''Good, this is much clearer and much more accurate. You can see, Mister Secretary, with the *Salinika* less than fifty miles south, there is no way she can clear the island with winds as they are.''

''Then we develop the option of clearing the grounding area and having the decontamination teams ready.''

Mitchell was momentarily stumped for a reply, but the chief of naval operations, Admiral Stewart ''Chip'' Collins, a thirty-five-year veteran of both surface and aerial operations, asked, ''May I comment, Mr. Secretary?'' With every superior he had ever served under, he had always had the flexibility of commenting whenever he wished, but with this SECDEF, and in the presence of his own senior, the chairman of the Joint Chiefs, he asked.

The protocol had been laid down as soon as the new administration had taken over. The chairman was SEC-

DEF's principal adviser, and it was expected that *he* would have the Joint Chiefs' position ready whenever the two consulted. It had been made clear that there was no need for any subordinate input at that point. And when SECDEF met or briefed the president, the protocol remained intact. The president expected his military adviser, SECDEF, to have been thoroughly briefed and have all the answers ready. Because of that strict policy, even the chairman of the Joint Chiefs was not normally present when a military situation was briefed to the president. The armed forces of the United States were under constitutional civilian control, the president had early on reminded everyone, and the national command authority consisted of the two top *civilian* military commanders—the commander-in-chief and the secretary of defense. The only other body concerned with matters before the NCA was the National Security Council, composed of selected cabinet appointees and the president's national security adviser. The president had more than once stated that generals and admirals, by the very nature of their profession, were always biased toward the military side of a question, and matters of national interest that were politico-military in concept required an equally intense political input to balance out the critical considerations.

Surprisingly, not only did SECDEF reply, "Of course," to Admiral Collins's request, he seemed genuinely interested in what the CNO had to say.

"Mr. Secretary, we not only have to consider the possibilities but the risks. Sure, it's possible the *Salinika* will ground and remain intact, but let's look at the risks. *If*—and it is a terrible if—any of the agent escapes, *any* at all, with hurricane winds present, it could travel to all parts of the island. Something as deadly as that which killed an entire ship's crew in a matter of what must have been a relatively short time has to be extremely potent. I don't believe we can take that risk, as relatively

small as you might think it is. And I don't make this
argument as just a military concern. The loss of one
civilian life—if we allow the ship to ground itself—will
have political ramifications that will certainly reflect
upon the judgment of this administration.''

"Thank you, Admiral. I am fully aware of any *political* ramifications. General Mitchell, what is your recommendation?''

"We sink the *Salinika* as soon as we get presidential
approval.''

"I believe you mean presidential permission.''

General Mitchell was obviously perplexed at the mild
rebuke. "Whatever, Mr. Secretary—whatever.''

The SECDEF stared intently at the small group of
military men before him. They were the most senior officers of all the services, and despite his gruff exterior,
he had developed the utmost respect for them and the
integrity of their advice and counsel. But he was not
only the services' buffer, he was the president's filter in
the relationship between the military and the administration. "Gentlemen,'' he began, "I know the urgency of
this situation has forced us to give only a minimum of
time to the considerations involved. But I want you to
know that I concur with your recommendation, and I
will present it to the president in the strongest of terms.''

7

USS FORD (FFG-54)
SEPTEMBER 5, 1420 LOCAL

It had been almost an hour since Dunne had talked to
Admiral Paterson, a very long hour during which Dunne
felt increasingly frustrated and extremely anxious. What
was the status of Paterson's request to the chairman of
the Joint Chiefs to obtain permission for the *Ford* to sink
the *Salinika*? Dunne knew that the elapsed time was not
unreasonable under normal conditions, but these were
far from normal conditions. It was after routine working
hours in the Pentagon and perhaps it was one of those
rare times when the CJCS had been able to leave in the
early evening. The duty officer would have to hunt him
down and then Paterson would have to brief him. Subsequently, the general would have to meet with the secretary of defense, and there would be another review of
the situation. Finally, the secretary would have to meet
with the president. Perhaps it was an impossible task,
getting through the bureaucracy in a matter of minutes
rather than hours, despite the critical nature of the problem. Yet that was supposed to be the nature of the military and its chain of command organization. Suppose
the threat was the avant-garde of a massive military at-

tack on the United States; the threat of the *Salinika* was no less an emergency.

And in that same hour, the *Salinika* had steamed fourteen miles closer to the southern shore of Oahu. The *Ford* had closed to within fifteen miles of the death ship and had opened a bit to starboard. The stress of the situation and Dunne's lack of sleep over the past twenty-seven hours had weakened his body, and he knew that his clarity of mind had to be suffering also. He tried to inject some reason into his predicament. There was nothing he could do until he heard from Admiral Paterson. Even a short nap would refresh him some. He had the time, but could he clear his mind? He had to try, because he would need a clearer head at the end of the next hour. Suppose the order didn't come?

He shut off the work lamp over the small desk in his sea cabin and lay down on his bunk. With no ports or windows there was complete darkness, but there was not complete comfort. The *Ford* was combatting the waves as fiercely as she had been doing for more than twenty-four hours. He must not *try* to go to sleep; any conscious effort would be counterproductive. Instead, he must just let sleep slip over him like a warm blanket. He needed to clear his mind, relax his muscles, give himself up to the darkness. He must not feel guilty. He must stop examining every detail of the loss of his six people. He must erase the mental image of the *Salinika* bearing down on Oahu. He even must stop praying. Ship's company could run the *Ford*; they were well trained and qualified, and at this moment he knew that rest was as essential to his ability to command as were his technical and leadership qualifications. God, he was tired. . . .

8

SECDEF waited impatiently in the Oval Office for the president to arrive. The chief of the White House staff had seemed very irritated that the president was being pulled from his meeting with several key congressional members who were presenting their views of the impending Iraqi negotiations.

"The president is extremely engaged at the moment," the chief of staff had stated, undoubtedly miffed at SEC-DEF's reluctance to tell him the subject matter relative to his urgent request for a meeting. Conversely, SEC-DEF was not about to release that information until the president was informed of the situation. There were too many leaks among White House staffers, and if news suddenly reached the public via some irresponsible radio or TV announcement, there could be panic in the streets of Honolulu.

SECDEF stood as the president entered. They sat opposite one another on the twin loveseats in front of the fireplace. It was also immediately apparent that the president was not too pleased with the interruption. "All right," he began, "this better be urgent. What do we have?"

Quoting from the *Ford*'s flash message to USCINC-PAC, and amplifying the information with the comments of CJCS General Mitchell, SECDEF took only a few minutes to lay out the situation. At the end, he stressed, "Mr. President, we have a terrifying time restraint on a decision here. That ship is less than two hours away from Oahu."

The president held up a hand, the palm toward SEC-DEF. "This smells."

"What do you mean, sir?"

"We have only a navy commander's word for all this. The words Tonkin Gulf come to mind. And his conclusion is based on the reports of others who may or may not have the ability to determine that the crew of the . . . ah, whatever the ship's name is . . ."

"*Salinika*, sir."

". . . of the *Salinika* died from a biological warfare agent. We have to proceed very carefully. You are proposing that we sink a Greek merchantman in international waters without any provocation?"

"We're not sure she is truly Greek, and there *is* provocation, sir. The ship is threatening the population of Oahu. We have a strong belief that the crewmen are Iraqis."

"We don't know that—we *suspect* that."

"Mr. President, this report is from a naval combatant that has eyewitnesses to the circumstances I have briefed you on. We have the body of the pilot. We have an attack map for Oahu."

"There is evidence of the biological agent in the pilot's body?"

"No, sir. He was not affected. Or at least, we don't believe he was. He died from a gunshot wound."

"But if we sink the ship, we have no unquestionable physical evidence. Maybe we should brainstorm for a moment. The body could be a plant, part of a conspiracy.

You've already stated that you don't even have any photographs of the ship or aircraft.''

"No, sir, they were lost in the helicopter accident.''

"How convenient. And we can't get any more?''

"No, sir. We had a coast guard aircraft try, but the weather is too severe.''

"How about from a satellite? We have the ability to read an automobile license plate from outer space, for God's sake.''

"Not through hurricane cloud cover. Besides, the satellite has to be in the proper position.''

The president rose and walked slowly around the office. "We have to give this situation our most grave consideration. I don't like it at all. We're finally making progress with Saddam Hussein, and now we suddenly come up with an Iraqi terrorist attack on Oahu—on Oahu, no less. From a ship only two people have seen and they want to sink it before its identity is confirmed. No, I don't like this at all. Why would the Iraqis want to do such a thing in the middle of our talks? Tell me that.''

"Mr. President, we aren't certain they are Iraqis. We are certain there is a threat and it appears to be Arabic in origin. It could be anyone from the Middle East. The navy has fortunately discovered the impending attack through diligence and positive action.''

The president still seemed suspicious. "How well do you know Admiral Paterson? I don't know anything about him.''

"Very well. His background and experience cover thirty-seven years of service. He's a Vietnam and Gulf War veteran. He has made critical decisions under stress. He is the type of person one likes to have available during a crisis like this.''

"If it indeed is the crisis you claim.''

SECDEF sat silently. What else could he say? But he had to provide the best advice to the president. "Mr.

President, the nationality of the terrorists can be determined later. We just need to act on this—immediately, sir.''

"I know, but as the president, I *have* to consider all possibilities. There is a significant political aspect to this situation.''

"I recognize that, sir. We still have a decision to make, Mr. President.''

"We have to consult the NSC on this; at least, with as many as we can reach in time.''

"Mr. President, we have so little of that left.''

"But we must do this right, with inputs from the proper people. If all is as you say, I will authorize the sinking—obviously. But we can't afford to be wrong on this. Think what that would cause us on the international scene.''

"I agree, Mr. President, but the authority certainly lies with you as the head of the NCA. If there is insufficient time to meet with the NSC, you, as commander-in-chief, can make the decision.''

"I know that. And I hope you understand. I am just being cautious. That is my job. I have the ultimate responsibility.''

"Yes, sir.''

"Have General Mitchell inform Admiral Paterson that the *Ford* must not take any further action until I issue the order.''

"Yes, Mr. President. Forgive me, sir, but you do understand the necessity for lead time?''

"For God's sake, do you take me for a complete idiot?''

SECDEF knew that he had phrased his question wrongly.

At the Pentagon, General Mitchell could only sit by his hot line to Admiral Paterson and trust that the president would see that there was no other solution to the problem of the *Salinika* except that proposed by USCINC-PAC. Even so, he kept running the particulars of the crisis through his mind. But his questions had done an about-face since he had first been contacted by Paterson. No longer did he seek more proof; instead, he was combing his memory for some bit of information or hint that would indicate the conclusion could not be accurate. There was always that possibility, of course, but he had to agree that the conclusion of the commanding officer of the *Ford* was logical. As for such an attack in the middle of U.S.-Iraqi negotiations, *why*? It didn't make sense, even though the bastards had already shown that they were not to be trusted. Then again, why not lull the United States into a sense of security and then strike the most devastating blow of all—a biological attack against helpless civilians? And the selection of Hawaii as a target was a stroke of genius. It was the easiest state to approach undetected. The guise of a Greek ship was clever; the Greeks were all over the Pacific, in practically every port. If the *Ford* had not accidentally encountered the *Salinika*, the plan would have been fool-proof. The Forger could have sprayed its deadly contaminant over Oahu and left the area completely undetected. There could have been a convenient rendezvous with another Iraqi ship, a legitimate one this time. At that point, the *Salinika* could have transferred its crew and been sunk, along with the Forger, and all traces of the contaminant in water thousands of feet deep. This thought triggered another. If the plan was so good, why not try it on other U.S. soil? Why not Guam? or Puerto Rico? Either would be the last place of any concern to U.S. security measures.

Mitchell triggered his intercom and said, "Sergeant, I'd like to see the deputy chairman immediately."

Kahiki was scouring Oahu clean of any loose objects, and in many places providing new debris, but Blackjack

Paterson was hardly taking note of the damage reports coming into the command center. His eyes were either on the wall chronometer or his wristwatch. The *Salinika* was only twenty-five miles from Oahu. He wanted very much to pick up the hot line to General Mitchell, but that would not make the time pass any faster, and he knew that if there was an order coming, it would come no sooner by virtue of him bugging the chairman. To hell with it—he had to find out.

General Mitchell answered immediately, anticipating Paterson's question. "Blackjack, I'm doing everything I can."

"General, I need a decision. The *Salinika* is only twenty-five miles offshore; that's only about an hour and a half away from Oahu. If she hits and breaks up and these winds pick up any of the agent remaining on board, the entire population of this island could die in a matter of a few hours. This is the most serious threat we have ever faced. I must have permission to sink the *Salinika*."

"Blackjack, I can't get past the secretary to present my input. He has given me direct orders to stand down, and he is presenting the problem to the president at this very moment."

"Then, when, for God's sake?"

"The president is meeting with as many of the members of the NSC as are present here in the District. The whole matter of our Middle East policy is at stake and the key is Iraq. . . . Wait . . . I've just received some feedback from the secretary. The president does not want us to sink the *Salinika* with just an excuse . . . no evidence . . . that it may be an Iraqi terrorist ship. . . ."

Peterson persisted, "But that's exactly what it is! And why aren't you there at the table? My God, is he making this kind of decision without direct military input? Who is providing the military input?"

"There is no uniformed input other than my briefing

of the secretary. The president feels this is too important a matter to allow the military to present their biased view. Even the secretary is out of the loop for the moment. The president has some lingering doubts about our conclusion, and his main reason is that we don't have one piece of hard evidence.''

"I have a witness."

"A witness who says she saw a Russian—that's *Russian*, Blackjack—aircraft on board a Greek freighter. That is all."

"I have the testimony of a naval officer who was on the ship and saw the dead and the spray equipment and the Iraqi insignia on the aircraft." Paterson had never experienced such anger. "We have the pilot. He's Arabic. We have his kneepad charts with flight lines drawn across Oahu. We have his time schedule and his rendezvous point."

"The president says that until the kneepad material can be translated, it could be all conjecture, that we may be taking advantage of a nonthreatening encounter to scuttle the settlement with Iraq."

"And the secretary?"

"I'm confident he is doing his best. But you know the president is supercautious these days. He's been burned. His foreign policy with respect to the Middle East has come under congressional scrutiny. He has to consider that. Believe me, he is not underestimating the threat."

"This is beyond belief. Fuck it. I'll authorize the sinking myself." Blackjack was on the verge of hanging up.

"No, you won't, Blackjack, because I am ordering you not to."

Paterson's eyes were shut tight against his tears of rage. "You're supposed to be one of us, General."

"Dammit to hell, I am! You don't know what it's like up here now. We're fighting for the very survival of the military as you and I know it, as we have served in it and loved it and fought this administration for it on so many counts.''

''But this is not political, this is a potentially national tragedy that will get the president impeached if he allows this ship to reach Oahu; but I don't give a damn about that. It is the lives of well over a million U.S. citizens. For the sake of almighty God, don't you people realize the magnitude of this crisis?''

''Blackjack, if the negotiations with Iraq fall through, it could be another Persian Gulf War and we don't have the forces we had in 1990—or the ability to deploy them in a timely manner. Saddam is poised and reinforced with Arab troops and hordes of Islamic extremists from practically every country in the Middle East.''

''That is exactly why the Iraqis or somebody are doing this—or were going to do it. They intended to kill millions of Americans, General. Within their twisted minds they think such a disaster would weaken our will. This has been coming ever since the bombing of the World Trade Center and the sinking of the Caribbean *Princess*. The talks are a hoax to buy time for the *Salinika* to reach Hawaii.'' Paterson felt pistol-whipped. If the chairman and SECDEF couldn't get to the president, Blackjack would have to give permission to the *Ford* to sink the *Salinika* and let the chips fall where they may. There was no way he was going to allow the population of Oahu to remain at risk.

SECDEF continued. ''Blackjack, I give you my word. The president has indicated he will give permission despite his misgivings. He just wants to cover all the bases.''

''You mean cover his ass.''

''Of course. Look, if the president drags his feet and we start to run out of time, I and all of the Joint Chiefs will back you on whatever decision you make.''

''One hour, General, and I give the order and you tell the president *that*.''

"Blackjack, listen to me. SECDEF is trying to keep me informed of progress. One of the remaining questions is: Is it possible—*possible*—that the storm may yet take out the *Salinika*? Just yes or no."

"Yes—any goddammed thing is *possible*."

Mitchell asked a second question, "Is it *possible* that even if the ship makes it the rest of the way and beaches itself on Oahu, that it will not break up or at least not break up to the extent that any contaminant would be released?"

"General, we can't count on it happening that way. . . ."

"Is it *possible*, Admiral?"

"Yes, sir."

"You have just agreed with the president on two counts. Now do you see the size of the argument SECDEF has on his hands?"

"Fifty-five minutes, General, and I do it. So, help me God, I will do it."

The members of the National Security Council that could be immediately rounded up sat around the conference table in the White House Situation Room. The president sat at the head and the First Lady had taken the seat to his right. The only other occupants of the room were the vice president, the secretary of state, and SECDEF.

The president gave the new members a brief of the situation, then declared, "We have very little time to discuss a course of action. In fact, unless someone can add something to my deliberations that I have left out, my decision is clear cut; despite some strong reservations I have about this situation, I must order the sinking of the *Salinika*."

The secretary of state leaned forward. "I don't like being in a box like this. There are so many things we should check, so many people we should talk to, but under the circumstances I agree that we simply do not have the time left. I can send for the Greek ambassador and brief him, of course, and assure him we feel the ship is sailing under false Greek colors. He may have time to double-check the registry. As for our talks with Iraq, I propose we tell them immediately what is going on and gauge their reaction. Damn, it's a hell of time for this to come up.''

The vice president added, ''How about the media? We have to tell them something.''

''Yes,'' the president agreed, ''but only after the fact. The situation is evolving too fast to bring in the media at this moment. I need every second for my considerations. But I would like very much to get an Iraqi reaction before I issue the order to sink the ship.''

''In that case,'' the secretary of state agreed, ''I must go. We're looking at thirty minutes or so.''

The president threw up his hands. ''I will wait until the last possible minute to issue the order.''

Within moments, the president and First Lady were left alone in the Situation Room. SECDEF had left to contact the CJCS in the event there had been any further developments on the scene. The president took his wife's hand. ''This is a real donnybrook. You're my right arm. How does it sound to you?''

''Very suspicious. But you really only have one course of action open. And I do think that when this is all over, you will need to emphasize that problem areas of this magnitude have to be identified much sooner than at the last minute. If that admiral in Hawaii drug his feet in reporting this, I would let him drag them right on into retirement. You shouldn't be placed in a position where you do not have the time to properly weigh all the factors.''

''That's just what I've been thinking. If this is some sort of tragic misunderstanding. . . .''

''I assume there is a record of all this, the secretary

of defense's initial briefing, your discussions with him, this meeting?''

"All on tape, as usual."

"You'll want it for your archives, if for no other reason."

"Yes—I suppose I will."

Forty-seven hundred nautical miles southwest of the White House, Joshua Dunne finally sank into deep sleep. The stress of the last day and a half had left him reluctant to leave the situation in the hands of his crew. The storm was still venting its fury, the *Ford* still pitching and rolling, at times violently, the crisis still unresolved, but Dunne was stretched out on his bunk in the darkened sea cabin, his hands clutching the handrails even in sleep.

The human body can go on only so long before it simply refuses to go any longer. It will then demand to be pampered just a bit. The nerves that lead from the sensory organs need to relax and reduce the volume of the tiny electrical signals that speed to the brain, otherwise when they reach that complex organ they arrive somewhat confused and in a bunch. There is a danger that some will take the wrong path through the judgment center. When that occurs, one can react without full consideration of the messages they carry. In a combat situation, or even in any life-or-death deliberation for that matter, a wrong decision can be made. The blood needs to slow and exert lower pressure on the walls of its thousands of passageways through the body. Lung expansion needs to be a little less forced. Muscles, stretched and contracted by pacing and standing and even sitting, must be allowed to rest and recover from exercise that has caused them to minutely grow and expand with the stimulus of movement. Otherwise, they will strain and stiffen, not because of their load necessarily, but merely because of prolonged low-level use.

It is this slowing and lessening and resting and recuperating that allows the body to lapse into that delicious state of absolute sleep.

Dunne slept for a million years, although the minute hand of his sea cabin chronometer had swept through only one hundred and eighty degrees of its customary circuit.

It was the *Ford*'s alarm claxon that startled him and then the call "General Quarters, General Quarters—all hands man your battle stations!" that caused him to rush to the bridge.

The rain was still falling, the winds still blowing, and the clouds were as thick and low as before, but the sea was strangely calm, and the *Ford* was knifing its way at maximum speed.

The OOD—one of Dunne's junior officers whom he did not immediately recognize in the dim light—saluted and announced, "Captain's on the bridge!" He then hurriedly briefed Dunne on what was happening.

"Captain, we have received orders from CINC-PACFLT to sink the *Salinika*. The crew is at battle stations and we are closing on the target ship. With your permission, sir, I intend to circle the *Salinika* one final time to check for any signs of life and then retire for the shoot."

Even as the OOD spoke, the terrorist ship came into view and the *Ford* raced up her starboard side and cut across her bow. Dunne joined the lookout on the port wing of the open bridge. As the *Ford* continued her sharp turn and then swept down the opposite side of the *Salinika*, Dunne stared in disbelief at a figure clearly standing in the enclosed bridge.

Dunne pointed, shouting, "There's someone on the bridge!"

The exec had joined him. "I don't see anyone, Captain."

"There! By the helm."

"No, sir, I think it's just a shadow."

Dunne knew that he must take command of the situation. "I have the deck and the conn!"

The *Ford* had completed its reversal of direction and was opening aft of the *Salinika*. Dunne climbed into his bridge chair. He could not sink the *Salinika* if anyone was alive on the ship. Suppose it was Chief Gantry! Maybe he was not dead—that could be it! Gantry had just been unconscious when Boats Lombardi had looked down upon him in the boiler control room. Lombardi had panicked. "Dear God," Dunne announced, "it may be Chief Gantry." The exec responded, "Captain, the message from CINCPACFLT directs us to sink the ship regardless of any other considerations. It doesn't leave us any choice. Besides, there is no way we can double-check. I really think it was an illusion. And look there—ahead."

Dunne's heart skipped a beat as he recognized the Waikiki coastline of Oahu on the horizon, probably no more than twenty miles ahead. Soon, they would run out of deep water, and the *Salinika* must be sunk in deep water. "Very well, we will continue the attack. Open to minimum distance for Harpoon launch."

Even if there was one life aboard the *Salinika*, it could not be compared with the masses that might die if the *Salinika* beached, broke up, and released the biological agent.

At twenty-nine knots, the *Ford* reached its firing position in a matter of just a few minutes. Dunne gave his preparatory command, "Combat, let me know when you have acquired your target."

"Harpoon is locked on, sir."

"Fire!" Dunne ordered.

The Harpoon sped toward the *Salinika*, just 30,000 yards away. In a matter of seconds, it reached the target ship—and continued on. It had failed to drop from its cruise altitude and flew over the *Salinika* a good one hundred feet above the ship.

"Ready with Harpoon number two, sir!" CIC reported.

But Dunne was transfixed. Oahu was dead ahead of the surface-to-surface missile and well within range! "Destroy the missile!" Dunne ordered.

There was a brief pause before Combat replied, "Self-destruct activated."

Yet the Harpoon continued on its course.

"Destroy the missile!" Dunne again ordered.

"Destruct feature inoperative," CIC reported.

"Oh, God . . ." Dunne leaped from his chair and raced to the open bridge. Unable to speak any further, he watched the missile cross the beach and plunge into one of the high-rise resort hotels. There was an intolerable flash of brilliant white light and then a shock wave struck him and knocked him to the deck. He rose quickly, and although he had little of his vision left, he could readily make out the boiling white cloud that was building heavenward at incredible speed. The top flattened and mushroomed out, its stem a montage of pale orange, red, and purple condensation. *Oh, Dear Jesus . . .* "Bastards! You used one of the missiles with the nuclear warhead! What have we done? Dear God, what have we done?"

The exec replied, "You didn't specify the warhead, Captain."

Dunne climbed upon the low steel bulkhead that provided shelter on the open bridge. He had preempted the president. Thousands were already dead along the Waikiki strip and all would soon die from the fallout of the expanding nuclear cloud. He stared down at the sea. It was still thousands of feet deep and it was calling his name.

"Captain!" the exec called out, grabbing him roughly

by the shoulder, "Don't do it! Captain! Captain! Captain . . ."

". . . Captain! . . . Captain! . . ."

Dunne woke in a thick, sticky sweat.

The junior officer of the deck was shaking his shoulder. "We couldn't raise you on the intercom, Captain. CINCPACFLT is calling you, sir."

Dunne sat up on the edge of his bunk, his mind struggling to return to reality. Even as he spoke, his words seemed a mile away. "I'll take it in here. Have the patch made."

"Aye, aye, sir." The JOOD hurried out. A moment later a single ring signaled that the patch was completed.

Still shaken, Dunne answered, "Yes, sir."

"Joshua, I wanted to update you. The president is meeting with the NSC. He has issued an order: you are not to take any further action until directed by him. I have a confirmation message on the way."

Dunne checked his watch. "Does he understand the time restraints, Admiral?"

"Yes. General Mitchell is standing by at the Pentagon to relay the order from SECDEF when the president directs."

"Then, the president intends to authorize the sinking?"

"We don't know. He is discussing his options now."

"Sir, he doesn't have any options."

"We have made our recommendations, Joshua."

"Yes, sir."

9

Dunne studied the bridge radar repeater. Although there was considerable sea return from the massive swells and wind-whipped waves, the pale green blip that was the *Salinika* remained prominent, twenty-five miles ahead. And just thirteen miles beyond the death ship there glowed the clear outline of the southern coast of Oahu, extending from Barber's Point eastward past the well-defined entrance to Pearl Harbor and on along the concave beaches of Waikiki to the point of land that jutted seaward just below Diamond Head.

Thirteen miles . . . less than an hour. And the ship was approaching the two-thousand fathom curve even more rapidly. That was where the *Salinika* belonged, on the bottom just this side of shallow water.

Did the president of the United States realize that time had all but run out? Given that he was forty-seven hundred nautical miles away and immersed in the bureaucracy and confusion of official Washington, could his mental picture depict anything that was close to the plain view of impending disaster continually being painted on the bridge scope by the *Ford*'s radar? Could the leader of the free world and the bearer of awesome responsibilities reduce the scope of his considerations to just one small naval vessel tracking a terrorist ship almost within rock-throwing distance of the Royal Hawaiian Hotel? Could he look at the threat from a tactical military standpoint? That was what the situation called for, although it certainly would not be a difficult military operation. Still, a decision had to be made in time for relay to the *Ford* and to allow the frigate the opportunity it would need to prepare for and execute the attack on the *Salinika*. Fortunately, that lead time would be small when one considered the almost instantaneous speed of communications and the well-trained and disciplined crew of the *Ford*. But if the president used up more of that time, Dunne would have to compensate, but only in a limited way—by going to general quarters in advance. And in ten minutes, that was exactly what he intended to do.

He still had no visual contact with the *Salinika*, but that presented no problem. Emotionally, he was having some difficulty in erasing the mental impact of his nightmare; it had been so terribly real—but not realistic. The McDonnell-Douglas built Harpoon SSM was the navy's primary surface-to-surface, antiship weapon with an established ninety-three percent hit accuracy and he would launch a pair. Both would not miss, and even if they did, those on the *Ford* carried no nuclear warhead but 510 pounds of semi-armor-piercing high explosive. With inertial guidance to a predetermined point for the first portion of its flight, and self-contained radar search, acquisition, and terminal capability, the Harpoon should have no difficulty in striking a merchantman with no ECM or defensive capabilities.

With each passing minute, Dunne became more impatient. He did not want to wait until the last moment, but he forced himself to give the situation his promised ten minutes. Then, it was time to prepare.

He ordered, ''Sound General Quarters,'' and the *Ford*

put on her warpaint. He called CIC, "Combat, this is the captain. I will remain on the bridge for the attack." This would not be a fight; this would be a turkey shoot. Then, he added, "Harpoon attack; two missiles, simultaneous arrival."

The Surface Warfare Officer in CIC would insure that his SWG-1 Harpoon fire-control computer operator programmed the missiles to arrive at the *Salinika* together.

On the fo'c'sle, the dual-tracked Mark 13 launcher went vertical and a pair of Harpoons rose from their cylindrical below-deck magazine and locked into place. The launcher lowered its tracks to firing position and swung unerringly toward the unseen *Salinika*.

Combat reported, "Number one and number two Harpoons at the ready."

"Very well," Dunne answered.

Normally, the exec would have been at his battle station in after-steering, the secondary conning space deep in the aft bowels of the *Ford*, but Dunne had instructed him to remain on the bridge. The exec spoke hesitantly, "Captain, are we getting ready to fire? There's no order, yet."

"I'm assuming that responsibility as senior officer on the scene and in tactical command. Note the time and have it logged."

"Aye, aye, sir." The exec turned around and received a nod of acknowledgment from the quartermaster, who had also heard the order. Dunne's decision was entered in the ship's log.

Dunne requested, "*Salinika*'s range from Oahu?"

"Eleven-and-one-half miles," answered the JOOD, who was manning the repeater scope.

"Area clear?" Dunne queried.

"Clear, sir. No other targets."

Dunne triggered his voice circuit to CIC. "On my order . . . Standby . . . Fire, fire, fire!"

The two Harpoons, each fifteen feet long, with a diameter of just over a foot, roared from the launcher, the subsequent missile less than a second after the first. Propelled by solid-fuel booster rockets, each providing 12,000 pounds of instant thrust, the Harpoons accelerated with an ear-shattering swish to their Mach .85 cruise speed. Precisely 2.9 seconds after ignition, the boosters were spent and the 600-pound-thrust turbojet engines were on line and speeding the missiles on their way. Six pairs of stability and steering vanes had sprung open immediately after launch and stubby wings now provided lift for the near-sonic SSMs.

The launcher tilted back and another pair of Harpoons slid upward into place. The launcher re-aimed.

Dunne followed the Harpoons in his mind. Already they would be dropping to wave-top height for their radar-guided terminal approach to the *Salinika*.

The JOOD sang out, "Both missiles on course, sir!" and almost immediately afterward, "Missiles have merged with the *Salinika*; we have two hits, sir!"

The bridge watch was too disciplined to call out, but all gave a punch in the air or a hearty but silent *"Yes!"*

Two Harpoons would sink a frigate; they should have blown massive chunks of hull from the *Salinika*. It became apparent that they had.

It took only another three minutes for the JOOD to report, "Target return diminishing, sir. She's going down!"

Two minutes later, the *Salinika* was gone.

Dunne felt great. Damn the consequences. "Enter the last position of the *Salinika* in the log and on the steaming chart." Turning back to his exec, he ordered, "Draft the message to CINCPACFLT, Jim: Sank *Salinika*, date-time-group, position recorded. Flash precedence. Release it, yourself."

The exec didn't say a word but turned away to carry out Dunne's order.

Dunne felt that he was standing a foot above the steel

deck-plating, a great weight having just left his shoulders. He wasn't sure why he should feel so elated, perhaps it was because the only disaster sweeping across Oahu now was a dying hurricane. That would be cause enough for concern. "Mr. Holly, secure from general quarters. Set the steaming watch and take us out of this storm." There was no need to search for bodies in such weather, and Dunne wanted nothing further to do with the *Salinika*. "I'll be in my sea cabin," he said.

Blackjack Paterson was as edgy as Dunne had been thirty minutes back. And like Dunne, he now decided that the situation was in extremis. Presidential or no presidential order, the *Salinika* must be sunk. He left his small office and walked into the PACOM war room, only to be met immediately by his chief of staff.

"I was just coming to see you, Admiral. We've lost radar return on the *Salinika*."

"What do you mean by 'lost'?"

"It faded and then disappeared."

"Oh, shit. Get me Commander Dunne."

Before the chief of staff could react, the command duty officer rushed up and handed an incoming message slip to Paterson. Blackjack already knew what it was, but he read it aloud anyway. "It's from the Ford. 'Sank *Salinika* 060126Z Sept. Last position logged and charted.' " Seconds later, his command phone rang. It was the chairman of the Joint Chiefs of Staff, General Mitchell.

"Admiral, the president has ordered the sinking of the *Salinika*."

Blackjack kept his eyes on the message report, "General, I have a flash report here in my hands. The Ford sank the *Salinika* just minutes ago." Immediately Blackjack realized his faux pax. *Damn!* He should not have relayed the message—not yet. *Dunne had preempted the president of the United States*. Blackjack's best course of action would have been to wait and send CJCS a copy of the *Ford*'s message with an altered date-time group, one that would have indicated the sinking had taken place *after* the president had made his decision. It would have been dishonest, disloyal, and a serious breach of official conduct, but no one would ever have known. Blackjack knew what was coming next.

Mitchell's words were very slow and deliberate, "Commander Dunne took it upon himself to sink the *Salinika*? He deliberately disobeyed an order by his commander-in-chief?"

"General, forget I said that."

"So you can send me a copy with an altered date-time group? Blackjack, forget I said *that*. Ah—this circuit is acting up. Why don't we start over? Did you understand that I said the president has ordered the sinking of the *Salinika*?"

"Yes, sir—the order is being relayed to the Ford at this moment."

"Good. I'll expect a report of the action as soon as it is accomplished. The president is waiting and insists that the matter remain under the highest classification. He wishes to inform key members of Congress and then announce it to the public by means of a special press conference at the White House later this evening."

Blackjack replaced the handset as soon as he heard the dial tone. Thank God, Mitchell had immediately understood the situation, but perhaps it was not unusual. Blackjack had reasoned that the subterfuge just entered into by USCINCPAC and the chairman of the Joint Chiefs was really academic if one analyzed it properly. Dunne *had* carried out the president's order to sink the *Salinika*. The chain of command from the commander-in-chief down to the commanding officer of the *Ford* had all been in agreement. So what if Dunne had anticipated the president's order? What harm was being done? But deep down in his soul, Blackjack Paterson knew that the ice had just become very thin, and he and his boss had better skate quite carefully until the *Salinika* incident was history. If the president ever discovered that they had conspired to cover-up Dunne's premature action, the commander-in-chief would have even more ammunition in what seemed to be his struggle with the military.

Fifteen minutes later, USCINCPAC readdressed the message from the *Ford* to the CJCS and SECDEF, date-time group of the sink time changed to: 060135Z Sept.

General Mitchell picked up his direct line to SEC-DEF.

"Yes, General?" SECDEF answered.

"The *Ford* has carried out the president's order."

"I have just been handed a copy of the message. I'll inform the president immediately. What was the position of the *Salinika*?"

"Approximately eleven miles south of Oahu."

"Any chance anyone on the beach saw the action?"

"Mr. Secretary, as you know, Oahu is under siege by Hurricane Kahiki. I doubt if there was anyone on the beach. Even so, the visibility is certainly below eleven miles."

"Good. The president wants to make this initial announcement himself. It will give him a much better commander-in-chief image."

The East Room of the White House was crammed with members of the print, radio, and television media, an anxious murmur of curiosity and interest filling the air. At precisely 11:30 P.M. EST, the president strode confidently down the red carpet from his office, followed by the in-town members of the National Security Council. His face as serious as at any time since he had taken office, he took his place behind the twin microphones of the mahogany podium, its blue-trimmed top the background for the presidential seal. SECDEF stood behind him and to his right, while he waited until the initial flurry of flash pictures had been taken and the room quieted. The president then stated:

"I have a written announcement, and I will consider only a few questions after it has been read: Early this morning, a surface unit of the United States Navy was involved in a near-collision with a foreign merchantman in international waters approximately two hundred miles south of the Hawaiian island of Oahu. The merchantman was acting in a suspicious manner and the naval unit closed to identify the vessel. Due to unique circumstances, the naval unit requested permission from the commander-in-chief of the Pacific Fleet to board the vessel. It was granted. The merchantman was boarded and all crewmen aboard were found dead, victims of their own terrorist biological weapon that was intended for use in an attack upon Oahu. Due to the extremely dangerous nature of the weapon and the inability of the boarding party to alter the merchantman's course or speed, our naval unit requested permission to sink the merchantman. . . ."

Reporters were writing furiously on their pads and laptop computers, a number holding up small recorders, and there was an atmosphere of extreme excitement in the room, so intense that it actually constituted a low rumble of movement and hushed voices.

The president continued. "There was a great probability that the terrorist ship would beach itself on the southern coast of Oahu and break up due to the heavy surf of Hurricane Kahiki. If that were to happen, there was a distinct possibility that any of the biological agent remaining on the ship could escape and endanger the population of the island. Consequently, acting as the commander-in-chief of the armed forces of the United States, I directed that the merchantman be sunk. I would point out that there was no resultant loss of life as the crewmen were already deceased."

The media people intuitively knew the president had finished reading his prepared statement and all began shouting and waving raised hands for recognition just before his last word. In response, the president held out both arms in protest against the disorder and pointed to the senior correspondent in the room. She remained seated while she asked, "Mr. President, I understand your statement to mean that the ship has already been sunk. What is the identity of the ship?"

"She was flying false colors and carried a false identity of a friendly nation."

"Can you identify the country of registry?"

"I will not at this time as we are still consulting with the ambassador. But the ship was not registered under the flag she flew."

From the back of the room, an alert reporter from the *Chicago Sun* beat out his contemporaries. "Who were the terrorists, sir?"

"We do not have positive identification at this time, but we do have evidence of the identities and are following up with a worldwide investigation." The president picked a new hand from the forest of upraised arms.

"Sir, was the merchantman armed?"

"As far as we know, only with the biological weapon."

"I have two questions, sir. Was the merchantman a threat to the naval unit, and can you give us the identity of the naval unit?"

The president paused and glanced at SECDEF, who gave a very slight nod. The president replied, "A U.S. Navy frigate, and she was not endangered. It was the threat to Oahu that generated my decision to sink the vessel."

Another voice outshouted the rest, "We sank an unarmed foreign merchantman in international waters without provocation, Mr. President?"

The president appeared uncertain as to how he should

answer. He motioned to SECDEF, who stepped up to his side and spoke into the bevy of microphones, "No, that is not correct. There was certainly provocation. At the time of the action, the terrorist vessel had penetrated our territorial waters around the Hawaiian Islands. And I would point out that although she apparently had no defensive weapons, she did carry the offensive biological weapon. It was a clear-cut threat to a significant segment of the citizens of our country."

"Then," continued the questioner, "will the sunken merchantman be examined for confirmation of the weapon or other evidence that might identify the terrorists?"

The president answered, "I understand that the vessel has been sunk in water normally considered too deep for salvage operations, but we will be looking at that possibility. . . . Thank you all . . . thank you all."

Despite the clamor and pleas for more information, the president left the podium and led his small entourage back down the hall toward his office.

There was near pandemonium as the media people rushed to be the first to get the news before the public.

10

Chief Petty Officer Gerome Sulley awoke suddenly, dry and hot and chewing on his tongue. Not hard enough to break the flesh, but painful. It was swollen and there didn't seem to be any moisture in his mouth. He stuck up his hand to test the air flow. One of the compartment ventilator outlets was over his bunk, the top of two racks that made up one of the tiny CPO quarters in the forward bowels of the *Ford*. There was air flow and it was cool. Why was he so warm? He sat up and stuck his face in the stream. Better. What he really needed was a drink.

Carefully slinging his legs over the side of the thin mattress, he dropped noiselessly to the deck, almost falling and surprised at the weakness in his legs. Must be coming down with something. He had swallowed some sea water when going after the helicopter crash survivors. Too much salt in his system, probably.

The *Ford* was rolling and pitching still, but even with experienced sea legs he was having trouble getting his bearings and kept weaving from side to side as he made his way forward and down several levels. There would be no one about in this portion of the ship, and he knew the route by heart so that even with his mild disorientation and the dimly lit passageways he made his way directly to the forward chain locker. The hatch was small but ample and he crawled inside. Where was the damn bottle? There. Two left. That'd be more than enough to get him to Pearl.

He sat on the coiled chain, the large steel links jutting into his buttocks. Uncomfortable as hell, but a CPO in this man's navy didn't sit in the chief's mess and guzzle joy juice. Not in the United States Navy. The fuckin' Brits, they had the right idea. If a man needed a drink, they poured it for him, even if it was watered down rum and barely enough to keep a coal warm in your belly.

The first swallow rode a bit bumpy on the way down, but the second slipped through the gullet with no problem at all. The third was routine, just like it was supposed to be, with a slight oak taste and smooth. God, it was good, and the chain locker was a man's castle at times like this, far at sea and tuckered out from a full day's work. Let the sumovabitch *Ford* rock and roll all it wanted. Chief Sulley, Yoonited States Navy, at your service, sir. Go over the side in fuckin' hurricane waters and grab any officer you can find? Aye, aye, sir. The fuckin' coolies didn't make it. They rode that piece of aluminum shit down to sleep with Davey Jones himself. The pilot got out. Saved her ass, she did. Shoulda been a golden opportunity to feel her up, but he had been too busy keeping from drowning. She had all the right parts though; he remembered that. He started to laugh but it came out as a cough.

The next swig took the bottle down to just a finger over half full and Sulley didn't have a care in the world. Except one. His hands were swollen, all puffy like, and he had trouble gripping the bottle. Must be an allergy. How could a seventeen-year senior swabby suddenly become allergic to anchor chain? That'd be the shits, wouldn't it!

Sulley gagged on the next mouthful. It didn't want to go down. And part of the other came back up. There was no air in the compartment. Hell, had he breathed it all up? The hatch was closed and he leaned toward it. But that was all. His body stopped responding and his throat closed completely as he toppled forward.

Gotta . . . get some air! . . . Sweet fuckin' Jesus. . . .

11

(WASHINGTON, September 5) (AP) At 11:30 P.M.
EST, the president announced that a frigate of
the U.S. Navy had sunk a foreign merchantman
eleven miles southwest of Oahu after determining that the unidentified ship was carrying a
biological weapon and was attempting a terrorist attack on the island. The identity of the
ship was not revealed nor was the nationality
of the attackers; however, confidential White
House sources indicated that Iraq is under
suspicion as the country of origin of the
threat.

The president, accompanied by several members of the National Security Council, caught
correspondents by surprise with his hastily
called late-night news conference and appeared
uneasy with several of the reporters' questions, deferring to the secretary of defense
on two occasions.

The head of the Iraqi delegation, currently
discussing possible diplomatic moves to ease

the tension between their country and the United States, later told reporters that the White House report with respect to Iraqi involvement was a complete fabrication and indicated that the delegation was suspending the talks until the president assured the chief of the delegation that the charge was unfounded. After that brief statement, the delegation retired to their hotel accommodations at the Washington Hilton.

Iraq has tentatively offered to sign a nonaggression pact with Kuwait and also has offered to cease its attacks upon the Kurds' northern sanctuary in exchange for the lifting of United Nations sanctions and inspections affecting Iraq.

While the talks have appeared to be progressing in a positive manner, this new development has raised speculation that further progress is at a standstill.

Baghdad has announced that Saddam Hussein is meeting with his top military advisers and will issue a statement at 8:00 A.M. Baghdad time.

Hawaiian authorities have stated that they had no knowledge of the threat prior to the president's announcement, and the governor has indicated his displeasure with the lack of notification, declaring that such neglect was irresponsible on behalf of the administration and needlessly endangered the population of Oahu.

Senior military officials on Oahu stated that the operation was immediately classified TOP SECRET by the Pentagon, and the rapid development of the threat left no time for residents of Oahu to have been notified. They cited as further justification that the threat was neutralized before it was in a position to attack Oahu.

Hawaii's Republican senator, Mele Kahakamua, livid with rage at what she called a "serious administration error that in the midst of a devastating hurricane carelessly placed thousands of Oahuans at further risk," demanded a Senate investigation into the president's actions during the crisis.

The White House chief of staff was sipping his third cup of coffee and reading the article one more time before Charles St. John, one of his younger researchers, knocked briefly and then entered. St. John, an avid campaign supporter of the president, summa cum laude graduate of Brown University, Rhodes Scholar, and the chief of staff's primary consultant on gay and lesbian matters, had early on established himself as a dedicated, meticulous assistant and was constantly eager to be of service to his president. Twenty-nine, an accomplished baritone of professional quality, he was prematurely losing his hair, and his high forehead added years to his appearance that were not warranted. Slim of build and with a ready wit, his gregarious personality and sense of tact and discretion were traits for which the chief of staff particularly admired him. He was also loyal to a fault, highly motivated, ambitious, and there was general agreement among the White House staff that he was destined for greater things.

"Charles, have you read this Associated Press release?"

"Yes, sir. I just placed it in my files."

"It's the lead story in the press and on all the network news, naturally. While I don't detect any great criticism of the president's actions with respect to the *Salinika*, I think we should jump ahead on this. Obviously, the governor of Hawaii and Senator Kahakamua are disturbed, understandably perhaps—they both called early this morning—and I want the president to be able to discuss the whole incident from a base of complete knowledge. You know, how the threat developed, how timely it was reported up the chain, the details of the *Ford*'s response.''

''Yes, sir.''

''Drop whatever you're doing. I want you to develop a complete file starting with the *Ford*'s first encounter of the *Salinika*, and on through the sinking. I want places, times, copies of any written communiqués—everything. Talk to whomever you wish. Go where you have to go. I'm sure that SECNAV will give you a letter of authority, and I would suggest you start at the bottom with the captain of the *Ford* and work this thing right up to the president's considerations and decision.''

''Then I start in Honolulu.''

''Yes, I would think so.''

''Sounds like a tough assignment.''

The chief of staff couldn't suppress his grin. ''I'll give you five bucks to change places for a week or so.''

''No way, sir. I'll get right on it. I don't want to be away too long.''

''You're a hard worker, Charles. A little perk is due. However, don't lie in the sun too long. I want this file completed as soon as practical.''

''I'll leave tonight—Hawaii weather permitting.''

''And this is not an investigation; we just need a chronicle of events. Don't step on any military toes.''

''I understand, sir.'' St. John left the office in a much better mood. Normally a workaholic, he had been depressed at the sight of the stack of paperwork that had greeted his 5:00 A.M. arrival at his desk. Now, he could delegate it to others in the lower echelon of the staff. It took only twenty minutes to clean up one urgent matter, then he was off. As he sat in the back of the cab, he began to make a mental list of what he should pack. It would be his first time in Hawaii. Perhaps he was clairvoyant: Just a week back he had bought himself a new swimsuit; a flaming red polyester swimsuit. He didn't feel he had a particularly good body, but his buns were great and that red brief would show them off to their very best advantage.

Of course, no one bought swimsuits in Washington in September. But he had done so, just on the spur of the moment.

Joshua Dunne was fully rested and joined the enlisted crew on the mess deck for a 0600 breakfast. He made it a point to take an unannounced meal with his people every month or so, and he expected his exec to do the same every few weeks. It was not only an opportunity to test the caliber of food prepared, but also a chance to let some of the men voice any concern direct to the commanding officer on an informal basis. And it seemed to him that breakfast was the best time to gauge the mood of the crew. If they were eating heartily and engaging in some mild horseplay, they were happy. If the mess were quiet and trays returned half-full, it was time to have the division officers make inquiries.

After the *Salinika* action, the *Ford* had turned and steamed south for several hours until the sea state was comfortable and then set up a racetrack pattern to await Kahiki's passing of Oahu. In the past thirteen and a half hours, Dunne had sent several amplifying messages to CINCPACFLT with respect to the sinking, including a recommendation that the area be thoroughly searched for debris once the weather permitted. Before falling exhausted into his bunk, he had checked on Kohn's and Long John's condition, then slept solidly for eight hours. Lt. Kohn had been released from sick bay short of midnight, although he imagined she was one sore and stiff young lady. Long John Childress was not so fortunate. The last word Dunne had from Chief Martinez was that Long John was restless, although sedated, and was running a slightly higher than normal temperature.

The men around Dunne were eating well and chattering, all relieved that the *Ford* was in calmer waters, but with mixed emotions about the sinking of the *Salinika*. Dunne had instructed the exec to brief the department heads at morning quarters on the findings leading up to previous afternoon's action; they, in turn, would have their division officers and chiefs relay the briefing to their men during the day's activities. Dunne suspected that they could enter Pearl Harbor well before nightfall, since the latest weather information indicated that Kahiki had passed clear of Oahu during the night and winds at Pearl were already down to the thirty-knot range with light rain. He knew that there would be an international uproar about the incident, and he wanted to make certain that all of his crew had the actual story straight. Once they hit Oahu and pulled liberty, they would be besieged by the media, and depending on the classification of the incident, they would have to be cautious as to what they would say.

At 0700, he met with his exec in his sea cabin. "Jim, I anticipate we'll enter Pearl Harbor in the late afternoon. But I'm worried about Long John. Chief Martinez has expressed some concern about his condition, and I want to see if we can get an air evac as soon as lift is available from Pearl. Work with McGregor on that and let me know when it is arranged."

"Should we send Lieutenant Kohn in, also?"

"No, I don't think so, unless she expresses a desire to go. Martinez says she's just bruised and sore. Also, practically the whole fleet will be returning, and we want to be sure we get some priority on entering the harbor. I suspect the CINC is ahead of us on that. And I want the crew thoroughly briefed on the entire incident. They know the general picture, but I want them all of one mind. No speculations. No rumors for the sake of popularity or a free drink from the press. It'll be a sensitive few days."

"Perhaps we should consider limited liberty, Captain."

"No, they've been on an extended training operation and have had a rough few days at sea, not counting the encounter with the *Salinika*. They'll need to let off some steam—just be sure they're cautioned that misconduct will generate extreme command interest. They're good troops; they'll get the message."

By 0800, Dunne was in sick bay, talking with Chief Martinez.

She was more concerned than before. "I can't break his fever; it's only a couple degrees above normal, but I can't budge it and his white blood cell count has gone up."

Dunne could see that Long John's breathing was labored. "I intend to air-evac him as soon as we can get a chopper from the beach. The weather is improving fast and we'll start north toward Oahu."

"I think that's exactly what's called for. He needs more treatment and expertise than I have."

At 0816, Dunne walked onto the bridge and climbed into his chair. Lt. Murray was the OOD.

"Good morning, Captain."

"Well, let's head for Pearl, Mr. Murray."

"Aye aye, sir." Murray ordered a left turn and gave the helmsman a heading for Oahu. There were large gaps in the overcast and to the east the sky was blue. "Permission for twenty-five knots, Captain?"

"What's the latest speed of Kahiki?"

"Fifteen knots and it's downgraded to a tropical storm, Captain, fifty miles north of Oahu and opening."

"Go to twenty-five knots."

"Aye, aye, sir."

The exec was concerned. The deck division had reported an absentee at morning quarters, Chief Gerome Sulley, one of the swimmers who, along with Charlie Two Shoes, had pulled Kohn and Long John out of the water after the chopper crash. An absentee CPO at morning quarters was not unusual; the senior petty officers often having early morning obligations or sleeping in after a full-duty night. Sessions was seated at his desk when the chief master-at-arms knocked and entered the office. The exec pushed back some papers and grabbed his coffee cup. "Chief Sulley show up yet?"

"No, sir. I have several people looking for him."

"When's the last time anyone talked to him?"

"Chief Sanders is his bunkmate. He says Sulley got up about oh-two-hundred; assumed it was a piss call."

"He didn't come back?"

"Not according to the chief."

"Not in any of the heads? He could be sick."

"We've searched the places he normally might be."

"He wasn't in his bunk at reveille?"

The chief master-at-arms shook his head.

"You don't just disappear on a ship as small as this. He has to be somewhere." The exec didn't like the wild thought that jumped into his head. "God, you don't suppose he went over the side?"

"We're still in storm condition, sir. Sulley wouldn't have gone out on deck in the middle of the night."

The exec stood and motioned for the chief master-at-arms to close the upper portion of the office dutch door. "Chief Sulley can be mean when he drinks. Has he had any runins lately?"

"No, sir, nothing that could be that serious, sir."

"You never know."

"He was last seen in his skivvies, commander. He'd not have gone out on deck like that. He'd have froze his ass off in the rain and wind."

"Well, keep checking. Everywhere. Even the voids if you have to."

"Aye, aye, sir."

Second Class Quartermaster Pee Wee Johnson was not a happy sailor. Just off the six-to-eight, he had been commandeered by the chief master-at-arms to help locate Chief Sulley. Johnson wanted breakfast, he was dog-tired, and Sulley was not one of his favorite people, anyhow. Poor example of a career chief. All blow and no show. How Sulley had made his chief's hat, Johnson could never figure out, and he would never forget being dressed down by Sulley in front of the whole division while they had been in Sidney. Sulley's breath had been so whiskey-soaked, it had almost faded Johnson's uniform. Maybe someone did throw Sulley over the side.

Johnson was about to give it up when he reached the forward chain locker. The hatch was closed but not dogged. That was a breach of the watertight integrity of the ship. No way the chief would be in there. But what the hell, the word had been passed to look everywhere. Might as well check inside before securing the dogs. Johnson yanked on the hatch.

Sulley lay sprawled atop the piled anchor chain. Beside him was a half-empty bottle of Jack Daniels. Wearing only skivvies, his skin white and his body bloated, he was dead. There were deep scratches on his neck.

Johnson grabbed a damage control phone. As soon as someone answered in Damage Control Central, Johnson reported his find. "I found Chief Sulley. He's here in the forward anchor chain compartment."

The chief master-at-arms was on the other end. "What the hell is he doing there?"

"He ain't doing nothin', chief. He's dead."

"Dead?"

"Dead and pickled, I'd say."

"Stay there. I'm on my way as soon as I notify the XO."

The chief master-at-arms and the exec reached the scene together.

"My God—" The exec felt a sour fluid rising in his throat, but he managed to keep it from going any further as he gazed down at the body. "Have you told anyone about this?"

"No, sir."

"Get Chief Martinez down here, with a body bag and an NBC suit—and not a word on this to anyone else. Understand?"

"Yes, sir," they replied in unison. The chief master-at-arms left to get Martinez.

The remaining crewman started to bend over and examine the body.

The exec held him back. "No, don't touch him."

"I've never seen booze do *this* to a guy," the sailor uttered.

"You never know," the exec said, amazed but very pleased that the petty officer had not connected the death of Chief Sulley to the deaths of the crew of the *Salinika*. "I'll stay here, you go ahead and resume your duties. Not one word of this, though, understand? I'll make the announcement."

Martinez and the chief master-at-arms arrived as the sailor left. Martinez gasped as soon as she saw the body. "My God . . ."

The exec stopped her from getting too close. "Put on the suit. Then put the chief in the body bag. Can you do that by yourself?"

"Yes, sir."

"We'll leave him here in the locker. I don't want either of you to mention how he died. Just say it was the whiskey. Chief, can you seal this compartment?"

"Yes, sir—but what if we have to anchor out at Pearl?"

"Shit." The exec hadn't thought of that. "We should be assigned a pier or an outside mooring. If not, we'll have to insist on one. I do not want the body removed from here until a medical team gets on board."

Martinez suited up and placed the open body bag beside Sulley. With one hand on his shoulder and the other on his buttocks, she rolled him over and into the bag face down. A couple of tucks and a hearty pull on the far side of the bag and he was enclosed and zipped in.

"I'll spot-weld the hatch secure myself, sir," said the chief master-at-arms. The chain locker was very seldom entered. It was unlikely that anyone would discover the weld.

Martinez removed her protective suit, left it inside out, rolled it into a ball, and placed it in the chain locker beside Sulley's body.

The exec lifted a hand and cautioned, "Remember, not a word of how he died. The crew doesn't need to know, yet. I'll go report to the captain."

Dunne was on the bridge.

The exec spoke softly, "Captain, I need to speak to you. We have a problem. Can we go out on the wing of the bridge?" There, in a hushed voice, he reported the details of the search for Sulley and the finding of the body.

Dunne was stunned, and like the exec, very frightened. "How did that goddamned bug get on this ship?"

"Sulley was one of the swimmers who rescued Long John. Long John had been on the *Salinika*."

"But Long John doesn't have the disease."

"He's very sick."

"But we've assumed it's because of his injuries." Dunne walked forward and leaned on the rail, facing forward.

The exec joined him. Now the lookout could not even see their lips. "It has to be Childress. Somehow, he's carrying it."

Dunne rubbed his eyes, trying to work out the problem. "Martinez and the other corpsman. They don't have it, nor does Lieutenant Kohn."

"I don't know what the hell is going on, Captain, but if this gets out to the crew, they could panic."

"Well, they have to know. We can't keep *this* away

from them. They have a right to know. Sulley may not be the last. Petty Officer Two Shoes also had contact with Long John.''

''And at least three others. They carried the litter to sick bay.''

The OOD stuck his head through the hatch leading to the enclosed bridge. ''Captain, we have an air-evac ten miles out, requesting landing.''

''Good. Coast guard or navy?''

''Coast guard air-evac nine-one-three, sir.''

''All right. Go to flight quarters for the recovery.'' Dunne continued his hushed discussion with his exec. ''Get down to sick bay. Have Martinez and everyone concerned with transferring Long John put on protective gear. Long John, too. You get back and brief the helo crew that we're transferring a man with injuries, plus a possible contagious disease, but that there's no danger to them because the patient is isolated in his suit. I want that chopper off as soon as possible.''

The exec started to leave, paused, then said, ''And then what, Captain?''

''We go to general quarters.''

''Sir?''

''Look, Jim. We had only a dozen sets of protective wear when we sailed. We left one back on the *Salinika*, lost two in the Seahawk crash. Martinez deep-sixed Long John's and her own. One's in the chain locker. Six left. They're not like loaves and fishes—they won't multiply—so we can't protect the whole crew. Thus, we go to general quarters; everyone is fixed in place. If there is another casualty, we may be able to confine exposure to a minimum of the crew.''

The exec was still confused but he had to supervise the loading of Long John onto the chopper. He hurried aft without comment.

Dunne stared at the sea. Was the *Ford* about to become another death ship? Why hadn't the salt water washed any contaminant off Long John's suit? Was Long John now a carrier? He wasn't having any difficulty swallowing. He wasn't bloated. Could Sulley have passed it on? Why the delayed reaction? Even now, was the damned thing creeping from crewmember to crewmember? Dunne was no stranger to prayer, but he had never prayed more fervently than he did now. He crossed himself. "In the name of the Father, the Son, and the Holy Spirit. Dear God, please don't let this happen. Don't forsake us. These are good men and women. . . ."

Admiral Paterson was the last to read the latest message from the *Ford*. His chief of staff and then the ACOS for operations had studied it just before bringing it to him. All were seated in his office off the command center.

Paterson broke the silence. "What time will the *Ford* enter the harbor?"

Captain Howard Silva, the ACOS for Ops, answered, "Fifteen-thirty. She's requested a moor; for some reason she doesn't want to anchor out."

Paterson responded, "In light of this, she'll *have* to moor or anchor out. We can't put her alongside a pier or another ship. Not until a medical team boards and takes whatever action it can. We don't have any idea of what we have or how many of her crew are affected. Obviously, it's contagious. Do we still have a mooring buoy in the East Loch?"

Silva spoke again, "Yes, we do, and we have the team standing by, Admiral; all will be in protective gear. The medical officer informed me the plan is to remove the casualty to Tripler. The army has doctors on the staff with biological warfare experience and they'll perform the autopsy. If they can isolate the virus or bacteria or whatever it is, hopefully there will be an antidote or vaccine. Assuming there is, they will treat the crew. After that, the investigative team can board and conduct their preliminary inquiry.''

Paterson nodded his concurrence. ''Is there a chance the ship is carrying the thing and not the personnel?

''Highly unlikely,'' Silva answered. ''The agent almost had to have been picked up by one of the boarding party on the *Salinika*; most probably it was Lieutenant Childress, since he's the only survivor of the four men who went aboard.''

''Others on the *Ford* may have been exposed,'' Paterson stated flatly.

''True. If so, we'll know soon. It just depends on how it is spread; touch? breath?''

Paterson declared his next step, ''Howard, I want you to take personal charge of the situation as soon as the *Ford* enters the harbor. The medical team and the investigative team will be under your direct command.''

''Aye, aye, sir.''

''You keep the chief of staff informed. I anticipate that I'll be busy with the Washington crowd. They'll be all over us on this. I want a private briefing every morning before the routine staff briefing and anytime something unusual comes up. And most importantly, I do not want whatever is on the *Ford* to get off the *Ford*. We just sank a ship to prevent it from carrying the agent to Oahu—for God's sake, don't let the medical team bring it ashore. They know what to do, but you stay right on top of them.''

''I certainly will do that, Admiral.''

Paterson inhaled deeply, then pursed his lips, forcing the air to puff his cheeks as his lungs emptied. ''One final thing. One of the president's White House staff will be coming out to familiarize himself with the details of the sinking of the *Salinika*. Inform everyone to be cooperative.''

The chief of staff's eyebrows rode high on his forehead. "I thought that was the function of the military by way of the secretary of defense."

At Reedy's remark, Paterson's eyes burned with anger and humiliation. "That was when we lived in the real world. Now, in never-never land, we serve at the pleasure of the president and his diverse staff of all colors, creeds, and *sexual orientations,* and on occasion the command chain be damned."

Silva caught the emphasis but wasn't sure of the meaning. "You mean our man from D.C. is a bit soft?" he asked.

Paterson snorted. "According to General Mitchell, as soft as fairy wings. A source of some pride within the White House staff and a person not to be underestimated. He is an extremely capable and intelligent young comer. He will do a good job and we will be hospitable, courteous, and cooperative. Just don't kiss him on the lips—or on any other part of his anatomy."

Dunne watched the air-evac chopper clear the *Ford* and head for Oahu. "General quarters," he ordered. "Jim, for this, you station yourself in sick bay." The exec's normal battle station was in after-steering where he could take over conning of the ship should the bridge be destroyed. But there would be no military attack on the *Ford* this day.

The *Ford* was only eight miles from the entrance to Pearl Harbor. Dunne listened as each department reported battle stations manned and watertight condition ZEBRA set. Then, he spoke to the crew: "Now, hear this. This is the captain. I have ordered general quarters to prevent a very serious condition from worsening. A short time ago, Chief Sulley was found dead in the forward anchor chain locker. It has been sealed, the reason being that we suspect the chief died of a contagious disease, possibly of a biological contaminant from the ship *Salinika.* There is no great cause for alarm. If the disease

were already spread by any extent, more of our shipmates would be showing symptoms. None are at present,
and that is a very encouraging sign. However, if anyone
starts to experience breathing difficulties, remain calm
while your shipmates notify sick bay. You will be immediately treated. It is imperative that those in your
space refrain from physical contact with anyone with
these symptoms. In this way, if the disease appears, we
will confine it to a specific battle station and all hands
at that station will recieve immediate medical attention.
I say again, there is no cause for any great alarm, but
you must strictly adhere to my orders. We expect to
moor in Pearl Harbor within the next hour and a half,
and an extensive medical team will board and we will
be under their care. At that time, I feel we will be out
of danger.''

Dunne noted the looks of concern on the faces of the
bridge personnel; without a doubt, they mirrored the ex-
pressions of the entire crew. He smiled reassuringly and
spoke to them, ''We have always been prepared to go
into battle together. This is no different, except I am
confident our casualties, *if any*, will be minimal. Now,
let's show the pencil pushers at Pearl how a man-o-war
enters and shows her colors.''

Charlie Two Shoes tried to make himself comfortable in
the cramped after-steering compartment. Normally, the
XO would be with him and one other quartermaster, but
the XO was assigned to sick bay and the other watch-
stander had been temporarily reassigned to Damage
Control Center for the remainder of the journey into
Pearl. It was just as well. Two Shoes had slept poorly
and had no appetite at breakfast call. He made himself
as comfortable as possible.

Almost with no warning, he choked on some phlegm
and coughed up a small amount of white residue. Immediately, he thought of Chief Sulley. He had been in

the water with Sulley and Lieutenant Childress. But Lieutenant Kohn was not sick.

Five minutes later, Two Shoes noticed his face was swelling, as were his hands. There was no pain in his chest, but he was having trouble breathing. He raised one hand to his forehead to feel for a fever but stopped it level with his face. His hand was white despite his naturally darker pigmentation.

Suddenly dizzy, he passed out for a moment, and in his loss of consciousness, a wolf came to him. That was his grandfather's sign. And the wolf spoke the last words his grandfather had spoken to him: "My grandson, you honor our people by serving this land. I am proud of you. You take with you the code of the Ute people and the white men you will serve and serve with will benefit from your example. You will show them the pride of your people. Do not listen to those who say we have been done a disservice. We have a share of the dishonor our ancestors brought upon our lives. The past is the past. You are our future, my grandson. Live as a warrior lives, and if it is the Great One's wish that you die, die as a warrior. Die as a Ute."

Two Shoes woke and his mouth and throat were as dry and raspy as the sand of his reservation.

I have the sickness, he thought.

No one had survived, and Charlie Two Shoes immediately knew that he would not survive, either. But he could protect his shipmates. He closed his eyes and could picture his mother standing at the door of his home. His grandfather was standing behind her, one hand on her shoulder. Beside them was the wolf. Two Shoes knew what he must do.

The bridge talker to after-steering called out, "Captain, after-steering wants to talk to you, sir, on the sound-powered phones." The talker removed his headset and held it out.

Dunne hesitated. "To me? Or the OOD?"

"He specifically said you, sir; no one else."

Dunne still hesitated. Why was after-steering bypassing normal procedure? "Charlie Two Shoes is in after-steering?"

The OOD confirmed, "Yes, sir. Charlie Two Shoes is our battle station quartermaster in after-steering. He and usually Commander Sessions."

Dunne's exec was stationed in sick bay. Charlie Two Shoes would be alone. Dunne took the headset. "This is the captain."

"Captain . . . this is Petty . . . Officer Two Shoes . . . I . . . my throat . . . I'm having trouble . . . breathing. . . ."

Oh, Jesus, no. Dunne's heart rate began to double-time. He forced himself to appear calm. "Have you contacted sick bay? I'll notify them immediately."

"No . . . sir. I know there . . . is . . . nothing they . . . do. . . ."

Dunne also knew that, but he could not take away any hope that there could be help. He also knew from his first words that Two Shoes was doomed. *How many more?* He directed the OOD, "Have sick bay send Chief Martinez to after-steering, but she is not to enter the compartment until I give the word." He directed his attention back to Two Shoes. "Two Shoes, hang in there, we have corpsmen on the way."

"My mother . . . on reservation . . . Ute Mountains . . . I honor her and . . . my grand . . . father and . . . die . . . a warrior . . . Captain . . . you must . . . seal the . . . compartment. . . ."

"No, Two Shoes . . ."

"I . . . understand . . . you must . . ."

"We're only a few miles from the harbor."

"No choice . . . Cap . . . Captain. . . ."

Damn it, God! Why now? Why Charlie Two Shoes? Dunne was overcome by the futility of anything he could do. Sealing the compartment was exactly what was called for. In battle, he could easily be faced with the decision of condemning one or more of his men to save the greater portion of his crew. That was the ultimate responsibility of his command. Was this situation any less demanding? No. He wanted to cry out in protest, to flail his arms at the cruelty of the terrorists who introduced death to his ship. For no purpose other than man's inhumanity to man. It was senseless. And the *Ford* was less than an hour away from medical assistance. Dunne's tears were those of anger and frustration, every muscle in his body pulled taut by the heroics of Charlie Two Shoes. But he was the captain, and in spite of all of his awesome responsibilites, he must maintain a captain's composure. The bridge crew could not but notice the moisture in his eyes and on his cheeks, yet they would not see his despair or any reluctance to do his duty.

He spoke as softly as the demands of the sound-powered intercom system would allow. "Two Shoes ... I will take care of everything. I will talk to your mother and grandfather and tell them of your warrior's courage ... they will sing songs of you around their fires." Dunne wanted to speak words which would reflect Indian tradition and beliefs, but he was not an Indian and his feeble attempt seemed almost ludicrous under the circumstances. He didn't know if Indians sat around campfires as in the old days. All he knew about Indian culture was what he read or saw in the movies or on TV. He cursed himself for his ignorance. Why were Americans so ignorant of one another, particularly of their brethren, the first Americans? And why so unfeeling? Raised in the squalor and poverty of the reservation, Charlie Two Shoes had overcome such obstacles and had become master of his own fate. As a member of the U.S. Navy, he had proudly served the very government that had oppressed his people. The Ute was a Native American who had been a model sailor, one who showed great promise, one who had saluted Dunne with pride— and now Dunne was returning that loyalty by leaving him alone in a tiny below-decks compartment to die. Dunne knew his captain's duty, but his humanitarian side was demanding that he rush down to after-steering and hold Charlie Two Shoes in his arms, comfort him, and in some way ease his passing.

But he could not.

Instead, he called over his OOD and spoke quietly into his ear.

The OOD recoiled. "Captain . . ."

"Damn it to hell—relay my order!" Dunne had kept his hand over the mouthpiece while voicing his decision. Now, he removed it. "Two Shoes . . . ?"

There was no reply. He tried again. Then again. And one more time. He handed the headset back to the talker. "No, don't put them on." He knew that there would be no further need for communication with after-steering. The OOD had his orders. The sound-powered phones were in essence a secure circuit. No one else had heard Charlie Two Shoes. There was no need to inform the entire crew—not yet.

Dunne walked slowly to the front of the enclosed bridge and faced the confused watch. "Petty Officer Charlie Two Shoes has a problem in after-steering. I have given specific instructions to the officer-of-the-deck as to what we can do to help him. He has symptoms of the disease that killed Chief Sulley. If God is merciful, Two Shoes will be the last. If not, then we still have an ordeal to face. For the moment, I would like this situation to remain on the bridge only. Those who wish to pray will not be violating any order of this ship, or in my mind any provision of the United States Constitution."

A half hour later, the *Ford* was sailing through the Pearl Harbor entrance channel at a steady six knots. Three fire-fighting tugs came alongside and began hosing down the ship in response to the first of a series of orders by CINCPACFLT. Despite having steamed through heavy rain during most of the time since the encounter with the *Salinika*, there was a possibility that a further wash-down would insure no contaminant remained on the exterior of the frigate.

There was considerable debris in the channel—the residue of Kahiki's passage—but there was nothing large or heavy enough to impede the *Ford*'s passage. To the right, Hickam Air Force Base was already cleaning up; work parties were loading stake trucks with palm fronds and broken lumber. As the *Ford* passed to the right of Waipio Point and into the harbor proper, Dunne's mind was whelmed with thoughts of Charlie Two Shoes, but he could not ignore his immediate duties. He was comforted to see less storm damage than he had expected. Several small craft were driven up onto the beaches of the Waipio Peninsula, but most structures seemed relatively untouched. The *Ford* passed just to the right of Ford Island and rendered honors to the 1,177 entombed sailors and marines, ancestral shipmates who lay within the sunken hull of the USS *Arizona*. Dunne felt the whole world was preoccupied with death at the moment. The most widely known casualty of the Japanese air attack on a peaceful Sunday morning more than a half-century back, the *Arizona* still flew her colors and remained on the navy roster as a ship of the line. The white National Memorial structure that ran athwartships of the rusting, barnacled sunken hull was bare of any visitors, undoubtedly closed until the hurricane debris was removed from the harbor. Off to the right, the personnel of the monument's visitor center were peforming their own cleanup; the main buildings were undamaged, but a number of the palms had been felled by the storm winds.

North of Ford Island was the East Loch of the harbor, and the *Ford* proceeded to a large steel cylindrical mooring buoy, one that was isolated and seldom used. Head-

ing into the wind, the *Ford* eased up to the buoy, and the
fo'c'sle crew tossed the guiding line to the line handlers
waiting on the buoy. They used it to haul the heavy mooring line from the *Ford* and secure it to the huge iron cleat
on the buoy. The *Ford*'s bridge crew stopped the ship's
engines and let the frigate drift backward until the line
was taut. From now on, the *Ford* would be secure, drifting slowly around the buoy with the wind changes.

As soon as the *Ford*'s accommodation ladder was
lowered, a naval harbor service boat tied up, and the
medical team, looking all the while like alien spacemen
in their protective suits, awkwardly climbed the ladder.
There, Dunne met them.

The chief medical officer asked, "Any more casualties?"

"One," Dunne answered. "We have the body isolated."

"How long ago?"

"The better part of an hour."

"What was the interval since the first casualty?"

Dunne had no idea when Sulley had died. "Probably
eighteen hours or so back. I still have the crew at general
quarters. I thought isolating them in small groups might
control the spread."

"Good idea. We have vaccine for all known biological agents and an antidote if anyone else comes down,
but I don't know if it'll be effective once symptoms
appear. You first, Captain, then we'll need members of
the crew to guide us around the ship."

Dunne held up the sleeve of his tropical khaki shirt
and felt the gentle prick of the first needle. There were
two more. The bridge personnel were innoculated next,
then several members of damage control center; then the
team dispersed to treat the rest of the crew. They returned to the bridge an hour later. The chief medical
officer removed his protective gear as did the other

members of his team. "Captain," he said, "unless this is something new, your men are out of danger. They're very lucky."

Dunne did not share the sentiment, but he understood its meaning. He gave a welcome order to the OOD: "Secure from general quarters, set the normal mooring watch, ship's company to normal in-port routine."

The chief medical officer announced, "We will be taking the two casualties. I will have an autopsy report for you as soon as we can. Until then, I must order all hands to remain aboard except for yourself. I suspect Admiral Paterson will want a personal report."

"CINCPACFLT has us quarantined until his order," Dunne replied.

"Then, we will advise him."

Dunne sadly watched the team leave with the bagged bodies of Chief Sulley and Charlie Two Shoes. Communication services were now being provided to the ship by buoy connections, and his first obligation was to report his arrival to CINCPACFLT. The *Ford* would be sending its own message, but Dunne had been directed to personally call Admiral Paterson upon arrival. He made his way to his in-port cabin, requested a cup of coffee from his messman, and picked up the telephone. First, the admiral's yeoman and then Rear Admiral Reedy answered.

"Commander Dunne, we're all concerned about the *Ford.* Your people have acted with a great sense of duty. I understand the medical team has left?"

"Yes, Admiral. All hands have been innoculated. The medical officer seems to feel we're out of danger."

"I know the loss of your people has been traumatic. But you must take considerable comfort in your actions that have perhaps saved thousands . . . here's Admiral Paterson."

"Joshua." Paterson's voice was deep and friendly.

"It's good to hear your voice again, Admiral, and these circumstances are considerably better than when we last spoke."

"We don't want to go into any detail over this line, Joshua, but as soon as the medical people advise lifting the quarantine, I want to talk to you. In the interim, have your people prepare an after-action report. Chuck Reedy will want to talk to your exec and operations officer. The sinking of the *Salinika* is the number one item on a lot of people's desks. I'm sure you understand that."

"Yes, sir."

"Now, get busy and call your wife. She got out of Balboa yesterday and should be home. Thank God she is responding to treatment. I'll get off your line, now."

"Thank you, sir."

"Annie?"

"Josh! You're in Pearl! Are you all right? Oh, I've been so worried. The *Ford* has been all over the news, and the other ship. Everyone is talking about what will come next. The president held a special news conference . . ."

"Annie! Slow down. I want to know about *you*. I love you."

"I'm just pleased you're all right."

"Your father says the treatment is going well. That's the only news I'm interested in. How do you feel?"

Annie Dunne hesitated.

"The truth, Annie."

"I'm awful tired, Josh. But the latest chemo has a good track record with my kind of cancer. I really feel encouraged. My appetite is back. You know what I fixed myself for dinner last night? Cajun shrimp! Just like we used to get at K Paul's in New Orleans. Well, almost like his. I took the recipe right out of his book. When will you reach San Diego?"

"I don't know, yet. We'll have some debriefing here

and then I would think we could leave. We have some obligations to PACFLT as the result of all this.''

"Let me know, Josh. If I keep feeling this well, the doctors say I may be able to meet you at the pier when you arrive.''

"No, Annie. I want you to stay there. I don't want you to exert yourself . . .''

"But I feel fine . . .''

"No, you don't feel fine; you feel good because we're talking together, and I feel good, too. But as soon as we make San Diego, I'll come straight to the hospital or home, whatever. You're still sick, Annie.''

"I'm not sick, Josh. I'm dying . . . and I want to be with you.''

"Stop that kind of talk. I promise I'll come to you as soon as we hit port. It'll just be a matter of a few more days.''

There was no sound, but Dunne knew his wife was crying.

So was he.

12

Commander Joshua Dunne was ushered into Admiral Blackjack Paterson's USCINCPAC office located within the confines of the Marine Corps' Camp H. M. Smith. It was a spacious room with birch paneled walls and a blue deep-pile carpet that must have felt great to bare feet. But there were never bare feet on that carpet, only spit-polished shoes and occasionally clean and shined combat boots. The admiral had already risen from behind his desk and stepped forward to greet his son-in-law. For the first few minutes, it would be a family reunion.

"Joshua, it is good to see you." Paterson took Dunne's hand in both of his and held it. "It's been a while."

"Yes, it has, Admiral." Despite their closeness, Dunne would never presume to call Paterson "Dad." It just didn't fit; the ties of the service were much stronger than the ties of in-laws, and there was a deep feeling of mutual professional respect between the two naval officers. The vast gap in rank was too ingrained to be set aside, even in their more intimate moments.

"Sit down. Iced tea?"

"Thank you."

"Joshua, I just wanted you to know that I am satisfied with the way you handled the situation with the *Salinika*. Tactically, I approve of everything you did. As for taking it upon yourself to sink the son of a bitch, I feel that was your prerogative as the on-scene commander, but the fact the president had ordered us not to act until he gave the command has to be considered. We may take some flack on that if the president finds out."

"I felt a lot of concern about that, Admiral. I just had no choice."

"Well, at this point no one knows about it. As you are acutely aware, the president finally did give the order even as I was reading your action message. I spoke with General Mitchell and we both agreed you were justified. It is unfortunate that the hurricane prevented any physical support, but that is academic as far as I am concerned. We have tried to keep as much of the details of the encounter as we can from the press, but naturally we have kept the chairman of the Joint Chiefs—and through him the SECDEF and the president—fully informed. But it all has happened in such a short time that there are lots of questions, and many of them are coming from the White House. Our public relations folks here in the command have been able to hold off the hounds of the press fairly well, but the administration has a more serious problem. With your implication that the terrorists were Iraqis, the talks may very well be scuttled unless Saddam can convince the administration that the terrorists acted independently. That's certainly a possibility, but hardly germane to the problem we faced. We had an immediate threat, regardless of who is behind it. Personally, the more I consider the situation, the less I am certain that the Iraqis were responsible."

"I could agree with that."

"It *is* of serious concern within the National Security Council. There is speculation, most of it from the press and a few so-called military experts among our retired brethren, that there may be a retaliatory air strike. I don't know. Certainly, there won't be one based on speculation as to who the terrorists were. You might want to direct your crew not to speculate on it in public.''

''Yes, sir. I have given them specific orders.''

''Good. The president was on the verge of achieving a really significant political success, the evaporation of the Iraqi crisis—and he needs something of that magnitude to restore his international standing. I think, since the attack was countered before it materialized, he will be willing to resume the talks if Hussein can convince him that it was an independent operation. And the president *wants* to be convinced—very much.''

''What if our intelligence provides evidence that Saddam orchestrated it?''

''Unless it's foolproof, I think the president will sit on that and go for Saddam's pitch.''

Dunne did not like to think of that possibility. ''That would be naive. I don't like to think that the administration would be that anxious for a political victory.''

Paterson grinned. ''So, what else is new?''

Dunne was not convinced. ''I don't see how the president could ignore the facts.''

''Well, our responsibility is to see that we provide as much information as possible to our superiors. Your after-action report will provide a solid framework for any other findings we have. The autopsy should verify the agent used. Your eyewitness, Lieutenant Kohn, can provide first-person verification of the ship, the aircraft, and the casualties.''

''We have two witnesses. Lieutenant Childress actually boarded the *Salinika*. He can give a firsthand account of what he found.''

''He could have. He died on the air-evac helicopter en route to Tripler.''

Dunne had not known that. No message had been received during the night and he had left the *Ford* immediately after having been cleared by the medics. Now, he had another letter to write. "I didn't know. He was a very fine officer."

Paterson leaned forward and Dunne was not sure what his frown meant until he spoke.

"You know, Joshua, with no photographs and no visual sighting of the *Salinika* due to the storm visibility and the distance the *Ford* stayed away from the ship, we don't have *any* hard evidence except the sighting by Lieutenant Kohn that the *Salinika* ever existed. Think about that for a moment."

"We have the pilot. We *sank* the *Salinika*. There are a number of witnesses who can testify to that. We can even play back the radar picture of the Harpoon attack."

"We have a body in discontinued Soviet flight gear with a fatal gunshot wound and no evidence of the disease. You sank *a* ship. Can the radar verify it had a VTOL airplane on board? Can it show us the spray equipment or the barrels of biological warfare agent? Can you, the commanding officer who ordered the attack, give any firsthand testimony about the last two items?"

Dunne realized that he could not. It suddenly occurred to him that he had formed his conclusions based on what he had been told by the helicopter crew and a very sick and possibly panicked Long John.

Paterson added, "I would take very good care of Lieutenant Kohn. I should add, Joshua, that when some members of the administration first heard of your encounter with the *Salinika*, their initial reaction was that the report could be an elaborate ruse by the military to scuttle the Iraqi talks."

Dunne was irate. "That's unbelievable."

Paterson's chuckle seemed artificial. "It would make one hell of a movie, wouldn't it?"

"And I deliberately sank the *Salinika* in deep water

where recovery, and even a revealing examination, could be impossible."

"Still a good decision," Paterson offered, "but I don't think we are completely out of the woods on this one, given the mind-set of our current administration. They've been wrestling with foreign policy ever since inauguration day. I'm just playing devil's advocate, mind you."

"At an academy award level if I may say so, Admiral. I hadn't thought of any of this."

"You didn't know the background."

Dunne brightened. "We have the bodies of Chief Sulley and Charlie Two Shoes!"

"Recall that I said 'elaborate' ruse. And the tabloid press could run with it. You know the game: How hard would it be for military intelligence to introduce a biological agent into two crew members? It would sell newspapers."

"That would be murder. The U.S. Navy doesn't murder its personnel. With all due respect, Admiral, I think you're reaching a bit far."

"Am I? Not one thing I've said originated with me. General Mitchell called me on the secure line last evening, and what I have just seemed to conjure up comes straight from reliable sources inside the Beltway. Sometimes, we clods in the military have our own mole in high places. Thank God."

"You're saying this scenario is actually being considered?"

"No. What I'm saying is that we want to stay ahead of everything and everybody. To begin with, as CINC-PACFLT I have ordered a UCMJ Article 32 investigation into your actions and conduct to insure that nothing improper occurred. Obviously, it hasn't, but the investigation is proper procedure. That will give us our first documentary evidence of statements by witnesses and a detailed account of the action to back up your after-action report.'' Abruptly, Paterson changed the subject. ''Have you talked to Annie?''

''Yes, it was great to hear her voice. It sounded strong.''

''I've kept in touch every week while you were deployed, and your calls from Australia were big morale boosters for her.''

''I wish I could have called more often.''

Paterson shrugged. ''Annie's a navy brat; she knows the price. I don't know what she told you. This new mix of chemicals is not exactly a last-ditch effort, but it is powerful and the side effects can be devastating. I talked to her doctor, and he is not as optimistic with me as he is with her. She does, however, seem to be tolerating it extremely well.''

''She's very tired and I suspect very weak.''

''Par for the course, Joshua. Before her mother died— just shortly before you two started seeing each other— she had no muscle strength at all. She was such a vivacious woman, even in her late forties. She would have liked you. Same goddamned type of tumor. I discovered it myself one evening after we had gone to bed. I raised holy hell as to why she had not seen a doctor; the damned thing was the size of a pea and hard as a marble. At least Annie caught hers sooner. In all honesty, I don't think the prognosis is any better. You have to prepare yourself for that.''

Dunne replied with a very sympathetic tone in his voice, ''How do you do that, Admiral?''

Paterson shook his head and sighed. ''You don't, really. But you try to think of the good times you had together and you always present an optimistic front. Take it one day at a time. Never consider the inevitable. You can't or you'll come unglued. When the last days come, you have to be a rock.''

The two men sat for a minute, united in thought, drinking their tea.

Dunne could easily see another week in Pearl. "Admiral, Annie has already asked me when we'll return to San Diego."

"I want you with her as soon as possible. The investigation as far as the *Ford* is concerned should be short. A couple days, max. There is a member of the White House staff coming out; he should be here any time now. He will want to talk to you. Cooperate, certainly. I can't imagine that he would need more than a day. He'll be talking to us, also, so I'll sic him on you first. I would think you could sail by the end of the week; that's four days. Add your en route time."

"Thank you, sir."

Paterson stood. "Thanks for coming right over, Joshua. I wanted to give you some of the behind-the-scenes considerations that may be occurring, and I wanted to talk to you about Annie. From here on out, I suspect we'll have little official contact since my staff will be handling things. Come and see me before you leave; in fact, let's try and get together for a couple drinks, maybe dinner, the night before you sail. I've a couple things I'd like to send with you for Annie."

"I'll look forward to it, Admiral."

"And I." Paterson's farewell handshake was as warm and personal as his first greeting, although Dunne got the feeling that he was being summarily dismissed.

After Dunne left, Paterson took a moment to make some notes on the meeting. His son-in-law could very well have acted a bit prematurely in sinking the *Salinika*. But the die was cast. As he finished his notes, his thoughts became more personal. He thought quite highly of Joshua Dunne. His daughter could not have a more loving and caring husband. Yet, he also thought from time to time that it would have been nice if Dunne had been black. He didn't consider it a racist thought at all; it was just that a black grandchild would have preserved his own African-American heritage a bit longer. Even that innocent opinion had weakened, however, after his first tour in cosmopolitan Hawaii. The mixing of the races there had resulted in incredibly handsome and tolerant people. Besides, Annie and Joshua had no children and, unfortunately, never would have any.

Dunne had planned on returning immediately to the *Ford*; there was much to do. But he needed some time to himself. A quiet drink and a leisurely lunch could be in order. For one thing, he needed to think through the situation with Annie. The officers club at the naval station was a bit too stuffy. The one at the Barber's Point Naval Air Station was scaling down for base closure and would probably have a limited menu, but the blue suiters at Hickam always took pride in their club and it had by far the best atmosphere and food of the three.

After checking his ever overflowing paperwork on the *Ford*, he hailed a cab outside the fleet landing gate and within a few minutes was seated on the spacious outdoor patio of the air force club, looking over the channel entrance to Pearl Harbor. He was not a great Mai Tai fan but it just seemed proper as the first drink to have when one visited Hawaii. And the one he was sipping at the moment was very good. Maybe his taste was changing. It was certainly sweet enough, but the fruity flavor was tart and diluted the sweetness to an acceptable degree. The rum flavor was rich and strong. And as always, the best part of the drink was the thick stick of fresh pineapple, saturated with the overall flavor of the fruit juice and rum.

Traffic in the channel was light. A lone destroyer was putting out to sea; Dunne recognized it as one of the Arleigh Burke class. Better he than me, thought Dunne, taking another slow sip of his drink. His father-in-law had seemed a bit reserved, almost critical when he mentioned that there was only one eyewitness to the disaster on board the *Salinika*. Maybe it was just a reaction from being caught in the middle of the situation, but that's why admirals were highly paid. He could be overly concerned about his career; it was possible that he had aspirations about being the next CNO. That would be normal, but that job required presidential approval and no doubt the president viewed the *Salinika* incident as a critical blow to his international goals. That could backfire on Paterson.

And the press! How could even the staunchest liberal investigative reporter entertain such egregious thoughts about an outrageous U.S. Navy conspiracy as opposed to the probable involvement of Iraq? Could they really be that paranoid about the military? To be sure, the Joint Chiefs had opposed the administration on many issues, but when the decision had been made they had loyally, if not enthusiastically, carried out their duty in every instance. The 1993 compromise on the military gay ban was an excellent example.

"Well, hello."

Dunne looked up to see Lt. Kohn approaching his table; she had a tall pink drink in hand.

"I'm not interrupting anything, am I, Captain? You looked like you were lost in space."

Dunne was embarrassed. "Something like that, Sheila. Please, sit down. I'm just trying to unwind." *Either that, dummy, or I'm going bonkers*, he thought.

Kohn sat and leaned back in her seat and let the breeze flow across her face. "This is great." She sipped her rum punch, swallowed slowly, and placed the glass on the table. Dunne could see the sadness in her eyes when she said, "We need something like this, Captain. It's been a hard last week."

"That it has. It's a wonder, isn't it, how fast such a peaceful transit can become a thing of horror? Thank God, it's over. How're you doing?"

"Well, I'll admit it has given me a different attitude about a career in the military, but I would guess that is normal. I really had second thoughts after Long John and I were pulled out of the sea.''

"You know Long John didn't make it? He died on the air-evac.''

"No . . . I didn't know. Damn.''

"I just spoke with Admiral Paterson. He told me.''

"You travel in high circles.''

"Well, it was mostly business. But he is my father-in-law.''

"I didn't know that. Which reminds me—how is Mrs. Dunne?''

"Holding her own for the moment. I'm anxious to get back to her.''

"I'm sure you are. I'll certainly keep her in my prayers. She must be a special person.''

Dunne didn't want the conversation to continue on its present depressing course. "We can nurse these for a while; it's very pleasant out here. Then, how about lunch? I'll buy.''

Kohn held her drink out toward Dunne and managed a smile. "I'll drink to the first suggestion, but we roll for the second, Captain. I believe I saw a dice cup on the bar when I came in.''

As Kohn left to get the dice, Dunne resumed his watch of the channel. Naval aviator Frosty Kohn was a good sort. She was every bit the performer he had heard about. Death was an inevitable part of their profession, even in so-called peacetime. She handled it well, if such a thing could be said about anyone.

Kohn returned. "Ladies first,'' she proclaimed and tumbled the dice from the leather cup in such a manner that they were hidden from Dunne. "Three aces,'' she declared, set the cup back over the dice, and slid them to him. Obviously, the game was liar's dice.

"I'll accept that.'' Dunne lifted the cup after his safe call. Two aces were showing, the rest garbage. He set the two snake-eyes aside and rolled the remaining three dice. Shielding them, he announced, "Three aces and a six."

Kohn was not about to dispute that. It was a good call. "I believe you." She lifted the cup and set the new ace aside with the other two. There was no six. She grinned, knowing Dunne had her boxed in a bit. She rolled the remaining two dice, peeked, and confidently declared, "Four aces."

"No way," countered Dunne and raised the cup. Kohn slapped her thigh. "Gotcha! . . . sir," she gloated. The fourth ace was staring at Dunne. He would buy.

It was early afternoon when he returned to the *Ford*. The exec was waiting on the quarterdeck. "Good afternoon, Captain. You have a visitor waiting in your cabin."

Dunne returned the salute. "Who is it?"

"A Mr. St. John." The exec spoke the next words with some anxiety. "He's a member of the White House staff and has a letter of authority from the secretary of the navy. CINCPACFLT's aide escorted him on board and verified his clearance."

"Is the aide still here?"

"Yes, sir."

The admiral's aide stood as Dunne entered his cabin. St. John remained seated, looking up only after he finished reading a paper he held. The aide made the introduction. "Captain, this is Mr. Charles St. John. He is a member of the president's staff. Sir, this is Commander Joshua Dunne, the commanding officer of the *Ford*."

Dunne held out his hand. "Welcome aboard, Mr. St. John."

St. John returned the greeting and commented, "This is an impressive boat, Commander Dunne."

Dunne was not impressed with St. John's misuse of naval terminology. "Thank you; we call it a ship." He didn't mention that the use of the term *captain* would also have been more appropriate.

"Of course. I'm afraid my naval knowledge is somewhat limited. Forgive me."

I'll bet it is, thought Dunne.

"Commander, I only need to impose on your *ship* for a short time. I have been asked to assemble a chronology of the events leading up to the encounter and the subsequent sinking of the *Salinika*. My boss—the chief of the White House staff—wants me to prepare a briefing folder for the president to assist him in any further dialogue with the news media. I thought this would be a good place to start."

"We're at your disposal, Mr. St. John. What can I tell you?"

"I don't need to bother you personally, Commander. Admiral Paterson has indicated that he will provide me with a copy of your after-action report. I would, however, like to see the ship's log and get copies of any messages sent or received during the incident."

Dunne leaned over and punched one of the buttons on his intercom. The duty yeoman answered. Looking across his desk at St. John, Dunne asked, "Hawkins, I have an official visitor in my cabin. Could you come here and escort him around the ship?"

"Right away, Captain."

St. John looked a bit puzzled. "Oh, have I made another faux pax? I read your insignia as that of a commander."

"No problem, Mr. St. John. I do hold the rank of commander. The commanding officer of a navy vessel is traditionally called 'Captain' by his crew, regardless of his commissioned rank."

"Oh, I can see where that would be certainly appropriate."

Dunne was relieved to hear the duty yeoman knock and then enter. "Mr. St. John, this is Petty Officer Hawkins. He will escort you to the bridge and wherever you wish to go. Please feel free to talk with any of my crew. We're out of quarantine, so most of the officers are probably ashore, but Hawkins will take you to the wardroom if you wish to speak to those who are on board.''

"Thank you, Captain." Turning to the sailor, St. John asked, "I suppose I should address you as Petty Officer Hawkins; is that correct?"

"Just Hawkins will be fine, sir. Welcome aboard."

"The ship is yours, Mr. St. John," Dunne added. "Perhaps when you have everything you want, you could join me for coffee before you leave?"

"That would be nice, Captain. Do you have tea?"

Dunne forced his face to retain its neutral expression. "Certainly. I'm sure my messman can scare up some biscuits or small cakes if you would like." Dunne immediately regretted his last statement. It was somewhat compromising. St. John did not seem to be in the least offended.

"That would be a treat. High tea aboard a navy ship. I shouldn't be long, Captain."

"Take your time. I have plenty to keep me occupied."

True to his word, St. John reappeared at Dunne's cabin in just over an hour. Dunne had alerted his messman, and freshly brewed hot tea was ready. The enterprising sailor had also confiscated some sugar cookies from the crew's mess.

St. John nodded in approval. "This is very nice."

Dunne poured and offered the White House staffer a cookie.

"I had an uncle in the navy," St. John commented. "He was a gunner or something like that. I never knew him real well."

"Did you get everything you wanted?" asked Dunne, disregarding St. John's personal comments.

"Oh, yes. Your crew is very cooperative. I even met one lad from my home state, Connecticut."

"I'm glad. Will you be returning to Washington right away?"

"I have to talk to Admiral Paterson, of course, and his staff. I didn't realize he was black."

Dunne choose to ignore the last comment. He didn't understand its pertinence. "He is an outstanding officer and has had quite a career. I would think that he would be in the running for our next chief of naval operations."

St. John accepted a warm-up to his tea and politely received another cookie. "These are good."

"The crew enjoys an excellent galley."

"The navy is quite civilized when it goes into battle, isn't it?" St. John stated. "Clean ship and sheets, hot prepared food, laundry, stainless steel latrines."

Dunne was about to challenge the statement but considered further discussion pointless. He sipped his tea while St. John finished his cookie; then he said, "It has been a pleasure having you aboard. Please convey our respects to the president. My gig is at your disposal."

St. John grinned sheepishly. "Gig?"

Dunne had to laugh. Mentally, perhaps he was being too hard on the man. There was really no reason why such a cloistered civilian should be an expert on the naval service. "A gig is the captain's boat; ours is just a converted motor whale boat, but I'll have it standing by for you. My yeoman is just outside to escort you to the quarterdeck."

St. John might be ignorant of naval ways, but he knew when he was politely being asked to leave and he had to admire Dunne's diplomacy. Standing, he offered his hand and took his leave. "I have enjoyed this. Please give me a call when you're in Washington. Perhaps I could arrange a private tour of the White House for you and Mrs. Dunne."

"We would feel very honored. Have a safe trip

back.'' Dunne walked St. John to the cabin door and they shook hands a final time. Dunne hoped that he had not been too abrupt with the White House representative. He had felt uncomfortable with the man. Nothing he could put his finger on. Before he went back to his paperwork, he grabbed another cookie and called his messman.

"Yes, Captain?"

"Would you take the tea, please, and bring me a cup of coffee?"

Having been medically cleared, the *Ford* had been given a pierside berth, and Dunne worked in his cabin until time to leave the buoy. He informed his messman that he would be having dinner ashore. At 6:00 P.M., the OOD announced: "The officer-of-the-deck is shifting his watch to the bridge. Set the special sea and anchor detail. We will be departing for our pierside berth at eighteen-thirty."

Dunne made his way forward and up the various passageways and ladders to the bridge and climbed into his chair. Lt. Murray was again the OOD. "Why don't you take her over, Mr. Murray?"

"Aye, aye, sir."

Dunne watched as the fo'c'sle crew took in the buoy line and Murray smoothly eased the *Ford* around and conned the frigate from the East Loch to the naval base piers. The young NROTC graduate was becoming a very skilled seaman. Once tied up port side to Pier 3, Murray secured the special sea and anchor detail and shifted his watch to the forward accommodation ladder. Dunne then went to his cabin to change into starched wash pants and an aloha shirt. By 7:30 P.M., he was sitting in the Warrior's Lounge at the military-dedicated Hale Koa Hotel on the grounds of the army's Fort Derussy at Waikiki. As he sipped his Mai Tai and thought of dinner, the past days seemed just a nightmare, an imaginary event that just could not have happened.

As Dunne was enjoying his early evening cocktail, it was early morning on September 8 in Frankfurt, Germany. Five-seventeen A.M., actually, in the Sachsenhausen section of the city, and in a small nondescript rooming house well south of the Main river off of Darmstadter Street, three men were talking in very low tones.

The first was Solomon Weisman, a modest Jewish merchant who dealt in semiprecious stones. However, if he had ever possessed a birth certificate, the name on it would have been Ahmad Libidi. His exact birthplace was unknown even to him, but he did know that it had been a dirt hut in Libya and his father had forced himself upon his mother. Ahmad had killed the man responsible for his miserable existence when he was eleven.

The second man carried a passport that identified him as Solomon's brother. But he was, in reality, a Jordanian by the name of Jamal Hussein. Both men were devout Muslims, but they found travel so much more convenient as Jews, particularly in their profession.

The third man was also an Arab, but his real identity was unknown and he did not bother to affect a Jewish name or appearance. He was reportedly of royal blood and moved about Frankfurt within exclusive diplomatic and financial circles. But to Ahmad and Jamal, he was their control, and on this cool morning he was dressed informally, wearing jeans, a flannel shirt, and a black leather jacket.

All three men served only one master: Allah. But their service was perverted by their bitter interpretations of certain passages in the Koran. True, there was only one God, Allah, and Muhammed was His prophet. But Ahmad and Jamal were disciples whose only purpose in this world was to eliminate infidels. They were a two-man army in their own very private *jihad*. And they were specialists. Anyone could be their sponsor if the target was the land of the devil, the United States.

Their control spoke. "You are aware that our brothers on the *Salinika* are all dead?"

"We saw the report last night on the news, although my inadequate German caused me to miss some of the details," answered Jamal.

"They are of no consequence. Our immediate goal is to insure that the mission continues. On a smaller scale, perhaps, but with equal drama. Then, those for whom I serve can rightfully claim credit." The control handed over a small business-sized card to Ahmad, who held it up to the overhead light. It was watermarked in one corner with a star and crescent and in the middle was impressed the location and identity of their target.

Ahmad did not hesitate. "Two million American dollars."

The control handed over a large manila envelope. In it was a deposit receipt for one million American dollars issued by a Swiss bank and identified with the proper account number. "The balance will be deposited upon completion of your assignment."

Ahmad replaced the deposit slip and withdrew the travel packet. It contained a pair of airline tickets—Delta Airlines coach—issued by Hapad-Lloyd Reiseburo, a local travel office, and four credit cards in the names of the Weisman brothers. They were issued by the prestigious Bundesbank, and any debits would be automatically satisfied monthly by an electronic transfer of funds from their sponsor's account with the bank. There was no limit on the cards.

"It will be a long flight," Ahmad commented. "Business class. We are merchants." The last five words were an order, not a request.

"The exchange will be waiting for you at the Delta counter."

Ahmad's lips formed the trace of a smile. "Two seats, exclusive, no one in front or behind."

"Done."

"The target. We need something better to go on. Description."

The control nodded. "In the bottom of the envelope, a key to a locker at Honolulu International. You will find what you need there."

"Weapons?"

"I would not be so presumptuous. That is your responsibility."

Ahmad pursed his lips and commented to his partner. "And properly so."

After the control had left and the two Islamic warriors had completed their dawn prayers, they packed only two small carry-on bags and retrieved a black leather case of stone samples from the closet. Everything else would be left in the room.

The ride to the airport, a short five-mile trip from their quarters southwest on the Koln-Munich Autobahn, put them in the international section of the continent's largest airport by eight in the morning, and they checked-in to the Delta counter. Their flight, the first of three legs, left on time thirty-five minutes later. In the business-class section, two humble Jewish merchants politely refused drink service and leaned back comfortably in their seats for the flight across the Atlantic. One held a black leather case tightly on his lap. The other dozed.

13

Nestled deep in the southwest corner of the mountain state, just a few miles south of the high-country town of Cortez, lies one segment of the Ute Indian reservation, and the occupants of that land are referred to as the Ute Mountain Utes. They live and raise their children on what was, a thousand years ago, the land of the mysterious Anasazi people. Mesa Verde National Park protrudes into the Ute Mountain reservation, and there one can walk among the remains of an Anasazi village and marvel at the artifacts of a great people who were one with the land, yet suddenly disappeared. The Utes are not descendants of the Anasazi but take great pride in following the ancient ones, and like all American Indians, are struggling to fit themselves into the modern world while still preserving their traditional culture and intratribal relationships.

The land of the reservation is harsh but unbelievably beautiful. It is hot and dry in summer, cold and snowy in winter. Outsiders, including fellow Americans, are welcome on the reservation but only with Ute permission and usually with a native escort, who will lead them into the depths of the reservation in Indian fashion. Day trips and overnight forays, living close to Indian ways, afford the visitor some insight into a life that was once the only life on this continent.

There are no custom homes, tract houses, or even single dwellings of the type that house other Americans. There are a few trailers and many pickup trucks, a number of horses, and many makeshift dwellings that the Utes have constructed for themselves. Many are quite comfortable, although the uninitiated eye may see them as shacks or even eyesores.

Such was the home of Carl Ortega and his daughter, Mary, known in the reservation by their Indian names, Man Who Rides Far and She of Many Graces. They had a third name, and their tribal name, secretly given to them at their birth but never spoken outside the tribe. Mary's only son had no non-Indian family name, and because he had been adopted he was given no secret name. As his grandfather had decided, he had been known only as Charlie Two Shoes. Two days earlier, they had received the telegram.

On this cool autumn day, one of the Ute guides had brought a stranger to the home of Man Who Rides Far and She of Many Graces. He wore the blue uniform of a United States naval commander and addressed them as Mr. and Mrs. Ortega. They offered him a cup of mountain herb tea and She of Many Graces placed a warm round piece of puffy fry-bread before the commander and pointed to the squeeze bottle of commercial honey that sat on the wide board serving as their eating table. The commander thanked the stately woman for the tea and bread but did not immediately drink or eat. In fact, he did not sit at first, not until he told them the circumstances of the death of Mary's son and presented her with a letter signed by the secretary of the navy and another less formal one signed by Joshua Dunne.

Even in their grief, the aging Utes insisted that the

commander sit and drink tea with them. She of Many Graces poured honey on the fried bread and held it out to him, for despite the tragic purpose of his visit he was their guest and he wore the blue color of a warrior's dress as had her son. He told them of the threat to the island of Oahu and how the men and women aboard her son's ship had pursued and sank the *Salinika*. The reservation Indians were confused by some of the words the commander used but they fully understood the nature of death of Mary's son and they were in a small way comforted by the heroism of her son, who had proven himself a loyal and honorable warrior. They were told that the United States government would give Charlie Two Shoes a military burial in a national cemetery if they wished, or a military escort would return the body to the reservation if they desired. That would be proper, Man Who Rides Far declared. His grandson would receive an Indian burial.

The commander also told them that there would be a sum of money arriving, the product of their son's military insurance, and just before the commander left, Man Who Rides Far requested a flag of the United States, for his grandson was both a Ute and an American. He would fly the flag in front of his simple dwelling, raising it every morning at eight o'clock and lowering it at sunset, just as his grandson had said was the custom on his ship. They would have one, the commander said, and he would personally bring it to them.

As he turned to leave, and his escort who had remained respectfully standing the whole time left to start the pickup, Man Who Rides Far and She of Many Graces stood erect, side by side, semiclosed eyes holding back their tears, and Man Who Rides Far saluted the commander.

"My grandson taught me," Man Who Rides Far declared proudly.

The commander blinked and returned the salute—the most crisp and sincere salute he had ever rendered.

14

The late morning hours on this day were not good ones for the president of the United States. Around the world there was still a morass of guerilla warfare that was making a mockery of United Nations peacekeeping forces, and a number of those forces included U.S. service personnel. Americans coming home in body bags were grim reminders that the warring factions were not intimidated by either international sanctions or presence, and a large segment of the American public was demanding that he pull U.S. troops out of a number of the engagements— U.N. commitment or not. Congress was continually questioning his foreign policies.

His ambitious domestic plans were not yet fully realized. Everyone was grumbling about tax increases. A watered-down economic bill had received the barest measure of congressional approval and was now law, but it was having no significant effect on either spending or the deficit reduction, and every day another of his party members in Congress was near defection and siding with the loyal opposition.

And the damned *Salinika* incident. The Iraqis were

still holed up in their Washington hotel and vowing not to come out until the president issued a public statement admitting that the United States had no evidence to link Iraq with the *Salinika*. The president could not do that for there *was* evidence: the dead Forger pilot was an Arab, and there was an eyewitness who had seen traces of the Iraqi Air Force insignia on the side of the VTOL aircraft on board the *Salinika*. He had immediately dismissed the tabloid press's navy-conspiracy theory after the members of the National Security Council had unanimously declared that there was absolutely no basis for such conjecture; several had even begun to have doubts about the soundness of the president's mind if he even entertained such a momentary thought, and one had even told him so. Thank God the media had no inkling of the depth of that discord.

Even so, he could not get over the feeling that somehow the navy was to blame. They had pressured him into approving the sinking of the *Salinika*. In retrospect, sinking the ship in shallow water would have been the prudent decision. Then it could have been recovered and conclusive evidence presented to the world and he would have caught the terrorists red-handed. At least, a deep submersible would soon be on the scene and attempting to recover evidence and take photographs to confirm the particulars of the encounter. If the Iraqis were involved, he could send them packing; to hell with any settlement.

The First Lady, concerned that he had been absent from their bed since the early hours, found him pacing the dimly lit Rose Garden. A pair of confused but discreet Secret Service agents were monitoring the president's activities.

"Dear," the First Lady said, "it's chilly out here. Come inside. We don't need a sick president."

The president put one arm around her waist and they walked together. Even though the morning light was not yet present, the capital city was awakening, and the conglomeration of sounds and acidic smells of the first morning traffic were building. "It's just not what I thought it would be," the president said quietly.

"What you thought *what* would be?" the First Lady asked.

"The job. The bureaucracy. Congress—and it's *our* Congress. The people. They just don't understand what I'm trying to do. I really thought we'd make a difference."

"We are."

"No. Sometimes there are so many demands upon me, I can't decide on any particular one. I try to satisfy them all, but I satisfy none. I'm spread too thinly. Every president is spread too thinly. I just didn't know it until now."

The First Lady pulled her robe more tightly around her. "We should go inside; it is starting to get light. People will be coming. We can talk inside."

The president abruptly stopped and looked at his wife. "I must show that I can lead, that I can meet a problem head-on and solve it. I must have the people's confidence. And you know what? I'm starting with the Iraqis. They've jerked us around long enough. Today, I'm booting their asses back to Baghdad. No one will criticize me about that. And I'm not ever going to let the military put me in such a position again."

"But you said the evidence that it was the Iraqis is inconclusive."

"I need to do *something*—and the bastards want an apology. No way. Not yet."

The president seemed a bit cheered at breakfast, perhaps because he had decided upon a course of action with respect to the Iraqis. The White House chief of staff joined him for coffee.

"Any critical changes to today's agenda?" asked the president.

"No, sir. I do expect St. John back from Hawaii, and we'll have the chronology for you this evening."

"St. John? Oh, yes. He's a bright young man. I thought he was one of our experts on domestic matters. Why use him on the *Salinika* problem?"

The chief of staff accepted a warm-up of his coffee from the president's steward. "Nothing new happening in his area; he has things pretty well under control, and he was available. Frankly, he needed a few days away from the office; he's here when I arrive and works late . . ."

"Like all of us," the president interjected.

"Like all of us. But I knew he would be thorough, and it's a routine matter. Might give his mind a rest. He feels so strongly about the issues he's involved in."

The president wiped his mouth, neatly rolled his napkin into a smooth white linen cylinder, and placed it back inside the silver napkin ring. "I'm throwing out the Iraqi delegation today."

The chief of staff was caught off guard. "Sir? Are you sure you want to do that? We don't have any conclusive evidence that Saddam was involved. We could salvage the talks."

"No. I've decided. Look at the media. They all report that the people are incensed about the *Salinika*. I admit I had some confusing thoughts at first. But this is my opportunity to be decisive. No more flip-flopping. For the first time in a long while I can act with every American behind me."

The chief of staff nodded. "When will you announce it?"

"Right after I meet with Senator Kahakamua. Set up for ten-thirty."

"I'll have to adjust your eleven o'clock. Will you take questions?"

"Leave eleven as is. No questions. I'll hit them hard with the announcement, that's it."

"Will State inform the Iraqis prior?"

"No. At the moment I am making the announcement, I want a State Department representative and immigration officials standing by at the Washington Hilton. They will take the Iraqis in custody, drive them to Andrews, and the air force will fly them to one of their embassies—perhaps in Jordan."

"Mr. President, that is highly irregular. They have some diplomatic status."

"Revoked. If I have to, I'll do it by executive order. As of this moment they are parties to a terrorist act against the United States. They accept immediate deportment or they will be arrested and charged with conspiracy."

The chief of staff could only wonder what had happened during the night to effect such a change in the president's attitude and sudden abandonment of normal procedures. "Have you consulted with the attorney general on this? There are an awful lot of arrangements to be made."

"Have the attorney general in my office at eight. Cancel everything before Kahakamua. Have State contact the Jordanian ambassador; SECDEF can arrange transport. No VIP treatment. Use a troop cargo aircraft—and give the bastards standard box lunches. They take with them only what they can carry from the Hilton."

"I better get on this." The chief of staff hurried out. The president may have been disregarding protocol on this one, but somehow it seemed like a guts decision—and a damned good political move.

The president called for his steward and settled back for a third cup of coffee.

Senator Mele Kahakamua was an imposing woman, almost pure Hawaiian and with a hefty build that made one wonder why there were no female sumo wrestlers. The president was concerned about the Queen Anne armchair as the senator accepted his invitation to sit. She was certainly not intimidated by her first visit to the Oval Office.

"Mr. President, my calls and mail from my constituents are overwhelming. They are very angry that their lives were placed in jeopardy without their knowledge."

"Senator, I can understand that. I have already explained that the situation developed so rapidly there was no time to alert anyone."

"You were alerted, Mr. President."

"Of course, it was my responsibility, and combat communications circuits were used. A decision had to be made and I needed all possible input. There was no time for anything else."

On her second try, Senator Kahakamua managed to stand; then she said, "What will I tell my people? That ship would never have gotten so close to the mainland—or Alaska. We are entitled to the same protection. We are members of the same union."

"I have already ordered the military to review their peacetime surveillance around the islands. If there are weaknesses, they will be corrected, I promise you. And because of alert military and civilian authoritative action, the people of Hawaii were never at risk. The ship was being tracked before it entered our territorial waters, and at that point it was promptly attacked and sunk."

Kahakamua walked over to the facing loveseats in front of the fireplace. "Could we sit over here, Mr. President?"

"Of course." The president sat across from her and continued. "I consider the attempted attack upon Oahu an act of war, and there is sufficient reason to retaliate provided we can gather additional evidence that will corroborate our current feeling that the government of Iraq—not independent Iraqi terrorists—is behind the mission of the *Salinika*. The navy has a deep submersible on the way to probe the bottom of the Pacific for the ship, and at the very least I anticipate it will bring back pictures that will confirm the vessel as an Iraqi instrument of terrorism.''

"The people of Hawaii will be pleased.''

"Senator, I am going to make an announcement in a few minutes that will result in the immediate deportation of the Iraqi delegation. I would like you by my side.''

Kahakamua's smile indicated her satisfaction. "It would be an honor, Mr. President.''

The chief of staff had arranged for the announcement to be made in the Rose Garden, despite a few threatening rain clouds to the west of the district. The president strode to his position behind the podium and motioned for Kahakamua to join him. She did so, remaining respectfully to his right and one step behind him.

"As of this moment,'' the president began, "the Iraqi delegation has refused to reply to our inquiries concerning the September fifth intrusion of a terrorist ship into our territorial waters around the state of Hawaii. Our investigation to date has substantiated our belief that the government of Iraq may have conspired to conduct a biological warfare attack upon U.S. citizens. We anticipate momentarily the receipt of evidence that will conclusively support our contention. Consequently, I have revoked any diplomatic status the Iraqi delegation has enjoyed with respect to their presence in the United States, regarding certain concessions by the Iraqi government in return for the lifting of United Nations sanctions against that country. I have ordered immigration officials to take the delegation into custody and deliver them to Andrews Air Force Base, where they will be provided transportation to the Iraqi embassy in Jordan. I am every bit as outraged as the people of this great country, and I have asked that an emergency session of the United Nations Security Council be convened as soon as possible. At that time, with the support of further conclusive evidence, the United States will request additional and more strict sanctions against the government of Saddam Hussein. I will take no questions and my White House spokesperson will issue amplifying statements periodically during the day.''

The president wheeled and motioned for Senator Kahakamua to precede him back into his office. His short announcement and immediate departure stunned the White House press corps and left them frantically jumping up and calling out their questions for amplifying information.

''Mr. President, are you considering military response?''

''Is the *Salinika* being recovered?''

''Will there be another Desert Storm?''

Despite their frustrated shouts, they quickly dispersed to file their reports.

As soon as he returned to the Oval Office, the president felt much better. He had been decisive. Senator Kahakamua had left satisfied, and there was no doubt in the president's mind that the next polls would show a significant increase in his public support index.

''This would not be a bad time for a TV report to the public, Mr. President,'' the chief of staff suggested. ''There is much speculation as to how you would respond and they are unsettled. After all, the terrorists came very close to a successful attack upon Oahu.''

The president nodded thoughtfully. ''We need to have some options on further action. If this were indeed an effort by Saddam—and now we've kicked his delegation out—I would think he will plan some sort of immediate response. Let's set up a conference with the NSC for this evening. I want recommendations from the Pentagon on increased security around our coastlines and a list of graduated responses ranging from a retaliatory bombing of military targets in Iraq to a declaration that we consider the attack an act of war.''

"I'll start making the calls."

"That chronology of events you have your man working on, is it ready? I want to be up to speed on those particular details."

"I'll see that you have it the moment it's complete."

"This afternoon?"

"I would think so."

"I'll expect it then."

Back in his office, St. John began a review of his notes. Something was not quite right. He rechecked the sequence of messages. There *was* a serious discrepancy— or was it merely an error in assigning date-time groups to several of the *Salinika* incident messages? He was trying to reconcile the differences when the chief of staff called him.

"Charles, the president wants your findings by early afternoon. Any trouble with that?"

"It's complete, but I'm having a problem."

"What kind of problem?"

"I better come to your office."

"Bring everything you've got. We have to get the report completed by this afternoon."

St. John set the folder on the desk in front of the chief of staff and placed copies of two messages on top of it. Then he said, "This is the *Ford*'s report of the sinking. Note the date-time group. *This* is the message from US-CINCPAC reporting the sinking. Notice its date-time group. It is the one the chairman of the Joint Chiefs gave SECDEF and was in turn given to you. There is a nine minute difference."

The chief of staff studied the message copies, shifting back and forth between the two several times. "These are accurate copies?"

"Right off the originals, and the *Ford*'s message confirmed by the entry in the ship's log. I would say that is the correct time.''

The chief of staff let a low whistle escape his pursed lips. ''Then why is General Mitchell's report different? Error?''

''I thought so at first, but in reconstructing the sequence and considering the navy's view of the situation, it may well be that the *Ford* sank the *Salinika* before the president gave the order. The only place the actual time could be verified is the ship's log. That's the bible on such things.''

''We need to check with SECDEF on this.''

''Shall I call?'' St. John asked.

''No, not at all. I'll contact him. You go on back and smooth out the report; leave spaces where the conflicting times will go. We haven't been asked for any evaluations or conclusions, so let's don't volunteer them yet. I'll get the clarification.''

St. John left and the chief of staff hesitated before calling the secretary of defense. Maybe it would be best not to try and clarify the difference in times. The president had just taken a bold step in foreign policy that would show he could be a decisive leader. Perhaps this was also the time for him to whip the military into line. Someone, in all probability the commanding officer of the *Ford*, had deliberately disobeyed a direct order of the commander-in-chief. If so, General Mitchell would have to have known about it. Could he possibly have sanctioned the action? Was SECDEF involved? Could there be a major effort to cover up a premature rash action by the navy? The president would be furious—and the chief of staff would receive credit for uncovering the subterfuge. Yes, the chief of staff decided, he would have St. John insert the correct times and when he, himself, delivered the report to the president he would point out the discrepancy. It would be a delicious moment.

And the military fuck-heads would finally get their just due.

The president reread the chronology, performing some mental computations with respect to the particular log entry of the *Ford* that recorded the sinking of the *Salinika* and the CJCS message that reported the sinking. "You're right," confirmed the president, raising his head to look steadily into his chief of staff's eyes. "The *Ford* sank the *Salinika* four minutes before I actually gave the order." Angered, the president continued, "And the CJCS gave SECDEF the time as five minutes *after* I gave the order. Nine minutes total. Mitchell definitely altered official records."

The chief of staff nodded. "That he did, sir."

"Damn! When will it stop? The military thinks they are dealing with some jerkwater politician from the sticks. Did they really believe I wouldn't find out about this?"

"I suspect they didn't see it as a big deal. They knew you were going to authorize the sinking."

"The hell they did! Even so, that gave them no right to take such action. There is no way I will sit still on this. I am the commander-in-chief. They may not like it, but they sure as hell are going to realize it. I won't stand for them bad-mouthing me—they should know that by now—and I surely won't stand for insubordination and downright lying! It's another clear case of violating the Uniform Code of Military Justice. If it takes a court-martial or a string of courts-martial to whip these prima donnas into line, then that's what it will have to be. The chairman of the Joint Chiefs had to be in on the cover-up."

"I would think so."

"As of today, he's retired."

The chief of staff was pleased with himself and his president. Action, decisive action, that was what was needed to give the administration a backbone.

The president held up a finger. ''I want the commander of the *Ford* brought back here to the Pentagon and charges filed by the secretary of the navy.''

''I'm not sure that is the proper procedure, Mr. President.''

''It is if I say so. I want a high visibility court-martial that sends a message, and this is a cut-and-dried case. First, the military—the navy, mind you—embarrassed me when I made that initial trip to the aircraft carrier; then that high-ass air force general decided he could publicly denounce the character of the commander-in-chief, and now some low-grade ship's captain decides to ignore my direct order. With all of my responsibilities, keeping my military house in order is still paramount. Have SECNAV in my office this afternoon—and get me SECDEF on the phone. General Mitchell is history.''

''Yes, sir.''

General Mitchell was incensed. ''The president has every right to be upset. I admit I went along with the doctored date-time group, but it was for everyone's good. The captain of the *Ford* was in tactical command, and we dragged our feet in getting the president to authorize the sinking. We *all* did, and you know that.''

SECDEF sat behind his desk with a completely unsympathetic expression. ''The man is determined to establish his authority. Would you rather face the loss of your retired pay? He'll court-martial you unless you hang it up right now.''

''Oh, I'll hang it up all right. And you know why? Because I know I did wrong, despite the good intention. But I don't deserve to be treated this way. I've given thirty-nine years to this country. I should be allowed to leave with some dignity. He's mishandling this like he mishandles everything else.''

Without waiting for a response or a statement by SECDEF that the meeting was over, Mitchell turned and angrily stalked out of the office. He'd be out of his own office by the end of the day, but he still had a few cards to play.

"Blackjack, I've just been fired."

Paterson had been surprised to get the sudden call from his boss, General Mitchell; now, he was shocked. "What do you mean?"

"Our beloved commander-in-chief just fired my ass, effective immediately. He found out that Commander Dunne sank the *Salinika* on his own and figured I knew about it—which is goddamned correct and I'd do the same thing over again."

"I better pack my own bags."

"No, he didn't mention you. He's too dumb to figure these things out in any detail. And I called to tell you that you have to court-martial Dunne."

"What?"

"He's going to have Dunne transferred to the Pentagon and is ordering SECNAV to press charges: failure to obey a direct order of a superior officer. It'll be a hanging trial, Blackjack, and the presidential noose is destined for your son-in-law's neck."

Paterson's anger was rapidly rising to the level of Mitchell's. "Joshua was the on-scene commander. He made a valid tactical decision and it can be justified."

"Not to a Pentagon court. Believe me, Blackjack, when it gets to secretary level, the president pulls the strings."

"Shit fire, I can't court-martial my own son-in-law when I agree with his action."

"You have to. You'll preempt the Pentagon. It'll be your court. A fair trial and a proper verdict. You'll have control. Once Dunne gets orders, you've lost him."

Paterson knew Mitchell was right. "I guess we blew

it, General. I sure as hell hate to see Dunne suffer. But I'll order the charges immediately. I'm really sorry you're taking the heat.''

"I've enjoyed working with you, Blackjack. You're a good man. The deputy will take over here until a new chief is appointed. He's up to speed on all this and will keep you informed just as I have. He's okay.''

"Good luck to you, General.''

"And you hang in there, Blackjack.''

Paterson buzzed for his PACFLT chief of staff. When Reedy arrived, Paterson stunned him with his order, "Prepare general court-martial charges against Commander Dunne: failure to obey a direct order. I want him served as soon as we have the paperwork. Effective immediately, he is relieved of command of the *Ford* and confined to quarters to await the call of the president of a general court-martial.''

Reedy was hopelessly confused. "Charges? Admiral, the board of investigation has come up with no charges.''

"My prerogative.''

Reedy's next thought seemed trivial, but he blurted it out. "Commander Dunne has no quarters ashore. BOQ?''

"Yes. No—wait. We want to keep the media away from him. Put him in one of the beach cottages over at Barber's Point. They're remote and can be justified as officer's confinement. We can assign some security.''

"Admiral, what is this all about?''

"The president has discovered Joshua sank the *Salinika* before he received White House permission. He's ordered a court-martial and we want it *here*.''

"Has the president reviewed all the tactical considerations in Commander Dunne's decision?''

"He doesn't have to and I suspect he doesn't want to. He sees only the affront to his authority and he wants a yardarm hanging. And we have to beat him to the punch. Get the papers prepared immediately and served. I'll make up a list of the court. Send in Captain Fargo; he'll be the president."

Reedy hurried out and Paterson sat down to make out some notes. The Pearl Harbor-based Naval Legal Service Office could provide a designated military judge and Paterson would select another four members for the court. The legal office also could provide qualified trial and defense counsels as well as a reporter. Within just a few minutes, he had the information necessary for preparing the charge sheet and had his yeoman fax them to the NSLO.

He had just taken his chair to give his body and mind a rest when Captain Robert "Dutch" Fargo arrived. As Paterson's senior command-post watch officer, Fargo was a surface warfare specialist and had among his many qualifications considerable experience with the naval justice system.

Paterson waved him to a chair. "Dutch, I've just ordered a general court-martial for Commander Dunne. I want you as the president of the court. The legal office is preparing the charge sheet and the convening order. I'll give you four other members and I want the court convened as soon as possible."

Fargo was a hardheaded, no-nonsense career officer who was not easily rattled, but such an unexpected announcement momentarily numbed him. *Commander Dunne, the CINC's son-in-law—a general court-martial?* He lost none of his composure, however. "The charge, Admiral?"

"Failure to obey a lawful order."

Fargo nodded. "I had no idea this was in the works. I just read the draft of the investigation report. It completely exonerates Commander Dunne of any wrongdoing."

"You don't know the whole story. It'll come out in

the court proceedings. I shouldn't discuss it any further."

"I understand, Admiral. This is something of a shock. I am sure it is not easy for you."

"No."

"Can I be of any assistance in picking the members?"

"No. My chief of staff will handle that. I wanted to notify you personally and stress that I want the court convened as close to my convening order date as possible. That's September fifteenth."

"I'll be ready. How about the judge?"

"He'll come from the legal office. It's not a complicated case, so there should be no difficulty with witnesses or evidence."

Fargo was well aware that the guidance and procedures for the court were rigid and delineated in the UCMJ Court Martial Manual. Like anything in the military, all was spelled out in precise language. Certainly, he could be spared from the command post for the necessary time. "Then, I'll get to work, sir."

"Thank you, Dutch."

Fargo hesitated for just a second. "Is there anything you'd like to tell me—off the record, Admiral?"

"No."

"By your leave, sir?"

"Yes, of course." Paterson watched Fargo walk out the door. There would not be a better man than Dutch Fargo to head the military jury in his son-in-law's trial.

Now the question was how to handle Dunne. His son-in-law certainly would be caught by surprise and undoubtedly angered when the papers were served. He wanted to phone Joshua aboard the *Ford* but decided against it, at least for the moment. To avoid even the slightest hint of favoritism, they would have to have very little contact, if any, between now and the trial. He decided to have the papers ready and then have the server deliver a note with them to Dunne. Orders. He almost forgot. Buzzing his personnel chief, he ordered, "Contact the bureau of naval personnel; have a set of orders cut, relieving Commander Dunne from command of the *Ford*. He will report to CINCPACFLT relative to administration action concerning general court-martial order number one-ninety-five. Info copies to type commander and Surface Forces, Pacific."

The *Ford* would have to be held in port. Key witnesses were aboard the frigate and the helicopter pilot would have to be retained. He ordered his personnel officer to take care of those details.

From his office within the Pearl Harbor naval reservation, Paterson could see across the Kamehameha highway and the Halawa Gate to the naval base. The *Arizona* Memorial Visitors Center was to the right and beyond that the swaybacked white memorial itself, and just behind it was Ford Island. One of the fifty-foot navy-operated launches was approaching the memorial, its benchseats crammed with tourists. Off to his right, now that the *Ford* had left its moor, the East Loch of the harbor was clear and the water a calm blue. It was a scene he never tired of looking at, for Pearl Harbor *was* the U.S. Navy and that infamous December 7 more than fifty years ago had sanctified it to all Americans. The view almost always calmed him, but the business at hand was too disturbing. Beyond the obvious, how would his action affect the relationship with his son-in-law? Or with Annie! God, he must call Annie and explain. But the time difference made it too late to call San Diego; she might be resting and she needed rest. He would speak to her first thing in the morning.

Military judge Captain Fritz Rarick had recently taken over the Pearl Harbor Naval Legal Service Office on the first of September, and he was still in the process of getting settled. Now, CINCPACFLT was convening a general court-martial and needed a judge. It would have to be him or his lone commander on the staff. The accused was also a commander; that called for a military judge of higher rank, so it appeared that Rarick was going to have to plunge right into the business of his office. Still, it was nice to be back on the islands. He reviewed the charge sheet prepared by his staff. It was correct and complete and ready to go back to PACFLT for the CINC's signature. Rarick knew of Commander Dunne and the *Salinika* incident; everyone on Oahu was intimately familiar with that near-disaster. But what order had Dunne failed to obey? No matter at the moment; he would know soon enough.

15

Joshua Dunne was alone on the open bridge of the *Ford*, idly watching the comings and goings of the sparse harbor traffic that passed the destroyer piers. A steady sea breeze muted the humid warmth of the late afternoon sun. It was a good place to reflect, and his mind was on Annie. The fact that she was sharing her ordeal with so many women made it no less a personal tragedy. Outgoing, life-loving Annie, struck down just as her mother. And so young. What would it be like without her? Dunne held no illusions about the inevitable result of Annie's rampaging cancer cells. They were eating her up. Radiation was eating her up. Chemotherapy was eating her up. She needed him and he needed her. Surely, the *Ford* would be released in a day or so. The investigation was complete.

The vibrations and metallic sounds of footsteps climbing the steel bridge ladder interrupted his thoughts. It was the OOD's messenger, leading a commander wearing tropical whites and a tan-clad enlisted marine, a sun-bronzed lance corporal who obviously was very conscientious about working out daily.

"Captain Dunne, I'm Commander Powers, a designated trial counsel from PACFLT legal. I have some orders for you." He held out a single sheet and Dunne read:

From: Bureau of Naval Personnel
To: Commander Joshua Dunne,
United States Navy,
Commanding officer, USS
Ford (FFG-54)
Via: Commander in Chief, Pacific
Fleet
Subj.· Command, relief of.

1. Effective upon receipt of this order, you are relieved as commanding officer of the U.S.S. Ford (FFG-54) and ordered to report to CINCPACFLT for duty relative to CINCPACFLT General Court-Martial Order 195 dated this date. No travel time, leave, or delay is authorized in these orders. You will proceed to Naval Air Station Barbers Point for quarters as assigned by the commanding officer and restrict your movements to the confines of that Naval Air Station. You will further report to the Administrative Officer, Pacific Fleet, at 0800, Thursday, September 11, for duty.

Dunne was as surprised by the signature on the CINCPACFLT endorsement as by the order: Admiral Jack Paterson. His world, which had been in no fine state just a few minutes ago, was now in complete collapse. "What is this all about?" he asked.

The commander handed him a small sealed envelope.

Dunne ran his thumbnail down the top crease and pulled out the single sheet of notepaper. At its top was the embossed blue flag with the four white stars of the CINC.

Dear Joshua,

Do not despair. Trust me. My action is to protect you. I will explain personally as soon as possible. Destroy this note.

Blackjack

Admiral Paterson had never signed anything, even personal letters, to Dunne with simply "Blackjack." And *do not despair*? He had a dying wife, and now his own father-in-law was giving him a court-martial?

The commander handed Dunne a manila folder. Inside was the general court-martial charge sheet and the convening order. "Lance corporal Martin is your driver, commander. He will assist you in getting together your gear and transport you to Barbers Point. Your quarters are ready."

Dunne could only shake his head in confusion. "Forgive me, I had no warning of this."

"Take your time, Commander Dunne."

Dunne looked around, obviously upset and unsure about himself. "Ah . . . I'll have to turn over my ship to my exec."

"I understand, sir. Can I help in any way?"

"Help? No, thank you. Are you to escort me?"

"No. You are not under arrest, sir."

Dunne felt completely helpless. He was supended in space; the earth was spinning a million miles away.

16

If one had to be under house arrest, the beach cottages at
the naval air station on the southwest tip of Oahu seemed
ideal lodging. Dunne was in one of eight; his was to the
right end as they faced the beach, and the surf lapped to
within ten feet of his front lanai. The Pacific extended
ahead of him all the way to the mainland. Of redwood
construction and raised on stilts to protect against storm
waves, the cabin had three bedrooms and a complete
kitchen. The remote NAS was at the point on the southern
coast of Oahu where the sand and craggy lava beach
turned and climbed northwesterly. Hurricane Kahiki had
struck heavily on the west coast, but amazingly enough
the naval air station had received minimal damage. Only
one of the beach cottages was damaged, its roof shingles
in disarray and the front louver windows broken.

Dunne did not intend to use the kitchen, although he
had picked up a jar of instant coffee at the NEX facility.
He was indeed isolated, both on the base and on Oahu, but
the commanding officer of the air station had provided
him with a small scooter for any necessary travel around
the base. During the day, he could see the hazy blue pro-

file of Diamond Head eighteen miles to the east and the jumble of steel, glass, and concrete hotels along Waikiki, as well as the packed high-rises of Honolulu. Tourists would be paying premium prices for such a prime location; Dunne, an accused violator of Article 92 of the Uniform Code of Military Justice, had been assigned the quarters in return for his housing allowance, and he felt a bit angry about that; he was there by judicial order, not choice.

None of the other cottages seemed occupied, although there was a gently curving beach in front of all of them, and some hundred yards to the left of his, a few young men, most obviously beginners, had been late-afternoon surfing. He reasoned they were station personnel, and none seemed to have paid him any notice.

As the long dusk gave way to a moonlit night, the sound of the surf masked the approach of a private car. It parked at the back of his cottage, and a lone figure emerged and walked across the clipped grass and ice plants to the beach side of the cottage, where Dunne was sitting. The figure was already on the covered lanai before Dunne became aware of anyone near.

At first startled, Dunne stood and said with some relief, "Admiral." He had been extremely anxious for some contact.

Blackjack Paterson was in shorts, sandals, and a multicolored aloha shirt. "Like my disguise?" he asked, reaching for Dunne's hand.

"Admiral, what's going on? You have consistently indicated that my actions were proper and appropriate under the conditions encountered. Why wasn't I informed that charges might be pending? I'm really upset about—"

Paterson held up his left hand. "Whoa! Calm down. I expected you to be upset, and I don't blame you. But let me tell you what's happened and how I intend to counter it."

Dunne was in no mood to be calm. "Admiral, this ruins

me. My career—everything I've worked for.''

Paterson stood silent, waiting for Dunne to realize that he had an explanation to give.

Dunne continued, ''I really feel betrayed. This is shitty, Admiral.'' He flopped down onto one of the two webbed beach chairs provided on the lanai. Paterson drew the other alongside and lowered himself into it.

''Joshua, the president has been informed of the fact that you sank the *Salinika* before he actually issued the order.''

''You knew that—''

''Of course. Settle down, please. But along with General Mitchell, I felt the president didn't have to know it. We agreed on a subterfuge—we reported the time of the sinking as after his order.''

''Oh, Christ—that pretty boy from the White House staff that went through my ship's records . . . I had an uneasy feeling about him.''

''That's part of it. In any event, the president was furious and fired Mitchell on the spot. Why not me at the same time? I don't know; he just hasn't made the connection yet. Fortunately, our source in the White House alerted both Mitchell and me that the president was directing the navy to issue you orders to the Pentagon and there you would be court-martialed for disobeying his direct order.''

Dunne protested, ''There were extenuating circumstances. I had that authority as commander on the scene encountering a direct threat against the United States. I took an oath to defend the—''

''Joshua, shut up and hear me out. Circumstances or not, you get tried in D.C. and you become a sacrificial lamb for a domestic political victory that the administration sorely needs, the unquestionable subjugation of the military to civilian leadership.''

''That's the way it's supposed to be. For Christ's sake, that's the way it is! But a military commander in the field

has to have some leeway; if Vietnam taught us anything—''

''You listen to me, Joshua! I'm trying very hard to save
your ass.''

''By giving me a general court-martial? Admiral . . .''

''Exactly. By beating the Pentagon—namely the politically influenced office of the secretary of the navy—to
the punch. By charging you and taking you to trial, I insure that you get a fair trial with no political pressure.''

Dunne grunted. ''You don't think *you'll* get any pressure?''

''I don't give a shit. Once the court is convened, no one
can stop it, and there isn't an operational, combat-
seasoned officer on earth that would hold you guilty of the
charge, and that's what my court will consist of.''

Dunne had to let his mouth drop. ''You've rigged the
court, Admiral?''

''No, Goddamn it! I haven't rigged the court. I've just
made damn good and sure the sea lawyers in the Pentagon
don't get a chance to rig the court. You will get a fair trial
and be judged by your peers, and I've already said what
your peers will decide. Put yourself in their shoes.''

''I would gladly do that.''

''You know what I'm saying.''

Dunne indeed did. ''But I wish you had told me first.''

''Didn't have time. I felt I could have been fired any
minute and my priority was outmaneuvering the administration. I think we've done it.''

''*Think*, sir?''

''There may be some legal technicality I've overlooked.'' Paterson looked away from Dunne and stared at
the reflected moonlight flickering on the waves in concert
with the night surf.

With the explanation, Dunne could see the dilemma
that had faced Paterson. It had to have been a terrible decision. He wanted to lean over, place his hand on Paterson's shoulder, and say, ''Thank you, Blackjack.'' But

they were not quite close enough for that level of inti-macy.

Paterson sighed. "They have to go through me, Joshua, before they hurt you and my Annie. And I'm one tough son of a bitch when it comes to family *and* the navy. I'll go to the mat on this if I have to."

Dunne felt better, but not good.

Paterson sighed before continuing. "I know this is hard for you; and for me, too. I just don't see any other way. It's a sad commentary on the state of things when we have reached the point in history where our president just doesn't have a grasp of the military and egregiously sees us as adversaries. We're not blameless; after all, General Mitchell and I did violate our trust by falsifying the date-time group of the action report, something I thought I would never do. But the man has us on the defensive. That shouldn't be."

"No."

Paterson watched the waves a while longer, then stood. He and Dunne had never relaxed with one another. He was surprised to hear himself ask, "Want to go get a beer?"

It was the last thing Dunne expected to hear, and he suspected it was an effort for Paterson. Perhaps this was the time—but there were other considerations. "Should we be seen together?"

"Pearl City's just down the road. A bar in every block and no one gives a shit who you are as long as you're a good tipper."

"Sounds like you've been there before, Admiral."

Paterson grinned. "I wore bell-bottoms when I started out."

"Thirty, forty years ago, sir? You weren't the CINC then, and I suspect Pearl City is not quite the same."

"I'll drive. Come on. We need to bond."

*   *   *

Paterson dropped Dunne off at the cottage shortly after twenty-three hundred. It was the first time that Dunne had ever spent any private time with his father-in-law, and he came away from the evening with a new appreciation for Paterson's achievements and his love of country. Dunne also found that they had several shared interests besides the sea and ships. Professional football and the music of Roger Whittaker. Cross-country skiing and Coors beer. They had differences as well. Paterson was a Baptist, but didn't thump the Bible as one; Dunne was a lukewarm Catholic. Paterson felt that North Korea would be the next major threat to world peace; Dunne saw the Middle East in the fore and had used the *Salinika* to emphasize his point.

And they had one thing very much in common: Annie Mae Paterson-Dunne. Their evening conversation could not avoid the subject of Annie's illness.

"After this is over," Paterson had said, "you're due a shore assignment. I don't know what will happen to me but at least one of us will be there to take care of Annie. She needs to know the background behind all this. You want me to tell her?"

"I don't know, Admiral. Either way, it's going to add to the stress. But she'll know about it, of course. Maybe it would be best if you talked to her. You have *me* feeling better."

"All right."

Once inside his cottage, Dunne knew that he would not be able to go right to sleep. He stripped to his shorts and sat on the lanai. The night air was chilly and he could smell the familiar taint of sea salt. The beach cabins were just off one end of the air station's runways, and the low-pitched whine of turboprops preceded the passage of a P-3 patrol aircraft as it steeply banked overhead and headed out to sea on a night exercise. Despite all of his problems, Dunne felt secure in the night. He sat, alone with his thoughts, until his eyelids became heavy and he began to slip in and out of sleep. He went inside and stripped the top covers from the bed. Little of the night breeze was flowing through the cottage and within minutes he was dripping with sweat from the high humidity. The bed was old and overly soft and lumpy. There was no way he could rest. Exasperated and very tired, he dragged the mattress onto the lanai and let the sound of the surf give him the relief he sought.

Paterson also had enjoyed his rare night out and was pleased with his increased consciousness of his son-in-law's personality and inner feelings. They had never had an opportunity to really talk before, even when Dunne was courting Annie, and after the marriage their respective duties had kept them apart. He slept well.

The next morning, September 11, his first order of business was to insure that all members of the court had been notified and issued temporary additional duty orders. After that, he checked on the status of the deep submersible that would attempt to locate and photograph the sunken *Salinika*. One factor that he had not counted on was in the morning message traffic. It confirmed an earlier phone call he had from SECDEF. A new CINCPACOM had been ordered in and soon Paterson would be relieved of his double duty. He could devote his attention to the trial and countering any further Washington moves; and although he had yet to learn of it, one was in the works.

Man Who Walks Far was not at all pleased as to what the two white men before him and his daughter, She of Many Graces, were claiming. His grandson, Charlie Two Shoes, had just been taken to the sacred place and placed on the burial platform and he and his daughter were in a state of mourning. The men had insisted on an audience, however, and now they were disavowing the navy story of how Two Shoes had died.

"In effect, Mr. Ortega," the uglier of the two was saying, "your grandson died because he was refused his civil rights, his rights to medical attention and treatment." The man spoke with the squeaky voice of the weasel and his face had the same pointed snout feature. The other man was also small in stature and would nod at every sentence of the ugly one as if he had no mind or say of his own. "We want to help you bring this matter to the proper authorities. There will be compensation for you and his mother."

The last sentence particularly angered Man Who Walks Far. "The officer who brought us the news of the death of our beloved warrior told us of the circumstances. My grandson chose to refuse medical attention."

"He was not in his right mind. Even if he did refuse, it was the commanding officer's obligation to see that your grandson was attended to. The navy had that obligation; the government had that obligation. Regardless of your grandson's words—and I remind you that no one heard them except the commanding officer—civil rights are inherent within our status as citizens."

"I will not sign anything and my daughter will not sign anything. My grandson was a warrior and he died a warrior's death. I will not dishonor him by bringing discredit upon his leaders. He always spoke of them as honorable men."

"Sir, we can prefer these charges ourselves—without your permission."

"Then you will have to do so."

"It could lead to a large sum of money, Mr. Ortega."

Man Who Walks Far stepped forward until he could smell the breath of the weasel. "Get off our land. This is sovereign Ute territory and you are not welcome. I have been patient out of courtesy, even when your words cause pain to my daughter. Now, you must leave."

The young Ute who had escorted the men to the meeting with Man Who Walks Far and his daughter echoed the command, "Now, you must leave," and pointed to the pickup. The ugly man shrugged but said nothing as he and his companion climbed into the cab.

Their Indian escort sped back toward the tribal park entrance, ignoring the ridges and ruts in the dirt road until the jostled men asked him to slow down. Instead, he stopped. In the distance, the far distance, they could see the gate and their parked vehicle.

"I have other duties, now," their escort said. He reached across them and opened the door. "You will walk the rest of the way."

"In this heat?" the ugly man protested. "It's several miles to our car. I can barely see it."

"Out."

"You can't do this."

"When I return, if you are still on our property, you will be trespassing and subject to our tribal laws—and my errand is a short one."

"I shall report this to the Bureau of Indian Affairs."

The driver closed the door after them and spoke through the open window, "When angered," he said solemnly, "there are those among us who still take scalps."

The two men started quickly in the direction of the gate. The young Ute waited until they were out of earshot before he spoke to himself, "What a couple of dumb dudes! 'We still take scalps'—that's rich." He shouted after the two men, "And we hunt buffalo and raid wagon trains and rape the settlers' women—Ayyeeeeeee!" Flooring the accelerator, he spun a half-doughnut with the pickup and raced back up the road. *Man Who Walks Far will get a charge out of this*, he thought.

"This is ridiculous," complained the ugly one, already perspiring heavily. "They don't understand a thing about their own rights. They'll always be savages."

The other man nodded. "We don't need their participation."

"Oh, shut up."

The long hot walk back to their car completely exhausted them; the drive to Durango, even though a short distance, added to their fatigue; the commuter flight from Durango across the Rockies to Denver was just one long stretch of turbulence, and the four-hour flight in a completely full DC-10 to Dulles International Airport was a test of extreme patience. The only seats available were two smack in the middle of the pack, the five-seat-abreast center section of the long main cabin. It was the red-eye special, and the sun was still an hour below the horizon as they grabbed their carry-on bags and muscled their way off the giant aircraft that had just flown 664 armpits and half as many groins from Denver to Washington, D.C.

There was no trouble corralling a cab; they were lined up at the terminal, most of the drivers asleep. As they finally reached the Beltway, the early morning traffic crush was just gathering momentum and they decided to go directly to their offices in the Justice Department. Even so, it was just a few minutes short of eight o'clock when they arrived, smelly and spent and desperate for a cup of coffee.

Each cleaned up as best he could in the men's room and the ugly one put on a fresh shirt that had been squashed in his briefcase for the last thirty hours.

"Good Lord," the chief of their section commented when they walked into his office, "I told you to go see the Indians, not crawl into bed with them."

The ugly one did not smile. "Funny, chief, very funny."

"So, how'd it go?"

"They won't press charges. Refused to cooperate."

"Then we'll take it ourselves. I'll inform the division head. Get the paperwork started."

The two low-level United States assistant district attorneys sat quietly for a moment, contemplating their fate, before the ugly one pleaded, "Chief, could we go home and shower first?"

"I was just about to suggest that—and while you're there, burn those clothes, okay?"

The United States Attorney General was right on time for her late-afternoon appointment with the president. "Regarding the Dunne case, Mr. President—the Ortegas refuse to file charges."

"Then, we must."

"The papers are complete and ready to be filed, but I understand CINCPACFLT has already convened a general court-martial with respect to Article 92 of the military code."

"Where does that put us?" the president asked, obviously angry at the news.

"At the moment, on the sidelines. We can't interfere unless there is just cause and the CINC is going by the book."

The president pushed himself away from his desk. "Can't we add the charge as a friend of the court?"

"I think I have a more positive move, sir."

"What is that?"

"One of my senior staff is Tom Marshall. He's my number-one prosecutor, and he is a commander in the U.S. Naval Reserve. I recommend we have him called to temporary active duty and assigned to CINCPACFLT. I can go through SECNAV and have him instruct the CNO to cut orders that would specify that Marshall has been recalled specifically to act as trial counsel in the court-martial."

"Is that necessary?"

"Sir, I think that CINCPACFLT rushed into this court-martial to keep Dunne from standing trial here. In the administration's interest, we need a prosecutor who is enthused about this case. I should mention that I have learned that Commander Dunne is Admiral Paterson's son-in-law."

"Are you saying there may be command influence upon the court?"

"No, sir. There is no sign of that. But it is in the interests of justice to have someone in that trial who is not beholden to Admiral Paterson, and the perfect place is that of the trial counsel."

The president smiled and shook his head. "The military plays the same silly-ass games we do, don't they?"

The attorney general glanced about the Oval Office and gave only a silent nod in response.

"I want this Dunne," the president declared. "His conviction is just what I need to pull a few more military teeth."

"Marshall will be able to add the charge of a violation of civil rights. That gives us a stronger case and a very sensitive one. The abused was an American Indian."

"I appreciate you making this one of your priorities."

"Well, Mr. President, we may have lost the first round when CINCPACFLT beat us to the punch on filing charges and issuing the convening order. But it's only a preliminary round."

"Do you think CINCPACFLT will go along with Marshall?"

"The UCMJ provides for such a maneuver and SEC-NAV can put pressure on the CNO to encourage the CINC to go along with the assignment."

"And if he doesn't?"

"You have Admiral Paterson relieved and a new CINC assigned. That does not invalidate the court-martial."

The president was pleased that his attorney general was on top of the situation. He folded his hands on his desk and looked her squarely in the eyes. "One thing I wish to make clear. I want Commander Dunne. That's obvious. But regardless as to how both sides maneuver in this, CINCPACFLT or us, I want a fair trial. I don't want my enthusiasm for a conviction—I believe he is guilty—to be taken out of the context of the military justice system.

When you brief Commander Marshall, I want that point stressed. Despite my displeasure with Commander Dunne, I have been informed that he is an honorable and very capable naval officer and he will have public sympathy. However, this court-martial is the result of his actions and he must be prepared for any consequences. Off the record, I admit this trial has political overtones, but the first aim of any court is justice."

"I am fully aware of that, Mr. President."

"Then, I leave the matter up to you. At the first sign of any adverse reflection upon this administration—"

"There will be none, Mr. President."

Commander Thomas Peter Marshall, United States Naval Reserve, received his recall to temporary active duty as a well-earned gift, long overdue. Six feet tall, ramrod straight, he carried his one hundred and seventy-two pounds with the same confidence and singleness of purpose with which he prosecuted his court cases. Forty-two years old and with every single nongray hair still in place, he might be somewhat overage in rank but that was not uncommon in the reserves. If he read the CINCPACFLT court-martial opportunity correctly, he now held in his hands his ticket to promotion to captain and perhaps on to a star or two. He had never argued a case in a military court, but it could not be as difficult as representing the United States in a complicated securities fraud case or a constitutional-based appeal before the Supreme Court. As for his opposition, it would probably be some PACFLT JAG simpleton who was counting his active duty days until he could retire after twenty, go into private practice, and start pulling down the big bucks. A defense counsel with dollar signs in his eyes would lack the conviction to seriously challenge the proven thoroughness with which Marshall normally devastated his courtroom opponents.

Law so very often was not a matter of innocence or guilt; it was a contest of abilities in presenting evidence and testimony to a jury. And that involved psychology, intense playacting, a bit of showmanship, intimidation, and the reading of other men's souls. A little ridicule and tongue-in-cheek review of defense arguments also helped. The practice of trial law was an art, and Marshall had an array of legal brushes that could paint bold swaths across a courtroom canvas or insert delicate thin lines that highlighted just the right part of the picture he wished to emphasize. His gray eyes would have twinkled had not their color been so dull, but they did shine with anticipation at the plum he had just been handed. Several weeks in the islands. All expenses paid—and he could wear his uniform. And he had just purchased several tailor-made polyester uniforms, anticipating a Navy JAG legal seminar in Jacksonville. He would not miss that at all. The Hawaiian duty would take care of his annual active service requirements quite nicely.

He hummed as he took care of last-minute details. He could send his eleven-year-old son back to his ex-wife; she certainly wouldn't let Marshall take the boy off the mainland, and he had no desire to. As for his current live-in companion, she would want to go, but he could convince her that he would be much too busy to share any time with her; it was really time to break off their relationship. The woman was becoming too possessive; his life was no longer as exciting as when they were first adapting to one another. Besides, she was too much a fixture in his Old Towne townhouse. It was time for a new face—and a new body. There should be ample cruising opportunities on Oahu. He would have to take one of his Justice Department staff to prepare the daily briefs. That should leave most of his evenings free. He finished packing and checked his brief case. The fax copies of the charge sheet and the convening order were in one of the top pockets. He would study them on the aircraft. All that remained was for the department travel desk to deliver his tickets and the packet of traveler's checks.

                    *   *   *

Admiral Paterson spoke as soon as he knew the CNO was on the line. "Admiral, what is this bullshit about a special trial counsel being assigned to my staff?"

Admiral "Chip" Collins had expected the call. He had been a senior at the Naval Academy when the feisty Paterson had entered as a plebe and they'd formed their first preordained relationship. Later, as a buck ensign, Paterson had served with Collins on a guided-missile destroyer out of Naval Base Norfolk; Collins had been Paterson's department head and had formed his first professional opinion of the junior officer who had already been christened Blackjack. Even back then, Paterson had been a superb junior officer who showed considerable promise. Later on, they served together again during the early post-Vietnam years, Collins the commanding officer of a nuclear-powered guided-missile cruiser, Paterson his operations officer. The bond strengthened, and as Collins had climbed the promotion ladder, he had never forgotten his younger shipmate who was gaining on him rung by rung, partially because Collins never failed to aid the career of Paterson whenever the occasion presented itself. Now, they were equal in rank, with Collins having only the advantage of seniority—and duty as the navy's number-one naval officer. The CNO was quick to reply, "Blackjack, this order has come from the highest authority. Don't fight it."

"I'm the convening officer of this court-martial and it is my prerogative to assign the members."

"Partially true. That is why Commander Marshall has been activated and ordered to report to you for duty. He is—or will be when he gets there—on your staff."

"Whoa! Activated? He is a reservist?"

"A reservist who is a killer trial lawyer and handpicked by his boss, the attorney general, in response to the request of the president."

"They really want to get my Dunne, don't they?"

"That implies prejudice, Admiral. I won't comment on that."

Paterson felt the acids in his stomach start to swirl and eat into the lining of what over the past twenty-four hours had become a very sensitive organ. "I already have the composition of the court. Commander Marshall can work on some of my less complicated legal briefs."

"Blackjack, his orders specifically require you to assign him as trial counsel to the court."

"You approved?"

"Yes—off the record, under duress."

"That's not legal."

"I'm afraid it is."

"I won't do it, Chip."

"Damn it, Blackjack, you will or I'll relieve you and ship your black ass so far away from Hawaii, you'll think you're on another planet."

"Ha! How many remote billets do you have for a four-star, Chip? You're bluffing—and I don't appreciate that type of reference to my ass. It smacks of racism."

"Pull down your trousers and moon a mirror, Blackjack. Your ass is black, the same color as mine. I used the term to emphasize, not to insult. It would only be racism if my buns were that sickly pale pink that most of my officers have. Besides, we're all the same color in this man's service—navy blue."

"You're also a sexist! It's this man's and this *woman's* service. You're a throwback, Chip, to the dark ages."

"And I miss 'em."

"Me, too, but we're getting off the subject."

Collins intensified his argument. "Look, you don't want to fight this assignment. If you do and you are relieved, you will lose personal surveillance and that little bit of control you have over the court. Neither of us wants that. They're stacking the deck against Dunne. You must ensure that the letter of military law is applied without exception. They can't get him without going emotional and clouding the issues with idealistic arguments and their own personal interpretations of the Constitution. Military law is factual and direct. This Marshall will be lost without spectators to cheer his circus or the media to worship at his feet. You have a measure of control there, Blackjack. And I've looked at his record; he has never tried a case before a military court. A jury of professional military officers is not as likely to be swayed as a group of housewives and white- and blue-collar workers. Isn't that why you jumped the civilian-oriented gun that would have been aimed at Dunne by the secretary of the navy and the Justice Department?''

Paterson knew that was true. "So, I'm supposed to greet this Marshall genius with a hearty 'Welcome aboard'?''

"And a smile.''

"All right. I see your point.''

"Keep me posted,'' CNO Collins requested.

"Yes, of course. I'll talk to you later, Chip—God bless America.''

"And all the ships at sea, Blackjack.''

17

(HONOLULU, September 12) (AP) Admiral John J. Paterson, Commander-in-Chief of the United States Pacific Fleet, has ordered a general court-martial for Commander Joshua Dunne, United States Navy, the former commanding officer of the frigate, U.S.S. *Ford*, the naval vessel that successfully intercepted and sank the terrorist ship *Salinika* off the southern coast of Oahu on September 5. Commander Dunne is charged with the violation of certain civil rights of one of his crew members, a Colorado Ute Native American, and also with disobeying a direct order of a superior officer.

Of interest is the fact that Commander Dunne is the son-in-law of Admiral Paterson and the order that Commander Dunne is alleged to have disobeyed originated with the Commander-in-Chief of the Armed Forces, the President of the United States.

This is the latest of several unusual twists that have been involved in what has come to be known as the *Salinika* Incident. Washington sources have revealed that a special trial counsel has been assigned from the office of the United States District Attorney and that there have arisen several areas of ad-

ministration-military conflict with respect to
jurisdiction and make-up of the court. White
House spokesperson Agatha Andrews has dis-
counted such reports and has emphasized that
the court-martial is properly the function of
the Pacific Fleet Commander and that while the
president is naturally interested in the proceedings, his interest is of concern that Commander Dunne, a national hero since his
foiling of the terrorist attack upon Oahu,
will receive a fair and just military trial.

She further stated that despite the popularity of the young frigate captain, the main issue was civilian control of the military, and
the President was deeply concerned that there
might be some misunderstanding of that provision of the United States Constitution by mid-
dle-rank military officers.

Annie Mae Paterson-Dunne threw the newspaper onto
the foot of her Balboa Hospital bed, dabbed her eyes,
and blew her nose noisily into a wad of Kleenex.

"Oh, Joshua," she pleaded aloud, moving her head
from side to side with worry, "what are they trying to
do to you?"

18

Commander Marshall—with his white-covered bridge cap tucked neatly under his left upper arm and his shiny black alligator-skin briefcase held casually in his right hand—came to attention before the desk of Blackjack Paterson and announced his arrival. "Commander Thomas P. Marshall, United States Naval Reserve, reporting for temporary active duty, sir." He placed just the right amount of respectful emphasis upon his last word.

"Sit down, please," Paterson responded in kind. "I'd like to say welcome aboard, Commander, but you're not welcome in this command."

Marshall could be equally blunt. "I can understand that, Admiral—under the circumstances."

"And what the hell are those?"

"The relationship between you and the accused; the bad light this is casting upon your command; your desire to keep it all in the family, sir."

"Two balls and one strike, Commander. There is no bad light being cast upon this command."

"As you say, sir."

"As I damn well say. I want the court convened as soon as possible. You will advise the president when you are ready."

"I am ready now, sir."

Paterson did not for one minute believe that. "Have you read the results of the pretrial investigation?"

"No, sir. I just received a copy. I intend to digest it tonight."

"Oh? Do you have advance knowledge of the details of the case?"

"Not yet, sir, except for the media accounts—and of course they are not a reliable source for a legal action of this nature. I did get some briefing before I left Washington. When I checked in with your admin people, I also met your staff legal officer, and he has provided me with a copy of the *Ford*'s after-action report. Those two papers should give me a good feel for what witnesses I will call and indications of hard evidence that are available."

"Then, you're *not* ready. When you *digest* the pretrial report, you will see that it does not conclude that there has been any wrongdoing by Commander Dunne. It was my decision to override the conclusions of the investigation. My personal decision as the CINC."

"That's unusual, Admiral."

"No, not in the light of what transpired after the report was complete and not in the light of conclusions made by persons outside this command, in fact, outside the naval service."

Marshall allowed a slight rise of his eyebrows. "I would not say that the commander-in-chief of the armed forces is outside the naval service, not in *that* capacity."

Paterson glared back. "Strange, he doesn't seem to have a service record."

"He has one since January twentieth, several years ago."

Paterson bristled. The heat of his anger was slowly

melting the thin ice that Marshall was treading upon. "Commander," Paterson said evenly, "I don't like your mouth. You may be God Almighty when you're throwing your weight around in a federal court—and I suspect you are quite good at what you do—but that is not the relationship here—"

"Admiral—"

"I'll tell you when you can speak. At this moment, we are two naval officers, one junior and one a hell of a lot senior. And UCMJ recognizes that relationship, so don't forget for one moment that insubordination is a punishable offense and it doesn't have to come from a general court-martial. I have that court authority myself. If you don't want to start off your duty here with an admiral's mast, I suggest you reevaluate your position, shit-can your ego, and be a little more receptive to what I'm saying."

Marshall wasn't sure the pause meant that Paterson expected a reply, but he gambled. "I meant no offense, Admiral. I didn't exactly get a warm reception when I walked in here."

"What did you expect? A fucking hug?"

"No, sir. But I am just trying to do my duty."

"Good. You'll get no complaint from me on that. Just don't ever tell me again that you're ready to go to trial when you haven't even read the pretrial investigation report."

"I meant that I, myself, was mentally prepared to undertake my responsibilities as trial counsel. Certainly, I have some background preparation before I advise the president of the court that I am legally prepared."

Paterson's dark brown eyes were black holes. "All right. You are my representative in this court-martial and I expect you to represent this command with fairness, accuracy, and yes, enthusiasm. That is your job: to prosecute. But I don't want you going into that courtroom with any misgivings. Joshua Dunne is my son-in-law.

That doesn't mean diddely when it comes to the trial. If—*if*—he is guilty of the offenses he is charged with, then he must pay the price. I have no trouble with that. I have no desire to influence this court in any way. I convened it, thus I must feel there is just cause.''

''Yes, sir.''

''Have you been assigned quarters?''

''No, sir. I prefer to stay off base.''

''Your prerogative. You have a vehicle?''

''A rental, sir.''

''Then, I suspect our business with one another is over for the moment.''

Marshall stood, placed his bridge cap back under his left arm, picked up his briefcase, and came to attention. Anxious to be militarily correct, he asked, ''By your leave, sir?''

Paterson nodded but never took his eyes off Marshall. ''Good afternoon, commander.''

Marshall executed a smart about-face and left the office.

Paterson rose and walked over to where he could see the *Arizona* Memorial from his office window. The flag—actually attached to the *Arizona* and not the memorial—was limp. There was no breeze. That was rare. Paterson wondered what the men still entombed in the battleship shrine would think of the modern-day navy. Much more sophisticated and high-tech. Operationally saturated and budget poor. Along with the other services, a vehicle for social experimentation. Men and women serving equally; he liked to think that they would approve of that, but in his heart he knew that not a single man would have wanted women on his ship on December 7, 1941. The carnage would have been even more horrible if mutilated bodies pulled from the water had included the oil-covered and burned remains of females, stripped of their uniforms, their lives, and their dignity. He could only imagine the anguish as men tried to cut through the bottom of capsized ships with both men and women trapped inside. In those days, women were wives and sweethearts and sisters and mothers and were much more than equals in the hearts of practically all males. Now, they were just equal—by official decree.

Marshall seemed all that Chip Collins indicated: intense, proud, confident, egotistical, a bit showy. But not naval. As a reserve JAG officer he carried himself with an air that probably didn't quite smell fresh to the combat line officer. That was a shame, for Paterson knew that Marshall was not typical of the hardworking, dedicated JAG people he had been associated with in the past. But Paterson also knew that despite his flippant demeanor, Marshall would be most serious and ready to go when the court-martial convened. He would have his prosecution all laid out in his mind and a program of evidence and witnesses to back up every statement he would make in his opening and closing arguments. If he weren't so dangerous, Paterson would dearly love to see him in action. But as the CINC, he could only read the daily transcripts and they would lack the color of the trial. A source of some comfort was the knowledge that the designated defense counsel had something of a legal reputation of his own—and was regular navy.

Marshall walked from Paterson's office with hat in hand in more ways than one. For the first time in his life there was heavy moisture coating his armpits and soiling that area of his uniform shirt. The admiral had established his dominance in no uncertain terms, but he had not said anything that Marshall could use to say that the old boy was trying to influence the court. Their talk, while hostile, was more a difference of personalities than of legal views. Marshall could find no fault in that. He also knew that when he left PACFLT, he would have a fitness report signed by Admiral Paterson; Marshall could bend a little to keep from jeopardizing that. After all, that piece of paper would either make or break his quest for a fourth stripe, and Marshall knew that for a promotion he could kiss ass—even black ass—with the best of them.

His first chore would be to study the documents referred to in their conversation. From what he already knew, he had an open-and-shut case. The commander-in-chief of the armed forces had said don't do it yet—and Dunne had done it. Refusing medical attention to the Indian, regardless of circumstances, made that offense a fait accompli. All Marshall had to do was structure his case to convince the members of the court that there were no mitigating circumstances, and from his preliminary view, there were none. The defense would argue that there were—that was all the defense had. At least, there would be some challenge to that aspect of the trial.

He tossed his briefcase into the back of the convertible, shaking his head in disapproval at the car's heritage; a Ford Mustang, no less. A college kid's car. And metallic brown, for God's sake. Who ever heard of a brown convertible? Where were the BMWs and Mercedes? Avis had none; Hertz had one left and it was reserved for the month. Marshall's one-hundred-dollar bribe had failed to alter the situation.

He became hopelessly confused leaving the CINC-PACFLT compound. The Pearl Harbor interchange was a morass of exit and entry lanes leading to and from intertwined and multilevel roadways worthy of Los Angeles, and the rush-hour traffic afforded him little time to consult his road map. Consequently, he wound up heading the wrong way on the Kamehameha Highway. He didn't notice it until he saw a Highway 99 sign—he had been shooting for Interstate H1—and just beyond it one that said: Pearl City, 3 Miles. Pearl City? *No! I want to go to Honolulu.*

The first turnoff was to the left into a shopette area that featured several small service businesses and a trio of bar lounges. *What the hell.* He was upset about the reception he had received from Admiral Paterson, pissed that he had taken the wrong turn, and still tired from the long plane trip. A drink would help. He stopped in front of one of the bars called Happy's. Inside, a half-dozen male customers sat scattered along a single bar. One of the five tables was occupied by two more. Marshall grabbed a stool.

"What'll it be, Commander?" asked the bartender, a surprisingly well-groomed young man probably in his mid-thirties. As Marshall's eyes grew accustomed to the dim light, he could see that Happy's was quite a pleasant little place. In addition to the tables there was a pool table set at the back of the room, well lit by a green-shaded bulb that hung over its center. There were an English pub-style dartboard and various beer signs arranged haphazardly on the walls, some lighted by neon accent strips. Behind the bar were several pictures of naval ships, neatly displayed in eight-by-ten black metal frames and nestled among the three tiers of liqueur and whiskey bottles.

"Scotch, rocks—Chivas," Marshall ordered.

The bartender set a small tumbler of ice before Marshall and poured a generous two-fingers.

"Thanks."

"For new customers, first one's on the house at HAPPY's."

Chivas Regal, free? Marshall lifted the glass in appreciation. Such generosity would never surface in the district.

The bartender replaced the bottle on the lower glass shelf. "Navy's always welcome. Your boss even came in late last night."

"*My* boss?"

"Admiral Paterson; he's the boss of all you navy guys here, right?"

"Ah, yes. You know the admiral?"

"By sight. His picture's been on the paper and TV almost every day since that ship was sunk. Yes, sir, he came in with a younger haole in tow. They had a couple belts, talked a while at that table right over there and left. Five buck tip. He's okay."

One thing Marshall possessed was an instinct for recognizing small, seemingly innocent details that later became rather usable items in his various court cases, and right now the fact that Paterson had come into the small neighborhood bar, late at night, with a white companion, triggered his curiosity. "They were in uniform?"

"No. The admiral was in shorts, sandals, and aloha shirt. Just like anybody else. The other guy in wash pants and, ah, sport shirt."

"You didn't recognize the other fellow?"

"No. In his late thirties. Nondescript. Pleasant."

Marshall sipped his Scotch. Could it have been Dunne? It wasn't necessarily out of the ordinary that a father-in-law and son-in-law would have a drink together. But why late at night? And wasn't Dunne under any kind of restriction? Maybe the other person was the admiral's aide. Puzzling. The bottom line, if it had been Paterson, and the bartender seemed pretty sure of himself, was could Marshall use it in any way? Especially if the second man was Dunne. Marshall decided he would have another Scotch at Happy's in a day or so—when he had a picture of Joshua Dunne with him. He ordered a second, not wanting to walk out after the complimentary double shot, drank about half and left a generous tip.

He drove the highway back toward Honolulu, and this time successfully intercepted Interstate Highway 1. He followed it until he reached the Nimitz Highway exit. Then, it was straight in toward Waikiki, the Nimitz Highway becoming Ala Moana Boulevard. He turned right on Kalia Road, and just before entering the army's beachfront Fort DeRussy he hung another right into the main entrance of the Hilton Hawaiian Village. A parking valet gave him a receipt and Marshall walked over to the Tapa Tower, one of several high-rise units within the sprawling Hawaiian Village complex, and rode the elevator to his top-floor suite.

Before he stripped and entered the shower, he dialed the room number of his working assistant and had delivered some material the man had spent the late afternoon gathering. After the shower it was a third Scotch from the room bar, and he sat by the window-wall overlooking the early evening Pacific, studying the reports that would give him a more comprehensive understanding of the *Salinika* incident. As he read, he scribbled various names and questions on a yellow legal pad, occasionally a comment, at times nodding with satisfaction as he ran across an item that would be part of his prosecution. He took dinner in his room and continued to study the papers until he was satisfied with his approach. By then, a great silver moon was high overhead Waikiki, and he sat for another thirty minutes out on the private lanai, watching the moonlight shimmer on the waves while he savored the coming days. He would talk to his witnesses, review the material evidence, and sketch out his game plan. It was Tuesday night, and by Friday he would be ready. That should please the admiral.

The next morning, September 14, Marshall had a brief breakfast of fruit, juice, and coffee before heading back along Ala Moana toward Pearl Harbor. Once again, he navigated the interchange correctly, and by 0830 had entered the naval base, located the destroyer piers, and approached the *Ford*. After the traditional gangway salute to the ensign flying on the stern, Marshall saluted the quarterdeck. "Permission to come aboard?"

Lt. Murray was the officer-of-the-deck. "Permission granted. Good morning, Commander."

"Morning. I'm Commander Tom Marshall, the trial counsel assigned to Commander Dunne's court-martial.

I wonder if I could speak with the commanding officer.''

"Our exec, Commander Sessions, is acting CO, sir. Just a moment.''

Murray rang Sessions' office. "This is the OOD, sir. There is a Commander Marshall to see you; he is the trial counsel for Commander Dunne's court-martial. . . . Yes, sir. Thank you, sir.'' Murray motioned for the duty quartermaster. "Escort Commander Marshall to the executive officer's office.''

Sessions was waiting with certain misgivings. He knew he and others aboard the *Ford* would be called as material witnesses. *So, now it is beginning.*

He greeted Marshall and led him to the captain's inport cabin. "We will have more privacy here,'' he explained, "and less disturbance.''

Marshall took the offered chair opposite Sessions.

"Commander, I would like to speak to certain crew members with respect to the actions of Commander Dunne during the events that led up to the sinking of the *Salinika* and the subsequent deaths of Chief Sulley and Petty Officer Two Shoes.''

"Certainly. If you have a list of names, I will have the master-at-arms round them up. You can speak with them right in here if you wish.''

"That would be fine. But first, why don't we start with you, Commander?''

Joshua Dunne enjoyed the ride from Barber's Point to the Pearl Harbor Naval Station. Despite his relative freedom aboard NAS Barber's Point, he still felt cooped up spending most of his time at the beach cottage. The driver let him out at building 1746, the site assigned to the Naval Legal Service Office. He was led to a small conference room and there welcomed by his defense counsel.

"Good morning, Commander Dunne. I'm David Soto.''

"Joshua Dunne. Good to meet you."

Commander David Soto, navy law specialist and JAG-designated defense counsel, first son of Japanese-American parents, radiated friendliness, warmth, and concern. About the same height and weight as Dunne but with darker hair and eyes, he carried himself with an air of confidence and competency. Dunne liked that; if it were *his* first impression, it would most probably be the court's. He didn't realize it at the moment, but Soto's boyish good looks masked a mature legal mind that was finely honed, experienced, and steel trap quick. Dunne read the three rows of award and service ribbons Soto wore above the left pocket of his khaki uniform shirt and was surprised to see the navy parachute insignia over the ribbons. Among others, Soto wore two naval unit commendations and was a veteran of the Persian Gulf War; there was probably an interesting story there. Legal officers with combat decorations?

Soto smiled. "Commander . . ."

"Please, call me Joshua."

"Joshua, I've tried to bring myself up to speed before we met, and I believe I have a pretty firm grasp of the events behind the charges. In the light of the pretrial investigation and the *Ford*'s after-action report, which indicate you acted properly in all respects, I was first at a loss as to why CINCPACFLT even preferred charges. But, off the record, I have been made privy to the political background of the situation. For that reason, I think we have some problems. None that I don't intend to overcome, but I need you to give me your word-by-word description of everything that happened from the time the *Ford* encountered the *Salinika* to the time you moored here in Pearl Harbor. We need to compile a list of defense witnesses and I need your input to any evidence or precedents we may have that will substantiate your innocence. I'll show you what I already have. Then, later on, we'll visit your ship and talk to some of your crew.''

The phrases "your ship" and "your crew" rekindled Dunne's affection for the *Ford* and the men and women who manned her, but he knew the words were academic.

Soto continued. "I'd like to meet with the trial counsel tomorrow, and if all goes well, inform the president of the court that we'll be ready Friday. That's the date the CINC has in his convening order. But it isn't rigid. We have legal leeway. We'll be pleading 'not guilty' obviously. Any questions at this point?''

"No.''

"Incidentally, I've had your base restriction lifted. There is no reason for that except to maintain a distance from the media. You should continue to watch yourself when you're off base. No comments if you're cornered. Okay? So, let's get started.'' Soto placed a small tape recorder on the table between them and pushed the REC-ORD button. "Start on the morning of the fifth.''

Dunne collected his thoughts and began: "I was trying to get some sleep in my sea cabin when . . .''

Marshall looked back at the *Ford* as he walked away. A very well-kept ship and a sharp crew. Sessions did not impress him. Chief Martinez would certainly be a key witness as would several of the bridge crew that were on duty during the course of the incident. And Lt. Kohn; she wasn't on the *Ford*, having moved to the naval base BOQ. He wondered why. Most of her squadron detachment was still aboard, their return to the mainland delayed by the court-martial. He definitely needed to talk to her. The female aviator was the only person aboard the *Ford* who had actually seen the *Salinika*. Marshall began to see a delicious twist to his prosecution plan.

19

The manager of the Harbor Arms Apartment Hotel was manning the reception desk when the two Jewish gentlemen walked in. They certainly were not Orthodox Jews, having only mustaches and short beards; but they were wearing black yarmulkes.

"May I help you?" she asked.

"We would like a room," responded the older.

The manager pushed a three-by-five registration card across the counter and laid a ballpoint pen beside it.

The older man filled it in and slid it back to her while his companion waited silently.

"That will be seventy-seven dollars a day," the manager stated. The older one merely nodded his acquiescence and handed her a credit card. "Will you be staying with us long?" she asked.

"Perhaps several days."

The name of the older man, probably forty or so, was indicative: Solomon Weisman. His companion was a few years younger. Something about them bothered the manager, something she could not quite put her finger on, and she had always prided herself as a pretty fair judge of character. Jews were normally peaceful looking people and polite in their inquiries. These two were abrupt and unsmiling.

The one named Solomon asked, "Is there a temple nearby?" and when he was met by a blank stare, he added, "A synagogue."

The manager knew of none within her community of Aiea, west of Honolulu and near the north reach of Pearl Harbor. "None around here. The phone book should list them."

Solomon nodded. "Kosher restaurants?"

"I'm sorry, no. I would try Honolulu proper." The manager watched as they left with their key. They were driving a rental car and she had given them a room she could see from the office. They had only two small suitcases and a black leather bag of some sort.

Only a few minutes passed before the phoneboard lit up. They were calling long distance. After a few minutes, the telephone data appeared on the computer. They certainly had wasted no time. Why Frankfurt, Germany, of all places? the manager wondered. But then, perhaps that was not so odd considering the unification of Germany and the new freedoms.

They stayed in their room for the next hour. When they left, the manager watched their car disappear down the street. They were probably off on business. Her own business was slow. She called her niece from the back rooms. "Linda, watch the desk. I want to make sure one-seventeen is clean."

She entered their room and looked inside the suitcase that they had placed on the collapsible stand, being very careful not to disturb anything, even the tiny piece of toilet paper one of them had placed between the lid and the bottom. It had fluttered to the floor when she opened the case and to an innocent invader would not have been noticed. But it was an old trick, very familiar to the manager who liked to learn a little more about her occupants. She never took anything—that would have been unethical, even criminal if she did. She was just curious, and in the suitcase, lying on top of neatly arranged layers of pants, shirts, underwear, and socks, were two Israeli passports with German and United States visas. Solomon's companion carried the same surname; possibly he was the older Jew's brother; he was too old to be a son. She replaced the scrap of toilet paper and closed the case. Satisfied, she returned to the office.

The Weismans returned that evening. The one named Solomon smiled upon realizing that their suitcase had been opened and their passports examined—the minute piece of chewed gum he had placed on one of the hinges had been disturbed. They wanted someone to have confirmation of their aliases when the search started. Ahmad Libidi and Jamal Hussein had never in their life been to a Jewish temple or knowingly eaten Jewish food.

Ahmad sat on the bed while Jamal went into the bathroom. When he returned, Ahmad looked up and the trace of a smile softened his face. "It is good to be here."

"I did not like New York. The people are rude and godless," Jamal observed.

"It was a necessary stop."

"True enough. Still, we were held there unnecessarily long."

"Frankfurt calls the shots up to this point. Now, we do. We avenge the loss of the *Salinika*. The ship's mission has been costly, and several years of planning and preparation have been destroyed." Ahmad moved to a chair by the small table and sat opposite Jamal.

Jamal seemed disgruntled. "I don't like our target. A more spectacular response is called for, a bomb attack on the frigate, for instance."

Ahmad disagreed. "That would be impractical, even foolish. The *Ford* is moored in Pearl Harbor and even a clandestine underwater assault would be a substantial undertaking and one with great risk. Besides, my brother, we do not swim that well. This is better. Our sponsor wants something more unexpected. Something foolproof.''

"Something suicidal.''

"That concerns you? The salvation of our souls is at hand and you hesitate?''

"No,'' answered Jamal. "I am concerned only about success. What happens to us is the will of Allah. I *would* have preferred one more mission in Israel. There we have friends.''

"We may very well survive this. Americans are stupid. They lack the ability to anticipate.''

Jamal countered, "They are quite good after the fact. I can personally attest to that. My cousin was a member of the World Trade Center group.''

Ahmad unfolded the *Honolulu Advertiser* and tapped the front page. "I will never understand the devils. One of their naval officers intercepts our ship, sinks it, and saves the people on this island—and they reward him with a military trial.''

Their mission had suddenly become simpler and much more attractive. The image of their target had been spread all over the front pages of the paper and television screens. Now the cursed devil was going to undergo a military trial, thus keeping track of his whereabouts would be easy. In fact, a routine would be established each day when he would arrive and depart at the court.

They had brought in no weapons; that would have been too risky. But getting weapons in America was as easy as getting a hamburger. Ahmad had already set up a contact. That evening, acting on information supplied him by a Palestinian intelligence brochure on Honolulu, he visited the city's Chinatown section and purchased a service from one of the young ladies who routinely patrolled Hotel Street. A slightly overweight dirty blond Caucasian, she and another working girl were quite conspicuous among the endless streams of Chinese and small curious groups of mainland tourists along Hotel and Maunakea streets. It was merely a matter for him to stand as if waiting to cross the street, and he was immediately approached.

The young woman placed her hand on his. "Party?" she inquired quietly.

Ahmad stared straight ahead at the traffic light. "Relaxation would be nice. I'm very tense this evening."

"I can fix that—guaranteed."

"I am not a rich man."

"You will feel like one. My reward will be your satisfaction—plus one hundred dollars."

She led him to a small room over one of the open markets on Bishop Street and the smell of rice, fish, and suspended orange-glazed ducks competed for his nostrils with the musty smell of her room. There was no air-conditioning. The single window was open but there was no air movement within the room. At least the sheets were clean; perhaps he was her first customer for the night.

Afterward, as he was paying, he made sure the prostitute got a glance at his stuffed wallet.

"You are an enthusiastic and innovative young woman," he said, handing her three one-hundred dollar bills. It was triple her standard fee for straight sex.

"Well, thank you. Tell your friends."

"I'm afraid I have no friends. I have just arrived."

The woman cast her eyes toward the wallet. "You'll make plenty friends, I would say."

"Perhaps. But, I do have a more urgent need."

She chuckled. "I'll say—you almost broke my back."

Ahmad managed a smile. Despite his performance—that came instinctively—he was revolted at being with a whore. "No, not that. I am alone and travel the islands with a great deal of money. In these times, one needs protection, even here in Paradise.'' He peeled off five one-hundred-dollar bills.

"Perhaps you could help me. I am not privileged to be an American citizen, and obtaining a weapon . . .''

The woman avariciously eyed the money. "You need a piece?'' Then, she giggled as if suddenly very pleased with herself. "In addition to the one you just had?''

"You have a sense of humor.''

"And a friend who can help you.'' She picked up the bills. "He will want a name.''

"I told you: Weisman.''

"No. You don't screw like a Jew—and you're not circumcised.''

Ahmad shrugged. "I can pay cash.''

"You'll have to.''

"You have my money. Do we have a deal?''

Unabashed by her own nudity, she sat up on the bed, crossed her legs in a lotus position and began toweling off the perspiration. "There's a restaurant right around the corner; Wo Fat's. Be there tomorrow at noon. Take a table by the north windows. Order a Tsing Tao beer. You will be joined.''

"I'll be there.''

The woman rolled the bills into a tight cylinder, reached over and stuck them in her small handpurse. Keeping eye contact with Ahmad, she lay back on the bed, spread her legs slightly, and raised one knee. "One for the road?'' she suggested. "On the house.''

Ahmad turned away and left the room. *What Yankee decadence*, he thought, then offered a silent conciliatory prayer to Allah.

Wo Fat's was not at all hard to find, being at the corner of Hotel and Maunakea and just a short distance from the prostitute's dingy quarters. Honolulu's oldest Chinese restaurant, it normally featured dining rooms on the first three floors; however, only the second floor was open. Ahmad reasoned that a drop in tourism was responsible. He took the single small elevator and stepped out into a large rectangular dining area with windows on the west and north sides. He requested a table on the north side and was promptly seated. Only four other tables among the thirty or so were occupied, and they were all along the west wall. He ordered his beer from the elderly lady who brought him water and a menu. "There will be one other," he said.

Five minutes later he was joined by a man who materialized from a small foyer near the kitchen area. He was obviously Chinese but not purebred. The wide nose, thick lips, and darker coloring, not to mention his bulk, were Polynesian in nature; most probably he was Hawaiian. He wore black wrinkled pants and suitcoat and a white dress shirt, unbuttoned at the top. One part of his front shirttail was struggling to escape the tight confines of his belted trousers. He sat opposite Ahmad, and the woman wordlessly brought him a pot of tea, a porcelain handleless cup, and a large bowl of thick hot-and-sour soup.

The man poured his tea and tried the soup. "Very good. The best in Chinatown. You should try some, brudder."

"Perhaps I will," Ahmad replied.

The man swallowed several spoonfuls of the soup before again speaking, this time almost in a whisper. "What does a Jew want with a gun?"

"Protection. Personal protection."

"We have no real crime problem here—as long as you stay away from certain places."

"I may not have that choice. My business takes me to several areas I have heard are not quite safe for the tourists."

"You don't look like the kind of a person who can handle a weapon."

Ahmad was very careful not to let his face reveal that

he could handle *any* weapon—very well. "Do you have something for me or not?"

"Do you have twenty-five hundred dollars?"

"That's outrageous."

"Then you should order some soup and we can enjoy lunch together—but that's all."

"All right, what do you have?"

The man lifted his napkin from his lap and wiped his mouth. "U.S. Army 9-mm automatic, still in the preservative. Two boxes of ammo—hundred rounds."

"For *twenty-five hundred dollars*? I'll go to a gunshop."

The man laughed softly. "Here? On Oahu? With an Israeli passport for identification? You not very smart, brudder."

Ahmad mentally reviewed his times with the prostitute. She must have seen his room key. These people were much more cautious and thorough than he had imagined. One of them had been to the Harbor Arms and either talked to the manager or searched his and Jamal's room. Jamal had also been gone from the room for considerable lengths of time, his task being to determine how they could gain access to the naval base, if that was where the court-martial would be.

"All right. When do I pick it up?"

"You don't. I'll deliver it. Tonight."

"What time?"

"Just tonight. Watch some TV. Play cards with your companion. Whatever."

Ahmad did not like being fleeced, but he was careful not to show his anger. He rose and took a bill from his wallet to leave for the beer. The half-breed Chinese waved it away. "Allow me, haole," he offered.

Ahmad dropped the bill on the table and walked away.

* * *

The man from Wo Fat's came earlier than expected. Ahmad admitted him and the man took a shoe box from a paper shopping bag and handed it to him. Ahmad examined the automatic. "You said it was still in the preservative."

"It was. I did you the courtesy of cleaning it for you. Part of my service."

The gun was new and unscratched. Ahmad tilted the barrel under a lamp and squinted unto it. There was no indication that it had even been fired. He opened both boxes of bullets; they were undisturbed. He ejected the clip, filled it, reinserted it and chambered a round. He pointed it at the seller. "Feels good." He lowered the gun and handed the half-breed a thick white envelope.

The man merely glanced inside at the stack of one-hundred dollar notes. Holding up the envelope in salute, he smiled. "Enjoy your stay in Hawaii. Aloha."

Back in his car the man considered what he had just seen. Two solemn and mean-looking "Jews," one giving the 9-mm a careful examination and handling the weapon as if it was anything but strange to him. The other sat on a sofa, wordless throughout the transaction. In front of him had been a copy of the Honolulu paper, open to the page where there was a picture of a naval officer. With only the one glance, the half-breed had read the heading of the article next to the picture: FORD CAPTAIN CHARGED IN COURT-MARTIAL. The one on the sofa had reached over and casually closed the paper.

The man from Wo Fat's could easily count to four. It was merely a matter of adding two plus two. The men were not Jews but they were definitely from the Middle East—and they were terrorists. They could have something to do with the terrorist ship people. At the first pay phone, the man called his contact in the Honolulu Police Department. A tip of this nature, he reasoned, would gather a rich return when needed.

*   *   *

Ahmad Libidi began throwing the few things they had unpacked back into the suitcase. Trying to anticipate every possibility, he had replaced the license plates of their rental car with stolen ones and had parked it down the street. "We need to get out of here," he announced. "That infidel will turn us in for sure."

"Where will we go this time of night?"

Ahmad stared into space for a moment. "The room above; it should be number two-seventeen, yes?"

Jamal nodded. "I would think so."

Ahmad dialed the number. A man answered. Ahmad apologized as he said, "Sorry to call at this late time, sir, but I have a message for you. I will bring it right up."

The young man, not expecting any message, asked, "What does it say?"

"It is in a sealed envelope, sir. The envelope has the logo of Aloha Airlines. May I ask your name?"

It never occurred to the sleepy young man that the front desk could have checked the name by merely glancing at the room registration card. "Jack Phillips."

"That is the name on the envelope, sir. Aloha Airlines sometimes has very good promotions. I'll bring it up, sir."

When the unsuspecting occupant opened the door, Ahmad held out an envelope and as the man reached for it, Ahmad stuck the 9-mm in the man's stomach.

"Wha—"

"Inside—one sound and you're a dead man."

Jamal followed Ahmad into the room and immediately noticed the closed bathroom door. He pointed to it as his eyes asked the question, "Someone in there?" he asked.

Before the man could answer, a woman's voice came from behind the door, "Is it a free trip, Jack? What is it?" She stepped into the main room, wearing a white terry-cloth robe and drying her hair with a large motel towel. Jamal had his hand over her mouth before she even saw him. He dragged her back into the bathroom as Ahmad smashed in the left side of the man's skull with the barrel of the automatic. There was the sound of a struggle in the bathroom, but it only lasted a few seconds. Then Jamal appeared. "Bring him in here."

The woman was in the bathtub, crumpled in a pool of her own blood. Ahmad placed the man on top of her and Jamal drew a straight razor across the unconscious man's throat.

It was 3:00 A.M. when FBI senior agent Jason Orr rang the night bell at the Harbor Arms. There was no sound within the office. He pushed the button and held it down until there was a light and a very upset and frumpy Oriental woman appeared at the night window. Orr held up his identification and the night woman pushed a button that unlocked the door.

She became more agitated when she realized Orr was dressed in all black, including a flak jacket, and carried an automatic weapon.

"One-seventeen; Solomon Weisman and a second party. Check your registration," Orr ordered.

Hurriedly, the woman produced a registration card and slid it across the counter. Orr scanned it for only a moment. "Are they in?"

"I don't know."

"Is it their habit to be in this time of the morning?"

"I don't know. They are very quiet. I've seen little of them. What is going on?"

"Who's on each side?"

The woman checked her file. "No one in one-sixteen; Mr. and Mrs. Fredericks in one-eighteen."

"Give me the keys to one-sixteen and one-seventeen. You stay right here. I'll put an officer with you." Orr left the office and a uniformed HPD police officer walked in.

"It's all right, ma'am; please walk into the back room," the officer directed. "I'll be right here."

Orr led an eight-man assault team toward one-seventeen. Being careful not to produce any shadows across the window, they split and took position, four to a side, outside the door. Orr unlocked and quietly entered one-sixteen, and placed his ear against the wall common to both rooms. Nothing. He returned to his team and carefully inserted the key into one-seventeen. Ever so slowly, he turned it and gave the door a very gentle push. It gave. No dead bolt. Good. There could be a chain-lock, but that would snap instantly when the two lead men crashed through the door. Keeping the key turned to the open position, he gave a nod of his head. Two agents, the biggest on the team, slammed into the door with their shoulders with the precision and power of NFL linemen. There was no resistance. The door flew open and the two off-balance men fell forward but kept their weapons under control. Orr burst in behind them, followed by the remainder of the team, all yelling "Freeze! FBI!" and shining flashlights into the dark. Within moments they had passed through the small sitting area and entered the bedroom, kitchenette, and bathroom. There was no enclosed closet. Orr flicked on the lights as did the others. The apartment was empty except for fast-food remains scattered around the sitting room. Two room keys lay on the top of the TV. There was a crumpled newspaper in the bathroom waste can. Orr unfolded it. It was the morning edition of the *Honolulu Advertiser* and a picture and article had been ripped from page three.

Orr handed it to one of his men. "Find out what's missing, although I have a pretty good idea. Lift any prints and have this place scrubbed. The bastards are pros. Make a contact, then get out. Standard operating procedure. They had no way of knowing we'd been tipped." He placed his weapon back in its shoulder holster while commenting bitterly, "The fucking needle just dove into the haystack."

When the first FBI agents had approached 117, Ahmad had spotted them from 217. "I knew the unholy one was going to turn us in. He had it in his eyes."

Together in the darkened room, he and Jamal listened to the raid, peeking out of the window only once. Immediately after the raid, the FBI had all occupants advised that all was well, but that they should stay in their rooms with doors locked until further notified. Shortly before six, they cleared the occupants to leave, but ordered them to stay away from the raided room, citing the disturbance as being domestic. Later, Jamal complained, "We should have left before they came. They will find the bodies tomorrow."

"No. It was too late. By the time we found someplace, a late check-in could have aroused suspicion. This way, we start out this morning, arriving at a decent hour. I will check-in alone. You can join me after I'm in the room." A number of the Harbor Arms occupants were already checking out, frightened and unsure as to what had been going on in the early morning. Room 117 was cordoned off by yellow police tape and several agents were scouring the room for clues as to who the occupants had been. A uniformed HPD officer was patroling the area outside of the office and in the parking lot.

"We might as well shave now." Ahmad went into the bathroom, lay his razor on the sink, and started massaging the wet bar of soap to build up a lather. Afterward, while Jamal removed his own beard, Ahmad changed into a loud tourist aloha shirt. Then he ripped open the lining of the suitcase and retrieved new identifications, all plastic: drivers' licenses, credit cards, library cards, and membership cards to the Italian-American League. Both he and Jamal spoke fluent

Italian, and they were now clean-shaven vacationers from Chicago—Anthony Lurasci and Leo Perroni. On their way to find new accommodations, they would stop and purchase a couple of cheap cameras. As they left the room, Ahmad hung the DO NOT DISTURB sign on the outer door handle.

Jamal continued to complain as they drove away. "We should not have killed those two. They are bound to connect it with the Chinaman's tip and that will be confirmation that we exist."

Ahmad angrily glared at Jamal. "I *want* them to know. I want them to sweat and wonder what is coming next. I want them to kick their own asses for letting us get away. They are stupid. I would give my mother's soul to see their faces when they realize that we were only a few feet away when they made their raid."

By noon, they had settled in a suite in a large apartment hotel in the town of Kaneohe, on the windward side of Oahu. Their movements would be lost in the many comings and goings of the other occupants. When Ahmad had checked in as Lurasci he had taken a studio suite and made a show of buying several rolls of film at the front desk and asking directions to the Polynesian Cultural Center and several other north coast tourist attractions. He had then joined Jamal at a nearby fast-food restaurant and given him the room number. By late afternoon, they were discussing their next move.

"I have read that the court-martial starts in two days," Jamal said. "It will take place in a navy courtroom within the naval base. I still have to locate the building."

"Tomorrow, we rent another car. That way we can operate separately and return here every night to debrief. I think maybe I will contact our Chinaman again, first to see if he can feed us any information on what the police and FBI are doing—and then I owe him a swipe of my razor."

"I will check on vendors entering and leaving the base. As soon as I find a suitable one, I'll have our passes."

Ahmad had no difficulty in again contacting the Caucasian prostitute. She was as much a fixture of the Maunakea-Hotel street intersection as the traffic light. Within minutes, they were in her room.

Ahmad spoke immediately. "Don't bother to undress. All I require is another contact with the man at Wo Fat's."

"Johnny Wu?" the woman asked.

So, that is the devil's name. "Yes. But I meet him here."

"He will need a strong reason to come to my room."

"Tell him the gun he sold me is defective. He will know why I cannot meet with him in a public place. Tell him I am not overly disturbed, but I insist on a replacement weapon." Ahmad handed the woman a hundred-dollar bill. "There's another two after I meet with him."

She placed the bill in her handpurse. "Wait here."

Ahmad was uncomfortable in the dirty and disarrayed room, but he used the time to examine the hall and stairs in the event he had to leave in a hurry. He did not completely trust a woman who made her living lying on her back, faking orgasms. He spent the rest of the time searching out the single window for any suspicious activity on the street below. It was an hour before he spotted the woman returning. She was alone.

"He is not happy," she declared. "I had to do a lot of talking. I told him that you would hurt me if he did not come."

"Is he your pimp?"

"No! He is my husband and he is one purely pissed-off Chinese. You better have some good excuse after he gets over here. He doesn't buy the defective gun story, and Johnny Wu can be one bad dude when someone fucks with him.''

"Is he coming or not?"

"He'll be here. Just wait. I need to get back to work, so don't tie up my room too long. Okay? Just leave the bills under the mattress."

A few minutes after the woman left, Johnny Wu entered the room, closing the door very quietly. "What's this shit about a defective weapon? And you rough up my wife, you're a dead man."

Ahmad held up his hands in a gesture of submission. "I need some information. The gun is perfect."

Johnny Wu tilted his head and narrowed his eyes. "What kind of information?"

"Police activities. FBI."

"I don't have those kinds of connections."

"I think you do. You tipped them on my weapon buy after you found out where I was staying. You are a big fat ass, Wu, but there is five hundred dollars in it if you can provide one last service for me."

Johnny Wu swung a solid softball-sized fist with no warning. Ahmad had only a split second to prepare himself, but with Ahmad Libidi, a split second was enough for him to avoid the full force of the blow. It knocked him off balance, but he rolled and sprang to his feet. Wu rushed forward, his face contorted with rage. Ahmad stepped inside his next swing and slapped both hands against the sides of Wu's face. Locking his forefingers in the Chinaman's ears for leverage, he pushed the man's eyeballs back into their sockets until he felt them collapse, and then with the hard edge of one hand he delivered a vicious blow to Wu's windpipe before the big man could cry out. Wu fell to the floor, gasping for air and trying with his hands to stem the flow of blood running down his face.

Ahmad straddled and then sat on Wu's mountainous stomach and placed the straight razor against Wu's throat. Ahmad was not sure that the half-breed was conscious of his presence any longer, but just in case he placed his mouth close to Wu's face and whispered, "Allah will have no mercy on you." He calmed himself enough to realize that if he cut Wu's throat, he would be sprayed with blood. Instead, he watched Wu desperately trying to inhale through his crushed windpipe. He could not, and Ahmad pressed a pillow across Wu's face.

Before leaving, he used his razor to slice the bed covers and mattress into shreds.

20

Joshua Dunne sat across the small oak conference table from his defense counsel, David Soto. The two commanders were now bound in a common cause, and Soto knew that if he was to prevail in the trial he would have to know as much as possible about his client and in particular Dunne's attitudes and actions during the *Salinika* incident. Soto had studied the after-action report and the pretrial investigation. He had copies of all the message traffic. He had interviewed and prepared his witnesses. He was convinced that although Dunne was technically guilty of disobeying the president's order, he was innocent of any wrongdoing in light of mitigating circumstances. As for the violation of civil rights charges, Soto had already armed himself with what he felt was a solid argument backed up by a number of precedents.

In the few days that he had to prepare, one of his priorities had been to find out as much as possible about the trial counsel, Tom Marshall. What he had discovered within the limited time was enough to convince him that

Marshall was a consummate prosecutor, who had a record of overwhelming his opponents with a combination of thorough research and preparedness, a powerful presentation of testimony and evidence, and a chameleon-like ability to adjust his court manner to the collective personality of the jury. Marshall truly believed that the individuals of the jury, reacting with one another in their deliberations, developed a collective consciousness, and he wanted his arguments to appeal to that collective personality. In fact, Marshall went after the jury, not the defense. In his civilian role, the pre-selection questions he asked of prospective jurors were skillfully orchestrated not to determine any preconceived notions a candidate would have but to ascertain if that person would respond to Marshall's engaging personality. This was a particularly effective tactic when the evidence and testimony of the prosecution's case were weak. Damn the evidence and testimony! The jury would then vote for the counsel most credible to them.

That was Soto's ace in the hole. Marshall had no say in the appointment of the members of the court—the military jury. That was the exclusive purview of the convening authority. In Soto's mind, if there were such a thing as a collective personality to a jury (and he thoroughly disagreed with such a notion), Marshall would have no hints as to what it might be, any more than Soto.

Soto spent the first half hour reviewing Dunne's personal history prior to his appointment to the naval academy. Routine childhood in a stable home; religious upbringing; straight-A student in high school, with an emphasis on math and science. Lettered in football, baseball, and track. Dated, but no steady. Exemplary performance at the academy, graduated number three in class of 723. Here, Soto ran into his first concern. Dunne had requested and been assigned to flight training, completed it again near the top of his class, and had been assigned to jet fighter operational training. Yet Dunne wore no wings, and his service history since 1982 had been in surface warfare. His service record contained only an entry that reflected a switch in orders from flying duty to surface duty.

Soto asked, "You are a naval aviator?"

Dunne answered but did not elaborate. "Yes."

"You are not wearing wings."

"No. I have been medically grounded since 1982."

Soto leaned back in his chair. "What happened?"

"Right after I joined my first squadron, flying F-4s, I had an engine explosion and fire. I ejected along with my rear-seater. The canopy didn't jettison. I suffered a neck-vertebrae injury that restricted my side-to-side head movement. At first, my movement to the right was only forty degrees. Not enough for flying status."

"I'm sure it was a big disappointment."

"Yes. But you play your hand with the cards you're dealt. I'm very happy as a surface officer."

"Any chance of ever returning to flying status?"

"No, not now. I have achieved sixty-five degrees of movement through physical therapy. Another fifteen degrees and I would be medically qualified, but I'm too old and senior to start out again. It would be a fatal career pattern switch."

Soto agreed. "I'm surprised you don't wear your wings."

Dunne grinned. "Surface personnel have enough trouble reconciling themselves to fly-boys driving carriers; the hard-charging frigate navy might have second thoughts about an aviator reject as one of their COs. It's no problem with me. I'm very proud of my wings, but they have no part in my career now."

Soto decided it was a strange attitude but would be no problem to his defense. The revelation, however, increased his admiration for Dunne. It was an adjustment few aviators ever made well.

Another hour was spent reviewing questions that Soto

planned to ask defense witnesses. They were straight-forward and logical. Finally, he said, "I want to put you on the stand."

"Why? I'm innocent until proven guilty. Let the prosecution try and prove his case. I thought that was what it is all about. I acted professionally and with full justification in every action I took. Let him prove otherwise. You put me on the stand and a lot of doors open up."

"For one thing, you are the only person who heard Petty Officer Two Shoe's statements and requests. That's essential testimony."

"Testimony that the trial counsel will claim is self-serving."

"He has a witness that can testify to what you said, and without Two Shoe's side of the conversation it can mislead the members of the court. You specifically ordered Martinez not to enter the compartment without your permission—in effect, not to render medical assistance without your permission."

"What witness?"

"Your bridge talker. He was standing next to you after he gave you the phones. Without any rebuttal, Marshall can insinuate all sorts of ideas into the minds of the members. Two Shoes could have been desperately pleading for his life, for help."

Dunne's eyes flashed. "That's not the way it was!"

"Sez who?"

Dunne calmed. "Sez me." But, Soto's point was made.

"I don't like it," commented Dunne.

Soto did not want to ask the next question but he had to. "Joshua, is there any reason I don't know about why you shouldn't be placed on the stand?"

"Of course not. It just galls me that, as an officer who has served to the best of his ability, I have to subject myself to an examination of motives and rationale for my actions. I acted properly, and this whole trial is the result of political pressure. I resent it. It'll ruin my career. It's put an incredible strain on my relationship with my father-in-law and perhaps even my marriage.'' Dunne stood and slowly walked around the table. ''No, that's not true. It's just my ego. Admiral Paterson had no choice. It was a hell of a decision he had to make. Prosecute a member of his own family whom he knows is innocent. I should be grateful he kept me out of the hands of the D.C. crowd. I guess the president's pretty ticked I acted on my own, but he just doesn't understand the position of an officer in the field. He has no experience to fall back on. The commander-in-chief should not enter into tactical matters. That cost us our ass in Vietnam.''

''Be that as it may, Joshua. You need to take the stand, maybe even just to voice such concerns.''

''And place myself in a pissing contest with the president?''

''If it means acquittal, yes.''

''David, I don't want to go against my president. I respect his efforts in the godawful job he has, even if I do feel he would screw up a two-car funeral. I didn't even think of it as going against his order when I fired those Harpoons. I just knew the *Salinika* could not be allowed to beach herself on the coast of Oahu, and I was the only man on the face of this earth who really knew how close that was to happening. I meant no disrespect or insubordination. You know, we're bouncing all around here; one minute we're talking civil rights and the next, failure to obey a lawful order.''

''That's exactly what Marshall may do. He'll try to get you confused; he'll try to get you off balance.''

''Not if I don't testify.''

The session had lasted all day with only a brief coffee break for lunch. Dunne liked the quiet but efficient Soto and felt confident in the ability of his defense counsel. There was some mild disagreement between them, particularly Soto's insistence that Dunne would have to testify on his own behalf. It was galling to him that he would have to subject himself to what he considered an indignity. The testimony of others and the evidence available should all be sufficient to prove he acted properly. Still, he knew that if he had to direct Soto in conning the *Ford* around the ocean, he would expect the legal officer to take his advice whether he agreed with it or not. Dunne tried very hard to convince himself that Soto's advice in court matters should carry as much weight.

Now that he was not confined to Barber's Point, he had a rental car, and after returning to the beach cottage and a change of clothes he could at least get off base for a decent meal. He did notice that a car was following him as he accessed Interstate 1 and headed west for the NAS exit. The damned press were a determined lot. But even if they got on base, there was no one there who would tell them where his quarters were, and the base security police would turn them back if they stumbled upon the remote beach road. They would probably pick him up again when he left the base, but he would deal with that when the time came.

He swung into his parking area and walked the seventy feet or so to the seaward side of his cottage. That was the front entrance and he never tired of looking out over the water and the surfers to the east.

"Hi, sailor, buy a thirsty girl a drink?"

Dunne could not believe his eyes. Annie Mae Paterson-Dunne was sitting in one of the reclining beach chairs on the lanai.

"Annie!" He rushed to her and knelt before she could sit erect. Her lips were as delicious as ever, but he was startled to feel as if he were hugging a skinbag full of sharp bones. She had so very little flesh. "What are you doing? This is crazy."

"Doctor's permission." She gave him another quick kiss before continuing. "I'm between treatments. There may even be a remission. I'm stronger than I've been in days. Daddy has kept me up to date on developments— unlike some *other* people I know—and I just decided I wanted to be with you, even if it's only for a few days. Daddy pulled some strings and I rode an air-evac from NAS North Island to Hickam."

Dunne fingered the plastic hospital ID bands that were around her left wrist. "How did you know where I was?"

"Daddy. He met me at the terminal and we had some words. I'm not happy with his treatment of you, Josh. He walked away in a huff, but at least he had his driver bring me here. I insisted he not say anything to you. I wanted it to be a surprise."

"Well, it sure as hell is. You shouldn't have come." As soon as he spoke, Dunne saw the disappointment in Annie's eyes. "I don't mean that like it sounds. I'm so pleased and I love you, Annie. But this is too much of a strain for you."

"And I suppose being lonely and scared and worried back at Balboa Hospital is not?"

"I'm sorry. It must be terrible. I promise as soon as this is over, I'll get an assignment where we can be together."

Annie smiled and raised Dunne's hand to her lips. "I'm a navy wife, Josh. You will go where you have to go, and if I am with you, that's God's final gift to us."

"I don't want you talking like that."

"Why not? Death is a part of life. The last part, but the longest part—and maybe the best part if it means we'll be together forever."

Dunne wished that Annie's faith and resignation

would somehow bleed into him. "You are one of a kind, Annie."

"As are we all. Now, where'll we go for dinner?"

Dunne studied his wife's face. Despite her illness, the flesh was smooth, although drawn slightly over her high cheekbones; her lips still full and impish. Her dark brown eyes radiated her happiness at being with him, but they could not hide the pain that was her constant companion. Her light bronze skin was still soft to the touch and a complimentary contrast to the eyes and normally the hair—her wig was true to her natural color; Admiral Paterson had always joked about that. He and her mother had been unmistakably African—handsome and dark and full-featured—while Annie had uncharacteristically delicate features and a lighter skin. "There has to be a white boy in the woodpile somewhere," Paterson would declare, giving his daughter a deliciously playful hug.

Dunne had to treat himself to another kiss. Then, he stood. "Let me shower and change. What would you like to eat?" He could only imagine her lack of appetite and general disinterest in food.

"Oh, I don't know. A piece of fish. Perhaps mahi-mahi. It's been a long time since I've had that."

"I'll just be a minute. Relax and enjoy the view."

"I already am." For the first time in months, Annie was glad she was alive.

Dinner at the military-exclusive Hale Koa Hotel on the army's Fort Derussy at Waikiki had been an unusually pleasant and satisfying time, although Annie did little more than toy with her mahi-mahi. She and Joshua had reminisced about their early days together and the good times of maturing within the special social confines of the naval service. She asked him about the *Salinika* incident and expressed horror at the tragedy that would have occurred had the terrorists been successful. Where would it all lead? she had wondered out loud.

After dinner, they had walked for a short while along the beach, then sat for some time and watched the evening joggers and late strollers who were also enjoying the light of a full moon and a cool sea breeze. By ten, Dunne knew she had enough activity for the day; she had to be tired from the long plane ride, although on an air-evac she would have had some rest and perhaps even sleep. Surprisingly, she was still a bit keyed up when he suggested that they return to Barber's Point. She insisted they sit on the lanai; but she soon dozed off and Dunne helped her into bed. As he lay beside her, he realized he was very glad she came. Annie Dunne radiated courage and strength and stubbornness of purpose, traits that her husband aspired to as he completed the last full day before his court-martial.

About the same time that Joshua and Annie Dunne were giving themselves up to sleep, Ahmad Libidi and Jamal Hussein were discussing their tactics for the assassination of the devil who had sunk the *Salinika*.

Jamal was not confident that they had selected the best course of action. "I really think, my brother, that we will need a more aggressive attack. A single weapon will force us to depend upon very favorable conditions, perhaps even ideal. A timed attack from two directions with automatic fire would take care of a lot of 'what ifs.' "

"True enough, but it would increase the risk of detection. We must blend into the background; you don't hide an automatic weapon under a thin flowered shirt. The secret to this success shall be precision. I can kill the man with a single shot if I am close enough and no one is suspicious. I prefer it that way. It will give me great satisfaction. I want to see his head explode, and perhaps an instant before that the fear that will be in his eyes. He will not be so brave as he was firing on our defenseless ship and comrades."

Jamal managed a wry smile. "I don't think our dead comrades were concerned."

"How do we know—how did the infidel know—that they were all dead? Well below decks, some could have been alive, praying to Allah for some chance to complete their mission."

"Then I am to provide some diversion?"

"Yes. I must have time to pull my weapon, aim, and fire. After the first shot, I will close and fire a second and, assuming the American is dead, I will kill as many around him as I can. We will have the advantage of surprise, but we must anticipate that the day we select for this mission will be the day we will be with Allah. You must follow my lead once the attack commences."

"I have no weapon."

"Yes, you do." Ahmad lifted a blanket-wrapped object he had earlier brought into their small suite. He unwrapped the blanket and tossed it onto the bed. In his hand he held a well-used and slightly rusted machete. "This is a sugar cane harvesting weapon. They are everywhere on this island. I had only to express a desire for one as I toured the cane fields. The field hand wanted but a few dollars. You can hide it nicely down one leg of your trousers. Then, with surprise and swiftness, you can send three or even four American souls to eternal punishment. This will be a great triumph for Allah, for we will show that His disciples can select even a single target in the midst of American military might. Psychologically, this will make more of an impact than bullets. The Americans have no stomach for slashed and severed bodies. You, Jamal, will attack with the sword of Allah!"

Jamal took the machete and held it out. The feel of it slicing human flesh would be good. And even if it did not kill, the wounds would be infected by the rust and fester in a painful reminder of the viciousness of the attack. The thought appealed to him. He felt much better.

His victims would see his face and cringe before the justice in his eyes as he struck. His own death would be that much sweeter. "When?" he asked.

"That we must determine. I want it to be at a special time, one that will give us maximum effect with respect to the media. We could accomplish this at night with stealth. But the world must not just read of our sacrifice, they must see and hear it. That requires television cameras. There will be a permanent record of this holy deed, Jamal. The court-martial starts tomorrow. We must first be able to gain access to the naval base. What have you determined?"

"I have selected the vendor. It is only the matter of taking his truck and pass. He is an independent who services a different part of the base every day. He has no employer, so he will not be missed. His goods are simple—nuts and candies for machines. We will be able to decide upon the best place to wait for our opportunity."

"That is excellent. Now it is time for our prayers. Allah will be pleased."

For the second time within the past twenty-four hours Jason Orr was back at the Harbor Arms, this time in the room directly over one-seventeen.

Captain Davey Isaka, Honolulu Police Department, stood with him, viewing the bodies of the young couple. "I called as soon as I got the report. Can't be a coincidence. Too brutal. No robbery. The men you were searching for in one-seventeen did this."

Orr was not a big man, but he was a solid six-footer and he seemed taller as he drew himself up in anger. "You can bet the family jewels on this. Senseless brutality. The murder of innocents. The mark of a true terrorist. God, I've had my fill." Only two years away from retirement, Orr had been tempted to say "to hell with it" on several occasions. This was another one.

Isaka shook his head. "Animals." The stocky Japanese-Hawaiian cop was a veteran of fifteen years on the force. "We'll do what we can but I doubt if we'll find anything."

"You won't find a goddamned thing." Orr knew he was dealing with professionals. There had not even been a suspicious print in one-seventeen. Not even a hair. "There's some whisker bits on the sink. Probably the young man's."

"We'll check them out."

"I need some air. Thanks, Captain. We'll see more of each other." Orr walked outside and leaned on the guard rail. Twelve years a Marine. 'Nam from '68 through most of '73. He thought he had seen it all. Women and old men hacked to death. Kids torched. But the Muslims . . . he checked himself. That wasn't fair. The great majority of the followers of Islam were decent, caring, moral people. Most Catholics and Protestants were, too, but they sure loved to kill each other in Northern Ireland. And the tribal blacks in Africa. The serial killers in America. The diehard Communists in China. The whole fucking world was becoming a killing field.

Well, he had work to do.

21

Lieutenant Commander Phil ''Flipper'' Toohey, USNR, Officer-in-Charge of the U.S. Navy's Deep Submergence Vehicle FOUR was the last of the three-man crew to board the minisub. The DSV-4 was still attached to the launch-and-recovery structure that would swing the *Turtle II* over the stern of its mother ship, the recondi- tioned, seagoing, fire tug, *Laney Chouest*. Identical to the original *Turtle*, the second deep submersible was slightly more sophisticated with improved search-and- recovery capability. Seagoing tugs were not the world's fastest water vehicles, and the voyage from San Fran- cisco had taken ten days. Toohey had not been pleased to cut short the *Turtle II*'s routine maintenance period, but he certainly understood the priority that required the sudden departure on the early morning of September sixth. Fortunately, the *Turtle II* had no major discrep- ancies despite having just completed a twenty-day pro- ject in conjunction with the Woods Hole-Massachusetts Institute of Technology project off Baja California. Just as advantageous, the 235-foot-long navy-leased mother ship had enjoyed favorable seas and light winds during the crossing, and now she was positioned over the site of the *Salinika* sinking. Before Toohey closed the hatch he could see the southern coast of Oahu just 11.83 nautical miles away; the *Laney Chouest*'s precise satellite navigational gear had the same exquisite capabilities as any modern naval vessel.

The 50,000-pound, twenty-seven-foot-long *Turtle II* was anything but the fat, bulky, irregular craft she appeared to be. In her element—the darkness of the deep sea down to her dive limit of two miles—she was a highly maneuverable steel submersible that could use her pair of hydroelectrical manipulating arms to drill, cut, and retrieve objects from the seafloor. She was equipped with high-intensity lights, and she could use her self-contained sonar to avoid unseen underwater obstacles. Her other exploratory equipment included television cameras and a monitor as well as 35-mm still cameras. In addition to Toohey, her crew consisted of pilot Lt. Bob Evans and support systems operator Master Chief Petty Officer Manuel Valdez. The *Turtle II* could stay submerged for well over sixteen hours, her life support system including air purification and oxygen supplemented recycling equipment. Free-diving, she could roam at will, and her mission on this day was to locate and photograph the Iraqi terrorist ship.

The launch cradle lowered the *Turtle II* into the Pacific and the small, noncombatant submarine detached itself and floated with its tiny entrance tower awash, while the crew made their final checks. Everything was green, and Toohey gave the dive order. At one hundred and five hundred feet, he executed routine communications checks with the mother ship. All was well, and the life-support and propulsion systems were functioning properly. Now it was a matter of patience as the outside pressure increased and filtered sunlight decreased until soon there would be none.

A prominent sonar return was guiding the *Turtle II*; it had to be the *Salinika*, unless there was an unrecorded sinking in the area. That was always a possibility. Toohey thought back to World War II and could not recall any mention of a sinking that might confuse them among the reference material he had hastily glanced at before leaving San Francisco, but there was always the possibility that a ship had been lost and unaccounted for. The December 7 attack had come from the north of Oahu, and there had been no record of combat action he had ever heard about in this vicinity except for the possibility of an unknown Japanese midget submarine. But the sonar echo was too prominent for that.

The ride down to one mile was a relaxed ride with routine monitoring of the submersible's systems. The *Turtle II* was every bit the performer that her namesake had been, although this was only her sixteenth dive and the first that was programmed to exceed 8,000 feet.

A pre-dive check of the *Salinika*'s position confirmed that Dunne had sunk her just inside the 2,000 fathom curve south of Oahu. The actual depth had been measured as 10,921 feet, well within *Turtle II* design limits.

At 8,000 feet, all hands made a careful check of systems and equipment. The cabin was cramped but afforded enough room for the three men to twist and turn and thus reach throughout its entirety. MCPO Valdez had a puzzled look.

"Anything wrong, Master Chief?" Toohey asked.

"No, sir. It's just that there seems to be a bit more humidity than before. The gauge reads forty-three percent, but even without looking I can feel it."

Toohey shrugged. "Seems normal to me. What about you, Bob?"

Lt. Evans was at the controls. "Haven't noticed it."

At 9,500 feet, Toohey had the high-intensity lights turned on and Evans slowed the descent as they neared the seafloor. It was relatively level but with some undulations that caused their height above it to vary from 1,300 to 1,000 feet. The sonar profile had the *Salinika* down and ahead at four hundred yards. Evans placed the *Turtle II* one hundred feet above the floor and eased the tiny craft forward. An occasional luminescent fish was caught in the light beams and one very unusual creature that was long and slender as a sea snake. But there were ventral and dorsal fins, yet it had no eyes.

Evans was the first to see the ship. "Contact . . . look at that."

They were approaching the starboard aft side of the hull and it loomed over them like a gigantic steel cloud. The waterline, with dull red paint below it, was clearly visible and Evans eased the *Turtle II* aft and around the stern. Toohey called off the letters, reversed in order as they came into view: "A-K-I-N-I-L-A-S. Salinika." He made his contact report to the *Laney Chouest*.

The *Salinika* was upright and the sea sand bottom was up to the eight-foot marker on her stern depth line.

"Let's move forward," Toohey directed.

Evans guided the submersible along the starboard side of the hull, raising his height to parallel the lifeline. Suddenly, there was only jagged metal. "The bow's gone," he stated. "That must be where she took the missiles. They blew it clear off."

"Or weakened it so that it ripped off on the way down. She would have been dropping at a good clip once all the air was gone from inside. Look at the waterline markers; she's down seventeen feet at the bow."

Evans had lifted to just over the foredeck. "There's part of the collapsible deckhouse. Where's the airplane?"

"I bet the hummer was torn off or ripped off by the explosions of the missiles. We need to find it. CINC-PACFLT was pretty explicit about that."

"I dunno," responded Evans. "We're almost two miles down, and if it broke away near the surface it could be a good distance from here. Hell, with its wings intact, it could have 'glided' a mile or more."

MCPO Valdez interrupted, "I've got an unusual hiss back here."

Toohey turned and made eye contact with Valdez. "Air hiss?"

"Must be. There, now it's stopped."

"All your gauges normal?"

"Yes, sir."

"Let me know if you hear it again."

"Aye, sir."

Toohey reported topside. "We have pictures of the starboard side. Bow apparently blown off by Harpoons. No sign of aircraft. Will inspect port hull and topside structure."

"Roger, Turtle." The detached voice was loud and clear.

It took another hour to examine most of the *Salinika*.

Toohey made his decision and said, "We have enough pictures; let's make a sonar sweep around the area and see if we can pick up the aircraft."

"With this bottom, it could be half-covered," Evans commented.

Four hours of further search revealed no sign of the *Forger*, but a sharp drop-off three hundred yards directly ahead of the bow of the *Salinika* was discovered. It was an extensive canyon. When Evans got into position to have a sonar look downward, it measured another three thousand feet in depth with some ledges and outcroppings along the one wall they could detect. "It's big," Valdez declared.

"And too deep for us," Toohey added. "But let's go down another thousand feet and see if we can pick up anything along the wall. The airplane could have hung there." He knew it was a very remote possibility.

Evans voiced a caution. "That's getting close to design limits."

"We've had *Turtle* down to twelve thousand feet several times," Toohey responded.

Evans eased downward, more than a little nervous. He had not been on any of the DSV-3s two-mile dives. There was always a safety factor built into design limits, but he was still uncomfortable. He leveled at 11,900 feet. They hovered a half mile from the canyon wall and began their sonar sweep.

Valdez suddenly announced, "There's that hiss, again."

Toohey began training the outside video camera around the *Turtle II*. "Okay, we got bubbles rising aft."

"That shouldn't be," Valdez said with considerable concern. "We're self-contained."

"What's our cabin pressure?" Toohey asked. He had a gauge directly in front of him. The reading was normal.

"I think we should start up," Evans suggested. Any unidentified noise was always cause to abort a mission.

"I concur, Bob. Let's sur—"

Toohey never finished his sentence. His words froze in his mouth as the hiss became a high-pitched scream and then there was a loud bang followed by an extremely high-pressure stream of sea water that immediately expanded into a deluge. It filled the cabin within a heartbeat. The three crewmen died instantly as the pressure crushed them, although the *Turtle II* remained intact, its hull designed to withstand the depths, and with penetration by the seawater the pressure had equalized inside and out. All systems were instantly rendered inoperative and the pudgy gray submersible headed for the bottom of the sea canyon.

In the control center aboard the *Laney Chouest*, all *Turtle II* monitoring indicators went to their OFF positions—a complete shutdown of all incoming signals.

The duty communicator immediately pushed the alarm button and called the submersible. "Turtle II, this is Mother. Do you read? Over.'' Nothing. ''Turtle II, say your depth. Do you read?''

The center rapidly became crowded. The dive-monitor officer looked at the readout of the last recorded depth: 11,900 feet. ''They should be okay,'' he spoke hopefully. ''Could it be power failure at their end? Ours?''

The communicator removed his headset and looked over his shoulder. ''They're gone. No way we could lose everything like this unless they're gone.''

''Good God,'' the monitor exclaimed, ''it had to be catastrophic. It just can't happen. We've been down this deep before.''

''Not with *Turtle II*,'' a low voice from the group declared.

The dive monitor cursed. ''Shit! The fucking Iraqis have taken another three lives—without even lifting a finger.''

Admiral Paterson was busy in his CINCPACFLT office when his chief of staff was announced.

''Good morning, Chuck,'' Paterson greeted. ''You look like your cat just died.''

''Admiral, we just lost the *Turtle* with all hands.''

''Oh, my God. What happened?''

''We don't know, yet. She made the dive early this morning just as we briefed you. She found the *Salinika* a few hours ago and then started into a nearby canyon.''

''Why did she do that?''

''The bow of the *Salinika* was gone, apparently blown off by the Harpoons. The Forger was gone also. They thought it might have dropped into the canyon and there was a possibility it could have been caught on the canyon wall. The *Turtle* stayed within her design depth but something went wrong. There was no warning, no Mayday call.''

''This thing just won't end, will it? Draft a message

for me to Commander, Deep Submergence Group ONE. That was their second *Turtle*, wasn't it?''

"Yes, sir. *Turtle II*.''

"Be sure we render any assistance we can. How about the mother ship?''

"She's remaining on station, but there's nothing they can do.''

Paterson had felt matters couldn't get any worse. His son-in-law's court-martial was set to convene at 1000, just an hour away. Before he could fully explain, his daughter had raised holy hell with him for charging her husband with serious UCMJ violations. Even now, after he had arranged for her to come to Oahu, she was very cool toward him. She was her mother's daughter, all right. The media were demanding television coverage of the court-martial. Paterson was just as adamant in his refusal. He would allow only five pool reporters. Washington was even pressuring him about that. To hell with them. The do-gooders were up in arms, the local liberals screaming to high heaven that if Charlie Two Shoes had been a white man, he would not have been denied medical attention. On the other side of the fence, several civic groups were condemning the admiral for court-martialing the man who had saved Oahu. Paterson's official car had been struck twice with rocks; either group could have thrown them. Now, three additional lives had been lost and there would be official and media inquiries about that, although PACFLT had been only in an administrative role with respect to the deep dive. His personal phone in his quarters had been ringing day and night until he had the number changed and informed his staff that he would personally shoot the man or woman who leaked it again. Then, he felt guilty about being so angry with them. They were his buffer during working hours and he knew they were loyal. One of his friends could have given the number out. Not all of them were happy with him, either.

He had counted on *Turtle II* bringing up some pictures of the *Salinika* and the Forger. They would have given Dunne's defense counsel additional hard evidence, although Paterson doubted that their existence would have been a deciding factor. He also wondered if any of the biological agent could have escaped, assuming there had been any remaining on board. His medical officer had assured him that, in all probability, any released agent at such depths would be so diluted and dispersed by the time it reached the surface that there would be no threat. Another factor disturbed Paterson. Why were no bodies found at sea? Surely some of them, especially those observed on the weatherdecks, would have floated free. PACFLT search units had recovered none. None had washed up on any beaches—thank God. He doubted if sharks would have eaten such contaminated meat.

He also continued to worry about the international ramifications, particularly the Iraqi reactions to the expulsion of their Washington delegation.

The FBI had alerted Paterson to the possible presence of two terrorists on Oahu, and it seemed their purpose might tie in with the sinking of the *Salinika*. Paterson had to admire the agency for keeping that and their counterterrorist activities low-key. Even their early morning raid at the Harbor Arms had been passed off as a response to a domestic disturbance. In any event, he had directed that a U.S. Marine contingent be assigned to provide security around the court-martial building, half of them to be in civilian clothes. He would not have Dunne informed; no reason for that additional worry; and even if his son-in-law knew, he could do nothing to counter the threat. So, best he remain ignorant. Besides, he might not be the target.

Paterson could at least call the CNO and bring him up to date on developments. It would be late afternoon in Washington.

"Admiral, this is Blackjack."

"I was just about to call you."

"You first then," Paterson offered.

"I was wondering if the court had convened."

"No, sir. In an hour. I have to report a tragic development, however."

"What is that?"

"Chip, we've lost the deep submergence vehicle that went down to the *Salinika* this morning."

"Jesus, Blackjack, you're going to be a basket case if this keeps up. Lose the crew?"

Paterson briefed the CNO on what he knew.

The CNO asked, "You going to try again?"

"I don't think so. I doubt we could complete the mission before the court-martial is over, and I don't think any further evidence will add anything. The *Turtle* did confirm the presence of the *Salinika*."

The CNO's voice was compassionate. "I'll check with personnel about family notification and assistance. I'm sure they're on top of it. I understand your daughter arrived. How is she?"

"Mad as a wet Rhode Island Red with me, but I couldn't talk her out of it. She's doing okay at the moment, but she has an appointment for a CAT scan at Tripler this afternoon."

"Give her my love, Blackjack."

"Of course, Chip. I'll be in touch, Admiral."

"Thank you for the call, Admiral."

It had helped to speak with Admiral Collins. Blackjack and he were practically lifelong shipmates, and Collins had been Annie's sponsor at her baptism. Collins had been Paterson's mentor throughout their distinguished careers, and it was almost preordained that Paterson would follow Collins into the number-one billet of the United States Navy. *Not now*, reckoned Paterson. He had escaped the president's wrath about the attempted cover-up of the real time of the *Salinika*'s sinking, but he could no longer be in favor with SECDEF.

Actually, Paterson did not give a rat's rear about that.
He had performed his duty as he had seen it, and if his
present job were his last he would go back to Louisiana,
find himself a good Cajun cook, and go for the big
bucks. Blackjack's on the Bayou. It might not be bad at
all. He could certainly count on all of Chip Collins's
business.

Blackjack chuckled at the thought as he sat back down
at his desk. The damned IN basket seemed to have a life
of its own, breeding directives and orders and procedures as if that was the most important task of the four-
star leader of the Pacific fleet. It wasn't. Defending his
country from its enemies abroad and from within was
his primary task. And he sure as hell was going to continue to do that to the best of his abilities. Taking the
first paper from the top of the stack, he signed it without
reading a word.

A glance at the wall chronometer confirmed his in-
tuition. It was ten hundred. The court-martial of Joshua
Dunne was about to convene.

22

CINCPACFLT Courtroom #1 was smaller than Joshua Dunne had imagined it would be. At the front was the judge's bench; to the left of that, the witness podium and seat. The court reporter's position was to the right, facing to the left. Behind all three positions, there was a richly paneled wall and high at its center was a three-foot logo of the Pacific fleet. To the observer's left was the gold-fringed flag of the United States, the stained and lacquered pole resting in its stand, the flag under the watchful and protective eyes of a brass bald eagle. Spaced equally on the opposite side were the blue colors of the U.S. Navy. Along the left side of the trial area were the seats for the members of the court, nine in all but only five would be occupied. An appropriate distance from the bench were tables and chairs for the defense—to the observer's left, opposite the U.S. flag—and the trial counsel on the right, opposite the navy colors. Both sets faced the judge's bench.

There was a wooden railing that separated the court area from the observer area, and there were three rows of bench seats with an open aisle down the middle.

There was room for probably eighteen observers. The entire deck was carpeted with a commercial grade, navy blue, close-weave carpet. Matching color venetian blinds, their plastic louvers open, hung loosely at each of the four windows, two to a side, all spaced on the side walls opposite the observer seats. Six large fluorescent light fixtures were imbedded in the overhead. Except for the wood paneling at the head of the room, the walls were painted light blue. The room was very similar to those normally associated with civil courtrooms. And as would be expected, there was ample room between the judge's bench and the other positions for the display of charts or slides or whatever was necessary to the proper conduct of a court-martial.

When Dunne and his counsel, Commander Soto, had arrived, Commander Marshall and a lieutenant, who was most probably his assistant, were already seated as were a dozen or so observers and prospective witnesses. Lt. Kohn, along with several of the *Ford*'s officers, was seated in the first row of observer seats behind the defense table. There were five men who appeared to be press people behind the trial counsel's position and several navy personnel scattered in the rear rows. A U.S. Marine guard in green service uniform and wearing a sidearm was stationed beside a door at the front. Dunne assumed it was the entry for the military judge and the members of the court. He was a little surprised to see two more marines, also armed, standing at parade rest in the back corners of the room. There had been another two just outside the main entry. Five seemed a bit excessive for a court-martial concerning nonviolent charges and a defendant not under any kind of restriction.

Lt. Kohn and the ship's officers all rose to greet Dunne. Kohn seemed to speak for them all. "Good morning, Captain. We're certainly behind you in this, sir. It's an outrage."

Dunne had only time for a brief "Thank you" before Soto led him to their table. Almost immediately the marine stationed at the wall entrance walked over and said quietly, "There will be just a short delay, sirs. The judge is meeting with the members of the court."

"Thank you," replied Soto, placing a manila folder in front of Dunne. "Short bios of the members. I thought you might like to read them."

Dunne wished that Annie were present, but she had an appointment at the army's Tripler Hospital in Aiea. She would turn in her health records and spend a few minutes with several of the staff doctors, enabling them to be prepared if she needed an immediate treatment while she was on Oahu. There was a routine chemotherapy scheduled for the twentieth of the month.

Dunne opened the folder and read the contents.

The military judge was Captain Fritz Rarick, USN, so designated by JAG and the senior judge attached to the Naval Legal Services Office at Pearl Harbor Naval Base. A graduate of Harvard, thirty-one years of active service including duty on a number of naval and joint staffs as well as the office of the CNO.

The president of the court was Captain Robert "Dutch" Fargo, regular navy, surface warfare specialist whose sea commands had included the USS *Missouri* during the Gulf War; presently assigned to CINCPACFLT command and control center.

The members were:

Captain Henry "Hank" Billings, regular navy, rear admiral-selectee, naval aviator, and former commanding officer of the nuclear aircraft carrier USS *Enterprise*; wore the Navy Cross from the Vietnam era.

Newly promoted Captain Roy "Buck" Jones, regular navy, surface warfare specialist, former commanding officer of the guided-missile frigate USS *Reid*, sister ship of the *Ford*; veteran of the Gulf War; prospective chief of staff to CINCPACFLT.

Captain Jack "Duke" Wayne, reserve officer on active duty, naval aviator, former commanding officer of the amphibious assault ship USS *New Orleans*; wth three Distinguished Flying Crosses and eleven Air Medals, all from Vietnam era.

Commander Mary Margaret Dice, captain-selectee, regular navy, unrestricted line officer; veteran of Gulf War; former executive officer of the ammunition ship USS *Kiska*.

All were veteran line officers with combat experience. Dunne knew he could not have picked a more sympathetic jury.

He spoke softly to Soto, "I would hope they can relate to my situation."

"I would have settled for all 0-5s. Four stripes sometimes makes one think more of regulations and duty than circumstances."

"That's comforting," Dunne said, rolling his eyes.

"No, it's nothing to concern yourself with. I just relate better to 0-5s. They would be closer to your experience. Marshall has the worry; I've never run across a senior combat officer yet who has any love for flashy JAG types who wear custom-made polyester tropical whites." Soto had conspicuously worn the standard GI-issue, heavily starched, cotton uniform. The front crease in his trousers would slice right through a $2.99 steak special. Dunne squirmed a bit. His whites were crisp and spotless cotton and nylon, off the rack at the NEX in San Diego. But his Gulf War service ribbon, nestled among the three rows of service decorations and awards, would make him a blood brother to three members of the court.

Several more observers entered and sat in the rear observer's row. Dunne was puzzled that two were in civilian clothes, the other a khaki-clad navy warrant officer.

Commander Tom Marshall sat with nonchalance at

his seat as if he were waiting for a restaurant table and kicking himself for not making a reservation. He was doodling on a yellow legal pad. He paid no attention to any other person in the room, and when his assistant started to say something, Marshall cut him off with an upraised arm as if to say, "I need no further preparation, just relax."

Dunne was far from relaxed despite Soto's gentle attempt to reassure him. Dunne was unaccustomed to being in a position over which he had no control. His fate was completely in the hands of others, and now that the moment of truth was just on the other side of the door in the paneled wall he found himself suffering from what he imagined to be a sort of stage fright. He didn't like the feeling at all. There was a faint odor of some lemony dusting spray and he had noticed that the room was operating-room clean. He leaned over and sniffed the top of the table. It was the source of the odor.

The marine at the wall door came to attention. "All rise!" he commanded.

Oh, shit, Annie, thought Dunne, *here we go.*

The members of the court filed in and stood before their seats as Captain Fritz Rarick entered and walked behind his bench. He gently rapped his gavel before announcing, "This Article 39a session is called to order. Be seated, please.

"Pursuant to CINCPACFLT order one-dash-niner-five dated September eighth, this general court is convened to try the accused, Commander Joshua Dunne, on two counts of violation of the Uniform Code of Military Justice, specifically Article 92, to wit: Failure to obey a lawful order; and Article 134, general article, to wit: conduct prejudicial to good order and discipline, specifically the denial of certain civil rights to personnel under his command.

"A copy of this convening order is in the hands of the members of the court, the trial counsel and the defense counsel. Accordingly, if there are no objections, the reading of the names, ranks, and units of all participating parties is waived." Rarick paused before continuing. "Also pursuant to Article 39, pretrial arraignment has been waived. Is that the understanding and request of counsels?"

Soto and Marshall stood and answered in unison, "Yes, Your Honor."

"All concerned will stand to be sworn." Rarick administered the oath and directed, "Be seated." Then, he continued. "Does the accused understand his rights?"

Dunne answered, "I do, Your Honor."

"Very well, does the accused wish to enter a plea?"

Dunne again answered, "Yes, Your Honor. I plea 'not guilty' to both charges."

"Very well. The plea is accepted. There is one motion before the court. That motion by the defense, to dismiss the charges due to insufficient evidence and political overtones to the charges is denied. Does the trial counsel wish to make his opening statement?"

"Yes, Your Honor." Commander Marshall stood and faced the members of the court. "Gentlemen and lady, at first glance this court-martial seems a relatively simple one with respect to charges and the elements of proof of each charge.

"Disobeying a direct order requires only that: one, a lawful order was issued; two, the accused was aware of the order; and three, the accused did not obey the order.

"The violation of civil rights charge involves only three elements of proof: one, that the victim was entitled to certain rights under the supreme law of our Constitution; two, those rights were denied by the accused; and three, the victim did suffer as a consequence of the denial of those rights.

"The defense will claim mitigating circumstances that voided one or more of those elements of proof in each charge. That is simply not the case. All remain valid and the prosecution will show evidence and produce testimony that clearly and irrevocably support the validity of the charges and the guilt of the accused.

"Commander Dunne is a national hero. He sank a ship that the *defense* will claim posed a lethal threat to the inhabitants of the island of Oahu. That claim is so far from the truth that it may even constitute fraud. Commander Dunne is pictured in the media, indeed even within his own service record, as an outstanding officer of superb ability and considered judgment who has been twice early selected for promotion and for command well ahead of his contemporaries. The prosecution will show that during the period of time now referred to as the *Salinika* Incident, Commander Dunne repeatedly erred in judgment and the results of those judgment errors cost the lives of eight of his crewmen, young men that he was sworn to protect and care for. And when several of those crewmen voiced their concerns directly to their captain, they were ignored. . . ."

Dunne leaned toward Soto and said, "That's a bunch of rubbish."

Soto nodded.

Marshall continued, walking over to face the members of the court. "The first duty of an officer is to take care of his men. They willingly place their lives in his hands and in return they expect, and they have *every* right to expect, competent leadership, careful consideration of their needs—and I include medical assistance in those needs—and skilled direction and guidance whenever that leader takes them into harm's way."

Dunne doubted that Marshall even had the slightest understanding of the term.

"A leader leads by example. He conducts himself in such a manner that he can expect his men and women to also conduct themselves. He is loyal and he is faithful to his obligations. Remember those two words, gentlemen and lady, *loyal* and *faithful*. Commander Dunne apparently forgot them—among other things."

Joshua Dunne began to bristle. "Who in the hell does this paper pusher think he is?"

Soto whispered back, "The number-one prosecutor in the Justice Department. Don't get upset. He is just sowing seeds. We'll get a crack at the terrain before he starts his harvest."

Marshall was droning on. ". . . and let his ruffled feathers take advantage of his common sense. That is a very dangerous trait for a combat officer."

Dunne started to open his mouth again but Soto pointed to a note he had just scribbled: *Write questions or comments—the judge has already given us one cautionary glare.* Dunne glanced at Captain Rarick, who pointedly slid his right arm over and wrapped his fingers around his gavel. Dunne gave a submissive nod and it appeared that Rarick concluded the silent exchange with the hint of a smile, although Dunne had never thought such an act could so easily convey a threat.

Marshall had paused for emphasis. It was one of his techniques. When he thought he had made a particularly good point, he would pause and let the jury digest it without the distraction of a following point too close. But Dunne had missed Marshall's words in trying to comment to Soto, so he had no idea what several of the members of the court were nodding about to themselves.

Marshall was continuing with his definition of military leadership. "A leader cannot lead unless he has learned to follow; he cannot expect his subordinates to obey unless he obeys his superiors. If he does not, then that fault filters down and soon, instead of discipline, we have chaos.

"Commander Joshua Dunne has failed on two counts of leadership: loyalty and obedience. He was disloyal to Petty Officer Charlie Two Shoes, perhaps even prejudicial, and he deliberately disobeyed a direct order of the commander-in-chief of the armed forces of the United States.''

Soto was not fast enough.

Dunne was on his feet. ''That's a lie!'' he cried out.

Captain Rarick smashed his gavel on the bench with such force that a chip of wood flew across the length of the courtroom and ricocheted off the rear wall. Several of the observers ducked as the minute missile sped through the air.

''Commander Dunne! You will sit and be silent! Counsels will approach the bench.''

Under his breath, Soto muttered as he stood, ''Good on ya, Yank. We're five minutes into the trial and about to be cited for contempt.''

Dunne responded with a barely audible ''Bastard.''

Marshall joined Soto and they stood before the military judge.

Rarick leaned over and spoke in low tones, ''We're just getting started, gentlemen, and I think a few words of caution are in order. First, Commander Soto, your client will refrain from audible contact with you or anyone else in this courtroom while arguments or testimony are being presented. You know the rules. That is why God made pencils and paper—so that I may have a quiet court. May I add that if Commander Dunne does not want to openly support just about everything the trial counsel has said of him, he will control himself. You might mention to him during a brief recess I am about to call that his arguments concerning the matters before this court will receive ample consideration when you present his defense.''

Soto was surprised and relieved not to be cited with contempt. ''Yes, Your Honor. I apologize for my client. Thank you, sir.''

Marshall was trying to hold back a smile of satisfaction. Captain Rarick immediately helped him.

''Commander Marshall, it is already apparent to this

court that your prosecution will rely heavily on questioning Commander Dunne's integrity and fitness as an officer, thereby rendering any defense arguments ineffective. That is fine; in fact, within limits that is your duty. I allow considerable leeway in opening arguments but be warned that your closing argument will be more closely scrutinized. I see by your expression, you are somewhat confused. I will clarify. I strongly suspect that your use of the word 'prejudicial' set off Commander Dunne. I do not believe that aspect of this case has been anticipated. Perhaps it will be one of your tactics. Perhaps it will even be a factor. But for the moment, we are all aware that Petty Officer Two Shoes was a Native American and your thinly veiled reference was offensive to this court. Now, please, don't let this little talk dampen your enthusiasm, but do not stretch your innuendos too far at this point.''

''Thank you, Your Honor.''

As Marshall and Soto walked back to their places, Marshall was embarrassed about the mild censure. A civilian judge would never have called him on such a minor point. He shook off the feeling and continued. ''Gentlemen and lady, in light of Commander Dunne's outburst, I should also emphasize that another trait of a good leader is self-control.''

Captain Rarick almost banged his gavel again. Chastising a defendant was *his* prerogative. But he did not want to appear overauthoritative and besides, he recognized that Marshall had just scored a very good point. It would not be proper to take it away from him.

Marshall was ready to complete his opening argument. He had returned to his table and stood behind his chair. ''This is much more than a simple violation of two articles of the Uniform Code of Military Justice. There are aggravating factors that the prosecution will bring out during its conduct of the case. Factors that make the two offenses more than just letter-of-the-law violations. Commander Dunne was reckless in his command of the *Ford* during the chase, investigation, and premature sinking of the *Salinika*. His anxiety, perhaps even his ego, would not allow him to exercise the kind of restraint that was called for. By sinking the *Salinika* in deep water, two thousand fathoms, he has denied the United States of evidence that could be presented to the United Nations with respect to the murderous conduct of the perpetrators. We can't hold up the *Salinika* or the alleged death-dealing Forger aircraft and wave it under the nose of Iraq or Syria or Libya or whoever, and the international community. We don't have the slightest evidence of the origin or nationality of the terrorists. We can only say that we *think* the *Salinika* was a terrorist ship and we *think* it was going to attack Oahu. Sure, there is some circumstantial evidence to that effect, but Commander Dunne, far from performing a heroic deed, has done a disservice to the country and in doing so has disgraced himself and the naval arm of the military. Finally, by disobeying a legitimate order of the highest military command, our president, he has added to the stress between the military and the administration and cast doubts upon himself as a team player. A good officer salutes and says, 'Aye, aye, sir.' Commander Dunne has not even saluted.'' Marshall paused for effect, then raised his right arm until his hand was over his head, index finger extended. "Instead, he has defied his commander-in-chief with another symbol and done as he damned well pleased. Thank you, Your Honor.''

Captain Rarick was not pleased with the theatrics. The five members of the court sat expressionless. Marshall slowly lowered his hand and took his seat.

Rarick spoke to Soto. "Would the defense like to make its opening statement?''

"Yes, Your Honor. Thank you.'' Soto walked in front of the defense table and nodded to the court. "Members of the court,'' he began, "the trial counsel has made several statements that I wholeheartedly agree with. He has said that Commander Dunne is a national hero. I agree with that. He has said that Commander Dunne has been twice deep-selected for promotion and given a combat command well ahead of his contemporaries. I agree with that. He has also said that Joshua Dunne is depicted as an outstanding officer of superb ability and considered judgement, and I agree with that. All of his other statements—*all*—are incorrect. I have apologized to this court for Joshua Dunne's interruption, and I only add that Commander Dunne's reaction was certainly understandable, if not appropriate.

"We are all very fortunate that Commander Dunne is a conscientious officer who would not let a flagrant violation of the oceanic International Rules of the Road go unchallenged. His steady hand had already averted a collision at sea in very adverse weather. I suspect that none of you has any difficulty in conjuring up the mental image of the *Salinika* slicing into the *Ford* and spilling six hundred sailors into the sea in the dark of a very stormy night. It is every skipper's nightmare. But it did not happen and that near-collision was the first of several things that Commander Dunne handled *exactly right*.

"Let's imagine a second panic. A panic caused by the grounding of the *Salinika* on the southern coast of Oahu in hurricane-force winds. Most assuredly she would have broken up in the surf and released any biological agent remaining aboard to be blown across this island. Men, women, and children, bloated and white, lying in their beds, in the streets, in the open hotel lobbies, along Waikiki beach and in the parks. *That* did not happen. Why? Because Commander Dunne handled that situation *exactly right*.

"Finally, imagine yourself aboard the *Ford*. Two of your shipmates come down with the death agent. You are in a very confined space, the limits of a U.S. Navy frigate. How long before you begin to choke, bloat, and whiten? But *that* did not happen; not because you were not on board but because Commander Dunne did everything *exactly right*.

"Would you say that such a man was exercising poor judgment?

"My learned colleague, the trial counsel, has attempted to define leadership, but I say that he has tailored his definition to suit his own ends, and in doing so has misrepresented the duties and obligations of an unrestricted line officer. That officer's primary obligation is not to his men. His primary obligation is to carry out his mission and in combat to repel and defeat the enemy. He does have a very sacred second obligation: to execute that mission with minimal casualties. Most of the time, he has little or no control over that sacred obligation because the enemy does not honor it. However, that officer fulfills that second sacred obligation by seeing that his men are well trained, that their equipment is in apple-pie order, and that he has prepared himself to the ultimate. Certainly, he owes them no less. And he may very well be faced with the most agonizing decision a commander can make, that of sacrificing one or more of his men for the sake of saving the remainder of his crew.

"I know I am not telling this court anything new, but I feel it my obligation to correct the trial counsel."

Dunne silently cheered. *Go get him, Soto!*

"The defense will show that Joshua Dunne is a compassionate man who has a personal interest in every sailor and officer aboard the *Ford*. We will lay out the sequence of events as experienced by the crew, and we will ask certain of them for their reactions. We will offer testimony and evidence that substantiates the fact that the *Salinika* was a terrorist ship and her objective was Oahu. We already know that, you say? The trial counsel seems to have doubts, and he will attempt to implant those doubts into the minds of this court.

"Finally, I should like to voice an opinion and that is perfectly permissible in an opening statement. The press is calling this a political trial. They say it is a test of authority, the authority of the commander-in-chief of our armed forces versus the authority of an officer in tactical command at sea. That sells newspapers and keeps couch potatoes glued to their televisions through the evening news. But this trial is no such thing. The charges are legitimate. Military law is straightforward. The elements of proof are clearly defined. Our only job here is to see if those elements of proof exist in each charge. Military law is also just. Even if, *technically*, the elements are present, we must ask: do they represent all of the elements that must be considered when you take the letter of the law and test it with mitigating circumstances? The trial counsel has stated that the defense will bring such mitigating circumstances into the arguments. He is quite right on that claim because that is the heart of our defense."

Soto made eye contact with each of the members of the court as he continued. "Once the *Ford* made contact with the *Salinika* and identified the ship as a terrorist vessel with the capability of inflicting grave damage upon the property and citizens of the United States, the *Ford* and its crew were at war, with all of the obligations, responsibilities, and duties of a man-of-war engaging the enemy. The *Salinika* Incident is a wartime incident between two ships at sea, one intent upon an attack and one determined to foil that attack. And it is indicative of the viciousness of that attack that the crew of the *Salinika* intended it to continue *even after their deaths*. Commander Joshua Dunne found himself and his crew in a situation that called for impeccable judgement, and they acted with honor and in the finest traditions of the United States Navy. Thank you."

As Soto returned to the defense table, Judge Rarick announced, "We will take a short recess. Five minutes."

The members of the court took the opportunity to make a head call before proceeding to their deliberation room for coffee. The president, Captain "Dutch" Fargo, observed, "Rarick certainly has firm control. He seems like a good man."

Captain "Buck" Jones added, "He has a reputation. I checked with several of the legal officers. Where's Commander Dice?"

"Ladies room," Captain "Hank" Billing ventured.

Fargo lifted his cup but paused before sipping. "Ladies room. Men's room. Whatever happened to the head?"

Jones chuckled. "Y'know, several years back I was at an air force base with a joint inspection team and down on the flight line the damn place had a sign on the door that read TOILET. Toilet, for Christ's sake. Not latrine. That's some kind of obscene."

"They've always been progressive," said Billings as he lifted his cup in salute.

Commander Mary Margeret Dice walked in. "Gentlemen."

Fargo poured a cup of coffee for her. "What do you think, Mary Margaret, going to the 'ladies room' on a naval base?"

Dice grinned. "I think we are adding a little class."

Jones shook his head. "There goes the neighborhood."

Dice tore open a package of sugar substitute and added a small portion to her coffee. "Hey, I think 'Ladies Head' would be more appropiate. Tradition is tradition. I can live with that. Not to change the subject, but this Commander Marshall seems out for blood."

"Careful, we're not deliberating, yet," Fargo cautioned.

Jones nodded but added, "True enough, but I don't think general comments are out of order, do you, Dutch?"

"No, but the personalities of the members of the court should not be a factor."

"I certainly agree with that," continued Dice, "and meant the comment only as a passing remark. As for personalities, it will be a factor in how the case is presented."

Captain "Duke" Wayne lapsed into his namesake character, "Well, now, little lady, you just tell us pilgrims what you think of the rest of the court."

Dice could not suppress her grin but stuck to her guns, "Captain, this is serious."

Wayne returned to the business at hand. "I know, Commander. We have this Dunne's career in our hands. Forgive my levity."

"Your imitation is quite good," Dice remarked, "but we are about serious business."

Fargo changed the pace. "When do you put on that fourth stripe?"

"Any day, now," answered Dice.

Billings lifted his cup and said, "Well, it's well deserved, Mary Margaret. You did one hell of a job on the *Kiska*. She had her problems."

"Thanks, Hank."

Fargo stood. "We better get back in."

Everyone else except Rarick were back at their positions. Dunne and Soto were quietly conversing.

"Well, how do you think it went?" Dunne asked.

"Marshall scored a couple points we'll have to counter," Soto answered, popping a curled stick of gum into his mouth. "My mouth gets dry after a monologue that length. I think we're off to a reasonable start. Marshall gave me a good opening shot there when he tried to tell five senior combat officers the military definition of leadership. That was like a midwife trying to define birthing procedures to a group of obstetricians—he was a bit presumptuous. But opening statements are just to set the stage and perhaps establish some rapport with the members of the court. I think it went well for both of us. He's good.''

Commander Marshall was mentally reviewing his opening statement. In retrospect, referring to the members of the court as "gentlemen and lady" had sounded a bit awkward. Politically correct, certainly, but Soto's "members of the court" was more appropriate. He'd use that, also. The members had given him practically no facial feedback; he should have anticipated that. Still, it went well and in his mind he had been much more assertive than the defense.

"All rise."

Rarick had returned. "This court is now in session."

Marshall made the obligatory announcement, "All parties of this court-martial present prior to recess are again present."

Rarick instructed, "Commander Marshall, would you call your first witness?"

"Thank you, your honor. The prosecution calls Quartermaster Third Class David Andrews."

Dunne turned to see the young sailor stand and approach the trial area. He also noticed that the observer area was now full, mostly with uniformed naval personnel from the *Ford*.

After being sworn and seated, Andrews was approached by Marshall. "Please state your name and duty station.

"Quartermaster Third Class David Andrews, stationed aboard the USS *Ford*, sir."

"And were you in that duty status on the afternoon of September sixth?"

"Yes, sir."

"In what capacity?"

"We were at general quarters and I was at my GQ station on the bridge as the talker to after-steering."

"And who was on the other end of that circuit?"

"Quartermaster Third Class Charlie Two Shoes."

"Did you know Petty Officer Two Shoes personally?"

"Of course, sir. We were shipmates."

Marshall nodded knowingly.

"During the course of that watch, did anything unusual happen with respect to your communications with Petty Officer Two Shoes?"

"Yes, sir. We were still out a little ways when Charlie asked to speak to the captain."

"Was that a normal procedure?"

"No, sir."

"How did Petty Officer Two Shoes sound?"

"He was coughing and sounded hoarse."

"And what did you do?"

"I relayed his request to the captain and gave the captain the phones."

"By the captain, of course, you mean Commander Dunne?"

"Yes, sir."

"When Commander Dunne took the phones, were you near enough to hear what he said?"

"Most of it, yes, sir."

Marshall raised a finger of caution. "Now, this is very important, David. What did Commander Dunne say? Take a moment if you need to refresh your memory. Try and remember any exact words you heard."

Andrews nodded before he spoke. "I heard Commander Dunne ask Charlie if he had contacted sick bay."

"Have you any idea why Commander Dunne asked that question?"

Soto's interruption was immediate. "Objection."

"Sustained," Rarick replied.

Marshall did not seem to be concerned. "Please tell the court what else Commander Dunne said."

"Well, he answered 'no' once, but I don't know what

to, and then he said, 'We're only a few miles from the harbor.' ''

"That's good, David. What else?"

Andrews had to think for a moment before replying, "He told the OOD to send Chief Martinez to after-steering."

"And who is Chief Martinez?"

"She's a chief hospital corpsman, sir."

"Did not he also direct the officer-of-the-deck to order Chief Martinez not to enter after-steering until he—Commander Dunne—said so?"

"Yes, sir, he said that."

Marshall allowed himself a small triumphant smile and a pointed glance toward Joshua Dunne. "Anything else, David?"

"Ah . . . nothing else to Charlie, but I believe that I heard him order the OOD to have damage control seal the hatch into after-steering."

"*Seal* the hatch? David, think very carefully. You say you *believe* you heard the order. We need a more positive statement than that. Did you or did you not hear the order?"

Andrews looked at Dunne, his eyes saying *I'm sorry, Captain*. "Yes, sir."

"And what did you take that to mean?"

Soto interrupted again with, "Objection. Calls for a conclusion by the witness."

Rarick shook his head. "Overruled. The trial counsel is asking for an impression, not a conclusion."

Marshall glanced at Rarick. "Thank you, Your Honor. David, would you like me to repeat the question?"

"No, sir. I gathered that meant to secure the hatch in such a way that no one could enter after-steering."

"Or leave?"

"Yes, sir."

"Anything else, David?"

"Not to Charlie. Commander Dunne handed the

phones back to me and said, 'Don't put them on.' Then he told the bridge watch that Charlie was dying."

Marshall seemed to be waiting for more. "David, when we spoke before, when I interviewed you on the *Ford*, didn't you say that Commander Dunne said he didn't want the rest of the crew to know that Petty Officer Two Shoes had died?"

"Objection. The trial council is leading the witness."

"Overruled. The witness may answer the question."

"Oh, yes, sir. He said that."

"One last thing, David. When Commander Dunne handed back the phones to you and told you not to put them on, wasn't he severing communications with after-steering? Wasn't he denying Petty Officer Two Shoes any further opportunity to seek help?"

"On that circuit, yes, sir. But there . . ."

Marshall held up his hand. "That's all, David. Thank you." As he walked back to his chair, he spoke to Soto, "Your witness."

Soto removed his gum and placed it in its wrapper as he stood. "Petty Officer Andrews, did you observe Commander Dunne saying anything else into the sound-powered phones, words that you could not hear?"

"Yes, sir, he spoke a couple times in a low voice. I couldn't hear what he said."

"Thank you. And the sound-powered phones that were your communications link to Petty Officer Two Shoes—was anyone else on that circuit?"

"No, sir. That's the last-ditch circuit in case battle damage takes out all the rest."

"I see. Then, under normal circumstances, Petty Officer Two Shoes had other means of communications available. Is that correct?"

"Yes, sir."

"When Commander Dunne handed you back the phones and said not to put them on, there were other means by which Two Shoes could have contacted the bridge if he had wanted to or would have been able to; is that not correct?''

"Yes, sir.''

Soto approached the witness. "Then Commander Dunne was not, as the trial counsel has insinuated, denying Petty Officer Two Shoes an opportunity to seek help?''

"No, sir, I was trying to explain that to the commander when he cut me off.''

It was Soto's time to smile. *Thank you, David, That's exactly what I'd hoped you would say.* "Thank you, Petty Officer Andrews. That's all I have, Your Honor.''

"You may step down. Call your next witness, Commander Marshall.''

"The prosecution calls Chief Hospital Corpsman Juanita Martinez.''

Martinez took the stand, was sworn in, and stated her name, rank, and duty assignment.

Marshall stood before her. "Chief Martinez, you heard the previous witness recount the circumstances surrounding the death of Petty Officer Two Shoes, did you not?''

"Yes, sir, I did.''

"When you were ordered to proceed from sick bay to after-steering, what were your precise instructions?''

"The officer-of-the-deck ordered me to proceed to after-steering but I was not to enter the compartment until I received further word.''

"Did that seem strange to you?''

"No, sir. Not in the light of what was going on. I was quite aware of the danger of personally treating anyone affected by the biological agent.''

Marshall briefly referred to his notes. "When Chief Sulley was found dead in the forward anchor chain locker, you transferred his body into a body bag.''

"Yes, sir, but I was wearing protective clothing.''

"And you were not when you proceeded to after-steering?"

"No, sir."

"Why was that?"

Martinez was obviously uncomfortable with the question. "I reacted too fast, I suppose. I was halfway to after-steering before I realized I did not have on my NBC gear. And then, I had been ordered not to enter the compartment."

"When you arrived at the compartment, could you hear any signs of life from within?"

Martinez glanced nervously at Joshua Dunne before responding and then her answer was barely audible, "Yes, sir."

Captain Rarick leaned toward her. "Chief, please speak up so the court may hear your reply."

Martinez nodded. Her eyes were moist. "Yes, sir, I could hear Charlie Two Shoes moving about."

"And what else?"

Martinez seemed to apologize to Dunne with her eyes. "He was gagging and apparently trying to catch his breath."

"He was dying," Marshall suggested.

Soto stood. "Objection. Speculative, and the trial counsel is leading the witness."

"I'll rephrase, your honor," Marshall quickly interjected. "Were you concerned that he was dying?"

"Yes."

"Did you want to medically attend to him?"

"Yes, sir."

"Why didn't you?"

"I was under orders not to enter the compartment."

Marshall glared at the defense table. "In other words, Chief Martinez, in obeying the order from the bridge, an order that was relayed from Commander Dunne that you were not to enter after-steering, you were denying Petty

Officer Two Shoes the right to medical attention. Is that correct?"

Martinez did not want to answer. Marshall repeated, "Is that correct, Chief Martinez? You were denying him the right to medical attention?"

Reluctantly, Martinez answered, "Yes, sir."

"In obedience to Commander Dunne's order?"

"Yes, sir."

"Thank you, Chief Martinez. Your witness, Commander Soto."

Soto approached the witness. "Take a moment, Chief."

Martinez was on the verge of losing her composure. She used a handkerchief to wipe her eyes, then sat erect. "I'm all right, sir."

"Would you like a short recess, Chief?" Rarick asked. His bladder would appreciate one. To his disappointment, Martinez answered in the negative.

Soto asked, "Chief Martinez, what was the condition of Chief Sulley's body when you first saw him?"

"Ah . . . he was bloated and his skin seemed to be bleached."

"As were the bodies of the *Salinika* crew?"

Marshall sprung from his chair. "Objection, Chief Martinez at no time saw a member of the *Salinika*'s crew. Her only knowledge was hearsay."

Rarick agreed. "Sustained."

Soto took a different tack. "Chief, did Lieutenant Kohn or Lieutenant Childress, who had been on board the *Salinika*, describe the bodies of the crew to you?"

"Lieutenant Kohn did, sir."

"And did Chief Sulley's body fit her description?"

Marshall loudly objected. "No, sir, Soto! Objection, Your Honor. Defense counsel is thinly using subterfuge to get the witness to answer a question that the court has ruled improper."

Rarick was clearly disturbed by Marshall's manner.

"Overruled. Defense counsel is direct with the question and it can be directly answered."

Soto repeated his question.

"Yes, sir, it did."

"Then, you had every reason to believe that Petty Officer Two Shoes had come down with the same contaminant?"

Marshall again stated, "Objection. Chief Martinez could not see the body of Two Shoes. She had no idea what it looked like. It could have been any illness. It could have been a treatable illness. It could have—"

Rarick's eyes conveyed extreme displeasure as he interrupted. "I would advise trial counsel that an objection is not an opportunity for a lengthy argument. If I do not understand the objection, I will ask for elaboration." To Soto's surprise, Rarick added, "Objection sustained."

Disgusted with Marshall's repeated objections, Soto tried again. "Were you *afraid*, Chief, that Petty Officer Two Shoes was a victim of the biological contaminant?"

"Afraid, sir, in the sense that I was worried."

"I see. That's fine. Now, I ask you, if Charlie Two Shoes were a victim of the biological agent, could you have treated him?"

"No, sir. I had no antidote to any known biological warfare agent. We were returning from a routine training exercise. There was no need to stock such items before sailing."

"Was that your decision?"

"No, sir. That was in Warrant Officer Abbot's area."

"The ship's medical officer?"

"Yes, sir."

Soto was pleased to see that Martinez was warming to his method of questioning; he knew she had been uncomfortable as a prosecution witness. For some reason, he pulled his next question out of thin air, "Chief, did you make any effort to enter the compartment?"

Martinez glanced once more at Dunne for she knew

her answer would indicate she had violated her captain's order. "Yes, sir, I did."

Bingo! Soto said to himself. *Martinez had tried to render medical assistance!* He wasn't sure how he would use the admission. It didn't change the status of Dunne's order. But he decided to fish a little further. "What did you do?"

"I tried to open the hatch."

"And?"

"It was blocked."

Blocked! Soto was elated. The gods were with him. "How could that be?"

"Apparently, Charlie Two Shoes had jammed the dogs."

"Then, how was it finally opened?"

"The damage control party forced it open at Pearl after we had moored. They had to work with the latching handle a while. Whatever was obstructing it, fell away."

"You know that for a fact?"

"Yes, sir, I was there with the medical team that boarded the *Ford* and removed the body."

"So, Petty Officer Two Shoes was *resisting* medical help?"

Marshall was not about to let that question past.

"Objection. Calls for a conclusion."

"Sustained," Rarick intoned.

Soto could care less. He had planted the thought in the minds of the court.

"Thank you, Chief. No further questions."

Rarick could see Marshall fidgeting. "Re-direct, Commander Marshall?"

"Yes, sir. Chief Martinez, if you had been able to enter the compartment, what would you have done?"

"I would have just been there, I guess. Maybe my presence would have been of some comfort."

"Then, Commander Dunne's order not to enter would

have denied Petty Officer Two Shoes even that small assistance?''

''Yes, sir.''

''And isn't the right to die with dignity inalienable in our society?''

Soto wanted to object but knew that Rarick would overrule. The question was idealistic but legitimate even in Soto's mind.

Martinez answered, ''I believe it is.''

''Thank you, Chief. I have nothing further.''

Rarick asked, ''Commander Soto, do you have any recross-examination?''

''I do not, Your Honor.''

''You may step down,'' Rarick advised. He was not feeling too well. Maybe the pills he was taking for his prostate trouble had a side effect. ''How many more witnesses do you have, Commander Marshall?''

''Possibly four, Your Honor, plus I wish to admit some material evidence.''

''Then, this might be an appropriate time to adjourn. Our lunch recess would put us back here after two, and I believe you would appreciate a full day to further develop your argument.''

Marshall would have preferred to continue after lunch regardless of the late hour, but it was obvious that Rarick did not share that feeling. ''Thank you, Your Honor,'' Marshall replied. It never hurt to stroke the judge.

Hearing no objection from Soto, Rarick declared, ''This court is adjourned until oh-eight-hundred tomorrow morning.'' He accented his decision with a smack of his gavel.

The marine behind him came to attention. ''All rise.''

Dunne and Soto watched the judge and members file out of the courtroom, spent several minutes receiving the well wishes of the *Ford* crewmen and Lt. Kohn who were present in the room, and walked up one level to a small conference room that had been set aside for their use.

Soto produced a couple of Diet Cokes from the machine in the passageway. "I'm surprised Judge Rarick broke it up so early. I figured a couple hours after lunch."

Dunne didn't know if he should be surprised or not. "Well, it's thirteen-twelve; maybe he has a lunch date."

"Ha! Captain Rarick has a wife of thirty years and a grown son who is in private practice in Norfolk. The judge's pushing fifty-five and normally would be in mandatory retirement, but he's one of the best judicial authorities in the navy. He's rough and tough and hard to bluff, but he's fair and wise and knows the law like his wife's body. He'll keep this court on the straight and narrow, which is something Tom Marshall is beginning to find out."

"Did we win or lose today?"

"I'd be pleased if we broke even. You never know how the court takes opening statements. Our cross-examination of the witnesses went well, but if I had to call the race at this point I would say Marshall is out ahead of us by a long nose. Don't overly concern yourself about it. That's par for the course. If we have to, we'll play catch-up when he runs out of steam."

Together, the two men reviewed the morning's proceedings and the plans for the next day. By four in the afternoon, they went their separate ways—Soto to fine-tune his thoughts and Dunne to find his wife.

Annie had already left Tripler, and he suspected she was back at the Barber's Point cottage. When he arrived there forty minutes later, she had a cold beer waiting for him. "How'd it go?" she asked.

Dunne sat beside her on the lanai. "Good, I think. We only got through two witnesses."

"I thought it was early for you."

"What did the Tripler crew say?"

"Oh, we mainly went over my records and they called Doctor Fisher back at Balboa. CAT scan was broken. They poked some holes and took some blood and urine. When I left, they were smiling and telling me not to overdo any activity. If I'm still here on Oahu in a week, they want another CAT scan. But, Josh, I feel better than I have in so long a time. I picked up a pizza at the NEX. I'm keeping it warm in the oven. What say we just stay here and watch the water?"

"Sounds good to me."

With some effort, Annie Dunne pulled her deck chair closer to her husband. "Maybe later, we can give my battered constitution a real test. Ever made love to a bald-headed bag of bones before?"

Dunne took her hand. "In my dreams, a thousand times."

"Oooh, let's eat."

23

The long line of traffic was passing slowly out of the gate. Jamal Hussein sat quietly in his car on the side of the Kamehameha Highway extension that stretched past the gate toward the *Arizona* Memorial Visitors Center. After a short while, a small white panel truck approached the gate. On its sides, in multicolored letters, were the words: ANDY'S CANDIES. The driver was about Jamal's age and build but not quite as darkly colored. Jamal could live with that. The sentry, a civilian guard, merely glanced at his outstretched hand. "Another day, another dollar, eh, Andy?"

"You know it." The driver pulled back his pass and placed it behind the sunshade above his head.

Jamal eased his car out and fell in behind the candy van. The driver always took the same route home to a small apartment in Pearl City. Jamal followed at a discreet distance; there was no danger he would lose his quarry despite the heavy rush hour traffic. Jamal was now familiar with the route. As he drove, he mentally reviewed his notes on the man.

The man was the sole proprietor of a nice little candy machine business, servicing the Pearl Harbor Naval Base complex and several of its satellite activities. Three days of very boring surveillance and tracking had revealed that the man arrived and left by the same gate every day and at about the same times. Andy the Candy Man appeared to be single.

Jamal's other tasks were also largely completed. From reading the newspaper, Jamal knew the building number of the military courtroom. From *The Military in Hawaii*, a soft-cover welcoming book that was sent to every incoming serviceman and easily available in local hotels and temporary living quarters that catered to the military, he had a detailed street map of all military facilities in the islands, and he had already circled the place of the court-martial.

Today, he followed the candy truck with a more sinister purpose. He waited near the man's apartment until the candy man returned from his dinner alone. Soon Jamal knocked on his door.

The man opened it. Curious, he asked, "Yes?"

"Hello, is that your candy truck parked out front?"

"Yes, it is."

"I live just down the street. I noticed some teenage children walking around it, and I just wanted to make sure it was locked. They looked suspicious."

"Oh, thank you very much. I always keep it locked."

"I don't know. One of them tried the door on the passenger's side and it opened. They ran away when I approached."

"Maybe I better check. I'll get my keys. Thank you."

As the man turned to retrieve his keys, he left the door ajar. He went into his bedroom and lifted them off his dresser. That was his last earthly act. Jamal had quietly followed him and grabbed him from behind. Before the man could cry out, Jamal snapped his neck with one sharp twist. As did Libidi, Jamal liked to use his blade, but this was no time for a mess.

But what was he to do with the body? The apartment was not air-conditioned. The body would begin to smell in just a day. Then he saw the perfect place to stow the fresh corpse.

Jamal waited inside until after dark, ignoring the phone when it rang the one time. Then he took one of the man's white service coats, a matching Andy's Candies cap, and his keys, and drove away in the night.

Ahmad Libidi was waiting at his apartment. "You get the truck?"

"Yes. I put the cover over it." Jamal had purchased a protective dust cover at a local auto supply store. "Tomorrow, I will scout the court and plan for how we can keep from being too conspicuous. Then, we must be there every day until our opportunity arises."

Ahmad grinned. "We will be going into the lion's den, my brother."

"Allah will provide for us."

24

"The prosecution calls Lieutenant Commander James Sessions." As he spoke, Commander Marshall looked at Dunne and Soto as if to say: *Try this one on for size, gentlemen.*

The defense, of course, was aware that Sessions was on the prosecutor's list of witnesses, but not even Dunne knew what Marshall's purpose was or what his executive officer was going to say. When asked by Soto, Dunne had replied, "As a witness, Sessions is an unknown as far as I am concerned. He has been a very good XO, carrying out my policies without exception even when he disagreed with them. I have detected some animosity but it has been mild and never surfaced when we were in the presence of any of the other crewmembers. Sessions is a good officer."

The court had convened on time and Rarick had gone right to the trial counsel for his next witness. Sessions was sworn in, took the stand, gave his name, rank, and duty station as "Acting Commanding Officer, USS *Ford.*"

Marshall started routinely. "Commander, at the time of the *Ford*'s encounter with the *Salinika*, what was your duty assignment?"

"Executive officer to Commander Dunne."

"On September fifth, in the early morning hours, where were you?"

"I was in my cabin."

"Off duty?"

"As far as an XO is ever off duty."

Marshall nodded understandingly. "Were you asleep?"

"Part of the time. We were in extremely rough weather. I had been awake for the past fifteen hours and felt I should try to get some rest. I checked with the captain and turned in about oh-two-hundred."

"What time did you get up?"

Soto was confused. "Objection, your honor. Irrelevant. I don't see where this line of questioning is headed."

"Your honor," Marshall responded, "the purpose of my interrogation will be perfectly clear in a moment, if the court pleases."

"Overruled, but get to the point, Commander."

"I will, sir. Lieutenant Commander Sessions, let's jump ahead just a bit. When Commander Dunne was considering an order to launch the helicopter to investigate the target that later turned out to be the *Salinika*, did he consult with you?"

"No, sir."

"Was that normal?"

"Yes, sir. My primary duty was with administration, training, and discipline aboard the *Ford*. The operations officer was the logical choice for consultation and the carrying out of the captain's operational orders."

Soto could see that Rarick was becoming impatient. "Commander Marshall," Rarick interrupted, "this court is composed of senior naval officers. I don't believe we need an explanation of shipboard organization."

"That's not my intention, Your Honor."

"Good. Now, could we please get to the point?"

"Yes, sir. Commander, would you have launched the helicopter in such weather?"

Soto stood. "Objection. Speculative."

"Sustained."

"Your Honor, may I approach the bench?" Marshall asked.

"Yes. I was about to make the same request."

Soto joined Marshall before Rarick.

Marshall began his explanation, "Your Honor, it is the prosecution's intent to provide testimony to Commander Dunne's lack of judgement during the *Salinika* incident. It is that lack of professional judgment that led to his direct failure to obey the lawful order of the president with respect to the sinking of the *Salinika*. Lieutenant Commander Sessions is certainly a fully qualified professional surface officer, and I believe his testimony is pertinent and fully applicable to this case."

"Any comment from the defense?"

Soto shook his head. "No, Your Honor, but I am confused as to where this is leading."

Rarick sighed. "Very well, I'll allow you to continue."

Once both counsel returned, Marshall repeated his question to Sessions. "Would you have launched the helicopter?"

Sessions looked over Marshall's head at the spectators in the courtroom. "No, I would not have."

Marshall walked back to his table and picked up an inch-thick report. "Your Honor, I would like to enter into evidence a copy of the preliminary aircraft accident report conducted by FNADB—the Field Naval Aviator Disposition Board—with respect to the crash of the helicopter assigned to the *Ford* during the incident."

Rarick directed the report be handed to the court reporter and marked Navy Exhibit A.

Marshall handed a second copy to Sessions. "I direct your attention to the findings of the board; you will find them on page one-thirty-seven. Would you please read item number three under the subheading: contributing causes?"

Sessions read, "The failure of the commanding officer of the USS *Ford* to properly weigh the severity of the weather at the time of launch."

Soto passed Dunne a hastily scribbled comment. Two words: *That hurts*.

Sessions passed the report back to Marshall who turned to Soto. "Your witness, counselor."

Soto was not quite ready. "Your Honor, I have not seen that report."

Rarick looked at Marshall for an explanation. Marshall walked over and handed a copy to Soto with the explanation, "This report, Your Honor, arrived only this morning. I had not perused it myself until I arrived in the courtroom."

"You certainly had Commander Sessions at the ready," Soto complained.

"Gentlemen." Rarick followed his mild admonishment with a slight rap of his gavel. "I believe a ten-minute recess is in order to allow the defense to examine trial counsel's Exhibit A. Commander Soto, inform me if more time is needed. Court is recessed to reconvene at twenty minutes past the hour."

Rarick was barely out of the room when Soto confronted Marshall. "What kind of stunt is this?" he said angrily.

"Calm down. Let's step outside for a minute."

Soto followed Marshall out the main entrance. They stood away from several of the spectators who were taking a break. Marshall explained, "I truly did not know this would be here yet, although I admit I had asked for it from the FNADB.''

''You had an obligation to provide me with a copy immediately.''

''I have an obligation to prosecute the navy's case. This was not deliberate.''

''Then why the hell was Commander Sessions so conveniently handy?''

''He was my next scheduled witness. It's exactly as I told Judge Rarick in your presence—I called him for testimony relative to Dunne's judgment. The arrival of the report this morning is fortuitous, I grant you, but that's all it is.''

Soto turned to keep any of the others from seeing his face. ''Bullshit, Marshall. It's Hollywood stuff and you damn well know it.''

Marshall's self-satisfying smile was indicative of his pleasure that Soto seemed upset. ''Get with it, counselor. You have a loser for a client. Don't try to blame that on me. He killed six men in that crash.''

''Check the charges, Marshall. He's not on trial for manslaughter. Even if he were, your actions would still be out of order.''

Marshall wondered just how angry was Soto. Perhaps he could goad the defense counsel into doing something foolish. Maybe later.

When Soto returned, Dunne asked, ''What went on out there?''

Soto grinned, making sure Marshall could not see his face. ''I tried to pull his chain. He's a cocky one but smooth.'' Soto glanced behind them. ''I thought Mrs. Dunne was going to be here today.''

''She will. She wanted to sleep in.'' Dunne smiled to himself. No need to tell Soto why.

Soto busied himself, thumbing through the report.

''All rise!''

Rarick mounted the platform behind the bench, rapped

his gavel, and announced, "This court is again in session. Lieutenant Commander Sessions, I remind you that you are still under oath."

Marshall resumed his examination. "Commander Sessions, let's move ahead to when Commander Dunne made his decision to fire on the *Salinika*. Did you express any doubts you may have had to him?"

"Yes, sir. I reminded the captain that we did not yet have the president's release from his order not to sink the *Salinika*.

"The president's—or commander-in-chief's—order?"

"Yes, sir."

"What was Commander Dunne's response?"

"He replied that he was assuming responsibility for the attack."

Marshall wanted a repeat of that statement. "He what?"

"He was assuming responsibility for the attack."

Marshall had moved behind his table. "Thank you very much, Commander. I have no further questions for this witness, your honor, but I reserve the right to recall Lieutenant Commander Sessions at a later time."

"Commander Soto, cross-examination?"

Soto approached Sessions. "Isn't one of the obligations, indeed one of the *duties*, of an executive officer to advise his captain of any doubts he has about an operation?"

"Yes, I suppose."

"You *suppose*? My God, Commander, you've been a naval officer for fifteen years; surely you understand your duties."

"I do. I did advise him that we were still under the order not to take any action against the *Salinika*."

"But before that, you said nothing about your concerns with respect to launching the helicopter."

"I testified as to why."

"That you did. You graduated from the U.S. Naval Academy a year earlier than Commander Dunne, is that correct?"

"Yes."

"And yet, Commander Dunne is now a full year ahead of you in seniority."

"That is correct."

"Why is that, Commander?"

"Commander Dunne is an exceptional officer. He was deep-selected."

"And you were not?"

Sessions indicated his offense at the question by glaring at Soto. "No, I was not."

"Does that bother you?"

Marshall objected.

"Overruled," Rarick declared.

"Does that bother you?" Soto repeated.

"No."

"If you had doubts about the safety of a launch of the helicopter, why didn't you express them to your captain?"

"He had his operations officer available and the pilot of the helicopter."

"And you felt that negated your obligation as executive officer?"

"No! I just felt that their advice was more authoritative than mine."

"You didn't withhold your counsel did you, Commander Sessions, because you were jealous of Commander Dunne and would not at all have been disappointed if he made a bad decision?"

Marshall was instantly on his feet. "Objection! Irrelevant and immaterial. Despite any advice, Commander Dunne made his own decision."

"Sustained."

"I withdraw the question. Commander, do you know what recommendations the operations officer, Lieutenant

Commander McGregor, and the pilot, Lieutenant Kohn, gave to Commander Dunne with respect to launching the helicopter?''

"No, I do not.''

"Are you aware that in the final analysis, it is the pilot's decision as to whether a certain flight will be made or not, and thus it is his or her ultimate responsibility?''

"I understand that it is.''

"It always has been, Commander, and in referring to Exhibit A, I would like you to read under the same subheading: contributing causes, item one.''

It took a moment for Sessions to find the place. Then he read aloud, "Failure of the pilot to properly evaluate the weather prior to launch.''

"So, it appears that the pilot had agreed to launch, does it not?''

Marshall did not stand but held up a hand. "Objection, calls for a conclusion on the part of the witness.''

Soto was ready. "No, the report specifies that the pilot *had* agreed to the launch.

Marshall countered, "Then cite the report, not my witness.''

Rarick ruled, "Sustained.''

"Would you give me a moment, Your Honor?'' Soto requested, searching for the appropriate page.

Rarick appeared undisturbed by the request.

Soto resumed. "On page twelve, under the part of the report that is headed Sequence of Events, third paragraph from the top, and I quote: 'Lieutenant Kohn stated that she would ready the aircraft for launch and then abort prior to liftoff if the weather seemed too severe for safe flight.' End quote. We know that subsequently Lieutenant Kohn did fly, thus it is apparent to *me* that she considered the flying conditions to be safe. I believe that is consistent with item one of the contributing causes previously read. Do you agree, Commander?''

Despite some confusion, Sessions decided, "Yes."

"Let's turn our attention now to the matter of the death of Petty Officer Two Shoes."

Marshall strenuously objected. "The commander is my witness, Your Honor, and at no time in my examination did I refer to the death of Petty Officer Two Shoes."

"Approach the bench," Rarick directed.

Soto and Marshall did so.

"Gentlemen," Rarick began, "we have two charges here and they are quite dissimilar. I feel there is an obligation on your part to present the arguments in as orderly a fashion as possible. Commander Marshall, is it your intention to call Mister Sessions later with testimony on the death of the petty officer?"

"Yes, Your Honor."

"I admit we have a procedural problem, but let's solve it before we go any further. For the remainder of this trial, whenever a witness is called who will testify to both charges, he or she will be examined on the civil rights charge first, then the failure-to-obey charge. That also applies to cross-examination, redirect, and recross. Do either of you have any difficulty with that?"

"No, sir," replied both counsel.

"Very well. Despite the fact that this one examination is just the reverse, I would like you, Commander Marshall, to redirect on the subject of the civil rights charge—including any redirect on the failure-to-obey charge if you have anything. Then, Commander Soto, you can conclude with your recross. I believe that will put us back on the right track."

Marshall returned to a position before Sessions. "Commander Sessions, were you present at the discussions held between Commander Dunne and the ship's officers on September fifth after Lieutenant Kohn and her crew had identified and conducted an aerial examination of the *Salinika*?"

"Yes, sir."

"Please tell the court about that meeting."

"The captain had decided that we should board the *Salinika* and see if we could render any assistance."

"Why was that?"

"It was reported by Lieutenant Kohn that crewmen on deck were dead, possibly from a disease, and that the *Salinika* was steaming on a collision course with the island of Oahu. The captain felt we should change her course and speed toward open water."

"Did you agree with that?"

"All except the captain's request to bring back a body."

"Did you voice that objection?"

"Yes, I did. I was afraid that whatever killed the crew of the *Salinika* would be brought back to the *Ford*."

"And that is exactly what happened, is it not?"

"Yes, sir."

"In your judgment, was Commander Dunne's request to recover a body a bad decision?"

Soto objected. "Calls for a conclusion, Your Honor."

Rarick disagreed. "Overruled."

Sessions replied, "In retrospect, yes, but at the—"

Marshall did not wait for Sessions to finish. "When Petty Officer Two Shoes called from after-steering and spoke to Commander Dunne, where were you?"

"In sick bay."

"Did you hear any of the conversation?"

"No."

"Wasn't your GQ station in after-steering with Quartermaster Two Shoes?"

"Yes, but the captain had stationed me in the sick bay. We were not in a combatant situation."

"Thereby leaving Two Shoes alone?"

"Yes."

"Were you aware of Commander Dunne's order to

the OOD to send a medical party back to after-steering?''

''Yes.''

''And were you also aware that Commander Dunne had ordered the medical team not to enter after-steering unless he so directed?

''Yes.''

''No further questions.''

Soto addressed Rarick. ''I have no further questions, Your Honor.''

Rarick was surprised. ''You appeared to have, before I halted the proceedings.''

''The trial counsel has merely recovered ground he established with Chief Martinez, Your Honor. It's basically duplicate testimony. He has made no new argument that needs rebuttal.'' Soto knew his last statement would infuriate Marshall.

Rarick instructed Sessions, ''You may step down.'' He rapped his gavel. It was time to pump bilges. ''Court will recess until forty past the hour.''

''All rise!''

Before he sat down, Dunne turned to see if Annie were present. She was sitting directly behind him, between Lt. Kohn and Lt. Holly, wearing a flowered muumuu and colorful turban in place of her wig. ''My, you look festive,'' commented Dunne.

''Thought it might cheer you up,'' Annie remarked.

''Been here long?''

''Long enough to see you can be in deep trouble. That trial counsel handles himself well.''

''I'm in good hands,'' Dunne commented. ''This is Commander Soto. David, my wife, Annie.''

Annie offered her hand and kidded, ''I'll reserve judgment on you until this is over.''

Soto replied, ''Fair enough.''

''Can I offer anyone a candy bar?'' Annie asked.

Dunne took one. ''Where'd you get these?''

"There's a panel truck outside. Andy's Candies. Catchy, huh? I just walked over and bought them from the driver. He actually seemed reluctant to sell them to me. I just wanted something sweet."

Dunne rose and motioned for his wife to follow him. In a spot to themselves he asked, "Have you talked to your father lately?"

"Why should I?"

"Annie, he provides you with a car and driver. He pulled all sorts of strings to get you here. He made arrangements at Tripler."

"And he court-martialed my husband."

"We've been over that. He had to."

"There must have been some other way."

"No, Annie. I was really furious at first. But after I heard the facts, I knew it was to keep me from the Beltway wolves. There is obvious presidential interest in this trial, Annie. We live in a political world. You must not blame your father."

"I'm just so worried."

"Then make your peace with Blackjack. You know he's hurting, too."

"Why doesn't he contact us, then?"

"He's the convening authority of this court. He has to maintain his distance. The media would get a case of the double drools if they could uncover any signs of influence on this court. It's really a sensitive situation. You know that."

Annie took a bite of her candy bar. "I'll think about it."

"You'll feel better. We best take our seats."

"All rise."

Rarick settled himself.

Marshall remained standing. "Your Honor, I have a deposition from CINCPACFLT that states he relayed the president's order to refrain from any aggressive action toward the *Salinika* to Commander Dunne at 052313Z

September. I would like to offer it as Navy Exhibit B. A copy has been provided to the defense.''

Rarick took the deposition and handed it to the recorder.

''I offer in further evidence Navy Exhibit C. This packet of certified copies of official message traffic between the *Ford* and USPACOM and CINCPACFLT as well as a message from CINCPACOM to SECDEF. The defense has these copies as well, and I hereby provide copies to each member of the court.

''Finally, I offer as Navy Exhibit D a certified copy of the *Ford*'s official log on the date September fifth.''

Rarick received each of the exhibits and had them passed to the court reporter.

Marshall walked over to face the members of the court.

Soto whispered very low into Dunne's ear, ''Here come the big guns.''

Marshall began, ''I call the members attention to Exhibit B. Please note the time: 052313 ZULU. Dunne was well aware of his commander-in-chief's order from that point on. Please note the times on the messages in Exhibit C: the presidential order to sink the *Salinika* was issued at 060130 ZULU. The chairman of the Joint Chiefs reported to SECDEF that the *Salinika* had been sunk at 060135 ZULU. Finally, and this is the moment of truth, look at Exhibit D, the *Ford*'s log, at the entry opposite the time: 060126 ZULU, *four minutes* before the president issued his order. You will see it reads: fired two Harpoon missiles at terrorist ship *Salinika*. I want you to keep that four-minute differential in mind as I call the navy's next witness.''

Marshall walked to the center of the court area. ''The navy calls Vice Admiral George Bray, United States Navy, retired.''

The list of witnesses to be called by the trial counsel had been provided to Soto, and he had interviewed the admiral, but at that point the admiral had no idea why he was being subpoenaed.

The admiral was sworn in and seated. He gave his name and rank for the record.

Marshall radiated an air of confidence. He had just submitted irrefutable written evidence that Dunne had disobeyed the president's direct order. Now he would take care of any mitigating circumstances the defense could offer. "Admiral Bray, your credentials as an expert in naval tactical warfare are extensive. I will only read off a few. Please correct me if I am in error. You are a designated surface warfare officer in frigates, destroyers, and cruisers, including command of a guided-missile cruiser and the battleship *Wisconsin*. You have been on the staff of the Joint Chiefs as head of J-3, the operations directorate. You wear the Navy Cross as the result of tactical surface action during the closing days of World War II when, as a young officer, twenty-two years old, you took command of your old four-stack destroyer when all of your senior officers had been killed and fought the ship until it was shot from under you."

The admiral sat erect but showed no visible emotion. At seventy years of age, he could have passed for a man ten years younger. Marshall had requested he wear his uniform but the admiral had declined, feeling that it would intimidate the defense and the court.

"You operated in the waters around Oahu for many years did you not, Admiral?"

"Yes, I did."

"And you make your home here now?"

"On Maui."

"Are you familiar with the circumstances of the *Salinika* incident?"

"Only from the media and a conversation I had with my grandson who is on duty with the Pacific Fleet staff."

"I'm sure you are very proud of him."

Marshall walked over to an easel and removed the cloth that had been covering a large diagram of the tracks of the *Ford* and *Salinika*, from the time of the near-miss to the time of the sinking. Courses, distances, and times were lettered at strategic locations. The X, marking the sunken *Salinika*, was just inside the 2,000 fathom curve and the ship's sunken depth was recorded: 10,650 feet. The distance from the X to the southern coast of Oahu was designated 11.8 miles. "Admiral, can you see the chart clearly?"

"Yes, I can see it fine."

"In the *Ford*'s after-action report, it states that the speed of the *Salinika* at the time of the *Ford*'s attack was fourteen knots. That computes to be 466.7 yards per minute. In four minutes, the *Salinika* would have traveled 1,867 yards, that's point nine four miles. In your expert opinion, Admiral, would that less than one mile have constituted a greater threat to the island of Oahu than was present at the point the *Salinika* was sunk?"

"Objection."

Every eye in the room was on Soto. "Your Honor, the defense respectfully recognizes the expertise of Admiral Bray in the area of surface tactical warfare, and I join with the other members of this court in considering his presence here an honor. His service is well known. However, I don't believe it is claimed that the admiral is an expert in threat analysis and that is what the trial counsel's question refers to."

"Overruled," barked Rarick.

Admiral Bray also seemed to take exception to Soto. Soto sat back down. It had been worth a shot.

"To answer your question, Commander," Bray began while looking directly at Soto, "the difference would have been infinitesimal.

"Then, Admiral, in your expert opinion, did the commander-in-chief issue his order to sink the *Salinika* in a timely manner?"

"Yes, he did."

"Was there any overriding necessity, from a tactical standpoint, that you are aware of, for Commander Dunne to jump the gun in sinking the *Salinika*?"

"No."

"Your witness, defense."

Soto approached Admiral Bray and stood very close. "Admiral, in your expert opinion, *could* there have been any overriding necessity, one that you are *not* aware of?"

Admiral Bray pursed his lips and stroked one side of his full gray mustache. "I suppose so."

"No further questions, Admiral. Thank you."

"Is that all you're going to ask me?"

Soto stepped back a pace.

Admiral Bray shook a finger at him. "Young man, you have the reputation and future of a fellow officer in your hands and I've just offered damaging testimony!"

"Admiral," Rarick quickly interrupted, "you're excused, sir."

Bray gave Rarick a very disapproving look, then came out charging from behind the witness stand. He started to exit the court but said aside to Dunne as he passed, "Good luck to you, Commander, you'll need it with that idiot of a defense counsel!"

Rarick grabbed his lowered head with both hands and shook it. "Reporter, strike those last comments from the record. The court will disregard them." When he raised his head, everyone in the room was in disorder, some even laughing, including Soto and Dunne. Rarick banged his gavel. "Order . . . order . . . ten-minute recess." There was no way his bladder could retain its contents under the humor of the situation.

About the time Admiral Bray went stalking out of the CINCPACFLT courtroom, FBI Senior Agent Jason Orr was sitting deep in thought, studying material he had

chalked on a green board in his office. With him was
Captain Davey Isaka, the HPD liaison officer assigned
to Orr. The men were puzzling over the whereabouts of
who appeared to be two Middle East terrorists.

"Okay, Davey," Orr said at the end of a noticeable
exhale, "let's go over it, again." He prefaced his review
with a statement, "If we assume these two bastards are
connected with the *Salinika* incident, they arrived
sometime after the sixth because the *Salinika* was not
sunk until the fifth—unless they were already here,
which I doubt." He began referencing the chalked remarks as he continued. "They surfaced as Jews at the
Harbor House. One made contact with Johnny Wu by
way of the whore on Hotel Street and purchased a
weapon from Wu. Later, Wu was found dead in the
whore's room where, according to her, the Jew had returned and met with Wu a second time.

"We checked all the car rentals from September fifth
through the day of Wu's death. Twenty-three had been
rented to clients with probable Jewish surnames. All but
one checked out okay; a Hertz Taurus was rented by a
Solomon Weisman on the sixth. That was the name of
the registered guest at the Harbor Arms, the whore's
client and the murderer of Wu. We have an all-points
out on the Taurus, right?"

"Correct. Nothing yet."

"Next item: we raided room one-seventeen at the
Harbor House on a tip from the working girl. Nothing,
except for the missing newspaper clipping.

"Just a day later, the maid finds the couple in two-
seventeen slaughtered. In the bathroom sink, black
whiskers. The dead male was a blond. The bastards
shaved; Weisman was clean-shaven when he killed Wu.
So, they have a new identity." Orr shook his head in
disgust. "The fuckers were right there under our noses
all the time."

"They got balls."

"They're pros. Quite possibly, came to the island without a weapon and easily procured one. Wu's eyes were punctured and he was killed by a single chop to his throat that crushed his windpipe. They've changed identities and relocated. And I'll wager my pension they've ditched the Taurus. That's our best bet; we have to find that car. Barring that, we have to try and anticipate their target. That's a bitch. The whole island is covered with military bases."

Captain Isaka was staring at a map of Oahu on Orr's office wall. "What if we are looking at a continuation of the biological attack? Our water supply, for instance. They would need only a minute amount of the agent and could easily have brought it in through customs. Hell, in a bottle of shaving lotion, for example."

"God, that's all we would need. It's possible but I think unlikely. They came from Frankfurt; left on the day after the ship was intercepted and sunk. They would most probably have to have had some of the agent pre-positioned. I don't buy that. They're here to blow up something or kill somebody, maybe a lot of somebodies. And I have a hunch they want to make quite a media splash."

"Number-one military man is Admiral Paterson."

"Possibly."

"Commander Dunne?"

Orr's nose wrinkled; it always did that when he was confused. "Possibly. Dunne's a logical target and the person directly responsible for discovering the nature of the *Salinika* and sinking it. But maybe too logical. They may have torn the picture from the *Advertiser* to throw us off. That might leave the *Ford*, but it's too hard to hit while berthed at the naval base. One thing to our advantage is that we've been able to keep this quiet. The bastards know we acted on Wu's tip, but the media bought the domestic disturbance cover for the raid at the

Harbor Arms. The terrorists, however, don't know our level of effort.''

''You think they might try to hit Dunne at the trial?''

Orr shook his head. ''I doubt it. First, they would have to get on the base. They might be able to do that, but Dunne's surrounded by people. Navy security has five marines assigned to the court building. I have two agents monitoring the court-martial. It would be easier to take him while he's on the road between the naval station and Barber's Point. It's open freeway most of the way and the feeder road to the air station has a number of good ambush spots. So, we have a car covering him every day, around the clock. They can't get to Dunne.''

''I'll see if I can get a couple more uniforms pulled for the Taurus search.''

''Good. That'll be our next clue as to where they may have gone and possibly their intentions. Any questions?''

Isaka answered, ''Their one weapon; terrorists usually prefer weapons of mass destruction, car bombs, for example.''

''I suspect these two are elite assassins, and when it comes time to strike, it'll most probably be suicidal. They only need one weapon if they do it right. The strike will be clever and hard to combat even if we're ready. Hell, we can't even protect the president of the United States one hundred percent. History has proven that.''

25

Captain Rarick had extended the recess over lunch to give the court and spectators time to recover from the humor of Admiral Bray's out-of-order comments. The feisty admiral had completely disrupted the proceedings, and Rarick did not want the change of mood to dilute the importance of the trial counsel's examination of witnesses.

Captain Dutch Fargo and the other members of the court decided on lunch at the "O" Club and phoned ahead to insure they would have a private room, although each had subsequently gone through the buffet line in the main dining room. Now, they sat with their iced tea and coffee awaiting transportation back to the courtroom. Fargo rose and shut the door. "This might be a good time to discuss several things. We have something of a circus going on, and although Judge Rarick is keeping a steady hand on the helm, we must not let ourselves get caught up in anything other than the evidence and testimony of the trial."

Commander Dice added, "It makes for some excitement, I must admit that, but I'm not having any problem with the theatrics as his honor has referred to them.''

"Marshall has made some good points, despite his grandstanding. He probably does well back inside the Beltway," Captain Duke Wayne observed.

"Soto is handling him," Captain Hank Billings declared.

"Well," Captain Buck Jones interjected, "I would say both counselors are on their feet and well prepared. We may very well have a tough decision here when the time comes."

"I agree with Buck," Billings added. "I thought we had a cut-and-dried case when we sat, but now I'm having reservations."

"How about you, Duke?" Fargo asked.

"I have a problem. I don't want to bring it up until we start official deliberations, and at the moment I have an open mind. There are some very critical considerations that will warrant discussion, and you all may not like to hear what I have to say."

Fargo turned to Dice. "Mary Margaret?"

"I'm like Duke. This is not shaping up as what I thought would be an uncomplicated trial. Marshall rubs me the wrong way, but he is damn good. He knows the law."

Jones disagreed. "Civil law, maybe. But military?"

"What's the difference?" Fargo asked. "It should be all the same."

Jones elaborated. "In civil law, or criminal law, you have a culprit. Dunne isn't a culprit and certainly not a criminal. He's a poor bastard that went in harm's way, did an outstanding job, and now has his testicles caught in the wringer because of a technicality—excuse me, Commander."

Dice seemed to bristle. "I am fully aware of the sometimes sordid details of male anatomy, although I seldom hear them discussed with such emphasis. And I should add that I wouldn't call the deaths of his men a technicality.''

"It was an operational loss, Mary," Jones responded.

"I'm fully aware of that, Captain. I've been there.''

Jones did not like the retort. "I know you have. I didn't mean anything by that.''

Fargo held up a hand. "We're a bit tired. There will be time to disagree later.''

Dice knew she had jumped too fast and too hard. "I'm sorry, Buck, if I may still call you that.''

Jones had settled down also. "Captain-elect, you certainly can. I apologize. You can kiss me on the lips if you want.''

Dice smiled. "Drinks and dinner first. Sexual harrassment charges later.'' ''

"Oh, jeeeeeze . . .'' Jones moaned through mock agony.

"'You know,'' Billings said, "this may be Blackjack Paterson's court, but the commander-in-chief is watching these proceedings. I don't propose to let that interfere with my judgment or decision. And I know you folks don't either. But we do need to be sure we come up with a solid verdict, one based purely on the evidence and testimony. The fact that Dunne is an outstanding officer and a damned good combat sailor *and a shipmate* may make our decision hard as hell.''

"But, Hank, that's what we're here for. That's why we are a jury of Dunne's peers,'' Jones responded.

"True enough.'' Billings' final remark preceded a knock at the door. A young seaman stuck in his head. "Your transportation is ready, gentlemen—and, ah, Commander, sir—ma'am,'' the sailor stammered.

It was only a six-minute ride back to the courtroom.

As he continued the session, Rarick cautioned, "I would remind the court and the assembly here that they should not allow the remarks of the previous witness, after he had left the stand, to detract from the seriousness of the business at hand. The trial counsel will call his next witness."

"The navy calls Colonel Perry Dobbs."

The rotund and balding army medical officer took his seat after being sworn.

Dobbs gave his name and rank as requested by Marshall and his duty assignment as "staff pathologist, Tripler Army Hospital."

Marshall stood to the right of the witness stand, facing the members of the court. "Doctor Dobbs, I understand that your past duties have included responsibilities for monitoring U.S. developments in the area of biological warfare. Is that correct, sir?"

"Yes, I do have considerable experience in that area."

"You also performed the autopsies on Chief Gerome Sulley and Petty Officer Charlie Two Shoes, the two casualties removed from the USS *Ford*."

"Yes, I did."

"Doctor, what did you find?"

"Both died from coming in contact with a highly lethal and extraordinarily persistent biological agent."

"What was that agent?"

Dobbs looked at the five court members as he replied, "A mutant of the spore-forming bacterium, bacillus anthracis, which is commonly referred to as anthrax. As such, it is a common biological warfare agent."

"You say this particular version is a mutant?"

"Yes. Normally, anthrax manifests itself as lesions in the lungs or external ulcerating nodules. The mutated bacteria found in the two bodies has severely altered characteristics that cause it to ulcerate inward, attacking particularly the mucous lining of the mouth, throat, esophagus, stomach, and so on. The severe internal ulcerations rapidly produce a gas that is contained within the body by the closing of the throat and the lower intestine, also a mucus source. The body bloats and whitens due to—''

''I don't wish to cut your explanation short, Doctor, forgive me. But it is quite satisfactory without further elaboration. How is the disease spread?''

''Well, in nature, the unmutated bacterium develops in warm-blooded animals—cattle and sheep, for example—and it is transmitted to humans by the handling of infectious products such as meat or wool.''

''By contact, then?''

''Yes. As a biological warfare agent it can be used selectively by deliberate introduction of the bacteria into a person's food, for example. Or it can be used for mass distribution by introducing it into a liquid medium such as water or oil and spraying upon populated areas. It can also be delivered by artillery shells.''

Marshall stroked his chin. ''The mutated version that came from the *Salinika*—you mentioned that it was particularly persistent.''

''Yes. Normally, assuming it was brought to the navy ship by Lieutenant Childress, most probably by an oily coating on his protective suit, particularly the bottoms of the foot enclosures, it should have been washed off by the swirling action of the sea water. But if the medium were oil, as appears was the case, some could have remained. Sulley and the Indian lad, the swimmers who rescued Childress, wore only swimsuits and life jackets. The agent could easily have been transferred to their skin or even ingested if they swallowed some of the contaminated seawater in the struggle.''

''I see. Do we have a vaccine or antidote for the disease?''

''We have both for the unmutated version. The vaccine, among others, was given to the crew of the *Ford* as soon as they moored. We have no idea yet if the vaccine is effective against the mutated version, but we are testing. Incidentally, we do not know why the various delays occurred in Sulley and Two Shoes coming down with the disease. That's one of the unknowns about the mutated bacterium.''

''Is there any way personnel could have kept Petty Officer Two Shoes alive until the medical team boarded the *Ford*?''

''Perhaps, if they could have kept a supply of air going into the victim's lungs.''

Marshall immediately asked, ''Wouldn't a simple tracheotomy have accomplished that?''

Dobbs shook his head. ''No. The entire air passage itself would have been swollen shut and even part of the lungs. Help would require a skilled surgical team on site, and even then the outcome would have been doubtful.''

''*But*, had Commander Dunne requested such a team and it *had* been delivered to the *Ford* on the helicopter that transferred Lieutenant Childress to medical facilities ashore, could Two Shoes have been saved?''

''Possibly. There are so many factors that affect the question.''

''Thank you, Doctor. Your witness, Commander Soto.''

Soto stood. ''Doctor Dobbs, could a medical layman such as Commander Dunne have been expected to be familiar with the in-extremis treatment you just referred to?''

''No, I would think not.''

''In a practical sense, Doctor, was not Petty Officer Two Shoes doomed the moment he came in contact with the bacteria?''

''Yes, I would say so.''

''I have no further questions for this witness, Your Honor.''

Rarick leaned forward. ''You're excused, Doctor. You may call your next witness, Commander Marshall.''

Marshall stood in place. ''The navy rests, Your Honor.''

"Very well. Will the defense call its first witness?"

Soto turned to the observer area. "The defense calls Lieutenant Sheila Kohn."

After Kohn had been sworn, seated, and identified for the record, Soto spoke first to the military judge. "Your Honor, I have called Lieutenant Kohn for testimony concerning the second charge only, the matter of disobedience of a lawful order."

Rarick nodded.

"Lieutenant Kohn, you are the only eyewitness to the terrorist ship *Salinika* and the dead bodies aboard that vessel. One of the aspects of this case that we have been discussing is the matter of the professional judgment of Commander Dunne. The prosecution contends that Commander Dunne erred in judgment several times during the *Salinika* incident, and those alleged errors in judgment set a pattern of competence that forecast his decision to preempt the order of the commander-in-chief. My questions to you will concern those matters."

Soto paused and allowed his words to be absorbed. Continuing, he asked, "Did Commander Dunne consult with you before he ordered the initial launch of your crew to identify the ship involved in the early morning near-collision?"

"Yes, he did. He asked me about my evaluation of the weather with respect to safety of flight. I advised him that while the weather was marginal at the time, I felt we should attempt to ID the other ship and that I would evaluate the weather just prior to requesting launch. If I felt it was unsafe, I would advise him and abort."

"Then, subsequently, you did feel flight conditions were acceptable and you launched."

"Yes, sir."

"Did Commander Dunne's obvious desire to ID the *Salinika* have any bearing on your decision?"

"No, sir."

"You, of course, saw the *Salinika* and you saw the Forger aircraft on the foredeck—"

Marshall protested. "Objection. Defense is leading the witness."

"Overruled. But Commander Soto, I believe questions rather than statements that the witness must verify would be more in order."

"Thank you, Your Honor. Did you have visual contact with the *Salinika* and observe the Forger on its foredeck?"

"I did, sir."

"Did you observe the piping under the wing of the Forger?"

"Yes, sir."

"After you had returned the body of the Iraqi pilot to the *Ford*, were you beginning to suspect the nature of the *Salinika*?"

Marshall protested again. "Objection. It has not been established that the pilot was an Iraqi."

"Sustained."

"I withdraw the reference from my question. Would you like me to repeat it, Lieutenant?"

"No, sir. I was beginning to believe that the *Salinika* was more than just an innocent merchantman. Later on, after I was in sick bay and had a chance to see the pilot's kneeboard and papers, I came to the conclusion that it was a terrorist ship. In the wardroom meeting shortly thereafter of the captain and his officers, his analysis confirmed mine."

"Did you feel that the *Salinika* represented a threat to Oahu?"

"Absolutely, sir."

"Were you aware that the president had ordered Commander Dunne to take no action with respect to sinking the *Salinika*?"

"No, sir."

"Were you aware that an attack on the *Salinika* had taken place?"

"Yes, sir. I was in CIC."

"As an aviator who deals with rates of closure and threat analysis on a daily basis, did you believe that Commander Dunne acted too hastily?"

"No way, sir. I would have sunk the ship before then."

"In defiance of the president's order?"

"If I had been the on-scene commander, I would have sunk the *Salinika* before it reached the two thousand fathom curve, regardless."

"Why is that?"

"To ensure that no contaminant could escape the ship."

"Isn't that exactly what Commander Dunne did?"

"Yes, sir."

"Your witness, Commander Marshall."

Marshall deliberately took his time approaching the witness stand, letting his face express the pleasure with which he was going to cross-examine. "Lieutenant Kohn, what is your relationship with Commander Dunne?"

"Professional, sir. I am the officer-in-charge of the ASW helicopter detachment assigned to the *Ford*."

"Nothing else?"

"I consider Commander Dunne to be a role model."

"Nothing else?"

"What else could there be, sir? We are both naval officers; he senior, me his junior."

"He's a male, you're a female.?"

Soto jumped up. "Objection! What kind of question is that?"

Kohn's dark eyes were boring holes into Marshall's.

Rarick was quick to respond, "Sustained."

Marshall did not withdraw the question but continued,

"Lieutenant, on September seventh, where did you have lunch?"

Kohn could not immediately recall. The seventh? That was her first day ashore after the *Ford* moored in Pearl Harbor. Oh, yes. "The officers club at Hickam."

"Did you lunch alone?"

"No. I ran into Commander Dunne and we ate together."

"You *ran* into Commander Dunne?"

"Yes."

"How convenient. Did the two of you have drinks before lunch?"

Soto was confused. "Objection. I see no relevance in these questions, Your Honor."

Marshall turned toward the bench. "If you will just bear with me for a moment, Your Honor."

"For a moment only. Overruled."

"Did you and Commander Dunne have drinks together?"

"I had a rum punch. I believe the captain had a Mai Tai."

Marshall turned toward the members and spoke aloud his thoughts. "The day after arriving at Pearl Harbor, the first time you are off the *Ford*, you and Commander Dunne meet for lunch. What did you do after lunch?"

Kohn answered in measured words, "We didn't *meet* for lunch. It was an accidental event. After lunch, I returned to my quarters."

"And Commander Dunne?"

"I have no idea."

"Have you seen Commander Dunne since that occasion?"

"Only here in the courtroom."

"Lieutenant, I invite your attention to the evening of August twelfth. Where were you?"

"I don't remember, specifically. We were in Sydney."

"Perhaps I can help. Do you recall the Sydney Hilton Hotel?"

"Yes."

"Did you ever spend the night there?"

"Yes, I did. On two occasions."

"Was one of those occasions August twelfth?"

Kohn had no idea of the exact date. "I don't recall."

"Could it have been?"

"Yes, I suppose it could have been. It would have to have been before the fifteenth, because that is when we resumed operations."

"Did you spend the night there alone?"

"Of course."

"No, Lieutenant. I am prepared to have a witness testify that on that date, you and Commander Dunne shared a room."

Kohn cut Marshall in two with her eyes. "No, we did not, and I resent that implication."

"No implication, Lieutenant. Fact." Marshall quickly walked to his table and grabbed the piece of paper offered by his assistant. "This is a record of the occupants of Suite 544 of the Sydney Hilton. Would you read the names on the record of August twelfth?" Marshall shoved the paper toward Kohn.

Kohn spat the words, "Kiss my ass, Counselor."

Rarick banged his gavel and glared at Kohn. "Lieutenant Kohn, you will *not* address this court in that fashion!"

"I apologize, Your Honor, but only to you." Kohn had not taken her eyes off Marshall.

"No, Lieutenant, you apologize to this court."

Kohn looked at the members. "I apologize."

Rarick was not through. "One more statement out of order and you face brig time for contempt. Do you understand that?"

"Yes, sir. May I make a comment to the bench?"

"No, you may not. The prosecution will continue."

"Thank you, Your Honor. Are those the correct names on the list, Lieutenant Kohn."

Kohn checked the paper. "Yes, but—"

"Just yes or no."

Several of the spectators figured that Kohn was about ready to go over the railing at Marshall. Soto was desperately trying to make eye contact and warn Kohn to settle down.

Kohn's one word reply was more the hiss of an angry snake. "Yes."

"Let's stop playing with each other, Lieutenant. Aren't you actually more than just a subordinate to Commander Dunne. Weren't you on August twelfth actually his one-night stand?"

"No!"

"And are not the two of you still involved?"

Soto had to grab Dunne and restrain him while yelling, "Objection! Commander Marshall has established no basis for such a question. It is misleading and out of order."

Rarick rapped his gavel again. "I'll see both counsels in my chambers. Court is recessed for ten minutes."

Dunne was livid with anger. Soto hushed him with upraised hands. "Don't say a word. That's exactly what Marshall is trying to do. It's big-city stuff. I'll handle him."

Rarick led the way to his small chamber. "Shut the door," he commanded as he sat behind the desk. Marshall started to lower himself into one of the chairs. "I'll tell you when you can sit," Rarick warned. "What kind of language is that in a military court, Commander Marshall, calling an officer in the United States Navy a 'one-night stand'?"

"She asked for it, Your Honor, by her outburst. She assaulted me."

"Oh, and I suppose there was no provocation?"

"No, sir. I was asking a legitimate question."

"Where are you going with this?"

"I intend to show that Kohn is a biased witness. She had an affair with Dunne and that colors her testimony."

Rarick turned to Soto. "Any comment, Counselor?"

"Commander Marshall is digging his own hole, Your Honor. The defense has no objection to his line of questioning, just the manner in which he is conducting it."

Waiting in the courtroom, Dunne turned to Annie. "It isn't true, Annie."

Annie forced a smile and nodded, but her eyes were moist.

Dunne rose and took her hands in his. "You'll see, Annie, I promise you."

"I told you he was tough," Annie declared, dabbing her eyes with a handkerchief.

Kohn remained seated in the witness chair as Dunne approached and tried to comfort her. "Soto is ready for the bastard. We anticipated this."

"How can he draw such conclusions?" Kohn asked, obviously still beside herself with anger. "I'm really sorry, Captain."

"No. Neither of us need be sorry about anything this pervert implies. He's a caveman from the dark ages. Don't let him rattle you. Just answer directly and truthfully, then watch Soto tear him apart. It's going to happen, believe me."

Rarick was continuing his admonishment of Marshall. "I told you at the beginning of this court-martial what I expected. Perhaps I forgot to include the word *dignity* in my description. I know you, by reputation, Tom Marshall. And I admire you for the success you have had in a very high echelon of the practice of trial law. But, I suspect you are not too impressed with us career types who have given up the big bucks for legal service to the military. That's a shame. We serve our country—"

"As do I," Marshall angrily interrupted.

"As do you," Rarick conceded, "but we rely strictly on evidence and testimony to resolve a case. No theatrics. I believe you have heard that before from me. Perhaps, you've seen the movie *A Few Good Men* too often. You are not Tom Cruise, commander, and Lieutenant Kohn is not the type of officer portrayed by Jack Nicholson. This is a *real* navy court, commander, and a *real* naval officer's career is at stake here. I would remind you that no justice will necessarily be done just because you might seem to be a better lawyer than Commander Soto.

"Now, we are going back into court and finish this case with decorum and dignity. They won't make a movie about us but we can be proud we have lived up to certain standards."

"All rise."

Dunne returned to his seat as Soto and Marshall reentered. Rarick followed and gaveled the court into session. Marshall boldly resumed his questioning, "Did you sleep with Commander Dunne?"

"I did not."

"Are you and Commander Dunne lovers?"

"We are not."

"Did you and Commander Dunne share Suite 544 at the Sydney Hilton on August twelfth?"

"Yes, we did." Kohn was calmed. If Soto was truly ready for his cross examination, there was no need for her to qualify her last answer.

Marshall was satisfied. Four of the five members of the court were men. There was no way they would figure Sheila Kohn and Joshua Dunne shared a hotel suite platonically. "I have no further questions."

Rarick said to Soto, "You may redirect."

Soto was more than ready. "Lieutenant Kohn, would you describe Suite 544?"

"Yes, sir. It was one of three suites provided by the Australian government as a courtesy to the crew of the *Ford* while we were joint training with the Aussie navy. Two were for enlisted crewmembers, one for officers. All were three-bedroom suites with individual baths, a large sitting room, and kitchen facilities. We were required to sign in so that if there was any damage or anything, responsibility could be fixed."

"*Three* bedrooms?"

"Yes, sir."

"Was the third bedroom occupied the night you and Commander Dunne occupied the suite?"

"Yes, sir, by Lieutenant Childress."

"Your Honor, may I have a look at the sheet Commander Marshall just showed to my witness?"

"Certainly."

Marshall handed the paper to Soto.

"Lieutenant, you have identified your name on this list and, of course, Commander Dunne. Is there a third name for suite 544?"

Kohn gave the paper a cursory examination and stared at Marshall. "Yes, sir. Lieutenant Childress."

Soto tilted his head. "I wonder why the trial counsel didn't mention a third party."

Rarick was on the verge of censuring Marshall on the spot for unethical conduct, a deliberate attempt to mislead the court, but Soto seemed to have things well in hand. Rarick decided he would chew a little Marshall ass after the trial.

Soto followed his pointed question with, "I suppose I should ask, since the trial counsel will do so in a recross, were the three of you engaged in a ménage à trois?"

Several spectators laughed at the ludicrousness of the question and Rarick tapped his gavel on the bench.

Kohn replied, "No, sir."

"What did you do?"

"I watched TV for a while. The captain and Mr. Childress were talking about ways to improve the ship's performance in man-overboard drills. Later, the three of us played a few hands of quarter poker." Kohn directed a look of superiority at Dunne. "I cleaned their clock to the tune of eleven bucks. They left to go down to the bar for a nightcap. I went to bed and didn't see them any more as they both went back to the ship early. I slept in."

"Lieutenant, did you have any qualms about sharing the suite with two members of the opposite sex?"

"I really didn't give it a thought. We were all shipmates and naval officers with certain standards. Besides, if you look at the situation, we each had separate quarters. Commander Dunne is happily married to a lovely wife. This is the nineties. Men and women can share a relationship without sexual overtones. At least, I believe that. Don't you, Commander?"

Soto smiled. "Of course. And I ask you again, as a professional naval officer, do you feel Commander Dunne exercised proper judgement in his timing of the sinking of the *Salinika*?"

Marshall wanted to object vigorously, but couldn't see over the deep edge of the legal pit he had dug for himself.

Kohn answered clearly, "Yes, I do."

Soto concluded with, "I have no further questions, Your Honor."

Rarick asked, "Do you wish to recross, Commander Marshall?"

"No, Your Honor."

Rarick turned back to Soto. "Your next witness?"

Soto stood and announced, "I call Commander Joshua Dunne."

26

The two Italian tourists sat on the sand in the shade of several palm trees. They were munching on fried chicken pieces and both had cameras slung around their necks. One had his shoes off and they had deliberately picked a spot that offered them privacy as they gazed across Kaneohe Bay towards the U.S. Marine Corps Air Station. Several sailboats were tacking back and forth across the bay, driven by a strong northeasterly breeze, and the few bathers within the park were either taking the sun or walking in the shallows.

Anthony Lurasci and Leo Perroni had spent most of the day in the Pearl Harbor area. They visited the sunken *Arizona* and took a boat cruise around the harbor, busily taking pictures as if the scenery might disappear by the next day.

Now, Lurasci and Perroni were speaking of serious business and they addressed each other by their real names.

"Jamal, I am disappointed in you. I have never seen you so discouraged."

"I have never seen the impossibility of a mission before. We cannot do it, Ahmad. It is impossible."

"No, it is not. There has to be a way."

Jamal spat out a small bone fragment. "We will die before we get ten feet."

"I admit it looks difficult. The solution is distraction and timing."

"I insist we consider our secondary target."

"You must further convince me."

Jamal took another piece of chicken from the box. "Too many guards. Too many media people. Too many spectators."

"Since when have those factors stopped us before?"

"They know we are coming."

Ahmad sat back as if surprised. "Of course they know we are coming. But they do not yet know where. They cannot provide protection for everybody and everything."

Jamal persisted. "I am very willing to die on this mission; I ask Allah for it! I pray for it. But I will not do it if we cannot eliminate our target. It would be fruitless. The Americans would laugh at us."

Ahmad looked at the sand. "You sound quite firm."

"I speak only the truth."

"It will lack the impact we seek. It will cost us money."

"Not as much as failure."

Ahmad did not like to consider that Jamal might be right. But as a professional who had never failed an assignment, he did have a reputation to protect. Secondary targets had been chosen before. "We must make completely new plans. There could be a time delay and I must insist that we not abandon our primary target, not until we have completed arrangements to take care of Admiral Paterson."

Jamal smiled at his success in arguing with his partner. "The admiral is a dead man, as of this moment."

"Perhaps," Ahmad ventured. "I will make the final decision in the morning."

27

Soto began the questioning once the court was in session. "Commander Dunne, how well did you know Petty Officer Two shoes?"

"I knew him as a member of the crew of the *Ford*, perhaps somewhat better than most of my men. He was our special sea and anchor detail helmsman, so he and I spent a lot of time on the bridge together. He was our most skilled helmsman and a superb petty officer, who would easily have passed the next promotion exam."

"Did you know him in any personal way?"

"I knew he had a mother and a grandfather in Colorado on the Ute Indian reservation. We had very little time for personal conversation when on the bridge, but we had a few minutes during the quiet times. He was very proud of his heritage and considered himself a career sailor. So did I. I was very proud of him."

"Commander Dunne, we have heard testimony as to parts of your conversation with Petty Officer Two Shoes over the sound-powered circuit between the bridge and after-steering. You are the only person who heard Charlie Two Shoes's side of the discussion. Would you tell the court, as near as you can recollect, what Two Shoes said to you?"

"I can't recall the exchange verbatim but it was obvious he was in physical distress. He stated that he was having trouble breathing. He knew he had the disease. He asked that I inform his mother and grandfather that he was dying with honor. When I informed him that corpsmen were on the way, he strenuously objected and insisted that no one enter after-steering."

"And how did you feel?"

"I knew he was right. I was also angry and frustrated."

"Did you order Chief Martinez not to enter the compartment?"

"Yes, I did."

Soto could see the moisture in Dunne's eyes. "Why did you do that?"

"My crew was at risk. I prayed, I really prayed that Two Shoes was the last man infected with the agent. If that were true, I could end the risk to my crew by honoring Petty Officer Two Shoes's request."

"And what was the size of your crew?"

"In excess of six hundred men and women."

Soto repeated the number for emphasis. "Six hundred crewmembers. Do you consider Charlie Two Shoes a hero?"

Tears were hanging precariously below Dunne's eyes. "My God in heaven, yes. He gave his life for his shipmates."

"Have you recommended him for any award?"

"The Navy Cross."

"Thank you. I would like to direct your attention and memory now to the circumstances surrounding your decision to sink the *Salinika*. But before I do, Your Honor, I would like to enter several pieces of material evidence."

"Certainly, counselor."

"I have here the papers found on the dead body of the pilot of the Forger. They include a passport and a chart taken from his kneepad that is an overview of the island of Oahu with a number of parallel lines drawn east and west across the island. There are some other symbols as you will see and some Arabic notations. There is also a duplicate chart with English translations of the notes that was prepared by intelligence personnel."

Rarick received the papers, glanced at them, and handed them to the court reporter with his instructions: "Please enter these in the record as Defense Exhibit A."

Soto uncovered a large placard that sat on the court easel.

"I invite the attention of the court to this chart, which is a blowup of the chart just offered as Defense Exhibit A. It is the one with English translations. This position here is identified as the proposed launch location of the Forger with the time noted: oh-two-hundred. An early morning launch under the cover of darkness. Most of the island would have been asleep. These are obviously flight lines over the islands, and you will note the marking of certain geographical points used as guidelines to insure complete island coverage by the aerial spraying tactic. Finally, this is the rendezvous point with the *Salinika*, which is only a few miles from the launch point. Are there any questions?"

Hearing none, Soto returned to his witness. "Commander, you had this evidence before you, admittedly without the English translations, but was there any doubt in your mind that you had intercepted an Arabic terrorist operation directed against the island of Oahu?"

"None."

"Did your key officers concur?"

"Yes."

"Then what did you do?"

"I decided the vessel should be sunk and made that recommendation to CINCPACFLT."

"Then what happened?"

"My request was relayed up the chain of command."

"How far?"

"To my commander-in-chief."

"By that, you mean the president?"

"Yes."

"How do you know those details?"

"Some were relayed to me by Admiral Paterson by direct secure voice contact. The *Ford* was also an info addressee on all message traffic concerning the matter."

"What precipitated your decision to sink the *Salinika* without presidential approval?"

"I felt that if the *Salinika* were allowed to approach Oahu any closer than eleven miles, a failure of the missiles used in the attack could allow her to be too close to the island when a subsequent attack could be made. The explosions could propel contaminant into the air— the winds were hurricane force—and endanger the population of Oahu."

"You mean a technical failure of the weapons?"

"Yes. It happens rarely, but I wanted a cushion. The situation warranted that."

"Thank you. Your witness, Commander Marshall."

Marshall began his attack. "One thing bothers me about your neglect of the welfare of Petty Officer Two Shoes. After Chief Sulley died, apparently of the biological disease, an air-evac chopper came to the *Ford* to ferry Lieutenant Childress to Tripler Hospital. Would not that have been a good time to have requested a medical team? They could have been on board when Charlie Two Shoes became ill. Perhaps they could have even started their innoculations. Why didn't you request that, Commander?"

"We were only a short time out of Pearl. By the time the team could have been assembled and embarked on a helicopter, I figured we would be at our mooring assignment. No appreciable time would have been saved, in my opinion.''

"In *your* opinion?''

"Yes. It also appeared that Chief Sulley was to be the last victim. Hours had elapsed and no one had come down with the symptoms.''

"Yet, you went to general quarters just in case such an event happened?''

"Yes.''

"And it did.''

"Yes.''

"And you denied Petty Officer Two Shoes medical attention?''

"At his request.''

"Of course.'' Marshall let his eyes emphasize the innuendo in his last remark. "What else did you do?''

"I don't understand the question. I did a lot of things.''

"With respect to Charlie Two Shoes. What was the order you gave to the officer of the deck? The order that you whispered? The order that you wanted kept from the bridge personnel—and this trial—but which the OOD had entered in the ship's log?''

Dunne had not known the order had been entered, but such an entry was certainly proper and he would acknowledge it. "I ordered after-steering sealed.''

"Sealed? With Petty Officer Two Shoes inside?''

"Yes.

"You didn't give a damn about that Indian, did you, Commander?''

Soto was furious. "Objection! Inflamatory and speculative.''

The ruling was immediate: "Sustained.''

Marshall was nonplussed. "You not only sealed the compartment, Commander Dunne, you sealed a human being's fate, didn't you?

"I—"

Marshall threw up his hands in mock despair. "No need to answer that question, Commander."

Soto was still standing. "Objection. Commander Dunne has every right to answer that question. Your Honor—"

Rarick held up *his* hand. "Sustained. Commander Marshall, I have warned you about theatrics."

Marshall looked squarely at the members of the court. "I withdraw the question."

"Not until my client answers it," Soto insisted.

Marshall shrugged. "Your call, Counseler."

"No, Commander, *my* call," Rarick corrected. "Commander Dunne, you may ignore or answer the question as you wish."

Dunne was quite willing. "Yes, I sealed the compartment, but the fate of the brave sailor you refer to rather offhandedly as a human being was already determined. I had no hand in that."

Marshall then began his cross-examination of the second charge. "Commander Dunne, you deliberately sank the *Salinika* in defiance of a direct order of your commander-in-chief. You have just admitted that."

"Not in defiance."

Marshall ignored the clarification. "Did you make any last effort to get presidential approval for your attack?"

"No."

"Oh? And why not? Didn't you at least owe that as a courtesy to your president?"

"There was not time. By the time my request could be relayed up the chain and the response received, the *Salinika* could have beached on Oahu."

"You seem like a very capable officer. Why not info the commander-in-chief on your message? Or better still, have him made an action addressee? That way, he would have received advance notice immediately and could have acted accordingly."

Dunne looked squarely at Marshall. "I'm afraid I did not have that kind of confidence. I had already emphasized the criticality of the timing. The president, isolated from the scene of the action, could not have the picture I had."

"But you denied him that opportunity to act, didn't you?"

Soto rose. "Objection. Commander Dunne had no intent to deny the president anything. He has already emphasized the chain of command. The question shows complete ignorance about military command procedures."

"Sustained."

Marshall continued. "We heard Admiral Bray testify that another four minutes would have made no difference in the degree of the threat posed by the *Salinika*. Do you agree with the admiral?"

"I had no way of knowing permission would arrive in four minutes."

Marshall persisted. "Do you agree with that evaluation by Admiral Bray?"

"Yes, I do."

"Then, you *could* have waited longer, isn't that correct?"

"Only after the fact."

"Commander Dunne, what is your impression of the president as our commander-in-chief?"

Soto raised a hand. "Objection. Immaterial."

Dunne turned to Rarick. "I'd like to answer that, Your Honor."

Rarick nodded. "Overruled."

"I believe the current president, as our commander-in-chief, is an intelligent, highly motivated and capable person. I believe that he wants very much to establish himself in his responsibility as civilian head of the military and that his motivations are honest and patriotic. He is trying very hard to understand the military mind, and I admire him for that. I know that during this incident, he had international concerns and pressures placed upon him that were not placed upon me. My decision as the on-scene commander was easy. His was not. I respect him as my commander-in-chief and he has my allegiance. My action was not defiance and it was not deliberate disobedience. It was the action of a military commander who was the only person with the ability to foil a deliberate attack upon the United States of America and that is my sworn duty. I don't blame the president for not understanding that.''

Marshall was not sure he should have asked the question. He felt a need to regroup. ''Commander, you have recommended Petty Officer Two Shoes for the Navy Cross. Isn't that a wartime award? We are not at war.''

''Maybe you aren't, but I and my crew were. The award may be downgraded because of a difference of opinion on the subject, but Quartermaster Third Class Charlie Two Shoes is an authentic naval hero and he deserves recognition as that. I intend to see that he gets it.''

Somehow, Marshall was figuring that he was about to lose control. He needed to get back on track. ''Regardless of your high-sounding words of praise for Petty Officer Two Shoes and your own actions during the *Salinika* incident, I believe the matter of you disobeying a direct order is still before this court. I would ask you three final questions: number one, did you consider the commander-in-chief's prohibition against taking any further action against the *Salinika* until he so advised a lawful order?''

''I did.''

''And were you aware of the order before you took action?''

''I was.''

''Then is it safe to say that there was a lawful order, you were aware of it, and you disobeyed it?''

Dunne considered his answer very carefully. Marshall had just recited the three elements of proof of a violation of Article 92 of the Uniform Code of Military Justice. He would have to answer yes or no, for Marshall was not about to allow him any clarification. What the hell? That was Soto's job. He answered, "Yes."

Marshall's smile was that of Caesar entering Rome after a successful campaign. "One other *small* matter, Commander. Did you even give a moment's thought as to what could happen to sea life when you ordered a deadly biological agent to be dispatched to the seabed?"

"My concern at the moment, *Commander*, was the well-being of the people on Oahu. I must confess that the danger to sea life was not my primary concern."

Marshall chuckled. "I'm sure it wasn't. I wonder what is happening at the bottom of the sea right this very moment."

Soto raised his eyes and shook his head back and forth. *What was coming next?*

Rarick apparently was entertaining similar thoughts. "Do you have any further *questions*, Commander?"

"No, Your Honor. Thank you, Commander. I have no further questions."

"Does the defense have any redirect?" asked Rarick.

Soto could not let Dunne's last answers be the last answers the members of the court heard. "Commander Dunne, do you feel there were mitigating circumstances?"

"Yes, I do."

"In your mind, what were they?"

"The distance, physical and mental, that the commander-in-chief was away from the scene of the action and the life or death urgency of the requirement to stop the *Salinika*."

"Thank you. That concludes the defense's case, Your Honor."

"Very well. We have moved into late afternoon, and

if we take a break now, it would mean we would be getting too late a start on the closing arguments. I prefer that we have a full day to hear and consider those. This court is adjourned until oh-nine-hundred tomorrow morning." The sharp rap of Rarick's gavel signaled the end of the day's proceedings.

The marine beside the court's exit came smartly to attention. "All rise."

As Marshall, his assistant, and the spectators left, Lt. Kohn and Annie Dunne joined Soto and Joshua at the defense table. Kohn was first to speak. "Captain, I'm really sorry about losing control. I just couldn't stand that Neanderthal's line of questioning."

"No problem, Sheila. He had it coming," Dunne responded, taking one of Annie's hands in his. He smiled confidently at Soto. "David, I'm proud of you. I think we fought a good fight."

Soto smiled. "Well, it's not quite over. We sum up tomorrow, and I think Marshall will pull out all the stops. We punched some big holes in his case."

Dunne asked Soto, "Shall we get together this evening?"

"Not unless you have something specific you want to talk about. I think we're prepared. I need to clean up a few loose ends in my closing argument. Why don't you and Mrs. Dunne try and relax?"

Annie Dunne turned to Lt. Kohn. "Sheila, join us for dinner. I need some girl talk. After all, you've already spent a night with my husband. We can compare notes." The two women laughed and gave each other a hug.

After they left, Soto still sat at the table, deep in thought. He had tried to keep Dunne's spirits up but inside he was worried. Tomorrow, four men and a woman, all experienced professional military officers, would weigh his arguments and those of Marshall. They would pay close attention to the closing presentations, for in their minds there had to be some unclear aspects to the case. There always were and the members of the court would have to resolve those issues in their private deliberations. Soto knew that military officers were notorious for searching for that one stone that either counsel had left unturned. If they found one, irregardless of how the defense or trial counsels had argued, they were prone to give it considerable attention and that could sway their decision. Soto prayed that in his closing remarks he would leave them a clear field to examine, with no stones at all.

Blackjack Paterson studied the nighttime sky from the lanai of his naval base quarters. Low, broken cloud cover was drifting in from the south, not too common an occurrence. In between the formations of low-level cumulus, the heavens were black because of a high overcast. Occasionally, the silver shimmerings of distant stars appeared and almost immediately were gone. The weather was as unsettled as Paterson. In fact, he was miserable. From what he knew of the trial, tomorrow would be the final day of arguments. If the closing remarks didn't last too long, there could even be a decision by the members of the court. Suppose they found his son-in-law guilty? What would Paterson have accomplished by beating the administration to the punch? Nothing, except possibly alienating his daughter and her husband from him for all time. And how would such a psychological blow affect Annie's illness? Mental attitude was certainly a factor in fighting any disease. Was he killing his daughter?

What was going on back in the Pentagon? General Mitchell was gone. There apparently was no replacement yet, although the scuttlebutt had the army chief of staff as the number-one candidate. Certainly, the navy was out for a while.

Blackjack had many thoughts at the moment in addition to the concern for his daughter. She hadn't called since their first talks. What would he do if Dunne were convicted? Maybe that would be the time to hang it up. Travel, perhaps. That might seem a strange consideration for a man who had spent a lifetime in the navy. But he had never been to Africa. Most of it was too chaotic now to visit. But there were areas, some even still pristine, where he could walk the veldt and imagine what the world must have been when his earliest ancestors were the only people who roamed it and courts-martial were still a million years away.

28

"All rise."

To Commander Joshua Dunne, the alerting command of the marine guard was the trumpet of the angel Gabriel, advising the world that the career of a once highly favored naval officer could very well be about to go down the toilet.

The members of the court took their places. The familiar figure of Captain Rarick mounted the bench and called the session to order. The prosecution would lead off the closing arguments.

Annie leaned forward and gently squeezed Dunne's shoulder. She was seated with Lt. Kohn and the cadre of the *Ford*'s officers who were not on duty.

Marshall addressed the court. "Members of the court, when I made my opening statement just two days ago, I indicated that this would be a simple, straightforward case. You have heard prosecution witnesses testify repeatedly to the facts that Commander Dunne, in his capacity as commanding officer of the USS *Ford*, did violate the civil rights of one of his men, Petty Officer

Two Shoes. The defense has offered testimony that Charlie Two Shoes asked to be denied medical assistance when he was struck down by a horrible biological warfare agent. But from whom did that testimony come? From Commander Dunne, the accused. He was the only one who heard the words of Charlie Two Shoes, and I have to ask if there was not a vested interest in Joshua Dunne's testimony? I do not believe Commander Dunne deliberately lied. But he said himself that he could not recall verbatim Two Shoes's words. Could his memory, clouded by the predicament he now finds himself in, have misinterpreted the pleading words of a doomed man?

"Even so, was not Commander Dunne obligated by his 'sacred second trust' to render all possible aid to his stricken shipmate? I say he was. Our humanitarian instinct says he was. Civilization says he was. It was possible to offer the dying Charlie Two Shoes comfort without risking any of the other crewmembers. Chief Martinez said as much. She violated her captain's order and tried to enter the compartment, but even in his delirium Two Shoes had wanted to serve his captain and apparently did something that blocked the hatch. But we have to wonder. Was that his intention or was he trying to get it open and accidentally jammed it? We will never know. We do know that he died, alone and undoubtedly afraid, in a tiny steel compartment. And I say that he did not have to die alone, and Commander Dunne's attempt to shift the blame by recommending Petty Officer Two Shoes for a very high naval honor is a subterfuge to distract all of us from Joshua Dunne's shame."

Marshall had directed his last statement at Dunne and now he paused, his grim face apparently flush with anger. It was an old trick he used, tightening his stomach and neck muscles to trap blood in his head and holding his breath until he could feel that blood throbbing in his temples. He pointed his finger at Dunne as if to continue

but shook his head and pulled his lips tight as if he was
having difficulty continuing.

Soto was enjoying the performance. In fact, he reasoned, if the trial was ever the basis for a movie, Marshall should play himself. The Oscar would undoubtedly
be accepted with grace and humility.

After a show of trying to calm himself, Marshall
launched into the second charge. "With respect to the
violation of Article 92 of the Uniform Code of Military
Justice, Commander Dunne himself testified that the elements of proof were present in his refusal to obey the
order of his commander-in-chief. You heard it from his
own mouth. There was a lawful order; he was aware of
it, and he disobeyed it. Period. I would call that a courtroom confession.

"Quite naturally, the defense counsel attempted to establish two things: time had run out and Dunne *had* to
act, and there was no way the president could have understood the situation. No less an authority than Admiral
George Bray blew away that first excuse—and it was an
excuse, not a mitigating circumstance. And the president
was surrounded by his top military advisers and knew
full well the situation. That fact is confirmed in that the
commander-in-chief issued the order to sink the *Salinika*
just *four* minutes after Commander Dunne had disobeyed his direct order. Who was the better tactician?
Joshua Dunne, who *just couldn't wait*? Or his commander-in-chief, who had strategically waited until the
last minute to insure that all considerations of this potentially explosive international situation could be re-
solved. Commander Dunne said it himself: his job was
easy; the president carried the weight of international
consequences upon his shoulders."

Marshall stopped to sip from a glass of water that had
been placed on the trial counsel's table. He took the
opportunity to casually examine the reaction of the five
members of the court. Their faces were as fixed as those

of the four presidents sculptured in Mount Rushmore. But they were fixed on him. He had their undivided attention.

"Members of the court, this has, indeed, been a simple case. It is straightforward. Commander Joshua Dunne, one of the navy's so-called golden boys, under the pressure of a dangerous situation that called for patience and considered judgment, failed the test. The *Salinika* now rests under almost two miles of Pacific Ocean, with all hands, I might add. We lost a valuable deep submergence vehicle and another three precious lives in trying to retrieve valuable hard evidence that would substantiate the story of the *Salinika* and possibly identify the nationality of the terrorists. Instead, we have only a dead Arabic aviator and the defensive testimony of Commander Dunne and—oh yes—his star witness, the lovely Lieutenant Kohn.

"I submit to you, members of this court, that you have no choice but to find the accused guilty of both charges. Thank you, Your Honor."

Soto stood. "Your Honor, could we have a five-minute recess?"

"On what grounds?"

"It's of a personal nature, sir. A physical requirement."

Rarick could understand that. His own bladder was probably swollen to the size of a softball.

"Five minutes."

Soto left the courtroom as soon as Rarick disappeared. He returned in less than three minutes.

"That didn't take long," Dunne commented.

Soto's smile was that of the Cheshire cat. "It didn't take any time. I wanted to break the court's concentration. Marshall had them listening. They didn't move during his remarks. Now look at them."

The members were relaxed and chatting. Only Commander Dice had left.

"The judge will never make it back here in five minutes," Soto declared with some satisfaction. "It will be more likely ten or so. By that time, some of Marshall's words will be drifting around more casually in the minds of the members. When we present our closing argument, they will not still be considering his."

"You devil, you," Dunne mocked.

"Look at Marshall," directed Soto.

The trial counsel was glaring at the defense table, and if he had been capable flames would have been shooting from his nostrils. He was fully aware of Soto's tactic. He even placed one hand in front of his mouth to shield it from the members of the court and mouthed "Bastard."

Soto answered with a very slight bow.

The recess lasted twelve minutes.

Soto chose to remain behind the defense table as he started his closing arguments. "Your Honor, members of the court, I will not be taking much of your time, for it is not necessary to discuss in any great length the obvious. There is no question at all about the reputation of Commander Joshua Dunne as an exemplary naval officer. His service record speaks for itself. His testimony has indicated a great compassion for his crew and a deep concern about their welfare. So much so, that when he was faced by the heroic request of Petty Officer Two Shoes, Commander Dunne agonized in his realization that there was only one course of action open to him. If Charlie Two Shoes were the last infected crewman— and subsequent events have proven that true—then the insidious, terrorist-introduced disease—that had the potential to wipe out six hundred young men and women— could be stopped in its tracks."

Soto emphasized his last remark by smacking his right fist hard onto his open left palm. He paused for effect and then continued. "It was the moral equivalent of the dilemma of a ship's captain who must close and bar certain watertight hatches, even though one or more of his men are still in the flooding compartment, in order to prevent the loss of his wounded ship. And we must hold uppermost in our minds the fact that the man most affected by Dunne's decision introduced it and insisted that it be carried out. The trial counsel has tried to plant a doubt in your mind, implying that Commander Dunne's testimony with respect to his contact with Charlie Two Shoes is self-serving. He says he is not calling Commander Dunne a liar, but that is exactly what he is doing when he implies that Dunne's testimony is self-serving.'' Soto held out a hand toward Dunne. ''I ask you, does the man sitting before you appear to be that type of person, one who would so viciously lie to protect his own reputation?

''All of us know, even those of us who wear the insignia of a noncombatant branch of the U.S. Navy, that one day we may be called upon to make the supreme sacrifice for our country. It is part of our tradition, our heritage, our responsibility. Charlie Two Shoes knew that. Commander Dunne knew that. And you, the members of this court, know that. It may be that one or more of you have been faced with that type of awful decision.

''As members of the military service, we voluntarily give up some of our civil rights. We can't come and go as we please. We have certain restrictions on our free speech; we can't openly criticize in a derogatory way our commander-in-chief, for example. No matter how strongly we may feel, we can't decide whether or not we want to go on a particular deployment. And we know that there may come a day when we must carry out our duty to the extent to sacrificing our own lives or those of our shipmates for the common good of all. That is a *hard* thing to do, and none of us knows whether we can live up to that obligation until we are faced with it—but over the years thousands of our shipmates have done exactly that. And they were joined on the afternoon of

September sixth by two more, Commander Joshua Dunne and Third Class Petty Officer Charlie Two Shoes. We owe those two men honor, not punishment. They were shipmates on opposite sides of a life-or-death question but two men who came up with the same decision. Joshua Dunne is not guilty of violating the civil rights of Charlie Two Shoes, for Charlie Two Shoes set those particular rights aside when he told his captain to seal after-steering.''

Soto walked over to the right side of the court and faced the jury. ''As for the charge of failure to obey a lawful order, we have only to put ourselves in Commander Dunne's place on the bridge of the *Ford*, isolated at sea in the middle of a hurricane, with an enemy ship steaming toward Oahu. It must be stopped and it is to Commander Dunne's credit that he contacted his immediate superior for instructions. He did not act impulsively or in disregard for proper procedure, although there are those who would say he had every right to attack the *Salinika* of his own volition on the strength of what he knew about that death-ship and its target.

''Despite his many talents, Commander Dunne is not clairvoyant; he had no way of knowing that in four minutes his commander-in-chief would agree with the decision Dunne had already made. What is the problem here? Everyone from Dunne up the chain of command— CINCPACFLT, USPACOM, SECDEF, the National Command Authority, the president as commander-in-chief—all came to the same decision! And now Dunne is on trial for reaching it first? Will a technicality, especially one offset by mitigating circumstances, be allowed to ruin the career of one of the navy's most promising officers? Don't let the trial counsel's unethical attacks on the judgment and moral character of Joshua Dunne sway your considered judgment of the evidence and testimony in this case. Driving in this morning, as I turned into the gate, the radio news reported that our president has ordered a series of limited military strikes against targets in Iraq as retaliation for that country's blatant terrorist attack upon U.S. soil by the *Salinika*. Are we now going to say that Commander Dunne also preempted the president by attacking the *Salinika*? No, I think not. Joshua Dunne's judgment has been vindicated. I thank you.''

"*I'm* convinced," said Dunne as Soto sat beside him. He offered his hand and Soto took it.

Rarick charged the military jury: "The members of the court will retire for their deliberations. I will be in my chambers. Do the members require any clarifications at this point?"

The president of the court, Captain Robert "Dutch" Fargo, stood and answered, "We do not at this time, Your Honor."

"Then, this court-martial is closed."

"All rise."

Soto began putting some papers into his briefcase. "No chance of anything until after lunch. Why don't we grab something and be back here about thirteen hundred? I'll inform the court reporter."

Joshua and Annie Dunne, along with David Soto and Sheila Kohn, sat at a rail table at the Marina outdoor restaurant run by the Pearl Harbor Naval Exchange. The popular lunch eatery was located just north of the *Arizona* Memorial Visitors Center and the World War II submarine USS *Bowfin*, a celebrated diesel sub of that era. The Marina overlooked a cluster of berthed power- and sailboats owned by military personnel. The wide-open view was of the East Loch of Pearl Harbor and the east side of Ford Island. From most of the tables one could also see the *Arizona* Memorial. Despite the seafaring ambiance and reasonably priced entrees, Joshua and Annie were eating lightly while Soto and Kohn seemed to have more normal appetites. A nervous tension hung in the air despite several spirited attempts at conversation. Dunne finally pushed his plate away, the crab cakes and pasta only half-eaten. ''I wish this were over,'' he said.

Soto ventured, ''It will be soon, Joshua. I know how you must feel, and I don't want to get your hopes up, but I don't see how you can be found guilty of either charge. Trust me—and eat your lunch.''

''No appetite.''

Annie Dunne was eating a little more, but a similar anxiety as that of her husband was beginning to resist any hunger.

For a while the four sat and watched out over the water, each one wanting to comfort and encourage the others. The ride back to the courtroom was just as mute. It was one-thirty as they reentered the courtroom and took their places.

''We could go up to our conference room,'' Soto suggested. ''They'll call us.''

''I would just as soon wait here for a while,'' Dunne stated.

Captain Dutch Fargo led the other members of the court into the deliberation room. All took seats around a small green-felt covered conference table. Water, coffee, and iced tea were in place. To Fargo's left sat Commander Mary Margaret Dice and Captain Duke Wayne; across from Dice sat Captain Hank Billings. Captain Buck Jones sat opposite Wayne. Fargo started the proceedings. ''I sent out for lunch. If no one has any objections, we'll eat here. I suspect we're all anxious to get this over with.''

No one spoke.

''Before we begin, I'd like to take a vote to see where we stand. It'll be confidential, or at least as confidential as it can be with just the five of us. Each of you tear off two slips from the notepad in front of you. On one, write your verdict with regard to charge one: violation of civil rights. On the other, your verdict on charge two: disobedience of a lawful order. Fold the papers and pass them to me. I'll do likewise.''

It took only a moment for the others to comply. Fargo read the votes and placed his in the stack. "Obviously," he said smiling, "we have disagreement. And one non-vote until deliberations are over. So, let's start with charge one. Who would like to go first? . . . Duke? Okay, fine.''

"I like to speak plainly," Wayne began. "I think the civil rights violation is a trumped-up charge by the prosecution for political purposes. The fact that Petty Officer Two Shoes was an Indian has no bearing on the case at all. And it shouldn't have, and I could piss on the person that brought the ugly spectre of prejudice into the court. We in the navy have been fighting that problem for years, and except for an isolated case here and there, we have it licked. And this is not one of those cases.''

"I agree," Billings added.

Commander Dice shook her head. "No. I think we have to look closely at Commander Dunne's actions. Would he have sealed that compartment to let the man die if he had been white? This is a very sensitive issue.''

"We would have no way of knowing that even if it were a factor," responded Wayne.

Fargo recognized Jones. "Buck?"

"Nothing about Dunne's background or performance of duty indicates he has any prejudices. He's married to a black woman, for God's sake. Can't we *ever* get past this way of thinking?''

"Hear, hear," Wayne muttered, frowning directly at Dice.

Fargo intervened. "Can we all agree that whether or not prejudice is a factor, the question is: were Petty Officer Two Shoes' civil rights violated? That's the only question. There's no charge of prejudice.''

Dice agreed with a nod of her head.

"You want to go on, Commander Dice?" Fargo asked.

"I would like to say that in my opinion there were other courses of action open to Commander Dunne. He could have placed Two Shoes in isolation, administered what medical treatment there was, and allowed him to die in dignity, not welded inside a tiny lonely compartment."

Jones leaned forward. "Mary Margaret, what would you have done?" he asked.

"I'm not on trial."

"No, but you want to judge a man who is. I say that you have to judge him on professional standards. Would you have complied with Two Shoes's request—he *asked* to be left in the compartment, you will recall—if it had been your decision? Now, remember, you have a crew of over six hundred to consider."

"I don't know."

"Well, you damn well better decide. That fourth stripe is going to get you a ship. Dunne's problem on September sixth could be yours next month."

"When the time comes, Captain, I'll make my decision."

"Let me offer a thought," Fargo intervened, "and it is a thought that came up in testimony. Many ship's captains have faced the same problem Dunne faced; sacrifice one or several men for the good of the remainder of the crew. Yea or nea. What's the proper action? Why are you a naval officer? One answer is to make decisions. Hard decisions. That's exactly what Dunne did and I applaud him for it."

Dice was not ready to concede. "The man had a civil right to life until he drew his last breath. Commander Dunne preempted that right."

Billings spoke next. "Look, I think we're getting hung up on a technicality here. It's sort of like when you are terminally ill and ask that you not be hooked up to machines. We're all familiar with that situation. It's even been recognized legally by the living will document. It gives you a chance to go with dignity. I figure that's what Charlie Two Shoes wanted, to go with dignity. I couldn't criticize anyone who complies with a living will; I can't criticize Dunne for basically doing the same thing. You don't violate a loved one's civil rights by conceding to his wish or even pulling the plug if he's a vegetable. Society *recognizes* that. As a society, we do it all the time. Does that help, Mary Margaret?''

''I hadn't thought of it that way, and I'm not certain it's a parallel situation.''

Fargo waited for further comment. There was none. ''I think that's a good point, Hank, and I recognize Commander Dice's concern. Perhaps we should go on to the second charge.''

Buck Jones seemed ready. ''That's a tough one. In my mind, Dunne clearly disobeyed an order.''

''But there were mitigating circumstances,'' commented Billings.

''Being on the scene?'' Jones queried.

''Yes. Dunne was the on-scene commander. He had the best knowledge of the situation. He was in extremis.''

''But the commander-in-chief gave the order in time. Admiral Bray proved that,'' Jones retorted.

Wayne cut in. ''Dunne had no way of knowing the order was coming. He was hanging out there in the storm and on his own. CINCPACFLT shoulda jumped in. He knew the situation. Where was Paterson?

''Yes,'' Jones countered, ''but if we decide Dunne is not guilty, what kind of precedent does it set? And don't forget the political side, shipmates. We're talking about a presidential order. An order, that in retrospect, was justified.''

Dice wanted in. ''I believe that tactical decisions

should be made by the tactical commander, not some politician sitting several thousand miles away—regardless of political overtones. We're given grave responsibilities. We must have commensurate authority.''

"I agree," Wayne said.

Fargo smiled. "I remember that someone, I think it was a mud-soaked marine, remarked during 'Nam that President Johnson might be a great commander-in-chief but he was a piss-poor squad leader. You remember those days when the chain of command was violated daily by the highest authority? And look what happened. We lost thousands and thousands of young men because we were not allowed to do our thing. We have a duty to preserve that chain of command. Otherwise, the whole system falls apart.''

"I won't argue with that," Jones interjected, "but I just can't get it out of my mind that if Dunne had held off four minutes longer, we wouldn't be sitting here under a great big presidential shadow.''

"Screw the presidential shadow—"

"Mary Margaret!" Wayne exclaimed as Dice spoke.

"No, I mean it. The commander in the field must have tactical authority to act.''

A light knock on the door interrupted the proceedings.

"Well," Fargo concluded, "we may still be at an impasse, but let's have our lunch. We can continue our deliberations while we eat." As he ordered, "Come in," Fargo studied the faces of the other members of the court. He intended to bring in a decision that would stand up under any appeal. After lunch, he would ask for another vote, and if it were still undecided, he had a few things he would say. The situation looked like it called for a Solomon-like decision. The court must make every effort to uphold presidential authority even if it were at the expense of a fine young officer's career. But the court could not turn inward on itself. The members and those like them were on the front lines. Weakened tactical authority could mean the loss of other fine young people. He could not live with that.

Dunne and his party had reentered the courtroom and were quietly waiting when at 1538, one of the marine guards walked over. ''They've reached a decision, sirs.''

''That was fairly fast,'' Soto commented, checking his watch.

Tom Marshall and his assistant entered and took their places. Most of the original spectators took theirs.

''All rise.''

The members of the court filed in, their faces emotionless. Judge Rarick followed. ''This court-martial will come to order.''

Marshall proclaimed, ''All parties and members and the military judge are present.''

''Captain Fargo, have the members reached findings?'' Rarick asked.

Captain Dutch Fargo, his blond crewcut freshly waxed, stood. ''We have, Your Honor.''

Rarick further asked, ''Are the findings on charges pursuant to CINCPACFLT convening order 1-95?''

''Yes.''

''Would the trial counsel, without examining it, please bring me the findings, identified as Appellate Exhibit A?''

Marshall took the folded paper from Fargo and handed it to Rarick. The judge studied it for only a moment before handing it back. ''I have examined the Appellate Exhibit A. It appears to be in proper order. Please return it to the president of this court.''

Marshall did so.

Rarick looked at Dunne and said, ''Commander Joshua Dunne, would you and your counsel stand up, please? Captain Fargo, announce the findings, please.''

Fargo stood erect and read without hesitation, ''This court-martial finds you, Commander Joshua Dunne, to the charge of violation of Article 134, General Article of the Uniform Code of Military Justice, that is: executing a neglect prejudicial to good order and discipline, to wit, the violation of civil rights of a member of your crew—not guilty.''

Dunne felt Soto's hand touch his in subtle congratulations.

Fargo continued. "To the charge of violation of Article 92 of the Uniform Code of Military Justice, to wit, failure to obey a lawful order, we find you, Commander Joshua Dunne—guilty."

"Please be seated," intoned Rarick.

The world slowed and then stopped. The elation that had buoyed Dunne after the first announcement gave way to a dry-mouthed disbelief. *No. This cannot be happening.* Soto echoed his feeling with a barely audible "No."

The rap of Rarick's gavel brought Dunne back to the real world. "Does the trial counsel have any further remarks before the members retire to consider the sentence?"

"No, Your Honor."

"Does the defense wish to address the members with any mitigating comments before they retire to consider the sentence?"

Soto stood. "Yes, Your Honor. I wish to respectfully remind the members of Commander Dunne's outstanding performance over his past nineteen years of service and ask that their deliberations consider that performance in arriving at their sentence."

"Very well. I commend the defense counsel's remarks to the members. Sentencing will take place tomorrow morning at oh-nine-hundred." Rarick raised his gavel.

Captain Fargo spoke immediately, "Your Honor, if it pleases the court, the members are prepared to announce the sentence at this time."

Rarick lowered his head and peered over his glasses. "This is a serious departure from normal procedure, Captain. Are you confident the sentence has received the proper consideration? Does the sentence take into consideration the remarks just made by the defense counsel?"

"We have anticipated the factors mentioned by the defense, Your Honor, and the members of this court join me in this request."

"Very well. Do I hear any objections from counsels?" Hearing none, Rarick proceeded with the ritual. "Captain Fargo, is the sentence on Appellate Exhibit A?"

"Yes, sir."

"Will the trial counsel, without examining it, please bring me the sentence?"

Marshall took the second folded paper and handed it to Rarick. The judge glanced at it and for an instant Soto thought he saw Rarick's mouth hint at a smile. Marshall returned the paper to the president of the court.

"Commander Dunne, would you and your counsel stand up, please?"

There was dead silence in the courtroom.

"Captain Fargo, would you announce the sentence, please?"

"Commander Joshua Dunne, this court-martial sentences you to lose one unrestricted line officer running mate number on the next eligibility list for promotion to the rank of captain and to forfeit one dollar in pay for one month."

Soto whispered an enthusiastic "Yes!"

Rarick ordered, "Be seated. I will now advise you, Commander Dunne, of your posttrial and appellate rights."

Still stunned by the verdict, Dunne could hear the words but most of the meaning passed by him. He did hear the references to the "convening authority" and the

"Court of Military Review" and the "JAG"—but they were disjointed and at the moment, he could care less. He had a court-martial conviction on his record. The unthinkable had happened.

"Do you have any questions? Commander Dunne, do you understand your appeal rights and do you have any questions?"

Soto's poke in the ribs alerted Dunne to Rarick's repeating his question. He managed to reply, "I understand, Your Honor. I have no questions."

Rarick then rapped his gravel, which struck the hardwood pad. "This court is adjourned," he stated.

Soto instantly turned to comfort Dunne. "Joshua, don't you see? The court went by the letter of the law, but with such a token sentence they have sent a clear message. An appellate court cannot but help overturn the verdict. I have our argument all ready."

Dunne turned and walked away only to be stopped by Annie. "Let's stay here a few minutes, Josh. You are surrounded by friends. They want to offer you sympathy and encouragement."

Agent Jason Orr picked up his phone on the second ring. HPD captain Davey Isaka was on the other end. "Jason, we found the Taurus."

"Terrific. Where is it?"

"At a small apartment complex in Aiea, 320 Hikihiki Street. I'm on the scene."

"I'm on my way." Hurrying out of his office, Orr grabbed one of the agents working on the case. Eleven minutes later they pulled up beside Isaka's car and joined the captain by the Taurus. "Who found it?" Orr asked.

"One of the special-duty officers, routinely checking hotel and apartment lots in this area. Stolen plates."

Orr leaned over and peered in the driver's side window. "Anything yet?"

Isaka shook his head. "It looks clean, but I've got a team coming to scrub it."

Orr sized up the apartment building. Six apartments, three up and three down, 302A through 302F. A uniformed officer was checking 302C at the bottom right.

"We might as well wait until he finishes," suggested Isaka.

"Anything in the trunk?" Orr asked.

"Nothing."

"I wonder if they just ditched it here or traded it?"

Isaka shrugged. "My officer is asking if any of the occupants noticed it or saw anything."

"Damn. I wonder how long it's been here."

"A bit dusty. I would say a couple days, at least."

Orr agreed as he rubbed the windshield and dirtied the ends of his fingers. The uniform returned. "No one saw a thing, Captain," he reported. "But no one's home in 302B, lower center."

Orr noticed that the shades were closed in 302B. All the others were open. "Who lives in 302A?"

The policeman checked his small notebook. "A Mr. Arthur Nash."

"I'd like to talk to him," Orr declared.

Isaka instructed the officer, "Stay with the vehicle. As soon as the team arrives and gives it a preliminary look, they can take it to the impound."

Orr's first knock brought Arthur Nash to the door. Orr asked, "Sir, do you know who lives in 302B here?"

"Yes, Andy the candy man."

"Candy man?"

Nash chuckled. "Sorry, that's what we all call him. I don't know his last name. He has a candy route; you know, services machines."

"Is he home? We couldn't raise him."

"Well, his truck isn't in the parking lot."

"Truck?"

Nash answered, "Yes, he has a small panel truck that

he uses on his route. Has the name Andy's Candies on the side. A real nice fellow. Has machines on the naval base.''

Orr felt the small hairs on the back of his neck stiffen. Andy's Candies had a base vendor's pass! "Oh, shit," he murmured. "When was the last time you saw him?"

"Oh, it's been a couple days, actually."

"Is that normal?"

Nash shook his head. "No, he sort of has a daily schedule. Leaves around nine; back about four mostly."

Orr asked, "Who has the keys? Is there a resident manager?"

"No. A realty firm in Honolulu handles the leases."

Orr had *that* feeling. "Come on," he said urgently to Isaka. He knocked loudly on 302B. "Mr. Andy! Hello! Anyone in there?" He didn't expect an answer. Taking a small ring of metal probes from his pocket, he inserted one and jiggled the lock. It opened and he led Isaka inside.

All seemed in order except for the kitchen area. Isaka commented, "Looks like he might have a refrigeration problem."

The chromed reefer racks were on the table as were a number of bottles, jars, and covered plastic bowls. Catsup, mustard, soft oleo, all warm. Lunch meat turning green around the edge. Isaka picked up a milk carton and smelled it. "Ugh—sour."

Orr's eyes were fixed on the refrigerator door. "Davey, I don't like this." He pulled open the door. "Fuck it! I knew it!" The candy man's body was twisted and squeezed tightly inside the refrigeration compartment.

"Sweet Jesus," Orr prayed, his nose wrinkling as never before. "We have to get to the base!" Isaka could hardly keep up as Orr dashed for his car.

* * *

Joshua Dunne returned the warm handshake of Lt. Holly. He was the last of the crewmembers present with the exception of Lt. Kohn. After Holly left, Dunne stood and picked up his bridge cap. He stood for a moment, running his fingers across the gold braid on the brim. Inside, every muscle and tendon in his body was drawn tight and he felt that any moment he would explode. He wanted to lash out at someone, but who? Not Soto. He had done well and even now was preparing for the appeal that he felt would absolve Dunne of the guilty verdict. Dunne was not nearly as confident; in fact, he had no confidence left at all. It was a sad navy that would do such a thing to him.

"C'mon, Josh, let's go." Annie took him gently by the hand and they walked outside, followed by Soto and Lt. Kohn. A few of the crew were still standing on the sidewalk or in the grass. The two men off to the left were in business suits, probably journalists eager to write their views on the trial and verdict. *Screw 'em* was all Dunne could think of. Several TV crews, along with other members of the media, were set up but had been held at a respectable distance by the marines. Beyond one of the cameras was another stranger that Dunne could recall not seeing in court. He presented a striking figure, although a bit nervous, as his dark eyes stabbed into Dunne's. *What was his bitch?* Dunne wondered. One of the marines walked up and spoke, "We think you got the shaft, Commander; hang in there."

"Thanks." Dunne observed a dark blue navy sedan parked in front of the adjacent building. The four-star flag of CINCPACFLT fluttered from the short staff attached to the left front fender.

The other marine offered, "*Semper fi*, sir."

"Aren't we all?" responded Dunne, managing a weak grin but keeping his eyes on the sedan. For the first time he noticed the two outside marines were also wearing sidearms.

Annie was on his right arm, Soto and Kohn behind. Somewhere in the distance he could hear a car's racing engine and the faint squeal of tires. Some idiot was begging to attract the attention of the base police. The sky overhead was the same shimmering blue as always, and as he glanced around the area, a few sailors were going about their business. The world was still turning.

"Well," he said to Annie, trying to be lighthearted, "I could buy you a piece of candy." The white Andy's Candies truck was parked just opposite the place of the court-martial and the driver was crossing the street toward them, his tray of candy bars swung from around his neck.

At that precise moment, time slowed to a crawl and Dunne would forever remember each hour-long second for the rest of his life. When about twenty feet away, the candy man dropped his tray and shouted, "Allah Akbar! God is great!" His hand reached down into the top of one trouser leg and withdrew an evil looking rusty machete. "Die, devil!" he shouted, his face contorted with hate. He began to run toward Dunne. All eyes were on the man, all wide with horror and anticipation of what was about to be—and all were too far away to intercept the man. The TV crews whirled and focused on the man. Dunne grabbed Annie and started to push her behind him. That was when he heard the first shot. It came from his left.

"Allah Akbar!" Ahmad Libidi had shouted just before he raised his weapon. He was no more than fifteen feet to the left of Dunne but just as he squeezed the trigger, he was struck by a vicious body blow.

Dunne felt a sharp sting across the back of his neck and then heard the sickening impact of a bullet striking flesh. But it was not his flesh. He turned to see Annie with her mouth open, the left side of her head a mass of blood, bone, and ripped skin.

A volley of gunfire erupted as Dunne threw Annie to

the ground. To his left, Libidi fell when the two FBI agents emptied their guns into his head and body. A car careened into the curb and two men jumped out, one in the uniform of the Honolulu Police Department.

Dunne looked up. Incredibly, the machete man was still coming as the gunfire had been concentrated on Libidi. Dunne let go of Annie and when Jamal Hussein was only a few feet away, Dunne dove straight forward under the vicious arc of the machete and made a textbook twisting ankle-tackle of his assailant. The two men rolled twice and Dunne sprung to his feet—but Hussein had been faster. He was only three feet away with his machete raised. That was the position in which he died. The two marine guards blasted his chest at point-blank range.

Annie! Dunne rushed back to her. Kohn was sitting on the ground, cradling his wife's head in her lap, Annie's vivid red blood saturating Kohn's white uniform trousers and shirt.

"Oh, Annie," Dunne moaned.

For just a brief moment, her deep brown eyes seemed to sparkle, then they became fixed and unfocused. Dunne grabbed her and pulled her to him. "Don't do this to me, Annie! Don't do this!" Suddenly Blackjack Paterson was kneeling beside him.

"Annie, Annie . . ." the admiral cried.

But the terrible evil thing that had been slowly killing their Annie had been cheated out of its final weeks of pain.

Several hands helped Dunne stand while a trio of navy corpsmen covered his wife. Dunne looked around him. All were respectfully silent. Paterson was still on his knees, sobbing. The machete man lay on the ground face up, his eyes open. Dunne slowly walked to beside him and picked up the machete. "Look at me, you horrible inhuman son of a bitch! Look at me!" Dunne brought the machete down across the dead assassin's throat. The man's severed head rolled over once and stopped still face up. Dunne started toward Libidi but was restrained by Jason Orr and the two marines. One gently took the machete from Dunne's hand, saying softly, "I'll take this, sir." Dunne collapsed.

Joshua Dunne opened his eyes. He was in a navy hospital gown and lying flat on a very hard bed. He could feel a bandage on the back of his neck. Staring down at him was the large grief-stricken face of Blackjack Paterson. Dunne started to sit up but was restrained by the hand of Paterson and the more gentle one of a navy nurse. "Take it easy, son," Paterson said.

"Oh, Blackjack, she's gone."

"God's will sometimes confounds us, doesn't it? This way there was no pain."

Dunne was not sure. "What am I going to do?"

Blackjack still hovered over him. "I'll tell you what *we* are going to do. First, you will rest here. Then, you're coming to my quarters and we're going to talk. We're going to remember our Annie as she would want us to. Then, we're going to drink every drop of bourbon I have in the house and think how lucky we are to have shared such a precious life. Finally, we are going to give Annie a proper send off and get on with our lives."

"How do we do that?" Dunne murmured.

"Very sadly. But we will. Trust me—I've been there before. Now rest."

Dunne felt a slight prick in his upper left arm.

29

The *Ford* slipped silently from the entrance to Pearl Harbor and headed for the open sea, her bow slicing smoothly through the gentle swell as her acting commanding officer, Commander Jim Sessions, ordered, "Ahead, two-thirds." From one of the mainmast halyards fluttered the four-star blue flag of CINCPACFLT. Admiral Blackjack Paterson and Commander Joshua Dunne stood on the open port wing of the bridge and, like the entire crew of the *Ford*, wore crisply starched whites. The blue of the Hawaiian sky could only be described as tourist blue, a deep clear vibrant color that would be woefully understated if one used the term brilliant. It was as if the heavens were joyously awaiting a new arrival and indeed perhaps they were. Dunne held in his hands a small light-colored marble urn and inside were the mortal remains of his beloved Annie, reduced to ashes and a few bits of bone. Like him, she had always loved the sea and considered it a perfect resting place when the time came. And now it had come.

The green of shallow water gave way to deep-water blue and Sessions swung the *Ford* to face Diamond

Head, twelve miles away. All of Oahu was bathed in bright sunlight with only a single white cloud building over the deep-purple Pali pass. "All stop," Sessions ordered, and when the *Ford* had slowed to five knots, he directed, "Ahead one-third, make turns for three knots." He held the sleek miniature greyhound of the sea steady on a course that would put the ocean breeze off to starboard.

Paterson and Dunne stepped down the bridge ladder to the weatherdeck and proceeded aft until they were amidships. They faced outboard and over the 1MC came the bridge bo's'n's voice, "Attention to port, stand by to render honors." Those of the crew manning the lifelines stood smartly at attention, and as the PACFLT band, stationed on the helipad, began the first strains of the "Navy Hymn," the crew raised their right hands in salute. Paterson and Dunne took a step forward and joined in gripping the urn. Lt. Holly reached over and removed the cover. Together, father and husband tipped the vessel and let the ashes fall into the wind. They swirled briefly within the mild turbulence around the *Ford*'s hull, a light gray wispy cloud, but continued outboard and aft, blown away from the ship. Paterson released the empty urn to Dunne. The band began the second stanza of the "Navy Hymn."

"Remember the first time you called on Annie?" Paterson asked in a quiet voice.

"Of course. Annapolis. That lemon of a townhouse some shady realtor had pawned off on you. The two of you were in the backyard. Annie had forgotten about the time. She was in jeans and you were tossing a football back and forth. She was good."

The tears that had been hanging precariously just below Paterson's eyes began to slide down his cheeks. "She could catch like a wide receiver. God, what a tomboy, even as a young adult."

Dunne held out the urn to Paterson and grinned. "Admiral."

Paterson looked puzzled for only a moment. He took the marble vessel; it weighed close to three pounds. Loudly, he called, "Go out for a long one, Annie—a very long one." He waved his left hand forward in the familiar manner of a quarterback who was ready to throw the bomb. Then he cocked his right arm and gave the urn a mighty heave. It flew high against the blue sky and arced into the waters of the Pacific a good twenty yards away. Just as it splashed, the band completed the last strains of the hymn. Then a strange and completely unorthodox thing happened, something that would be a source of pride and comfort for Paterson and Dunne in years ahead. The seventy or so sailors manning the port lifeline, having just dropped their salutes with the last note of music, broke into spontaneous applause.

Paterson dropped a large lei of purple vanda orchids onto the water. Dunne reached out and released a single long-stemmed bird of paradise. It floated beside the lei.

The Pacific fleet band struck up a lively arrangement of "Anchors Away," Annie's favorite anthem. Four years earlier—to the day—she had selected it to be played at their wedding as they left the church.

It had never sounded more appropriate.

Epilogue

(WASHINGTON, SEPTEMBER 22) (AP) The President today, in his role as commander-in-chief of the military, granted a full pardon to Commander Joshua Dunne, U.S. Navy. A CINCPACFLT court-martial had convicted the former commanding officer of the USS *Ford* of failing to obey a lawful order. The President also stated through a White House spokesperson that he was strongly supportive of the Navy's selection of Admiral Jack Paterson, U.S. Navy, as the next Chief of Naval Operations.

Both moves were seen as conciliatory gestures by the President in lessening the tension that has existed between the administration and the military. The Secretary of the Navy hailed the decision ''as indicative of the compassion and concern that the President has for a national hero.''

The Navy announced that Dunne had been reassigned to his former command and would shortly receive orders to the Senior Course at the Naval War College, Newport, R.I., an assignment that is given only to the Navy's most promising officers.

Admiral Paterson issued a statement through his public affairs officer, saying only that

''I serve at the pleasure of the President and appreciate his confidence and that of the Secretary of the Navy.''

Lt. Sheila Kohn, U.S. Navy, heroic helicopter pilot assigned to the USS *Ford* during the *Salinika* encounter, will rejoin her San Diego squadron after being absolved of any primary blame for the crash aboard the *Ford* that cost the lives of her three aircrewmen and three ship's company Navy men.

Commander Joshua Dunne stood on the port wing of the bridge. The special sea and anchor detail was set and in a few minutes the *Ford* would get underway for San Diego. He was about to order, ''Single up all lines,'' when a figure bounded up the accommodation ladder. He recognized Lt. Kohn, and she was hurrying up the port side toward the bridge. ''Hold the accommodation ladder,'' he ordered.

Kohn took the bridge ladder two steps at a time. Saluting and almost out of breath, she greeted Dunne. ''Captain, I had to say good-bye and wish you and the crew a safe voyage home.

Dunne returned the salute. ''You can still ride back with us.''

Kohn nodded and laughed, trying to regain her breath. ''Thanks, but no thanks. I've got a C-5 seat out of Hickam. It has been a real opportunity for me to have served under you, and I'm as happy as your crew that the *Salinika* business is all over.''

''I appreciate that. It's been a pleasure to have you on board. Thank you for everything and have a safe trip. Maybe we'll do it again sometime.''

Kohn was breathing easy now. She looked for a long moment into Dunne's eyes. ''I'd like that. Good-bye, Captain.''

''Take care, Frosty.''

Dunne watched Lt. Kohn trot back down the port side and step up on the accommodation ladder. She faced aft and saluted the ensign, then gave a cheerful wave to all hands as she hurried down to the pier. A number of the crew waved back, there was a loud whistle, and a husky voice cried out, "Go get 'em, Lieutenant!"

Dunne turned to his OOD. "Mr. Holley, why don't you take us home?"

Holly sang out, "I have the conn. Single up all lines!"